Giorgio Faletti graduated with a degree in Law and went on to become a singer-songwriter, TV comedian and actor.

I Kill was his first thriller. Published in 2002, it topped the bestseller lists for over a year. The novel has since been translated into more than twenty-five languages, including Chinese, French, German, Japanese, Portuguese, Russian and Spanish.

Also by Giorgio Faletti

I Kill
I Am God

THE KILLER IN MY EYES

GIORGIO FALETTI

Translated by Howard Curtis

Constable • London

Constable & Robinson Ltd
55–56 Russell Square
London WC1B 4HP
www.constablerobinson.com

First published in the UK by Constable,
an imprint of Constable & Robinson Ltd, 2012

ISBN: 978-1-84901-998-9 (B-format paperback)
ISBN: 978-1-78033-387-8 (A-format paperback)
ISBN: 978-1-78033-522-3 (ebook)

Printed and bound in the UK

1 3 5 7 9 10 8 6 4 2

To Roberta, the only one

Song of the Woman Who Wanted To Be a Sailor

I stand here on this cliff
my eyes embrace the sea,
I dream the same old dreams
these dreams won't let me be
The surface of the waves
like craters on the moon,
like twisting trails of snakes
or trees cut down too soon.

And this strange old heart of mine
now sets sail upon the sea . . .

I stand here on this cliff
look down upon the sea,
I hear the mermaids sing,
singing their song to me.
Their song is sweet to hear,
as honey on the tongue,
Their song strong as the wind
that blows down old and young.

There's no glory or desire
that can tear my dreams apart.
There's no grindstone known to man
Can crush this rock inside my heart.

Connor Slave
from the album *Lies of Darkness*

PROLOGUE

The darkness and the waiting are the same colour.

One day, a woman will be sitting in the dark, and she will have had enough of both to be scared of them. She will have learned the hard way that sometimes sight isn't exclusively physical, it's also mental. Beyond the curtains in the place where she waits, beyond the windows, in the yellow glare of 1,000 lights, the dazzle of 1,000 neon signs, will lie the madness they call New York.

On the low table next to her chair, there will be a Beretta 92 SBM – a gun with a slightly smaller handle than usual, expressly designed for women.

She will have cocked it before putting it down on the glass table top, and the noise of the bolt will have echoed in the silence of the room like the sound of a bone cracking.

Gradually, her eyes will have grown accustomed to the darkness and she will have gained some idea of the place where she is, even with the lights off. She will be staring at the wall in front of her, sensing rather than seeing, the dark patch of a door.

Once, at school, she learned that when you look intensely at a coloured surface and then take your eyes away, there remains imprinted on your pupils a bright patch of colour exactly complementary to the one you have just been staring at. This cannot happen in the dark, however, since darkness generates only more darkness.

When the person she is waiting for has arrived, light will suddenly flood the room.

After an apparently endless road travelled, after a long journey down a tunnel where only a few paltry lamps showed the way, two people will finally emerge into the light. The only two people in possession of the truth.

A woman scared by the knowledge that she has it.

And the man she is waiting for.

The killer.

PART ONE

New York

CHAPTER 1

Stark naked, Jerry Ko slid to his knees on the huge white sheet he had taped to the floor and, after a moment's contemplation, plunged his hands in the big can of red paint between his legs and raised his arms towards the ceiling, letting the paint run slowly down to his elbows. There was something of the pagan ritual about the gesture, the transformation of the human form in order to achieve contact with a higher spirit. With the same fluid movements, he proceeded to smear the paint over his body, sparing only the areas around his penis, mouth and eyes. Gradually, the blood-red paint gave him the appearance he wanted: one single vast, festering wound.

He looked up at the woman. She stood there in front of him, also stark naked, her body painted a different colour, a particularly intense shade of blue.

Jerry reached out and touched her outstretched hands with his own. The sound as their palms came together was the sucking of liquid on liquid. The colours started blending into one another. Slowly he guided her until she was kneeling in front of him. The woman, whose name he had completely forgotten, was somehow indeterminate, both in age and physical appearance. In normal circumstances, Jerry would have considered her almost repulsive, but right now she was perfect for the work he was planning. To his mind, in fact, shrouded as it still was in the effects of the pills he had taken earlier that evening, disgust was an essential component of the work. As he looked at her slightly pendulous breasts, which not even that bright colour could improve, his penis started swelling. His arousal had nothing to do with the woman's nakedness, but everything to do with the sexual effect that making one of his works always had on him. Slowly, he lay down on the sheet, his mind engorged by the coloured shapes his body was tracing on what would become one single huge painting, subdivided into panels of equal size.

For Jerry Ko, art – creation – was above all a matter of chance, of chaos. That was why it needed two things intimately connected with chaos: sex and drugs.

Jerry Ko was completely crazy. Or at least, in his total narcissism, he liked to think so. He motioned to the woman whose name he couldn't remember to come closer. She lay down on top of him, placing her hands either side of him, her eyes half closed and her breathing slightly laboured. Jerry felt her paint-smeared hair lightly brush his navel. He grabbed her head and guided it towards his now completely erect member, which stood out white against his painted body. Her lips opened and he felt the sticky, worshipping warmth of her mouth envelop him completely.

Now he could see the two of them as superimposed patches of colour reflected in the large mirror on the ceiling. The slight movement of the woman's head was barely visible at that distance, but he could feel it. A sense of elation welled up in him. He pressed his hands, palms open, on the white sheet beneath him. When he looked up and saw the prints he had left on the sheet, his excitement increased.

6

Why waste time painting a body on canvas when that body could paint itself?

He saw in the mirror, and felt on his skin, the blue hands of the nameless woman move up his sides, leaving two coloured stripes on his red body.

He heard her say, 'Oh Jerry, I'm so—'

'Shhh.' He silenced her by placing a finger on her lips. Red paint on red lipstick.

The loft was dimly lit, most of the light coming from a bank of silent TV screens, linked together and computer-programmed to show a random sequence of colour mixtures, interrupted every now and again by a dissolve that reduced these mixtures to fragments and recomposed them into images of terrible disasters and atrocities – thousands of bodies floating along a river during the Rwanda massacres, episodes from the Holocaust, or the atomic mushroom cloud over Hiroshima – alternating with highly explicit sex scenes.

'Quiet, now,' Jerry whispered. 'I can't speak. I mustn't speak.'

He forced the nameless woman to lie down beside him, then pointed at their reflections in the ceiling mirror.

'I have to think. I have to *see*.'

He felt the woman's excitement clothe her like an aura. Turning abruptly, he opened her legs and penetrated her in a single violent movement. In so doing, he knocked over the can of paint he had used on himself. From her supine position, the woman saw the red paint spread across the white sheet, as if all the blood in her body was suddenly gushing out, and the almost liturgical purpose of their union overwhelmed her. Her desire turned to frenzy and she began moaning louder and louder, in perfect rhythm with the urgent thrusts of the man she held between her loins.

Even though she didn't know it, Jerry was convinced of the fact that both sex and art were destined to end in failure. That an artist carried within himself the seeds of his own destruction.

However many nameless women he screwed on sheets fixed to the floor, however much paint he applied to surfaces prepared to welcome them, the work he yearned for would forever remain beyond his reach, a fleeting idea immediately obscured by the images of everyday life.

With a long moan, the woman reached orgasm, trying in vain with her hands to grip the sheet. Jerry could resist no longer. Leaping to his feet, he masturbated frantically, scattering his seed over the marks their movements had left, as if trying in some unnatural, blasphemous way to inseminate the sheet.

The woman realized what he was doing, and the knowledge that she was part of that creation brought on another orgasm, even stronger than the previous one, which forced her to curl up in a foetal position.

Drained, Jerry slid to the floor until he was lying with his face turned towards the large windows that looked out on the East River. Even though they were on the seventh floor, he could still sense the reflection of the full moon on the dirty water. He moved his head slightly and there it was – a luminous disc in the middle of the window on the left.

The previous evening, the radio had said there would be an eclipse – which would be visible from that part of the coast. At that very moment, a thin black border was starting to gnaw at the impassive circle of the moon.

Jerry started trembling with emotion.

His mind went back to 11 September 2001. The clamour after the first plane struck – the screams, the sirens, the unmistakable sounds of panic – had come in through his open windows. He had gone up to the roof of his building on Water Street and from there had watched as the second plane struck – and then as the Twin Towers collapsed. It was a masterpiece of destruction, a perfect example of how civilization could only be redeemed through its own annihilation. And if that was true of civilization, how much truer was it of art, which represented the most advanced outpost of civilization. The fact that thousands of people had died in that collapse did not greatly concern him. Everything had its price, and those deaths were small change compared with what the world had gained from the event.

That was the day he had decided to change his name to Jerry Ko, a deliberately transparent play on words, evoking Jericho, the Biblical city whose impregnable walls had fallen at the mere sound of a trumpet. He was going to bring the walls down too, he had resolved – and himself with them.

As for his real name, he had preferred to forget it, along with the whole of his previous life. There was nothing in that life that was worth preserving.

The nameless woman was crawling towards him, her movements made awkward by the paint drying on her body. He felt her hand touch his shoulder, and then her breath, still hot with pleasure, next to his ear, saying, 'Jerry, that was really—'

Jerry clapped – and a sensor immediately switched off all the lights except for the shifting colours of the TV screens. Then he placed a hand on the woman's back and pushed her roughly away.

Not now, he thought.

'Not now,' he said.

'But I . . .'

9

The woman's voice faded to a whimper as Jerry pushed her even further away.

'Be quiet and don't move,' he ordered.

She lay there motionless and Jerry again looked at the circle of the moon, by now half swallowed by the darkness. He didn't care that the phenomenon he was witnessing had a scientific explanation. All he cared about was the allegorical significance of it.

He kept watching the eclipse, sinking into the after-effects of the drugs and the physical effort, until the moon became a black disc surrounded by light hanging in the sky of Hell.

He closed his eyes and, as he drifted into sleep, Jerry Ko hoped the moon would never return.

CHAPTER 2

The woman opened her eyes and immediately closed them again: the daylight coming in through the windows was too bright. She had drunk a lot of champagne the previous night, and now her tongue felt furred and there was an awful taste in her mouth.

She realized that she had been sleeping completely naked on the floor and that it was the cold that had woken her. She shivered and curled up, searching for warmth in the same position in which the previous evening she had sought escape from a truly overwhelming orgasm. It had been a shattering experience. For the first time ever, she had felt completely part of something, something she would remember for the rest of her life. She kept her eyes closed for a little while longer, as if to preserve the images of that amazing event, and her whole body broke out in goose bumps, partly from the cold, partly from the excitement.

Then, with a sigh, she cautiously opened her eyes again. The first thing she saw was Jerry Ko's back, still naked, the now congealed red paint looking scaly. The loft was lit by the blue glow of early morning, as well as the flashing of the TV screens. They had probably been on all night. The woman wondered if that was the work that had . . .

As if becoming aware of a change behind him, Jerry turned

and looked at her with eyes so red, she had the impression that the paint he had smeared himself with last night had gone inside him. He stared at her as if he had never seen her before. 'Who are you?' he asked.

The question unsettled her, and all at once she felt absurdly embarrassed by her own nakedness. She sat up and put her arms around her legs. Her skin felt strange because of the congealed paint, as though a thousand tiny needles were pricking her simultaneously. A few coloured scales fell on the white sheet beneath her.

'I'm Meredith.'

'Meredith, of course.'

Jerry Ko gave a slight nod, as if there was something inevitable about the name. Then he turned his back on her again and resumed dipping his hands straight into the pots of paint and spreading colours on the sheet. Meredith had the impression he was somehow erasing her presence from the room, or from the world.

His hoarse voice surprised her as she was trying to get up without causing abrasions to her skin. 'Don't worry about the paint. It's non-toxic watercolour, the kind children play with. Just take a shower and it'll disappear. The bahroom's at the back on the left.'

Jerry heard her steps as she walked away – then, after a while, the roar of the shower.

Wash and go, Meredith . . .

He knew the kind of woman she was. If he gave her the slightest encouragement, she'd stick to him like a tattoo, and he wasn't going to have that. She had been a means to an end and nothing more. Now that her usefulness was over, she had to disappear. In his mind, he had a vague memory of meeting her the previous evening at an opening to which his dealer,

12

LaFayette Johnson, had dragged him. Somewhere on Broadway, he seemed to recall. It was a photographic show, displaying the work of a journalist who had lived for a couple of years out in the wilds of Africa, photographing the members of a supposedly unspoiled tribe.

He had wandered for a long time among those faces and voices and clothes without the slightest curiosity as to who was who and what was what. After a while, the boredom of it all had started to cancel the effect of the ecstasy pill he had taken before leaving home and he longed to be somewhere more exciting.

'Are you Jerry Ko?'

He had turned towards the voice, to be confronted by a woman so grey, she seemed made of vicuna. Her bright red lipstick was the only splash of colour, although the worship in her eyes shone as brightly as it did.

'Do I have any alternative?' he had replied.

The woman had not picked up on the dismissal implicit in his words. She had kept going – in love perhaps with the sound of her own voice, like all the people around them. 'I know your work. I saw your last show. It was so . . .'

Jerry would never know exactly what his last show had been like. He had continued to stare at the woman's red lips as they moved, without hearing the words coming out of them . . . and that was when the idea had come to him.

Taking her by the arm, he had drawn her towards the door. 'If you like my work, come with me.'

'Where?'

'To be part of the next one.'

Jerry remembered how readily she had obeyed when he had asked her to undress, and her excitement when he had started to splash her with paint.

He could still hear the sound of the shower. The paint was swirling down into the drain, like excrement. *Art and shit are the same thing*, he thought. *And there's always someone who can sell either.*

His exhaustion was starting to make itself felt. His eyes were stinging, his neck muscles aching. He needed something – anything – to help him out of this physical impasse. And there was only one person who could get it for him. He stood up, went to the telephone and lifted the receiver without caring about the fact that he was staining it with the fresh paint on his hands. He dialled a number, and before long a drowsy voice answered.

'Who the fuck is this?'

'LaFayette, it's Jerry. I'm working and I need to see you.'

'Christ, Jerry, it's six in the morning.'

'I don't know what time it is. What I do know is, I need to see you – now.'

He put the receiver down without waiting for an answer. LaFayette Johnson would curse for a while and then get up and come running. Johnson owed most of what he had to Jerry, and it was only right for him to take care of his needs.

Jerry looked up and stared at his own image reflected in the mirror over the telephone. His painted face looked demonic. 'It's all going according to plan, Jerry Ko,' he grinned. 'All according to plan.'

Meredith's return, also reflected in the mirror, jolted him out of this dialogue with himself. She had washed her hair and was wearing one of his robes, which hadn't been laundered for a long time and was caked with paint.

Now that she had removed both the paint and any last trace of make-up, she looked vulnerable in the pitiless light of day.

14

Jerry felt a kind of hatred for her, for the adoration in her eyes whenever she looked at him. He hated her profoundly – and at the same time envied her for being such a total nonentity.

'Get your clothes and go. I have work to do.'

Meredith went red in the face. In silence, she started gathering her clothes from where they lay strewn on the floor, holding the robe with one hand to stop it opening as she bent. She turned her back on him and started getting dressed. Jerry watched as her nondescript body miraculously disappeared beneath her clothes. When she turned round to face him, she was again the grey woman of the previous night, but drained of the idea that had made her attractive to him for a few hours.

She held up the paint-stained robe. 'Can I keep this?'

'Of course.'

Meredith smiled. She hugged the robe to her chest and walked silently towards the door. Jerry thanked her mentally for sparing him a last look and a last nauseating farewell as she went out.

He was alone again. When he heard the noise of the elevator starting on its way down, he went and lay on his back in the middle of the sheet on the floor. Opening his arms wide, he gazed up at the image of his crucified body in the ceiling mirror.

He did not have the strength to pull himself together and get back to work. The TV screens continued to transmit their splashes of colour and their cruel, obscene images. The work – he thought of it as a totem – had been commissioned to be displayed in the huge lobby of the New York State Governor's Residence in Albany. The day it was installed, in the presence of the governor and a distinguished audience, there had been a murmur of anticipation when it was switched on. As the images had succeeded one another, however, the murmur had gradually been replaced by a stony silence.

The Governor was the first to pull himself together. His stentorian voice had echoed through the vast space.

'Turn that filth off!'

The totem had been switched off, but that did not put an end to the scandal. Jerry Ko was charged with defamation and obscenity, which had the effect of making him famous overnight. LaFayette Johnson, the gallery owner who was on his way now to supply him with drugs, had started to add noughts to the prices of his works.

The doorbell rang, and Jerry, without even bothering to put on any clothes, made his way through the chaos of his loft to the door. He was surprised to find it ajar. That idiot Meredith couldn't have closed it properly on the way out. But if it was LaFayette, why hadn't he come straight in without ringing?

When he opened the door wide, he saw a man standing out on the landing, shrouded in shadow. The light must be out of order and he couldn't quite make out who it was. It certainly wasn't LaFayette: this man was taller.

There was a moment's pause, a sense of time suspended, like the lull before a summer storm. Then:

'Hello, Linus. Aren't you going to let an old friend in?'

It was a voice he hadn't heard for a long time, and yet he recognized it immediately. Like everyone, Jerry Ko had fantasized often, especially under the influence of drugs, about his own death. He had wanted what every artist wants: to be the one to decide how it would happen – to choose, as it were, the colour and material of his own shroud.

When the man on the landing entered the room, Jerry knew that his fantasies were about to be overtaken by reality. As he looked the man in the eyes, he was barely aware of the gun he was holding. What he saw rather was a hand throwing a bucket of black paint over the questionable artwork he had called his life.

CHAPTER 3

LaFayette Johnson parked his brand new Nissan Murano on the corner of Peck Slip and Water Street, took his keys from the ignition and bent down to pick up a small package hidden in a compartment under the driver's seat. He got out of the car and locked it with the remote, then stretched and took a deep breath. A warm southerly breeze had risen, bringing with it a slightly brackish air and sweeping away the grey clouds of the past few days. Now, above his head, the sky was incredibly blue. But when you looked up, whether in the middle of the skyscrapers or in narrow streets like this one, all you could see was a small rectangle of it. In New York, the sun and the sky and a decent view were the privilege of the rich.

And that was what he had finally become. Very rich, thanks to that sleazebag Jerry Ko. Jerry's call had woken him but not surprised him. When, the previous night, he had seen him leave with a real dog, he knew perfectly well the function she had in Jerry's twisted mind. He, LaFayette, wouldn't have fucked a woman like that even with another man's dick, but he could hardly object if the goose that laid the golden eggs for him needed to mortify his flesh in order to turn out those daubs that LaFayette personally couldn't stand, but for which the public had an insatiable appetite. Jerry's work had given rise to a new interest in contemporary art, especially the work of young artists. People were collecting again, money was circulating. It was almost like the good old days of Andy Warhol. And LaFayette had bagged one of the winning horses for his stable. That meant he had to take care of him, pamper him and feed him, just like a thoroughbred. It didn't bother the dealer that Jerry's ideas were fuelled by almost every kind of drug on the market. LaFayette was shrewd enough to be devoid of scruples, and Jerry adult enough to choose his own means of destruction. It seemed like a fair exchange. He would supply Jerry with whatever he wanted to put in his body, and as a reward, he would receive 50 per cent of everything that came out of his fucked-up head.

LaFayette Johnson slipped the package into the pocket of the tracksuit he was wearing and turned right onto Water Street.

The section of Brooklyn Bridge straight ahead of him was lit by the sun, but there wasn't quite enough light yet to rescue Water Street from shadow. There were already cars on the bridge, and the low hum of morning traffic.

Johnson turned to look back at his shiny new car, and thought of the distance he had put between himself and his poverty-stricken upbringing. Now he could finally afford all the toys he should have had as a kid.

He was only seventeen when he had run away from the little town in Louisiana where he was born – a sleepy place where waiting seemed to be part of the inhabitants' DNA. You waited for everything. Summer, winter, rain, sun, the passing of the train, the arrival of the buses. You waited for the only thing that would never arrive: life. The community of Three Farmers consisted of a few tumbledown houses around a crossroads, where the mosquitoes ruled and the only aspiration of the locals was a jug of cold lemonade out on the porch.

There was his mother, grown old before her time, surrounded by the strong smell of Cajun cooking, and with stretchmarks even on the calves behind her knees. And there was his father, who conceived of the family only as something on which to vent his frustration and anger when he had been drinking. LaFayette Johnson had grown tired of fried potatoes and blows, and one evening when his father had once again raised his hand to him, he had broken the old man's teeth with a baseball bat and run away, grabbing all the money he could find in that stinking hovel he'd never managed to call home.

Farewell, Louisiana.

It had been a long slow journey, but at the end of the road, *Hello, New York.*

If he'd had a licence, he might have become a cab driver. Instead, he had been forced to do whatever he could, until he had struck gold. He had found work as an errand boy in a Chelsea gallery owned by an art dealer named Jeffrey McEwan – a middle-aged man, snobbish and slightly effeminate, always dressed in Savile Row suits.

Christ, what a hypocrite you were, Jeffrey McEwan.

Although he was married, that faggot Jeff had an ass you could have driven an electric train-set through and flabby white skin the boy had never managed to touch without repressing a shudder of disgust. But Jeffrey was rich and he liked good-looking young men with dark skin. Although LaFayette preferred women, he had immediately understood that this could be a crucial turning-point in his life. It was a great opportunity and he had to be careful not to waste it. And

20

so the game had commenced, a game of glances and silences, sudden advances and tactical retreats. After a few months of that, old Jeffrey McEwan was cooked and ready to serve. The climax had come when LaFayette had been caught naked in the shower in the bathroom of the gallery – just by chance, of course. The old queen had literally gone crazy. He had gone down on his knees in front of him, embraced his legs, and declared his love.

LaFayette had lifted the man's head and stuffed his cock in his mouth. After that, he had sodomized him, forcing him to bend over the wash-basin in the bathroom, holding him down with one hand on his back and pulling his fine ginger hair back with the other to force him to look at their images in the mirror.

At that point old McEwan had thrown caution to the winds, left his wife, and set up home with him in an apartment. They had become partners and had started working together, at least until Jeff had seen fit to make his exit in style, struck down by a heart attack at the private view of a highly rated painter to whom he had the exclusive rights.

Unfortunately for LaFayette, the stupid faggot had never divorced his wife, and the bitch had grabbed every bit of Jeff's inheritance that hadn't been left to him, which amounted to about 50 per cent.

All things considered, it hadn't gone too badly.

But there was something else that Jeff had bequeathed him, something that in this line of work was worth all the money in the world: he had taught him the value of culture. By the time his lover's widow had evicted him from the gallery in Chelsea, he had been in a position to stand on his own two feet. Following the trend that was slowly shifting the centre of gravity of the art world towards SoHo, he had bought a large space on the second floor of an elegant building on Greene Street, near the corner with Spring. There he had opened the L&J Gallery, determined that from now on he would be his own boss. Apart from the gallery, he also possessed the small apartment where he lived, and the seventh-floor loft on Water Street, where he had housed Jerry.

As he passed a steakhouse, closed at this hour, he looked at his reflection in the window. Saw a handsome, successful black man in his early forties, wearing a Ralph Lauren tracksuit. He uttered a phrase Jerry Ko often used: 'It's all going according to plan, LaFayette, all according to plan.'

Reaching the front door of Jerry's building – a sandstone edifice with faded paint and fire escapes on the front – he searched in his pocket for the keys and realized he had left them in the Nissan. He rang the doorbell, hoping that idiot Jerry wasn't completely sunk in a drugged stupor and would hear him.

He rang twice, but there was no reply.

He was about to go back to his car to get the keys when a figure emerged from the half-light of the entrance and pressed a button to release the door. It was a white guy wearing a grey tracksuit with the hood up and a pair of sunglasses. He kept his head tilted slightly forward, and throughout their brief encounter moved in such a way that LaFayette could not see his face. He came out as if he was in a hurry, shoving past him without the slightest apology. Once outside, he straightened his head and back and set off at a slow run.

Holding the entrance door open, so he could get inside, LaFayette watched him as he moved away. He noticed that the man was running in a strange way, as if he had a problem with his right leg.

Loser.

That was LaFayette Johnson's opinion of all runners, and this one in particular, as he entered the lobby and pressed the button for the elevator. The door opened immediately, which probably meant that the elevator had just been used by the guy who had shoved past him. Not so athletic as to use the stairs, apparently. Or maybe the problem he had with his leg prevented him from negotiating steps easily . . .

LaFayette shrugged. He had better things to think about. He had to get Jerry back to work as quickly as possible, since he was planning to mount a show for the fall. He had already sounded out some collectors he considered trendsetters, as well as arousing the interest of the specialized press. The time had come to make the leap from New York to America and the rest of the world.

The elevator door opened on the seventh-floor landing. Jerry's loft occupied the whole of the floor.

His door was ajar.

Suddenly and without any reason, LaFayette Johnson felt a strangely rusty taste in his mouth. If there was such a thing as a sixth sense, his had just been activated.

He pushed open the door with its peeling paint and entered the loft, to be greeted by the usual chaos, composed in equal measure of colour and dirt, which seemed to be the one environment in which Jerry could survive.

'Hey, you awake?'

Silence.

LaFayette moved slowly through that mess of canvases, plates, beer cans, leftover food, books, and dirty laundry. On his left were a set of metal shelves on which Jerry kept his cans of paint and the rest of the materials he used in his work. In front of him, on the floor, lay a white sheet covered in red and blue patches of colour.

23

There was a strong smell of paint in the air.

'Jerry? Man, you really shouldn't leave your door open. Any two-bit junkie hustler could get in here and grab all these masterpieces of contemp—'

He came past the shelves, to be greeted by a sight that made all thoughts of contemporary art flee from his head.

Stark naked and covered in dried red paint, Jerry Ko was sitting against the wall in a position so comical, only death could have made it tragic. The thumb of his right hand was in his mouth, and with his left hand he was holding a blanket to the side of his face in such a way as to cover his ear. His eyes were wide open, frozen in astonishment and horror.

On the white wall behind him, at the level of his head, was a thought bubble, drawn in blue spray paint. Inside the bubble, in the same colour paint, was written a number:

$$84336286747 \boxed{46}$$

LaFayette realized two things simultaneously. The first was that his goose would never again lay a golden egg. The second was that he himself was in big trouble. And there was only one way to get out of it. For once, he had to act according to the rules.

Taking his cellphone from the pocket of his tracksuit, he frantically dialled 911. When the operator replied in a polite impersonal voice, he reported that he had discovered a homicide. He gave his name and the address, promising that he would stay there until the police arrived.

Then he grabbed a camera and started taking photographs of the corpse from all angles. There would certainly be more than one newspaper ready to pay a fortune for these pictures, even if they weren't of outstanding quality. When he was done, he went to the bathroom, took out the pills he had in his pocket and threw them down the pan. He pressed the button that worked the flush and, as the water carried them away in a little whirlpool, LaFayette Johnson wondered how he was going to get Jerry Ko's latest works out of here.

CHAPTER 4

Standing by the window, Jordan Marsalis watched the removal truck reverse out of the parking space he had reserved for it in front of his building. Only a few minutes earlier, with the overheard comments of the removal men still ringing in his ears, he had signed the receipt the man in charge of the company had handed him. He was a huge black guy, with a wrestler's physique and big biceps that swelled the sleeves of the yellow and red coveralls he was wearing. On the back was printed the word *Cousins* – the name of the Brooklyn-based removal and storage company to which Jordan had entrusted the few items of furniture in his apartment that meant anything to him. The other things would be left for the new tenant. Jordan had scribbled his signature on the paper, giving his consent for part of his life to be hidden away in a warehouse somewhere, in some place he didn't know.

As he held out Jordon's copy of the receipt, the man had looked at his motorcycle leathers with a mixture of curiosity and envy. Jordan had put his hand in his pocket and taken out a hundred-dollar bill.

'Here, have a farewell drink on me and take a look at my things every now and then.'

The man pocketed the bill with a solemn gesture. 'Sure

thing, sir.' Then he had stood there, without making any move to go. After a moment, he had looked Jordan in the eyes and said, 'It's probably none of my business, but I get the impression you're going on a long journey. And you look to me like someone who doesn't know where he's going to end up.'

Jordan had been surprised by the sudden gleam of intelligence in the man's eyes. Up until this point, their dealings had been entirely professional.

'I confess I'd like to be in your place,' the man had continued, without waiting for a reply. 'In any case, wherever you're headed, have a good trip.'

Jordan smiled and thanked him with a nod of the head. Then, without another word, the big man had gone out and closed the door behind him – and Jordan was left alone.

As soon as the truck had turned the corner, he moved away from the window and walked over to the threadbare couch in front of the fireplace, grabbed the waterproof backpack in which he had placed the few clothes he might need on the road, picked up his helmet, and put his gloves and ski mask inside.

He had let his apartment through an agency to a stranger – an out-of-towner named Alexander Guerrero who was moving to New York. Although this guy had only seen the apartment in photographs sent as email attachments, he had enclosed, along with his references and the appropriate guarantees from the agency, a cheque for a deposit and six months' rent in advance – thus becoming the new tenant of a good four-room apartment on 54 West 16th Street, between Fifth and Sixth Avenues.

Well, congratulations, Mr Guerrero, whoever you are . . .

Jordan hoisted the backpack over his shoulder and headed

for the door, the sound of his steps on the bare wooden floor echoing strangely in the half-empty apartment. He had just placed his hand on the door when the phone on the mantelpiece rang.

He turned slowly and stared at it. He had sent AT&T a cancellation notice a few days earlier, and was surprised the number was still connected. The phone kept ringing, and Jordan debated with himself whether or not to pick up. He wasn't at all curious to know who was calling him, or why. In his mind, he was already on the freeway, shooting across the landcape, the white line in front of the bike reflected on the visor of his full-face helmet. He hadn't left New York yet, but it was already a memory – and not a very good one.

There had been a time when this city had meant something to him. After all, it had given him the opportunity to be what he wanted to be. Then, one day, he had been forced to make a choice – the kind of choice you cannot reverse – and he had learned that whatever life gives you, you have to pay back. And he had certainly paid more than his share. When he'd had enough of paying, he had decided to abandon the city and put his apartment up for rent.

With a sigh, Jordan threw the backpack and helmet down on the couch, and lifted the receiver.

'Yeah?'

He heard a muted rhythmical noise in the background, from which a familiar voice emerged.

'Jordan, it's Chris. I called you on your cellphone but it was off. Thank God you're still in the city.'

Jordan was surprised. His brother was the last person from whom he would have expected a call. There was a nervousness in Christopher Marsalis's voice and something new, something he would never have thought to hear.

28

Fear.

Jordan pretended not to notice. 'My cellphone isn't working too well right now. I was just about to leave town. What's up?'

Chris paused for a few seconds, which was also unusual for him. He didn't usually give anyone – himself included – a moment's respite.

'Gerald has been murdered.'

Jordan had a sudden feeling of déjà vu. He realized that, in a way, it was a piece of news he had been expecting for some time. He had felt it hovering over his head like a premonition every time he thought about his nephew.

He managed to keep his voice calm, not to let his brother's mood infect him. 'When?'

'Last night. Or this morning, I don't know. The gallery owner who handles his work dropped by his apartment very early and found the body.'

Jordan couldn't help thinking it was highly unlikely that son of a bitch LaFayette Johnson had been paying a social call at that hour of the morning. Nobody had ever managed to pin anything on him, but everyone knew how he paid for his protégé's work.

'Where are you now?' he asked his brother.

'I was in Albany for a meeting of local Democrats. As soon as I heard the news, I got on a helicopter. We're about to land at the Downtown Manhattan Heliport. Christ, Jordan, I was told they found him in a terrible state . . .'

Chris's voice shook, as if he was on the verge of tears. That, too, was new.

'I'll be right there,' Jordan said.

'Gerald was living . . .'

Jordan noticed that his brother had referred to Gerald in

the past tense. He himself felt strangely reluctant to bury him just yet. 'I know where he's living,' he said. 'At the end of Water Street.'

He was about to hang up when Christopher added, 'Jordan . . .'

'Yes?'

'I'm glad I found you.'

Jordan was not sure what to say, so he simply repeated, 'I'll be right there.'

Sometimes New York seemed like a living thing, which would continue to function even if all the human beings suddenly disappeared. The lights would still come on and off, the subway would still run, and the taxis would still cruise the streets even when there were no people waiting on street corners. In the same way, if he tried to leave now, Jordan had the strangest sense he'd find an invisible force-field around the city, making him stay somewhere he had no desire – and no reason – to stay.

He took off his boots, unzipped his leathers, slipped out of them in a single expert movement, and laid them over the back of the couch. Opening the rucksack, he took out a pair of sneakers, a shirt, a pair of jeans and a simple leather jacket – clothes he'd imagined he wouldn't need until he was many miles away.

As he sat down to tie his shoelaces, he saw something sticking out from between the cushions on the couch. He slid his hand under the seat and took out an old, slightly faded colour photograph. Jordan remembered it well. It had been taken at Lake George, where he and his brother had gone fishing with a group of friends. The two of them were standing side by side, the reflection of the water like a halo behind them. Both were smiling.

For a moment he sat looking at the faces as if they were those of two strangers. Physically, he and Christopher were very different. Only the eyes were identical. They had different mothers but the same father, and their blue eyes were the only inheritance Jacob Marsalis had divided equally between his sons.

Jordan stood up and placed the photograph on the mantelpiece, then picked up his helmet and headed for the door, with the absurd feeling that the images in the photograph were doing the same thing – that they were turning their backs on the room and walking away towards the lake in the background.

As he emerged onto the landing, from an apartment on the floor below came music, played excessively loudly. Jordan recognized a track by one of his favourite artists, Connor Slave, the new cult figure of American music – a sad, rather bitter song called 'Song of the Woman Who Wanted To Be a Sailor' – the story of someone longing for something they would never be able to attain. Jordan liked it. Maybe he identified with that woman standing on the cliff, looking at the sea on which she would never sail.

He went down in the elevator. On the street he was greeted by the light of a benevolent sun neither he nor the city deserved. As he crossed, he found himself thinking about the young man everyone knew as Jerry Ko, who had aspired to be the most significant figure in the New York avant-garde. A lot of things were going to be said about him and, unfortunately, almost all of them would be true. The newspapers would go to town on his difficult childhood and turbulent youth, his dependence on drugs and sex in spite of the fact that he belonged to one of the most high-profile families in the city.

On the opposite side of the street was a diner that was one of Jordan's regular haunts. He had often whiled away the hours there, joshing with the waitresses or just staring into the distance, searching for a solution he never found. Over time, he and the owner, Tim Brogan, had become friends, and Tim allowed him to keep his motorcycle in the little yard in back.

Walking past the windows, Jordan waved at a waitress in a green uniform who was serving two customers sitting at the table facing the street. As she had her hands full, she replied with a nod of the head and a smile.

He slipped into the alley and then turned right into the yard. Standing next to his motorbike, which was covered in a dust sheet, was Annette, another of the waitresses, taking a short cigarette-break. Jordan was familiar with her story. Her husband had long been fighting a losing battle with alcohol, and a few years earlier her son had been in trouble with the police. When she had turned to Jordan for help, he had taken pity on her and done what he could to help. Annette didn't talk about her husband these days, but her son had a job now and seemed determined to stay out of trouble.

'Hi, Jordan. I thought I'd find an empty place here this morning instead of your bike. I was sure you'd be gone by now.'

'So was I. But someone's decided otherwise.'

'Trouble?'

'Yes.'

Her face darkened for a moment. 'We all have our troubles, Jordan.'

Jordan approached the bike and started removing the sheet, until his shiny red Ducati 999 was revealed. Used to it as he was, he was still susceptible to its charms. It was the kind of

32

bike you loved not only for its performance, but even more for its appearance.

'It's a beautiful machine,' Annette said.

'Beautiful and dangerous,' Jordan replied, folding the sheet.

'No more than a lot of things in this city. See you around.' She threw her cigarette on the ground and carefully stubbed it out with her foot. Then she turned and went back inside the diner.

As Jordan switched on the ignition and buckled on his helmet, it struck him that he was about to do something he'd done many times in the past – something he'd thought he'd never have to do again: head out for a crime scene after taking a call. But this time it was different. This time, the victim was someone who was part of his life, even though he had long ago chosen not to be part of anybody's life.

But that was a minor consideration. The important thing was that Jerry Ko's real name was Gerald Marsalis and that, apart from being Jordan's nephew, he was also the son of Christopher Marsalis, the Mayor of New York.

CHAPTER 5

Jordan turned onto the final stretch of Water Street. By this time of day, the light was dividing the street exactly in half. Right and left, sun and shade, hot and cold.

The media were already out in force. There were print journalists moving about as best they could between the police cars, and trucks from *Eyewitness News* and Channel 4 parked on the square at Peck Slip. A woman reporter from the 24-hour news channel NY1, whose name he couldn't remember, was broadcasting live with the cordoned-off area in the background. Their prompt appearance had to be connected to the fact that there was always some cop in the force who was paying his mortgage or his son's college fees by playing the profitable role of 'reliable source'.

Jordan parked his bike where it would remain in the shade, in order not to find the saddle boiling hot when he came back. He then walked casually towards the building as if he was merely another curious bystander, keeping his helmet on his head in order to avoid being recognized. If there was one thing he didn't want or need right now, it was to be mobbed by a crowd of reporters wielding microphones.

Jordan had reached the barrier. There was an opening just in front of the main door of the building, where two officers were keeping guard. He knew one of them from Headquarters at

One Police Plaza, which was only half a mile away. The officer had already stepped forward to bar his way when Jordan's head emerged from the helmet. The other man recognized him and opened the barrier a little more to let him through.

'Good morning, Lieutenant.'

'I'm not a lieutenant any more, Rodriguez.'

'No, of course not, Lieut— I'm sorry.'

'It's OK, Oscar. Are they all up there?'

'Sure, on the top floor. The Mayor hasn't arrived yet.'

'I know. He should be here any minute.'

Officer Oscar Rodriguez's eyes narrowed. 'I'm sorry about your nephew . . . Mr Marsalis.'

'Thanks, Oscar. Can I go up?'

'Sure. Nobody said so openly, but I have the feeling they're waiting for you.' Rodriguez stood aside to let him enter the building.

As he went up in the elevator, Jordan recalled that he had never visited his nephew's loft. One evening, though, he had met him by chance at Via Della Pace, an Italian restaurant in the East Village. Gerald was with a group of young men and women whose appearance and behaviour seemed perfectly in line with his lifestyle. They all had the same expression on their faces – a mixture of arrogance and nihilism. From the way they deferred to Gerald, it was clear that he was their leader. When Jordan had approached the table, his nephew had interrupted the speech he was making to his friends and looked his uncle in the eyes, without surprise and without pleasure.

'Hello, Gerald.'

His nephew had grimaced. 'Gerald is history. It's a name that doesn't belong to me any more. Nothing's left of what I was before.'

'Nothing and everything are extremes. Sometimes it doesn't take much for them to meet.'

'Fine words, Father Marsalis. I didn't know you'd become a philosopher. If you came in here to give me a lecture . . .'

Jordan had shaken his head slightly. 'No, I came in here because I was hungry, but I think I came to the wrong place.'

'I think you're right.'

Silence had fallen, the kind of silence that always falls between two people who have nothing more to say to each other. Jordan had turned and walked away. In the indistinct buzz that had followed him, he had made out one phrase: 'Just a cop.'

That was the last time he had seen his brother's son.

When the elevator doors opened, the first thing that struck him was the strong smell of paint. The door of the apartment was wide open, and inside, the Crime Scene team could be seen going about their business. Given the identity of the victim, it was obvious that no effort would be spared.

Presumably Christopher had informed them of his arrival, because Detective James Burroni came out on the landing before the officer guarding the door of the apartment could bar his way.

'It's OK, Pollard, I'll deal with it.'

Jordan had known Burroni a long time and knew he was a good officer. They had worked together in the Ninth Precinct when that was still a frontier outpost, but had never been on especially friendly terms. Jordan couldn't blame the man for his attitude. Nobody readily forgave a colleague for being simultaneously a well-known figure in Homicide *and* the brother of the Mayor. It was obvious that many people thought his rapid rise had more to do with family connections than merit.

Jordan felt strangely like an intruder, being here at a crime scene, even though the crime concerned him personally. And he had the impression Burroni was thinking the same thing.

'Hello, James.'

'Hello there, Jordan. Sorry to be meeting because of something like this.'

Jordan made a vague gesture with his hand, as if to dismiss the awkwardness of the moment. They both knew the score.

'Come in. I warn you, it isn't a pretty sight.'

As he followed Burroni, Jordan took a rapid glance around. The indescribable chaos of the loft was illumined by a limpid spring light that seemed strangely peaceful in a place like this – a place from which Jerry Ko had waged war on himself and the world.

And then he saw him.

Jordan did all he could to remain impassive. He crouched beside his nephew's body and contemplated the wide-open eyes, the doll-like red paint, the grotesqueness of his position.

'So far,' Burroni said, 'we think he was strangled first and then arranged like that. Death took place a few hours ago.'

Jordan indicated the clear areas on the wrists and ankles where the paint had come away. 'These marks will have been left by whatever was used to immobilize him. Maybe adhesive tape.'

'Looks likely. That should come out in the post mortem.'

'What else is the crime team saying?'

Burroni shrugged, indicating the rest of the loft. 'Have you seen this place? It doesn't look as if it's ever been cleaned. Whatever we find could have belonged to anyone, any time over the past hundred years.'

'And what's this stuff?' Jordan pointed to the victim's

finger stuck in his mouth and the blanket he was holding pressed to his ear.

'Glue. They've taken a sample and should be able to tell us something once they've analyzed it.'

'And the paint?'

'He painted himself. His dealer says he often used this technique in his work.'

At this point, Christopher Marsalis himself arrived, followed as always by his right-hand man, Ruben Dawson. They heard him from the entrance, berating the Medical Examiner.

'Christ, doesn't it mean anything any more, being the Mayor of this fucking city? Do what you have to do! Get the body out of here as quickly as possible!'

Still crouching, Jordan waited for the moment when his brother walked past the shelves and was able to see the state his son had been reduced to.

And that was precisely what happened.

Jordan saw Christopher's face first turn to stone then somehow crumble, and his eyes become strangely opaque. He didn't know how much longer his brother had to live, but Jordan knew without a shadow of a doubt that he had died at that moment.

Chris turned abruptly and disappeared behind the shelves. Jordan stood up. Through the paint cans, he saw his brother hide his face in his hands. He went to him and put a hand on his shoulder. Christopher knew it was him without seeing him.

'Jesus Christ, Jordan, who could have done something like this?'

'I don't know, Chris, I really don't know.'

'I can't even look at him, Jordan. I can hardly believe that's my son.'

Christopher placed his arm on the wall and leaned on it with his back turned and his head bowed. He remained in that position while what was left of Jerry Ko was lifted, placed in a body bag, and taken out of the room on a gurney.

The four men – Christopher, Jordan, Detective Burroni and Ruben Dawson – were silent for a long moment. Christopher was the first to speak. He gestured at the wall against which his son's body had been propped and said thickly, 'What the fuck does this number mean?' There was anger in his voice, but he had regained some of his self-control.

Jordan took a deep breath and moved away from the others. Within a second or two, it was as if he was no longer with them. Over the years, he had discovered that he had remarkable powers of visualization. When he was still at the Police Academy, the psychologist conducting the aptitude tests had been astonished by his abilities.

Following his instinct, he stared at the wall until it disappeared.

He saw Gerald's body being dragged over and propped against the wall, then being placed in that absurd pose, and the hand drawing the cloud and . . .

'It's a Code T9,' he said, as if stating the obvious.

Three heads turned to look at him. 'What's a Code T9?' Ruben Dawson asked.

Jordan put his hand in his pocket and took out his cellphone. He started tapping quickly, every now and again raising his head to check the numbers. Only when he had confirmed his intuition did he look at them and say, 'It's an SMS dialling system. The telephone software recognizes the possible words from the keys pressed and reconstructs them without needing every letter.'

He approached the wall and pointed to the last two figures.

'There, you see? The last two numbers are in a square. Thinking of the position of the body and the numbers, I knew there must be a connection between them. I punched in those numbers and this is what came out.'

Jordan held up the open cellphone. On the display screen was a sentence:

the doctor is in

The three men all looked questioningly at him.

Anyone who knew him well would have understood that now Jordan wasn't so much talking to them as thinking aloud.

'The victim was placed in a position intended to recall Linus, the character from *Peanuts* who sucks his thumb and holds his comfort blanket against his ear.'

Jordan indicated the sentence on the phone display.

'These words are used by another *Peanuts* character – Lucy, the elder sister of Linus – whenever she sets up her psychiatric booth.'

Burroni was looking at him with what was meant to be a superior air, but his tone of voice when he spoke betrayed his admiration. 'And what do you think that means?'

Jordan put the cellphone back in the pocket of his leather jacket. 'I don't think the killer ever thought the message he left on the wall would be difficult to decipher. The pattern is so simple that any program used by the police or the FBI would have been able to decode it in a few seconds.'

Jordan took out a cigarette – a single cigarette, not the pack – lit it and took a drag.

'No, I think this was a kind of game for the murderer, a

little joke to show us—'

Jordan broke off abruptly. *I'm not a lieutenant any more, Rodriguez . . .*

'To show *you* his next move.'

None of the others seemed to have noticed that little correction.

Christopher took a step forward. 'What exactly do you mean?' he asked.

'The killer arranged his body to look like a *Peanuts* character,' Jordan explained. 'It's likely that the next victim will be treated the same way.'

Without realizing it, Jordan had taken the situation in hand and the others were hanging on his every word.

'I don't know who this next victim is, but if I'm right, two things are very likely. The first is that it's a woman . . .'

'And the second?' Christopher prompted.

'The second is that, in the killer's twisted mind, she's Lucy.'

41

CHAPTER 6

Lysa Guerrero was pushed slightly forward as the train stopped with a hissing of brakes. They had arrived at Grand Central Station, and Grand Central Station meant New York. A new city, more indifferent people, and another apartment full of furniture she hadn't chosen herself. But the choice was hers. It was a new start.

She stood up and, as she got her case down from the rack above her head, her long wavy hair moved as if alive. Out of the corner of her eye, Lysa caught a dreamy expression on the face of the man who had been sitting opposite her for part of the journey, a boy of about eight by his side, peeking at her whenever he thought she couldn't see. He was an average-looking man, the kind who wore a tie with a fake knot and a sleeveless shirt under his jacket. He seemed intimidated by her beauty, and the only time their eyes had met he had gratefully taken refuge in the answers that his son's questions demanded.

Lysa winked at him.

She saw him blush as red as a shrimp and immediately turn his attention to the backpack his son was having difficulty putting on by himself.

Lysa got off the train and walked along the platform, following the signs to the exit, indifferent to all the looks she was getting. There was nobody waiting for her, and at this point in her life she didn't mind at all.

She found herself in the vast main concourse – a monument of marble, with that staircase she had seen so often in movies, and that high ceiling depicting the sky. Pulling her case on its wheels, she turned right and headed for the subway. She knew that on the lower concourse there was a famous restaurant, the Oyster Bar. She decided that her arrival in the city should be celebrated appropriately. Oysters and champagne to start her new life. And maybe also to forget what she was here for . . .

Be brave, Lysa, it'll soon be over.

All her life she had been searching for a quiet place, somewhere to take refuge. What she wanted most in the world was something most people feared: to be ignored. Unfortunately, she had been gifted with a physical appearance that made that impossible. She had spent her life with everyone's eyes on her, all wanting the same thing from her.

And now, finally, she had surrendered.

If the world around her wanted her that way, then that was how she would be. Only, she would make them all pay dearly for her surrender.

She went down the ramp leading to the lower concourse. There was the restaurant she was looking for. She walked in through the glass doors of the Oyster Bar with an air of indifference, but none of those present was indifferent to her entrance.

Two somewhat aging yuppies, sitting at the counter just facing the entrance, stopped talking, and a plump man two seats further along dropped the oyster he was eating onto the napkin in his lap.

A waiter in the restaurant's uniform of white shirt and dark vest came towards her and escorted her through the large square room to a table in the corner, with two places set on a red-and-white check tablecloth.

Lysa sat down on the leather bench seat, ignoring the empty chair, and put her suitcase and purse down against the wall to her left. When the waiter held out the menu to her, she dismissed it with a gesture of her hand and gave him one of her sweetest smiles, which immediately won him over.

'I don't need it, thank you. I'd just like a selection of the best oysters you have and a very cold half-bottle of champagne.'

'Excellent choice. How does a dozen sound?'

'I think I'd prefer two dozen.'

The waiter leaned towards her conspiratorially. 'I'm well in with the maître d'. I reckon I could get you a whole bottle of champagne for the price of a half-bottle. Welcome to New York, miss.'

'How do you know I'm an out-of-towner?'

The waiter grinned. 'You have a case and you're smiling. You can't be from New York.'

'People leaving have cases, too.'

'Yes, but people leaving only smile when they've left the city behind.'

The waiter walked away, and Lysa was alone.

In the corner opposite was a table with half a dozen men around it. It was obvious they were out-of-towners, too. Lysa had spotted them behind the waiter as he was taking her order, had heard them talking, and had immediately recognized them for what they were.

Lysa took her time looking for something in her purse, until the waiter returned with a tray of oysters elegantly arranged on ice and a bottle in a chromium-plated bucket.

44

The men at the table waited until she had been served, and then one of them, a tall fellow with a receding hairline and a beer belly, got up from the table and, after conferring with his friends, came towards her.

Lysa had been expecting something like this to happen.

He reached her table just as she was serving herself a large Belon oyster. 'Hello there, darling,' he said. 'My name's Harry and I'm from Texas.'

Lysa lifted her eyes for a moment, then immediately dropped them and started seasoning her oyster. She spoke without looking the man in the face. 'I guess that makes you special?'

In his eagerness, Harry had not noticed the question mark at the end of the sentence and accepted it as a recognition of his qualities. 'You bet it does.'

'I thought so.'

Without being invited, the man sat down in the empty chair.

'What's your name?' he asked.

'Whatever you're planning to suggest, I warn you I'm not interested.'

'Come on, now. A man like me must have something to interest a woman like you.'

He was so sure of himself, he did not even notice the expression on her face. He was caught in a trap and didn't know it. Lysa leaned back in her seat, pushing her chest out slightly, and looked at him with eyes that made his legs shake.

Suddenly she smiled, a smile that was full of promise. 'You know, Harry, there's one thing I like in a man. Initiative. I think you have plenty of that, and that's what makes you such a smart guy.'

Harry smiled in his turn. Lysa did not miss the fleeting sideways glance he threw towards the other table: he was swanking to his friends.

'You can't even imagine how much,' he leered.

'That's what I thought. So it's only right for you to know that I'm pretty smart, too. Look at my hand.'

Lysa slowly ran her left hand across the table. Harry watched, fascinated by the route her nails were taking on the red-and-white check tablecloth. It was a simple movement, but her expression made it unusually sensual. He gulped.

'You see what I'm doing on the tablecloth? Just think – I could be doing it to you, on your back, in your hair, on your chest, other places . . .' Lysa half closed her eyes. 'Are you thinking about that?'

However limited Harry's imagination might be, his face made it clear that he was indeed thinking about that. Suddenly, Lysa's voice became a seductive sigh.

'And now just *think* what I could do with my other hand . . .'

She lowered her eyes, indicating a spot under the table. Harry looked down – and turned white. She was holding a switchblade in her right hand, aimed directly at his testicles.

'You have a choice, Harry,' she said. 'You can go back to your friends with your balls, or without them.'

Harry sought refuge in an ironic grin, but could not conceal the unease in his voice. 'You wouldn't dare.'

'Want to try me?'

For a few moments, the one movement in the world seemed to be a bead of sweat slowly trickling down Harry's forehead.

Then Lysa said, 'I'll give you a chance.'

'What do you mean?'

46

'Seeing as how you're not a bad person, just a moron, I'd like to do something for you. Put your hand in the breast pocket of your jacket and give me one of your business cards. I'll take it and smile at you. Your friends will see that, and you'll be able to tell them whatever you like. Maybe tonight you'll be able to go out on your own, go see a movie, and then tomorrow tell them what a terrific lay I was. I don't care. The only thing I want is for you to get out of my hair and let me finish my food.'

Harry slid cautiously out from the table and stood up.

Lysa put her right hand, now empty, back on the table. With a precise, highly suggestive gesture, she took the large oyster from her plate and slowly sucked it.

Harry turned his back to the table where his friends were and tried to recover some of his pride. 'You're nothing but a cheap whore.'

The angelic smile she gave him seemed incompatible with the woman who until a few moments earlier had been casually holding a knife aimed at his sexual organs. She slipped her hand back under the table. 'If that's what you think, why don't you sit down again?'

As Harry moved away without another word and returned to his own table, Lysa watched him with a smile on her face. When he sat down among his friends, she took the flute of champagne and raised it in his direction, as if toasting him. None of the other men noticed the grimace with which he responded to her gesture.

Then, calmly, Lysa turned her attention back to a huge Maine oyster that had pride of place on the metal tray.

Three-quarters of an hour later, a taxi dropped Lysa at the address she had given.

54 West 16th Street, between Fifth and Sixth Avenues.

She got out of the cab and, as the driver unloaded her case from the trunk, looked up at the roof of the building then let her eyes travel down to the windows of the corner apartment on the third floor. She put her hand in her purse, took out a bunch of keys, picked up her case, and walked to the front door.

She didn't know how long she would be here but, for now, this place was home.

CHAPTER 7

Jordan drove his motorbike into Carl Schurz Park and onto the short sloping path that led up to Gracie Mansion, official residence of the Mayor of New York. His brother had decided to live there during his term in office, even though he had a splendid penthouse on 74th Street. Jordan had kept a clear memory of his inauguration speech, when he had declared, in his best vote-catching voice, that 'the Mayor of New York should live where the citizens have decided he should live, because that's where they'll look for him when they need him.'

He stopped in front of the gate and took off his helmet. The security guard, a young man who still had a trace of adolescent acne on his cheeks, approached.

'I'm Jordan Marsalis. The Mayor is expecting me.'

'Can I see some ID, please?'

Without a word, Jordan put his hand in the pocket of his jacket and took out his licence.

As he waited for it to be checked, he saw that a number of police cars were parked beyond the gate, and that there were officers guarding the house. He wasn't surprised. The Mayor's son had been murdered and it couldn't be completely ruled out that the killer might come after the father.

The guard gave him back the licence. 'Thank you, sir. I'll open up for you.'

'Thanks.'

If the young man knew about him and his story, he gave no sign of it. Once the gate was open, Jordan drove through and parked his bike in the small open area in front of the main door of the mansion. As he approached, the door opened, and an impeccably dressed butler appeared in the doorway.

'Good day, Mr Marsalis. Please follow me. The Mayor is waiting for you in the small study.'

'You don't have to go with me,' Jordan told him. 'I know the way, thanks.'

'Very good, sir.'

The butler vanished discreetly. Jordan started walking along the corridor that led to the other side of the house, which faced the East River.

It was when he had left Gerald's apartment that Christopher had asked him to join him later at Gracie Mansion. Back out on the street, Jordan had once more escaped the onslaught of the press by using his helmet as a disguise – not that he had really needed to, because Christopher had come out immediately afterwards and the reporters had rushed towards him with all the blind frenzy of ants whose anthill has been destroyed.

Jordan had got to his Ducati and accelerated away without a backward glance.

And now here he was, outside a room he had no desire to enter. He rapped his knuckles softly on the shiny wood and, without waiting for permission, opened the door.

Christopher was sitting at his desk talking on the telephone. With his hand, he motioned him to come in. Ruben Dawson was sitting in an armchair with his legs crossed, as elegant and composed as ever. He gave an almost imperceptible nod of his head in Jordan's direction.

Instead of sitting down, Jordan preferred to walk past the desk and go to stand in front of the windows, which looked out towards Roosevelt Island. Outside, a barge was slowly descending the West Channel, heading south. A man was passing on the riverbank, holding two children by the hand, heading perhaps for the playground in the park. A boy and a girl were kissing against the railings.

Everything looked normal: a beautiful but ordinary spring day.

And behind him the cold voice of his brother, whose son had just been killed.

'No, I tell you. What happened mustn't be exploited. No photographs of the grieving father or anything like that. There are young American men at war right now, in various parts of world. The loss of any one of them is as important as my son's, the grief of a plumber in Detroit is no less great than the Mayor of New York's. All I'll let you say is that this city is mourning the loss of a great artist.'

A pause.

Jordan didn't know who exactly his brother was talking to, but it was clear that it was someone in his Press Office.

'All right. In any case, consult me before you decide anything.'

As he put down the receiver, the door opened and Police Commissioner Maynard Logan walked into the room, wearing a fitting expression. 'Christopher, I'm truly sorry. I came as soon as I—'

The mayor interrupted him without the slightest sign that he had even heard what he had said. 'Sit down, Maynard.'

Jordan had never seen the Commissioner looking so

embarrassed. When he noticed Jordan, his embarrassment increased exponentially.

Logan sat down. Christopher leaned forward, put his elbows on the surface of the desk, and pointed his index finger at him.

'Maynard, I want whoever killed my son to be caught. I want him locked up in Sing Sing. I want the other prisoners to beat the hell out of him every day and I want to be the one to give him the lethal injection when the time comes.'

Christopher Marsalis was a politician, and like all politicians he knew what to say when he was in the public spotlight. In private, though, his language wasn't always as refined.

'And I want Jordan to conduct the investigation.'

Three of the four men in the room were motionless for a moment: Jordan by the window, his brother with his finger raised, and Ruben Dawson looking with what seemed like great interest at the strap of his wristwatch. Only Commissioner Logan looked from one to the other.

'But Christopher—'

'Don't "But Christopher" me, Maynard!'

Logan tried to recover a little ground. 'OK, let's think about this for a moment. As a person, I have absolutely nothing against Jordan. We all know how good he is. But he isn't the only good police officer around, and what's more, there are procedures that even I can't—'

Logan seemed destined never to finish a sentence. Jordan saw his brother pounce on these words like a falcon on a henhouse.

'I don't give a fuck about procedures. Most of your men couldn't find their own asses even with an anatomy chart in their hands.'

'I have a duty to the community. How can I expect other people to obey the rules if I'm the first person to violate them?'

'Maynard, we're not at a police convention here. I know how the game works. Half the police officers in this city are taking bribes and the other half wish they were. Rules can be broken, it's a matter of necessity.'

Knowing it was his last throw of the dice, Logan tried to tackle the matter from another angle. 'Jordan is emotionally involved in this case and might not be able to keep a cool head.'

'Maynard, I saw what happened today. If Jordan was cool-headed enough to decipher that fucking number even after . . . after seeing what we saw, I don't think he'd have any difficulty in pursuing the investigation.'

'I don't know . . .' Logan sounded doubtful.

'Well, I do. Or rather, I know what I want. And you have to help me get it.'

For the first time since he had come in, Jordan spoke up. 'Don't you think my opinion matters in this discussion?'

Maynard and Christopher looked at him as if he had suddenly appeared out of nowhere. On Ruben Dawson's pale, impassive face, there was the merest hint of a smile.

Jordan left his place by the window and came and stood in front of the desk. 'I'm out of the game, Christopher. God knows I'm sorry about Gerald, but by now I should have been at least a hundred and fifty miles away from here.'

His brother raised his blue eyes towards him. 'The road will still be there, waiting for you, when this is all over, Jordan. You're the only person I trust. Could you excuse us for a moment, Maynard?'

'Of course.'

'Ruben, will you keep Commissioner Logan company and offer him something to drink?'

Dawson stood up without any change of expression and the two men left the room, probably grateful for the break.

Jordan sat down on the wooden chair that had just been occupied by the Commissioner.

'Logan will do what I tell him,' Christopher said. 'I can give you all the support you need. You just have to ask and you'll have every available means at your disposal. Officially, we won't say anything about you, but to all intents and purposes you'll be leading the investigation. If you like, Burroni can head it officially, but he'll be under your command.'

'I don't think he'll be pleased about that.'

'I just heard he's having some problems with Internal Affairs right now. He'll be pleased enough when we sort that out for him, and dangle the carrot of a promotion when all this is over.'

Jordan did not say anything.

'Jordan, you have to do it.'

'Why?'

'Because your nephew was killed this morning. And because being a policeman is your life.'

Jordan lowered his eyes to the floor as if he was thinking. In reality he was angry at himself for not finding any valid counter-argument. And there was a reason for that. What his brother had just said was absolutely true.

I'm not a lieutenant any more, Rodriguez . . .

'All right,' he said. 'I'll do it. As soon as possible, I need copies of the statements, the post-mortem report, and results of all the forensics tests. I have to do things my own way, but I'll let you know from time to time what support I require, and where.'

'Whatever you want. Ruben already has a copy of LaFayette Johnson's statement and the first findings of the Crime Scene team. The post mortem is taking place right now. The preliminary report might even arrive before you leave here.'

'Good. I'll keep you up to date with developments.'

Jordan stood up and walked towards the door. His brother's voice stopped him when he was in the process of opening it. 'Thanks, Jordan, I know you're doing it for me and—'

This time, Christopher was the one to be interrupted – something he wasn't accustomed to. Jordan looked hard at him, and his tone abruptly shattered the temporary solidarity that had been established between them.

'For once, let me be selfish. I'm not doing this to assuage your sense of guilt. I'm doing it to assuage mine.'

'Whatever the reason, I thank you. I'll never forget it.'

Jordan could not help making a bitter grimace. 'Seems to me this isn't the first time I've heard you say that.'

He saw a shadow pass over Christopher's face at these words. As he closed the door behind him, he hoped his brother did not have a conscience. Being left alone in that room to battle with it would be a hard trial, even for Mayor Marsalis.

CHAPTER 8

'Here you are,' Annette said, putting the cup of espresso down on the table in front of Jordan. 'Strong and black, no sugar, just the way you like it.'

'Thanks, Annette. Can I have the check?'

'The boss says it's on the house.'

Jordan looked at Tim Brogan, who was behind the cash desk, and thanked him with a gesture of the hand. On the TV set in the opposite corner, a Harry Potter movie was showing, with the sound turned down. Annette lowered her voice.

'We heard the news, Jordan. I'm really sorry about your nephew. A nasty business.'

'Life is one big nasty business, Annette. Just over twelve hours ago, I never thought I'd set foot in here again. And here I am.' He raised his cup in a toast as bitter as the coffee. 'To missed departures.'

'Postponed departures,' Annette corrected him.

A big bald man with a ketchup smudge on his cheek was waving behind them. Annette was forced to re-enter the world to which she belonged eight hours a day. Plus overtime, like this evening.

'Just coming!'

She walked away, and Jordan was alone again with his thoughts.

Even leaving aside the personal aspect, it really *was* a nasty business. To be handled with care. And if he was right, the heat was only just starting. When he had closed the door of his brother's office in Gracie Mansion, the post-mortem report had not yet arrived. He had preferred to leave Christopher to his feelings as a father and his duties as a Mayor. Jordan didn't know which of the two roles at that moment was the worse.

He had called Burroni and arranged to meet him here. He had just finished his coffee when the detective appeared, framed in the window.

He was wearing the same suede jacket and round-brimmed black hat he had worn that morning. He came in and looked around. When he spotted Jordan, he came over to the table with that strange walk of his, the centre of gravity low, like a soccer player's. He was holding a sports paper with a yellow folder sticking out of it.

Burroni came level with him and stood there. He looked as if he'd rather be somewhere else, with someone else.

'Hello, Jordan.'

'Sit down, James. What are you having?'

Jordan gestured to a passing waitress, who stopped to take the order.

'A Schweppes. I'm on duty.'

Burroni collapsed onto the chair facing him and put the newspaper down on the table. The folder slipped out a little and Jordan glimpsed the letters *NYPD* on the front.

'Let's get things clear straight away, Marsalis.'

'That's all I ask.'

'I guess you don't like me, but that's neither here nor there. The real problem is that I don't like you. And I certainly don't like this situation. I'm sorry about your nephew, but—'

Jordan lifted his hands. 'Stop right there. I don't know what you've been told and I don't care. But I would like you to listen to what I have to say.'

Burroni took off his hat and put it on the empty chair next to him. He leaned back in his own chair, folded his arms, and waited. 'All right, I'm listening.'

'I don't believe you're particularly sorry about my nephew. You think he was a freak who met the end he deserved, someone the world won't miss. That's your problem and I don't expect you to understand. But I think you'll have to get used to the situation. We're not getting married, James. But we have a job to do, and we have to do it together. We both have reasons for hoping it works out.'

Burroni put his elbows on the table and looked him in the eyes. 'If you're referring to this Internal Affairs business, you have to understand I—'

Jordan did not let him finish. 'I do understand. I understand it about you and lots of others. I understood all the years I spent in the Department. But I've always believed that a good cop, even if he sometimes falls victim to a few small weaknesses, gives more than he takes in the long run. If his weaknesses are big ones, then he stops being a good cop and becomes a crook. That's your problem, and a judge's. But there's something else that matters more.'

'Meaning?'

'Meaning I don't give a damn any more, James. For reasons of my own, I want to see this through and then draw a line under it. And the fact that the victim is my nephew is only part of it. When it's all over, I'll finally be able to leave on a journey that should have started this morning.'

The waitress arrived, placed a glass of fizzy liquid on the

table, and walked silently away. Burroni took a sip of the drink.

'That's my side of it,' Jordan went on. 'But you'll be the detective who caught the man who killed the Mayor's son. You'll be a hero, a star. And you'll be able to stop having to take kickbacks.' He pointed to the sports paper Burroni had put down on the table. 'What do you bet on? Horses or football?'

'You're a son of a bitch, Marsalis.'

Jordan made a small gesture with his head and gave a slight smile. 'Must be a family gift.'

There was a moment's silence. Jordan decided that, if a truce was necessary, this could be the right moment to wave, if not a white flag, at least a white handkerchief. He pointed to the folder sticking out of the paper.

'What's that?'

Burroni took it out, opened it and pushed it across the table. 'Copies of the statements. The post mortem was done in record time, and the first test results. It's all we have so far. Read it when you have time.'

Jordan decided that a bit of a boost to Burroni's self-esteem might be a good way of easing him into this forced collaboration. 'I'd rather you told me.'

Burroni's voice became slightly less tense. 'The PM confirms that the victim was strangled. To fix the thumb in place, his mouth was filled with strong glue. The same glue was used to attach the blanket and the hand to the ear. From the tests, it seems it was a very common brand called Ice Glue, which is found all over the country, so that doesn't give us any kind of lead. Plus, it seems you were right about the MO. There were traces of adhesive tape on the wrists and ankles – again, a very common brand. The killer probably immobilized him first and then killed him when he was unable to react. There are no signs of struggle on the body, apart from the strangulation marks on the neck. As for the testimony of . . .' he turned the paper towards him to read the name '. . . LaFayette Johnson, it hasn't been much use so far. He seems to have told the truth about what happened. The records show the victim called his cellphone pretty much at the time he said. When he discovered the body, he called the police. For the moment he can't be ruled out as a suspect, but . . .'

Jordan finished his sentence for him. 'But you don't think he would have killed his main source of income.'

'Precisely. He did tell us one interesting thing, though.'

'Which is?'

'As he was coming into the building, he almost collided with a guy in a tracksuit who was on his way out. He didn't see his face, but he said he ran off in a strange way, limping slightly, as if one leg was weaker than the other. We made enquiries in the building and the neighbourhood. Nobody of that description lives in the vicinity.'

'Seems worth pursuing. Anything else?'

'We managed to trace the girl who spent the night with your neph . . . with the victim. In fact, *she* contacted *us* as soon as she heard about the murder. They were questioning her when I left Headquarters.'

'What's she like?'

'Nothing to write home about. Quite plain, in fact. She's a secretary at a publisher's whose name I can't remember, with offices on Broadway.'

'Could she have strangled him?'

'Judging by her physique, no way.'

'And what are the Crime Scene people saying?'

'They have their work cut out. Thousands of prints, thousands of fibres, hairs, paint residue. It's going to take months to sort through everything.'

'So that's what we have, for now.'

There was no resignation in Jordan's comment. It was simply an observation. He knew from experience that most investigations started out with very little to go on.

'Do you think we're dealing with a serial killer?' Burroni asked.

'I don't know. It's too early to say. The MO does suggest the work of a psychopath. But it could be an acquaintance of the victim, or a fan, crazy enough to commit an isolated act, without there being any follow-up.'

'So what do we do?'

'It may not be pleasant, but we're going to have to look into the life of Gerald Marsalis. Everything. Friends, girlfriends, buyers, drug dealers . . .'

Jordan read the question in Burroni's expression.

'James, I know perfectly well who my nephew was and what kind of life he was mixed up in. I want to know everything. The rest is my problem.'

'I think you've made the right choice.'

Jordan thought he detected a touch of respect in these words. 'Do you have enough people?' he asked.

'Obviously, in this case as many as I want.'

'Then get someone to tail Johnson. He may not lead anywhere, but you never know.'

'OK. Are we done?'

'I think so, for now. Let's hope I'm wrong and we never find out who Lucy is.'

Burroni stood up and put his hat back on his head. 'See you, Jordan. Thanks for the drink.'

'We'll talk soon.'

Jordan watched as he went out without turning around and disappeared into the New York crowd.

On the TV at the back of the diner, someone had switched to CNN. After a brief item on the Iraq War, there were images of the murder of Jerry Ko, which was the big news of the day. From where he was sitting, Jordan couldn't hear the commentary, but he saw his brother outside Gerald's building, being swamped by a horde of reporters. Nobody, either in the morning or now, had paid any attention to the man with a helmet on his head slipping out of the front door of the building. The long shot was replaced by a closer shot of Christopher Marsalis getting into his car, leaving behind him a lot of unanswered questions.

As it drove off, the car bearing his brother away reminded Jordan of another car, in another place, on another evening. The exact moment nearly three years earlier when everything had started.

Or ended.

He had spent the whole of that weekend as a guest in Christopher's house in the country. The weather was fine and he had decided to stay on until Monday in that splendid villa near Rhinecliff, with its big windows that looked out on the banks of the Hudson, its extensive grounds, private jetty and annex for the security staff. The house and its interior had been designed by a European architect who really knew his business, and charged appropriately.

There was a difference of about twelve years in their ages and an equally big difference in their characters. Christopher was the rich one, Jordan the young athletic one. Christopher was a natural leader and, as such, needed people. Jordan didn't need anyone but himself. He was a lone wolf, who liked to pass unnoticed.

That evening, after dinner, Christopher had received a telephone call. Through the open door of the study, Jordan had heard him speaking in monosyllables. Then he had appeared in the living room, wearing his expensive camel-hair coat. Jordan had seen a couple of wads of banknotes disappear quickly into his pockets.

'I have to go out. Just make yourself at home. I'll be right back.'

'Is anything wrong?'

Christopher had finished buttoning up his coat. 'I have to see LaFayette Johnson,' he replied, without looking him in the face.

'You mean he's come all the way from New York?'

'For money, that piece of shit would be ready to accept an appointment on the *Titanic*.'

'Do you want me to come with you?'

'No point. He'll protect me.'

Jordan knew the reason for that meeting. Many of the paintings that Gerald sold were bought by Christopher himself. What Jordan had never understood was how much this was done to keep his son out of trouble and how much was due to his sense of guilt.

Christopher had gone out, and a minute or two later Jordan had heard the wheels of his Jaguar crunch on the gravel outside, then the noise of the engine fading away.

The house had sunk back into silence.

Jordan was used to the constant background hum of the city. Every time he was in that house he found the total absence of sound quite strange. It was a winter's night, cold and dark outside. Inside, it was warm and safe, with the flames leaping in the fireplace. He had switched on the TV and sat down on a couch to watch the Monday night football game. He had with him a bottle of the eighteen-year-old whisky blended specially for Christopher and, without realizing it, he had drunk half of it. He had not even seen the end of the game, but had drifted into a peaceful sleep.

He was jolted out of it by the ringing of the cordless telephone on the low table next to him.

'Hello?'

'Jordan, I'm in deep shit.' His brother's voice was agitated.

'What's going on?'

'I just killed a man.'

'What do you mean "I just killed a man"?'

'I was on my way home after meeting with LaFayette. At a traffic junction, this guy just shot out without giving way. I was going quite fast myself, and hit him straight on, but it wasn't my fault.'

'Are you sure he's dead?'

'Christ, Jordan, I'm not a doctor, but I fought in a war. I know when someone's dead.'

'Are there any witnesses?'

'At this hour, in winter? I'm in open country. I doubt they get more than three cars passing in a week.'

'Where are you?'

'Near High Falls, on the other bank of the Hudson, due south. Do you know where it is?'

'Yes, no problem. I'm on my way. Don't do a thing till I get there. And above all don't touch anything in the other car. Have you got that? If anything happens, call me on my cellphone.'

'Jordan . . . hurry.'

'OK. I'll be right there.'

He had grabbed a winter jacket, left the house and set off in his Honda. When he had reached the scene of the accident and got out, a glance had been sufficient to take in the situation. The Jaguar was in a ditch, on the opposite side of the junction from which Christopher had come. The left rear side was crumpled and a wheel stood out at a twisted angle. Across the road was an old pick-up in an equally bad condition, facing in the opposite direction. Through the shattered windshield, he saw a body slumped over the steering wheel. From the marks on the asphalt, it was clear what had happened. He could see where the Jaguar had braked, and where the pick-up had spun around after the impact. Pieces of glass and plastic lay on the ground.

He had gone to the pick-up and touched the neck of the middle-aged man at the wheel. There was no pulse. He looked around. There was no sign of Christopher.

'I'm here, Jordan.'

Christopher had emerged from a clump of bushes, his hands deep in the pockets of his coat.

'I wasn't sure it was you, so I thought it was best to get off the road,' he said, his breath turning to steam in the cold air. 'What do we do now, Jordan?'

It had only taken Jordan a moment to make up his mind. 'Take my car, go home, and stay there.'

'Do you realize what you're saying?'

'In the ultimate scheme of things, a good mayor is more important than a good cop. Do as I say.'

They stood there for a moment looking each other in the eyes. Two pairs of blue eyes, the only thing they really had in common. Then Christopher had got in the Honda and started the engine. Before driving off, he leaned out of the window.

'I know what you're doing and I'll never forget it.'

Jordan had stood there watching the car lights becoming smaller and smaller and disappearing into the distance. Then he called the sheriff's office in Rhinecliff, switched on the indicators of the two vehicles, and settled down to wait next to the half-wrecked Jaguar, with a dead man and his own thoughts for sole company.

He had lit a cigarette and smoked it all the way through as he waited.

By the time he heard the sirens approaching, he had known that this night was one he would never forget. He had given his personal details to the deputy sheriff and declared that he had been at the wheel of the car belonging to Christopher Marsalis. Naturally he had been given a breathalyzer test, and had had to admit he'd drunk half a bottle of whisky.

Fortunately things hadn't turned out so badly because the post mortem on the victim had revealed that he had died of a heart attack. In other words, the driver had lost control because he was already dead at the moment of the collision, which was why there had been no criminal proceedings againt Jordan.

All the same, the accident had involved a lieutenant in the NYPD driving while in a state of intoxication. As if that was not enough, this lieutenant was Jordan Marsalis, the Mayor's younger brother. The media had gotten in on the act, turning the case into a political football. The pressure from Christopher's opponents had become unbearable, and his own party had made it clear behind the scenes that it wasn't at all happy with the situation. So Jordan had eventually tendered his resignation and handed in his gun and his shield.

Since that day he had not drunk a drop of alcohol, nor driven a car. And he had hardly ever heard Christopher's voice until the latter had called him to announce that Gerald had been murdered.

Now, sitting at the table in the diner, Jordan reflected sourly that history was repeating itself. In the afternoon, his brother had thanked him with the same words he had used that evening.

I know what you're doing and I'll never forget it.

But he had.

CHAPTER 9

Jordan left the restaurant and crossed the street, to where light spilled out through the glass door of his building. As he moved his helmet from one hand to the other and felt in his pocket for his keys, he heard loud music coming closer.

Instinctively, Jordan knew that this music meant trouble. He turned and saw a dark, shiny Mercedes parking just ahead of him on his side of the street. From the open window came the electronic rumble of a techno track, played at high volume. The doors were flung open and two black men got out and came towards him, their lazy walk heavy with menace. They were both wearing bright tracksuits and jogging shoes. One had a woollen cap on his head and the other a black bandana.

One of the two, the man with the cap, he had never seen. The other he recognized immediately. Everyone knew him as Lord. It was Jordan who had put him inside for possessing and dealing heroin, as well as wounding two officers while resisting arrest.

'Hello, Lord. How come they let you out?'

'I was a good boy, Lieutenant. Six months off for good behaviour.'

'I'm not a lieutenant any more, Lord. And I hope that's the last time I have to say that today.'

'Oh, I know. They kicked you out on your ass. You're a private citizen now. Just like us – right, Hardy?'

Hardy said nothing, didn't react at all.

'Do you know what it's like to spend three years in the can?' Lord went on.

He didn't give Jordan time to reply. Not that he was interested in what he had to say anyway. He was enjoying himself. He turned to his friend as if sharing a joke.

'Oh, I forgot. Lieutenant Marsalis can't go to prison, because he's the Mayor's brother, so even when he's out driving, smashed out of his head, and knocks down some poor bastard who happens to get in his way, the most he gets is a little slap on the wrist – and then he's free to go off and kill somebody else.'

'Stop beating about the bush, Lord. What do you want?'

It was a dumb question, whose sole purpose was to gain time. Jordan could perfectly well have answered it himself. He tightened his grip on the chinrest of his full-face helmet, ready to use it as a weapon.

Lord took a step back and with a rapid movement unzipped his tracksuit top, took it off, and dropped it on the ground. Then he lifted his arms and stood there in his undervest, his biceps and chest muscles tensed, in a bodybuilder's pose.

'Do you see these, Lieutenant? Know how I got them? By working out four hours a day, every one of the thousand-something days I spent in the can. And you know what I used to think about when I was lifting weights?'

'No. Surprise me.'

'I used to think about seeing you again, knowing you didn't have your shield any more to protect you.'

Jordan saw the shadows outlined on the rectangle of light

cast on the asphalt through the glass door behind him. He didn't have time to turn before the door opened and two people stepped out and took him from behind, pinning his arms behind his back. His helmet dropped from his hand and rolled on the ground.

Lord came closer. 'I used to think about *this*.'

When Jordan had joined the police, he knew a cop sometimes found himself in difficult situations. The irony was that this was one of the worst situations he'd ever been in and he wasn't even a cop any more. He leaned back against the two men behind him, lifted his foot and planted it in Lord's face. He distinctly heard the sharp sound of the cartilage of his nose breaking and saw him disappear from his field of vision. As he tried to free himself from the grip of the two men, the previously impassive Hardy suddenly came to life. Taking up a classic boxer's position, he landed him a one-two to the solar plexus. Jordan felt the food he had eaten earlier rise to his throat, then saw, as if in slow motion, Hardy's fist heading straight for his face. It struck him and, even before he felt the pain, there was a blinding flash of yellow light in his eyes. The impact pushed him backwards against the two other men, dislocating his shoulder.

In the meantime, Lord had got back on his feet and was coming towards him with blood dripping from his broken nose and onto his uneven teeth. 'You motherfucking bastard, I'm going to —'

He didn't get a chance to say what he was going to do. On the other side of the street, a police car had stopped just outside the diner and an officer had climbed out.

'Shit, it's the cops,' a voice behind Jordan's back said. 'Let's get out of here.'

Lord came close to Jordan. 'We'll finish there for now. But this isn't the end of it, you piece of shit.'

He gave Jordan a backhander that knocked his head sideways. Jordan felt the grip on his arms loosen and he fell to his knees. The four men got quickly back in their car and disappeared in a slamming of doors and screeching of tyres.

His ears were humming from the blows and there was a dull pain in his shoulder. He saw bloodstains on the stone steps and realized that the blood was his. He stood up and went to get his helmet, holding it with his left hand. Then he staggered inside the lobby and leaned against the wall for support. Taking a deep breath, he gave his shoulder a quick, sharp jerk, stifling a groan of pain as the joint clicked back into place. A few drops of blood fell onto his jacket and shirt. He took out a Kleenex and dabbed his nostrils. Then he went up in the elevator, standing in such a way as not to see himself in the mirror.

Once back at his door, he went in and switched on the light. Here was his old apartment, waiting for him. He put his helmet on the couch and headed for the bathroom, where he was surprised to see a sliver of light under the door. Maybe he had forgotten to switch off the light that morning. But right now, he had other things to think about.

He opened the door, and there, in the amber light of the bathroom, was a naked woman. The most beautiful woman he had ever seen in his life.

She had her back to him and was reflected from the waist up in the mirror. She had been drying her hair with a towel and had stopped when he came in. She showed not the slightest reaction, either of surprise or fear, nor had she made the slightest attempt to cover herself.

71

'Should I consider you a danger?' she asked, in a soft calm voice.

Jordan was completely taken aback. He couldn't speak for a moment, couldn't do anything but stand there in the doorway, seeing his face reflected next to hers in the mirror as he pressed a pathetic bloodstained tissue to his nose.

'No, I'm sorry, I—'

'Then do you mind closing the door and waiting outside while I get dressed?'

Jordan did as he was told, feeling like a small boy caught peering through a keyhole. He took refuge in the other bathroom, the one next to the guest room. He switched on the light and looked at his face in the mirror. He was forced to admit that Lord and Hardy had done a good job on him. His eye was swelling up and his mouth and nose were dirty with half-congealed blood. He turned on the faucet and washed himself. The cold water felt good on his swollen face.

He took off his shirt and used the clean part to dry himself. As he went back along the corridor towards the living room, he heard the hum of a hair dryer. He opened the closet where he had put his backpack that morning, and from it he removed a clean shirt. As he changed, he couldn't stop thinking about the woman in the bathroom. He couldn't remember ever seeing such a stunning creature. Closing the closet, he put the backpack down on the couch next to his helmet.

At that moment, the woman appeared, wearing a blue robe. Her dark hair was still a little damp. Her large liquid eyes were the most incredible hazel, almost golden.

'Now then, are you going to tell me why you're here?' she demanded.

'I live here.'

'Strange, I thought I'd just rented the place. Maybe there's some detail I missed.'

Jordan felt the same sense of inadequacy he had felt a while earlier in the bathroom. 'Let me rephrase that. I *used* to live here.'

'Are you Jordan Marsalis?'

'That's right. And you must be Mrs Guerrero . . .'

'Not exactly, but more or less. My name's Lysa.'

Jordan shook the hand she held out to him. It was warm and soft, a tactile sensation that was complemented by the delicate vanilla scent she gave off.

'I was told you'd be here in three days.'

'That was the idea, but I decided to come earlier because the agency told me you'd be leaving today.'

'I was supposed to, but then . . .' Jordan made a vague gesture with his hand. 'Well, things don't always work out as planned. I'm sorry I startled you. I'm really embarrassed.'

'Do you always get a nose bleed when you're embarrassed?'

Jordan lifted a hand to his face, and when he took it away it was stained with blood. The wound had started bleeding again. He walked to the kitchen door and looked around for something to stem the flow.

'I'm sorry. I've had a really bad day.'

'I'd already guessed that. Sit down on the couch. I'll be right back.'

She left him for a moment, and when she came back she was holding a dressing-case that looked more like a first-aid kit. She put it down on the couch next to Jordan and took out some yellowish cottonwool.

'Don't worry. I used to be a nurse. Anyway, I don't think I'd manage to make it any worse.'

She stood in front of him. Again, he smelled that vanilla scent of hers. She gently touched his nose and eye, then put her hand under his chin and lifted his head.

'This is going to burn a little.'

Having applied the haemostatic agent, she stepped back.

'All done, the blood's stopped. Your nose isn't broken, you'll be pleased to hear. That would have been a pity, it's a nice nose. There'll be a bruise, but it should match your blue eyes.'

Jordan felt as if she was looking deep inside him, searching out his secrets.

'You look like a man who's had more than just a bad day,' she went on.

'Yes. Someone I knew was murdered today.'

'I watched the news on TV. They said Gerald Marsalis, the Mayor's son, had died. Was he a relative of yours?'

Gerald is history. It's a name that doesn't belong to me any more . . .

'He was my nephew. Christopher Marsalis is my brother.'

'I'm sorry.'

Jordan stood up and picked up the helmet and backpack. 'Well, I think I've disturbed you long enough. Good night, and thanks.'

He was on his way to the door when Lysa's warm, calm voice stopped him. 'Listen, I feel guilty about sending you away in that state. If you like, you can stay here tonight. You know the apartment. There are two bedrooms and two bathrooms and we won't bother each other. Tomorrow you can decide what you want to do.'

'Won't your husband mind if I sleep here?'

Jordan always looked in people's eyes. He could tell when a person was lying or telling the truth, revealing their state of

74

a mind or trying to hide it. And yet he couldn't have given a name to what he saw now in Lysa's eyes.

'Considering you've already seen me *half* naked, I think finishing the job might help to avoid any further misunderstanding.'

Lysa opened her robe. Beneath it, she was completely naked. Time seemed somehow suspended. Jordan had the impression that, if Lysa had let the robe fall to the floor, it would have stopped in mid-air, as if by magic. Then the moment came to an end and Lysa disappeared again inside the garment. When she spoke, her voice was as defiant as the expression on her face.

'As you see, I'm Mrs Guerrero *and* Mr Guerrero.'

Jordan searched frantically inside himself for words appropriate to the situation.

Lysa seemed to read his mind. 'You don't have to say anything. Whatever you might say I've already heard at least a hundred times.'

She bent to take a bottle of pills from the dressing case and went and placed it on the granite worktop in the kitchen.

'Good night, Jordan. If it hurts at all, take a couple of these pills.'

In silence, she walked along the corridor towards the bedroom. Jordan was alone, and the room where they had just been together went back to being a simple living room.

From the floor below, music drifted up. It was the same track as before, that song full of longing and regret. It struck Jordan as the perfect soundtrack for that moment. As he listened to the lyrics, with a new interest in their meaning, he wondered how many times Lysa had looked at the sea and felt herself dying inside for something that had been denied her.

I stand here on this cliff
my eyes embrace the sea,
I dream the same old dreams
these dreams won't let me be.
The surface of the waves
like craters on the moon
like twisting trails of snakes
or trees cut down too soon.

And this strange old heart of mine
now sets sail across the sea . . .

PART TWO

Rome

CHAPTER 10

I stand here on this cliff
look down upon the sea,
I hear the mermaids sing,
singing their song to me.
Their song is sweet to hear –
as honey on the tongue.
Their song strong as the wind
that blows down old and young.

There's no glory or desire
that can tear my dreams apart.
There's no grindstone known to man
Can crush this rock inside my heart.

A man's bare arm emerged from under the duvet and stretched across the bed towards the control panel in the wall that worked the stereo and the TV. A slight pressure of a finger on a button, and the music – the melancholy, slightly old-fashioned sound of a bandoneon and a string band – was cut off as it drifted towards the open window and out over the roofs of Rome.

Maureen Martini stuck her tousled head out from beside him. 'No, let me hear it one more time.'

'Darling,' Connor Slave said, without taking his head out from under the duvet, 'do you have any idea how many times you've listened to that song?'

'Never as many times as I need.'

'Don't be selfish. And please don't make me regret writing it. Just think how many times *I've* had to listen to it . . .'

At last Connor's curly head appeared. He yawned and rubbed his eyes in a way that made him look like a cat. Even though music was his medium, he had an instinctive knowledge of movement, which complemented the intensity of his onstage performances. But in private, he could be a real clown. Much to her surprise, Maureen had gradually discovered that the mysterious planet called Connor Slave had a bright side. Sometimes, he made her laugh until she cried, especially when he imitated a cat licking its own fur.

'Go on, do it!'

'Oh, no.'

'Please, just for a moment.'

'No, you'll have me prowling the rooftops next.'

Maureen shook her head, pretending to sulk.

Connor got out of bed and, completely naked as he was, walked to the window and looked out. She admired his slim, well-defined body – he could have been a dancer or a gymnast. His hair rippled as he lazily stretched his neck muscles. She looked at him, silhouetted against the light, and it struck her that that was what Connor Slave was: a silhouette, a shadow. There was a dark radiance about him, something enigmatic that went beyond appearances.

Maureen got out of bed, also naked, went to him and embraced him from behind, breathing in his smell. She laid her head on his shoulder, savouring the miracle of his skin against hers. There was respect and admiration between her and Connor, and sometime also a kind of shyness – they were at such different places in their lives – yet Maureen could not help quivering with pleasure at each embrace.

'There's something I've always wanted to ask you,' she said.

'Go ahead.'

'What's it like, writing a song?'

Connor replied without turning around, his voice seeming to come straight from the sundrenched panorama in front of them. 'I can't explain it. It's a strange feeling. First there's something that doesn't exist yet, or may exist already but is hidden somewhere in the darkness inside me, asking only to be found and brought out into the light. I don't know what others feel. For me it's something that comes without warning, and it's only after it's come that I realize I couldn't live without it. It's one of those things we think we control but that end up dominating us completely. It's like . . .'

He turned and looked at her as if it was only now, letting his eyes come to rest on her, that he had found the perfect definition.

'Writing a song is like falling in love, Maureen.'

Ever since their relationship had started, she had been reluctant to define it in any way, for fear that a noun or an adjective might give it a weight it didn't have. Now, hearing those words, hearing her name as part of them, she understood that what she had been feeling could finally be called love.

They stood there in each other's arms, looking out at that picture-postcard view of Rome, the red roofs, the blue sky, the sun. Maureen lived in the Via della Polveriera, on the top floor of an old house that had belonged to her grandfather. The place had been renovated and turned into a large duplex apartment. From the terrace, which occupied part of the roof, there was an incredible 360-degree view of Rome. In the evening, you could even have dinner there without any other lighting than the reflection of the yellow floodlights on the Colosseum. As they stood there, wrapped up in each other, they both felt that nothing – not Italy, not America, not the rest of the world – could ever reach in past the borders of that room and invade their intimacy.

Maureen recalled that amazing day they had met. Connor Slave was in Italy for a six-concert tour to promote the release of this latest album, *Lies of Darkness*. The tour had been organized by an agency called Triton Communications, run by Maureen's best friend, Marta Coneri. On the day he was due to perform in Rome, Marta had swept into Maureen's apartment in the whirlwind way that was typical of her and insisted that she come to the concert.

'Maureen,' she said, 'if I had an apartment like this, I don't think I'd go out much either. But between *not much* and *never* there's quite a difference. And this boy's worth going a very long way to hear.'

Maureen knew she would need a really good excuse to deter Marta – and off the top of her head she couldn't come up with a single one. So she had found herself sitting in a seat in the Teatro Olimpico, with an empty place beside her. Everyone who was anyone in Rome – or wanted to be anyone – seemed to be there.

Marta joined her just before the start of the concert, collapsing into the free seat to her right. 'Good. My work is over. Now let's enjoy the show.'

Maureen had no time to reply, because at that point the lights went down and the audience fell silent.

From the darkness had come a soft guitar arpeggio, a sound so delicate as to be quite sensual, with a delay effect that seemed to make it roll around the walls of the auditorium. Maureen had the impression it was echoing in her head. Then a light had struck the centre of the stage from above, and into that beam, so white as to appear fluorescent, Connor Slave had stepped, wearing a dark suit with a Korean collar that was almost monastic in its plainness. His head was tilted towards the audience and his arms hung casually at his sides. In his hands he held a violin and a bow.

A synth pad had been added to the sound of the guitar, a low electronic vibration that seemed to move straight from the ground into the spectators' bodies. Then Connor had slowly lifted his head and started singing. The unique charm of his hoarse voice had immediately relegated the accompaniment to the background. For a few blissful moments, Maureen had had the absurd sensation that the song was dedicated exclusively to her – then she had looked around at the dimly lit auditorium and saw from the expressions on the other spectators' faces that everyone there was feeling the same thing.

It was a song called 'The Buried Sky', a gentle melody with anguished lyrics that some critics had accused of being blasphemous. The song was about Lucifer, the rebel angel, meditating in the darkness of hell on the consequences of his act, an act not so much of rebelling against God as of daring to think for himself.

> How strange it was to choose a day
> and say, 'The day has come to pass' –
> a day that on the hill of heaven
> was nothing but a blade of grass.
> The day I disobeyed the rules –
> the game would never be the same.

How strange it was to see the sky
and say, 'Now I don't need the light' –
then stand and watch the sun go down
and bring about eternal night.
The day I took the rebel's mark –
condemned myself to endless dark.

Another voice had joined Connor's then, a voice as pure as crystal, and a beautiful female singer had appeared from the shadows at the back of the stage to share the spotlight with him. Their two voices were completely different in timbre and colour, and yet they had harmonized so perfectly as to make them one voice. That vocal union had embodied everything the song was about: the light and the dark, the regret and the pride, the sense of setting out on a journey from which there was no return.

Instinctively, Maureen had felt a sharp sense of jealousy towards the clear-voiced girl who was sharing a fragment of Connor's life with him on the stage. It was hard to believe that her obvious passion and devotion were just pretence.

But the feeling went as suddenly as it had come, because at that point Connor Slave had stopped singing and lifted the violin to his shoulder. When he started playing, it was as if he had disappeared, leaving only the music. His body was there, in front of everyone, but he was surely elsewhere, in some parallel universe. Perhaps influenced by the words of the song, and by that supernatural talent, Maureen had become convinced that, if the devil did really exist, at that moment He was there, playing the violin.

For the rest of the concert, Maureen was kept spellbound by this man. He was with the audience listening to him and with the band accompanying him and with the music he was playing, and he was with whoever wanted to go with him – and at the same time he was nowhere and belonged to nobody.

As she watched him receiving the tumultuous applause at the end of the concert, Maureen had found herself thinking that for someone like Connor Slave, real life was hard work, and the only time he felt free was during those few hours up there on the stage, making music.

Then the curtain had fallen, the lights gone up, and the magic had ended. Marta turned to her with a triumphant expression. 'What did I tell you? Is he great or what?'

'Absolutely extraordinary.'

'And there's more – a little surprise. That's why I wanted you to come. Guess where we're going for dinner?'

'Marta, I don't think I—'

'Maureen, your father owns one of the best restaurants in Rome, probably in the whole of Italy. You're my friend, and by some incredible conjunction of the stars, this evening I even managed to persuade you to come out. In your opinion, where else could I take a brilliant American who's hungry, in every sense of the word, for Old Europe?'

Marta wouldn't take no for an answer. She was in charge this evening, and that was it.

They waited outside Connor's dressing room for him to change, and after the introductions, Marta led them towards a dark Lancia Thesis waiting for them outside the theatre. She sat down next to the driver, leaving Maureen and Connor sitting side by side in the back. They had started talking and getting to know each other as they moved through the traffic of Rome towards her father's restaurant in the Via Dei Gracchi.

'How come you speak English so well?' Connor asked her. 'You sound more American than I do.'

'My mother's from New York.'

'And she not only lives in Rome but has you as a daughter? What a lucky woman.'

'Not exactly. She and my father are divorced. She went back to live in the United States.'

From the front seat Marta butted into the conversation in her Roman-accented English. 'You may have heard of her mother. She's a very well-known lawyer. Her name's Mary Ann Levallier.'

Connor had turned to her. '*The* Mary Ann Levallier?'

'That's right.'

From her tone of voice, Connor quickly gathered that this wasn't a subject to pursue. He opened the car window a little, as if to relax the slight tension inside the car: a touch of sensitivity that made him rise in Maureen's estimation. She had known other people in showbusiness, especially musicians, and had never felt especially attracted to them, coming to the reluctant conclusion that few of them were as good as their music.

Connor smiled. 'Well, you know what I do for a living. How about you?'

In her excitement, Marta had tried to answer for her. 'Oh, Maureen's a—'

From the back seat, Maureen had stopped her with a glance before she could launch into a sales pitch.

'Maureen's a . . . a really bright girl.'

At that point, they had arrived at the restaurant, and all conversation ceased. Once inside, Maureen and her friends were warmly greeted by the head waiter, Alfredo, who had been there forever and had known her since she was a child.

'Hello, Maureen,' he said, embracing her. 'What a surprise! Having you here is a real event. A pity your father is away. He's in France right now, selecting wine. I hope you'll accept this poor old man in exchange . . .'

He led them to a table, and she and Connor found themselves sitting opposite each other.

Over dinner, they had continued talking. As the conversation flowed and became increasingly intimate, Marta, bless her heart, had discreetly faded into the background. Maureen remembered the exact moment when Connor finally captured her heart. It was when she asked him what kind of music he listened to.

'My own.'

'Nothing else?'

'No.'

Maureen had looked at him, trying to read vanity and conceit in his eyes. And all she found was the serene gaze of a man who knew he had everything he needed.

'But it isn't easy music to listen to,' she said gently.

'Nothing's easy. Maybe I'm not easy either.'

'Then your success shows that people aren't as stupid as we think.'

Connor had smiled in amusement, as if at a joke he had been mulling over for some time. 'They aren't as stupid as we think – and they're never as intelligent as we'd like.'

Since that moment, they had hardly been out of each other's sight.

The telephone rang in the bedroom, reminding the lovers that, beyond that view that seemed to go on forever, there was still a world with its own agenda. Reluctantly, Maureen broke free of Connor's embrace and went to pick up the phone from the night-table.

'Hello?' she said in English.

'Hi, Maureen, it's Franco.'

Maureen sighed. The world could not be kept out forever, even from the happiest of rooms.

'Hi, Franco. What's up?'

'They've fixed the date for the hearing. Next Thursday morning.'

'So soon?'

'It's such a high-profile case, there's no way they'd have agreed to postpone it any longer. What about your end? Have they suspended you?'

'Officially, no. But I've been assigned to the Academy as a consultant. In practice, I'm a kind of janitor.'

'I know it's hard, Maureen. But if possible, I'd like you to drop by my office today. There are some proxies I need you to sign.'

'How about in an hour?'

'Perfect, I'll expect you and . . .' There was a pause at the other end of the line, then: 'Listen, don't worry.'

'No, I'm not worried.'

'Everything's fine, Maureen.'

'Sure, everything's fine.'

She put the phone down again, gently, although she would have liked to smash it down on the glass table-top.

Everything's fine.

But it wasn't.

It wasn't fine, because of the work she'd always done with passion and a desire for the truth. It wasn't fine, because of all the people who'd once assured her of their total trust in her, but who were now keeping out of her way. It wasn't fine, because of the sunset, and the wonderful man who was with her, and who had come so unexpectedly into her life.

It wasn't fine, because just two weeks earlier, Chief Inspector Maureen Martini, working out of the Casilino station of the Rome police, had killed a man.

CHAPTER 11

Maureen slipped into the gloom of the garage 100 yards from her apartment, where she kept her car. When he saw her come in, Duilio, the manager, emerged from his glass-fronted cubby-hole and came towards her. He was a man whose age placed him out of the running, but in his friendly way he had always made it known that he had a soft spot for her. Maureen had grown to accept this fictitious courtship, which had lasted a long time now without ever becoming invasive or suggestive.

'I'll get the car for you, Signora Martini. It's always a pleasure to drive a treasure like that.'

Maureen handed him the keys. 'Enjoy.'

Duilio went down the ramp and disappeared into the darkness. As she waited to hear the sound of her Porsche Boxster coming back up, Maureen couldn't help thinking about what a lucky woman she might be considered, in normal circumstances.

Her family had owned Martini's Restaurant for as long as she could remember, and over time her father Carlo had transformed it from a simple trattoria into one of the leading lights of Italian cuisine. When he had met and married her mother, the adventure had even continued beyond the ocean and there was now a Martini's in New York, a favourite haunt of movie and TV stars. In the meantime, her mother had become one of the best criminal lawyers in that city, spending more and more time over there, with the result that their marriage had gradually unravelled.

Maureen's relationship with her mother had never really been close. Mary Ann Levallier's cold pragmatic temperament left little room for the kind of affectionate give and take that existed between the girl and her father. And so, at the time of the divorce, Maureen had chosen to remain in Rome with Carlo and, after gaining her law degree, had decided to join the police.

Maureen remembered only too well how badly her mother had taken it when she had told her of her plans. They had been sitting in the restaurant in the gardens of the Hilton, which was where she stayed whenever she came to Rome. Mary Ann was, as always, perfectly dressed, in a Chanel suit, and perfectly groomed.

'The police, you say? What foolishness. I was thinking of a future for you in New York. In my firm we handle many cases in conjunction with Italy. There could be a great future for a bilingual lawyer with your training.'

'Just this once, Mother, can't you forget about what you want for me and think about what I want for myself?'

'On the basis of what you've just told me, I doubt you have a very clear idea of what you want.'

'No, unfortunately for you, I know *exactly* what I want. It's a question of attitude. I want a job that allows me to catch criminals and put them in prison, regardless of what I earn. Your work is the exact opposite: you help criminals to get out of prison, and make a good living at it.'

Her mother had surprised her by using what, for her, was very explicit language. 'You're an asshole, Maureen.'

The younger woman had finally allowed herself the luxury of an angelic smile. 'Maybe a bit, on my mother's side . . .'

She had stood up then and left, leaving Mary Ann Levallier to tackle a scampi cocktail that probably bothered her because the colour didn't match her blouse.

Duilio brought the Porsche, with the top down, up from the underground floor of the garage and parked beside her. He jumped out of the car and held the door open for her.

'Here you are. End of the forbidden dream.'

'What forbidden dream?'

'A nice run around Rome in a car like this, on a day like this, with a beautiful woman like you.'

Maureen got in, smiling at him as she fastened her seat belt. 'Sometimes you just have to dare, Duilio.'

'At my age, *signora*? When I was young, I was always afraid women would say no. Now I'm terrified they'll say yes.'

Maureen was forced to laugh, although her state of mind wasn't exactly conducive to laughter.

'Have a good day, Duilio.'

'You too, *signora*.'

The Porsche was a gift from her father. She loved it, even though it was the kind of status symbol that classified her as a rich woman. Maureen was, like many self-confident people, modest by nature, and so she had never used that car much, and certainly not to go to and from the police station. If she was going to get along with her colleagues, she certainly didn't want to intimidate them.

She joined the traffic and drove calmly through a tangle of small streets until she got onto the Via dei Fori Imperiali. Concealing her eyes behind sunglasses, she tried to ignore the looks that other drivers threw at her and at her car whenever she drew up at the lights.

As she drove down towards the river, her cellphone started ringing on the seat beside her. She put in the earphone and was surprised to hear Connor's voice.

'Hi. When are you coming back?' he said.

'I only just left.'

'You won't believe it, but that's the same excuse Ulysses gave Penelope when he got back after twenty years away.'

'Then we ought to synchronize watches. I haven't even been gone twenty minutes.'

'You're lying. It's been at least twenty-one.'

Maureen was grateful for the attempt to cheer her up. Connor knew perfectly well where she was going, and in what state of mind, and this was his way of making her feel she was not alone.

'Why don't you take a nice walk around Rome, eyeing up the girls, and then meet me in, let's say, an hour and a half outside my lawyer's office?'

'Promise me that after that, we'll go bum a dinner off your father.'

'Aren't you tired of eating there yet?'

'Not while it's free.'

Maureen gave him the address and hung up. In spite of his last remark, if there was one thing Connor didn't care much about, it was money. Even though his albums were starting to sell well, Maureen had the feeling he didn't even know how much money he had in the bank. When she had left the apartment, he had been on the phone, talking to Bono from U2 about a future project, his eyes shining like a little boy's.

She drove sedately alongside the river, accepting the intermittent glare of the sun through the branches of the trees lining the street. Despite the warm spring air in her hair, there was a slight feeling of cold in her heart.

She turned left onto the Ponte del Risorgimento, then along the Viale Mazzini, and by a stroke of luck found a parking space just outside the building where her lawyer Franco Roberto had his office.

When he saw her enter, ushered in by his secretary, Franco rose from his desk and crossed the room to greet her. He was a tall, thin, dark-complexioned man with brown eyes and black hair. He could not be called handsome, but his face and eyes were alive with intelligence. He and Maureen had studied together at university, from which he had graduated with flying colours. She suspected that, during their student days, Franco wouldn't have minded at all if their friendship had become something more. But Maureen's attitude towards him must have convinced him to discreetly set aside whatever intentions he might have had, and her suspicions had remained just that.

Now Franco kissed her affectionately on the cheeks. 'Good afternoon, Chief Inspector. How are things?'

'Sometimes good, sometimes not so good. And I'm sorry that right now you're part of the not so good.'

'I'll do my best to change that.'

He walked back behind his desk and opened a folder. Maureen sat down facing him, in one of the two elegant leather armchairs.

'The situation is somewhat confused, but I don't think someone with your service record should have anything to worry about at the hearing.'

'Franco, you're a naturally positive person and I'm not a naturally negative one. But I don't think I'm wrong if I define the situation as rather more than just "confused".'

'Do you feel like talking about it again?'

'All right.'

Franco stood up and went to stand by the open window. 'Try to summarize the facts.'

'There was this Albanian, Avenir Gallani,' Maureen began. 'He suddenly showed up in Rome and started going around in expensive cars, being seen in trendy clubs and showbiz circles, claiming to be a record and film producer. His behaviour and the money he was spending attracted our attention. From upstairs, we received orders to keep an eye on him, as he was suspected of being connected in some way with the Albanian Mafia, in particular with a big drugs ring. We ascertained that he had a fairly extensive criminal record in his country. We had him under surveillance for nearly a year, yet all we managed to discover was the likelihood that Avenir Gallani was a complete idiot. True, he had a lot of money – the source of which wasn't clear – but he was still an idiot. At the same time, he had a kind of low cunning and the trouble with such people is that, sooner or later, they can't help boasting about the fruits of their cunning. That was the trap he fell into. He'd started a relationship with a TV starlet, the kind of girl ready to do anything to further her career. Gallani fell in love with her and wanted to look good in her eyes. We had his apartment bugged, and one evening we heard him bragging to her that in a few days he'd be clinching a deal worth many millions of euros. When that was done, he said, he was going to produce a film to really launch her.

'We increased the surveillance and tailed him twenty-four hours a day,' Maureen went on. 'We finally managed to discover that Avenir was due to take delivery of a big drug consignment in Manziana forest, to the north of Rome. We set up an operation, in collaboration with the police in

95

Viterbo, and caught them all in the act. All except Gallani. When he saw us coming, he managed to slip through the cordon and escape. I followed him into the forest as far as a small clearing where a BMW was parked. He ran to the car, opened the door and leaned inside to get something. When he straightened up again, he had a gun in his hand. He aimed it at me and fired.'

'How many shots?'

'One.'

'And what did you do?'

'I fired back.'

'And killed him.' It was a statement, not a question.

'Yes.'

'And what happened then?'

'I heard a noise coming from the undergrowth on my right. I went back into the forest and took a good look around, but couldn't see or hear anyone. I assumed the noise had been caused by some animal scared by the shots.'

'What did you do next?'

'I went back to the car.'

'And what did you find there?'

'The body of Avenir Gallani in the same position he'd fallen in.'

Maureen would never forget that moment. It was the first time she had killed a man. She had stood there, motionless, looking at that body lying on the ground, the mouth wide open, a gaping hole over the heart, blood gushing to form a pool on the damp grass. All around were lights flashing, cries, orders being shouted, car tyres on the gravel. All she could do was stand there, her hand hanging by her side, still gripping her gun, faced with the immense responsibility of having cut short a human life.

'And the gun?' Franco Roberto asked, jolting her from her memories.

'The gun wasn't there any more.'

'Wasn't there any more or had never been there?'

Maureen leaped to her feet. 'What kind of question is that?'

Franco shook his head, and Maureen realized she had just failed a test.

'It's not my question,' he explained patiently. 'It's the kind of question the Public Prosecutor will ask you. And that wasn't quite the reaction I'd hoped for.'

Maureen fell back into the armchair. 'I'm sorry, Franco. My nerves are on edge.'

'I understand. But this really isn't the best time to lose control.'

'Franco, the man had a gun and used it on me! I'm not crazy and I'm not a liar. And I'm certainly not stupid. Why would I continue to insist on this version if it wasn't true?'

Franco's silence made her uneasy.

'You do believe me, don't you?'

'What I believe doesn't matter, Maureen. I'm paid to think and make other people think. And what I have to consider now is how to make the judges think that that gun was there.'

Maureen signed all the proxies and powers of attorney Franco needed, a formality that made the atmosphere in the office all the more unbreatheable. At last, it was all done, and she got up from her chair, went to the window and looked out. Below her was the traffic of a Roman evening, slow, chaotic and noisy. After a moment, she saw Connor coming up the avenue, his curly head bobbing up and down as he walked.

He stopped just below her and looked up to check that he had the right building.

For the first time since she had come into that office, Maureen smiled.

Franco came to her side and looked in the same direction. 'I get the impression that man is here for you.'

'Yes, I think he is.'

'I can't give a name to the way you said that, but I think you might like to know that I don't need you here any more.'

Maureen turned and gave him a light kiss on the cheek. 'Thank you, Franco. Thank you for everything.'

'Go. Nobody deserves the torture of waiting for you.'

She left the office and walked downstairs with a sense of liberation. The facts and the memories she had just had to confront had made her miss Connor. When she was with him, she felt different – she felt safe. Maureen smiled. How strange it was to feel protected by a man who faced life completely unarmed!

She opened the door and went out on the street. What happened next she would remember all her life, almost as a series of still images.

The door closing.

Connor waiting for her under a tree on the other side of the avenue.

Connor smiling at her and crossing the street to join her.

The light in Connor's eyes as he looked at her, the way she had always wanted a man to look at her.

Connor just a few steps from her.

A Voyager with blacked-out windows pulling up next to them with a squeal of tyres.

Four men jumping out and running up to them.

Four men putting black hoods over their heads and dragging them off.

CHAPTER 12

Darkness.

The vaguely mildewed smell of the cloth enclosing her head. The swerving of the vehicle as it accelerated through the streets of Rome. The noise of the wheels in a paved area. Tape had been tied round her wrists, and any attempt to scream had been frustrated by the gag that held the rough material of the hood over her mouth. Any struggle at all on her part had been put paid to by a voice in a slight foreign accent that had whispered in her ear, 'Don't move or your boyfriend dies.'

As confirmation of the threat, Maureen had felt the sharp point of a knife against her throat. She assumed that someone else had said and done the same thing to Connor, and the fear of his fear had filled her with despair, a despair darker than the darkness in which she was imprisoned.

She was motionless and silent throughout the journey. Encouraged by her lack of reaction, the man beside her eased the pressure of the knife after a while. At first, Maureen tried to remain aware of anything that could identify the route they were taking, but the drive had lasted so long, it was pointless trying to memorize any of it.

One thing she had been able to surmise was that, as they were stopping less frequently, they were moving away from the centre of the city. Then, when even these few stops were replaced by a long uninterrupted stretch, she assumed that they had left Rome completely.

At last, the Voyager made an abrupt turn and then came to a complete halt. Maureen heard the doors open, and sturdy arms pulled her up out of her sitting position. The same strong, pitiless arms almost lifted her from the ground as she took a few blind steps. The gag was removed, and then the hood. She breathed in the cool evening air. The first thing that struck her eyes, after all that darkness, were the colours: the red of the earth, the green of the vegetation. Then she saw three cars, arranged in a circle, their headlamps on, surrounding a large area of open ground, with two wide entrances through the bushes on opposite sides. Above, the trees leaned into the middle to form a kind of vault. Right at the top, through an opening, a few faded stars could be glimpsed.

On the opposite side of the circle, Connor was kneeling, his face and shirt soiled with earth. Maureen assumed that the man standing behind him had shoved him to the ground.

Between her and Connor, in the middle of the clearing, stood a man with his back to her.

He was tall and solid, but not fat. His hair was cut very short, and from under the collar of his leather jacket a tattoo rose from his neck towards his right ear like ivy on a wall. He lit a cigarette and Maureen saw the smoke floating in the light of the headlamps.

He stood like that, motionless, for a while, then, as if he had only just remembered that she was there, he turned towards her. He had sharp features and an unkempt beard.

His cold, deep-set eyes were perfectly in keeping with the cruel cut of his mouth. From his left ear hung a strange

100

earring, a stylized cross with a tiny diamond in the middle that glittered in the light as he moved his head, which he kept doing, as if nodding in reply to words that only he could hear. When at last he spoke, he had the same accent as the man who had held a knife to her throat in the Voyager.

'Well, here we are, Chief Inspector Martini. I hope my friends didn't mistreat you too much during the trip.'

'Who are you?'

'All in good time, Chief Inspector. Or can I call you Maureen?'

'I repeat, who are you and what do you want?'

The man ignored her question. 'Do you know where we are?'

'No.'

'Strange. I thought you might have recognized the place.'

The man gestured towards one of the entrances to the clearing.

'A few hundred yards in that direction, a few weeks ago, you killed a man.'

Silence fell for a moment. The man bent his head and moved the earth with his foot as if a body was buried there.

'Yes. We're in Manziana forest. Strange, the way we keep coming back to certain places, isn't it?' He looked up again. 'My name is Arben Gallani. The man you murdered, Avenir Gallani, was my brother.'

'I didn't murder anyone. You have no idea what happened.'

Arben threw the cigarette butt beyond the cone of light created by the cars' headlamps. 'Oh yes, I do. I was there.'

He put his hand under his jacket, took out a gun from the back of his belt and held it flat on his palm so that Maureen could get a good look at it.

'Do you recognize this?'

101

'I've never seen it before in my life.'

'Oh, but you have, even if only for a moment. It was the one Avenir was holding when you shot him.'

He dropped his arm down at his side, as if the gun had suddenly become too heavy.

'I was with him that day. I didn't agree with the operation, and he knew it. But he asked me to go with him and I couldn't refuse. We're always weak when it comes to the people we love, aren't we, Maureen?'

His gaze shifted to Connor for a moment. For the first time in her life, Maureen understood the true meaning of the word fear.

'I'd been waiting for him in the car, but then I'd gone into the forest to take a leak. I heard all the noise, assumed that something had gone wrong, and decided to stay hidden. Then you appeared.'

He took a pack of cigarettes from his pocket and lit one. He spoke calmly, as if the things he was talking about had nothing to do with him.

'Avenir was an impulsive boy. Too impulsive, sometimes. Maybe it was my fault. I should have kept more of an eye on him, made sure he didn't fuck up.'

Arben paused. He was looking straight at her but Maureen understood that he was not seeing her. He was reliving what had happened that day, just as she had relived it dozens of times in her mind.

'I threw a stone into the undergrowth to distract you. When you moved away, I came out, took the gun and hid again. I know you've had a few problems because of that, but that's not my concern.'

He smiled at her, quite gently, and that was the moment Maureen knew he was crazy. Crazy and dangerous.

102

'And now we come to the reason for this encounter of ours. Do you think I want to kill you? No, my dear.'

As he talked, Arben Gallani had slowly approached Connor.

'I think it's time you found out what it means to lose a person you love.'

Oh no.

Maureen started screaming, without realizing she was doing it only in her mind.

no no no no no no no no no no no no no no no no no no no . . .

Arben Gallani quickly raised the hand holding the gun and aimed it at Connor's temple.

no no no no no no no no no no no no no no no no no no no . . .

At the contact of the cold barrel, Connor instinctively closed his eyes. Maureen saw, or thought she saw, Arben's knuckle turn white as he pressed the trigger.

no no no no no no no no no no no no no no no no no no no . . .

One shot and Connor's head exploded, splattering blood and brain-matter over the car next to him, blotting out the light of the headlamps. Maureen's voice at last welled up out of her dry throat and, as Connor's lifeless body slumped to the ground, taking with him their dreams and plans, she screamed, screamed endlessly with anger and despair and powerlessness.

Arben turned and looked at her with one eyebrow slightly arched, an expression of sick pity on his face. 'Nasty, isn't it?'

Angry tears poured from her eyes as she gasped, 'I'll kill you for this.'

Gallani shrugged. 'That's possible. But you're going to live. In order to remember. And not only that . . .'

He dropped the gun on the ground and moved lazily towards her. When he came level with her, he struck her across the face with the back of his hand. Maureen fell back, surprised not to have felt any pain, as if her entire capacity for suffering had been absorbed in an instant by the death of the man she had loved. Gallani did not even grant her the dignity of fists. He continued slapping her across the face until she could no longer see his bloodstained hands. At last the pain came. She felt her body give way, and something hot and sticky covered her swollen eyes and coloured her tears. Arben Gallani gave a nod with his head. The man who had been holding her up let her slide to the ground, where he immediately pinned her down. Two other men came and lent a hand, squatting on either side of her to stop her moving her legs.

Arben took a switchblade from his pocket and snapped it open. The blade glinted for a moment in the light, like the diamond in his earring. He bent over her and started cutting her pants away from her body. Maureen heard the noise of the material tearing and felt the cold air on her skin as the blade stripped her. Through the veil of blood and pain that blurred her vision, she saw Gallani standing between her legs. Then she saw him loosen his belt and heard the noise of his zipper opening.

Arben then lay down on top of her. She felt the weight of his body, the roughness of his hands parting her legs, the pain as he thrust himself violently into her. Maureen took refuge in the memory of the beautiful things she had had and had now lost forever. The pain of that loss anaesthetized her temporarily against the physical pain she was feeling now.

The man couldn't take anything from her, because everything was already dead inside her. As the thrusts rocked her, the strange cross-shaped earring continued moving rhythmically a few inches from her face, glittering in the light of the headlamps, glittering, glittering . . .

Fate at last took pity on her, and she fainted. Before everything went dark, Maureen Martini found herself thinking how much it hurt to die.

CHAPTER 13

More darkness.

She was lying on sheets that felt slightly rough and, from the lingering smell of disinfectant in the air, she guessed that she was in a hospital. Her face felt strangely constricted. She tried to move her right arm, and heard the clinking sound of a drip knocking against the pole supporting it. With difficulty, she lifted her other hand to her eyes. She ran her fingers over what she realized was a bandage, held in place by a big Band-Aid. From somewhere in the distance, she heard voices whispering. That was immediately followed by footsteps, and then her father's voice, full of an anxiety that not even affection could conceal.

'Maureen, it's me.'

'Hi, Daddy.'

'How are you feeling?'

How am I feeling? I'd like to disappear forever in the darkness.

'I'm fine,' she lied. 'Where am I?'

'In the Gemelli Hospital.'

'How long have I been here?'

'They brought you here in a terrible state, and kept you under sedation for two days.'

'How did you know where to find me?'

'When they abducted you, your lawyer, Franco, was at the window and saw everything. He immediately called the police. Unfortunately he couldn't get the licence number, so all they could do was search for the model of car he described. Then the phone call came in . . .'

'What phone call?'

'A man with a foreign accent called your station and told them where they could find you.'

All at once, she remembered Arben Gallani's voice whispering, '*Nasty, isn't it?*' after the noise of the gunshot. And that cross-shaped earring swaying and sparkling in front of her eyes as he . . .

She asked the question she had been dying to ask, stupidly hoping as she did so that none of it had been true. 'What about Connor?'

'I'm afraid Connor is dead. The US Embassy has taken care of all the formalities. His body will be transferred to the United States in a few days' time. I don't suppose this is any consolation to you, but . . .'

'What?'

'Connor has already become a legend. A legend that will live forever.'

Maureen had to make an effort not to scream.

I don't want him to live forever. He was entitled to live his life and spend it with me.

And along with that thought came the terrible awareness that she was the cause of everything, because the day she had fired at Avenir Gallani, she had also killed Connor with the same bullet. She turned her head aside in order not to show the invisible tears she was weeping under the bandages, which became soaked with them. She wept in silence for herself and for that wonderful young man who had touched her life just long enough to say goodbye. Then her body yielded to the pain of it all, and even the tears ended.

'When will they take the bandages off?' she asked.

A second voice, a low one, joined Carlo Martini's.

'Chief Inspector, I'm Professor Covini, the Consultant Ophthalmologist here at the Hospital Gemelli. You're a strong person, so I'm going to be extremely frank with you. I'm afraid I have some bad news. It's quite likely you had a congenital weakness you weren't aware of, but the shock you suffered has caused what in medical terms is called a post-traumatic adherent leukoma. In layman's terms, irreversible damage to the corneas of your eyes.'

It took a moment for what the doctor had said to sink in.

Then anger took hold of her, more violently than any man could ever possess her.

No.

She wouldn't allow it.

She wouldn't allow Arben Gallani to deprive her, not only of her sight, but also her revenge. Her voice, a voice she finally recognized, emerged from her mouth through clenched jaws.

'Am I blind?'

'Technically, yes.'

'What does "technically, yes" mean?'

Maureen was glad not to see the expression on the doctor's face that would corrrespond with his tone of voice.

'There is the possibility of a surgical intervention, in other words, a transplant. It's a recognized procedure with a reasonable success rate. In your case, unfortunately, there's a problem. I'll try to explain how it works. The cornea of a donor is always a foreign body to the eye that receives it. That's why we have to use an appropriate cornea, in other words one compatible with the genetic type of the recipient. If we don't, then when the new cornea is implanted in the receiving eye and isn't recognized by the organism, we get the reaction that's commonly called rejection. We've discovered from blood and hystogenetic tests that you're a tetragametic chimera.'

'What does that mean?'

'It means you're the product of two eggs and two sperms. In other words, two different eggs from your mother were fertilized by two different sperms from your father. At a very early stage in their development the two embryos fused, giving rise to a single embryo in which two genetically different types of cell coexist. Unfortunately, in your case there exists a very severe problem of compatibility. In simple terms, there's only a very tiny percentage of people who share this characteristic.' Professor Covini paused briefly. 'As I said, that's the bad news.'

'You mean after all that, there's actually some good news?'

'Yes, there is.'

'I called your mother in New York,' her father said at this point. 'When I told her what had happened and explained your condition, she immediately got in touch with an acquaintance of hers, a doctor named William Roscoe. Right now, for someone with your pathology, he's the best man in the world.'

'That's the good news I was referring to,' Professor Covini said. 'From a scientific point of view, it's all highly complex, so I'm not going to bore you with facts you'd only find incomprehensible. The one thing that matters is that there is the possibility of a transplant. Professor Roscoe is one of the greatest experts in ocular microsurgery and has made incredible advances in embryonic stem-cell research.

Unfortunately, you'll have to go to the United States because here in Italy, thanks to the laws banning the use of stem cells in assisted fertilization, an operation like that is forbidden. The Professor and I had a long conversation on the phone, and what emerged from that is something not so much rare as unique.'

'Meaning what?'

'We have a donor who may be compatible. Professor Roscoe is able to use embryonic stem cells to inhibit the immune response to the donor's corneas, in such a way as to avoid any possible rejection.'

'The one condition is that we have to act fast,' Carlo Martini said. 'One of your mother's biggest clients has put his private jet at our disposal. We can leave for America tomorrow and the operation can take place the day after. If you agree, of course – and if you feel up to it . . .'

'Of course I feel up to it,' she said. *I'd feel up to it even if I had to suffer the pains of hell*.

'Good, very good,' Professor Covini. 'Now it's better if we let her rest, Signor Martini. I think she's had enough for today.'

'All right, Professor.'

She felt her father's lips on her cheek and heard his voice in her ear.

'Goodbye, darling. I'll see you soon.'

A thin hand she didn't know rested on hers for a moment.

'I wish you all the best, miss. And believe me, I'm not just saying that. Nobody should suffer what you've suffered.'

Maureen listened to their footsteps as they moved away from the bed. The noise of the door opening and closing left her alone in the silence of the room. The doctor must have put a sedative into the drip because she started to feel drowsy.

As she waited to drift into a few hours of non-thinking, she told herself she would do anything that was asked of her. Anything and more, for a single minute of sight.

That was all she needed.

Just one minute.

Long enough to see Arben Gallani's mocking face blown away by a bullet at close range.

Let there be darkness.

PART THREE

New York

CHAPTER 14

Jordan drove the Ducati at moderate speed onto the access ramp that led to Brooklyn Bridge. The traffic was light at this time of day and, despite the powerful engine beneath him, he was content to join the orderly line of cars streaming across the bridge.

He had already passed Police Headquarters at One Police Plaza – the building where he had worked for years – and City Hall – that smaller-scale imitation of the White House where his brother exercised the power the city had granted him – without giving either a second glance. Right now, Water Street was just below him. If he had turned his head to the right, he would have seen the roof of the building where a young man named Gerald Marsalis had died bearing a name that wasn't even his, but here, too, he kept his eyes fixed straight ahead.

It wasn't that he was indifferent, just that he didn't need to look at these places to know they existed. Each was clear in his memory, along with the price each had cost him.

Jordan Marsalis had often made decisions, knowing, but not caring, that he would have a price to pay later. That was why, one night three years earlier, he had taken the blame for an accident that was nothing to do with him.

He understood now that the journey he had been planning

to make, and had had to put off, had actually started a long time ago. New York had only been a stopping-off point, one where he'd had to stay in order to pay his dues, before setting off again.

And this strange old heart of mine now sets sail across the sea . . .

Jordan drove off the bridge and along Adams Street until after the junction with Fulton Street, leaving Brooklyn Heights on his left. He passed Boerum Place and continued southward until he reached the area where Detective James Burroni lived.

He had phoned Burroni after yet another conversation with his brother at Gracie Mansion. Ever since Christopher had seen the corpse of his son sitting like a cartoon in the loft where he lived, he had been acting like a wild beast in a cage, and Jordan wasn't sure if it was because of his anger as a father or because of his powerlessness as a Mayor.

After two weeks, the investigation into Gerald's death had reached an impasse. The police had examined his life from every angle, revealing all kinds of unsavoury things, but not coming up with any usable leads. The media had had a field day – even, because of Jordan's family connection with Jerry Ko, dredging up the old story of the automobile accident.

Then, when they could find nothing else to say, they had started making things up.

Luckily, LaFayette Johnson, although enjoying his sudden fame, had been prevented from causing any damage. Christopher had persuaded him not to talk to the media, thanks to the one incentive the man understood: money.

Jordan parked his bike across from Burroni's house, the first in a row of houses with gardens that lined the dead-end street in a working-class neighbourhood. He switched off the

116

engine and sat there for a moment, surprised by what he saw. He had imagined something different.

In front of the house was parked a white Cherokee, a fairly old model. All at once, the front door opened and a woman came out, holding a boy of about ten by the hand. She was a tall, blond, gentle-looking woman, with an expressive rather than pretty face. The boy, who was the spitting image of Burroni, had a metal brace on his right leg and limped slightly as he walked. Burroni emerged through the door behind them, carrying two suitcases.

When he looked up and saw Jordan, he stopped halfway along the garden path for a moment. Jordan realized he had recognized him in spite of the fact that he was still wearing his helmet. In the meantime, the woman and the boy had reached the car and opened the hatch at the rear.

Burroni put the two cases in the back. Jordan watched as he kissed his wife goodbye and bent to adjust a baseball cap on the boy's head. He heard him say, 'Bye, champ,' as he hugged him.

Mother and son got in the car and the boy leaned out of the window for a last wave to his father, who was still standing on the sidewalk. Jordan watched until the car got to the intersection and turned right, then propped his bike on its kickstand, took off his helmet and crossed the street.

As he approached Burroni, he noticed that there was a slightly embarrassed look on his face, as if he had been caught in a moment of weakness.

'Hello, Jordan. What do you want?'

His demeanour was cautious, his tone not hostile but not exactly cordial either. In spite of everything, Burroni still seemed to find it difficult to call him Jordan. Their relationship had neither improved nor deteriorated in the

117

course of the investigation: it simply could not be called a relationship. They were still just two people forced to work together temporarily.

'Hello, James. I wanted to talk to you – alone and in private. Do you have a moment?'

Burroni gestured in the direction in which the Cherokee had disappeared. 'My wife and son have gone on vacation to my sister-in-law, on the coast, near Port Chester. I don't have a moment, I have two weeks.'

Jordan shook his head. 'Unfortunately, I don't think we have two weeks, either of us.'

'As bad as that?'

'Yes.'

Only then did Burroni seem to remember that they were standing in the middle of the sidewalk. 'Want to come in for a drink?'

Without waiting for a reply from Jordan, he turned and led him into the house. Once inside, Jordan took a look around. It was a normal American house, redolent of friendly neighbours, inflatable swimming pools in the back garden, barbecues, cans of beer on Sundays.

On a low cabinet next to the door was a photograph of Burroni with his son. The boy was waving a baseball bat at the camera.

Bye, champ . . .

Burroni noticed what he was looking at. 'My son's crazy about baseball,' he said, with a slight crack in his voice.

'The Yankees?'

'Who else?' Burroni pointed to a couch. 'Take a seat. What would you like to drink?'

'A Coke would be fine.'

'OK.'

Burroni walked off and came back soon afterwards with a tray containing two cans of Diet Coke and two glasses. He placed it on the little table in front of Jordan and sat down on a slightly worn but comfortable-looking leather armchair to his left.

'Go ahead.'

'Any news?'

Burroni shook his head as he opened his can. 'None at all. We've questioned everyone who ever knew your nephew without turning up a single useful thing. The post-mortem results you already know. And there's still nothing from the Crime Scene team. You know how it is. Too many clues, too few leads.'

'Well,' Jordan said, 'I've been thinking over and over about the *Peanuts* connection, trying to figure out what link there could possibly be between my nephew and Linus, and the person we think may turn out to be Lucy. But I don't seem to have gotten anywhere. And I'm wondering how long we can keep the journalists away from all the things we've managed to keep secret so far. Including my involvement.'

'What does your brother say?'

'He can't say anything, because he was the one who wanted me in on this thing, however unofficially. But I think he's under a lot of pressure. Apart from personal feelings, his position isn't very good. You can understand what people are thinking: how can he protect our children if he can't protect his own? Politics is a nasty business.'

Jordan took a sip of his drink, searching for the words to express what he had to say.

'I want to tell you something, James. Whatever the outcome of this case, I'll make sure the promises that were made to you will be kept.'

Burroni said nothing for a moment, staring down at his can. 'Those things I said the other evening in the diner across from your apartment, I—'

'Don't worry. I made a meal of it, too. It happens. We all say things we regret.'

Burroni's gaze shifted for a fraction of a second to the photograph showing him with his son, ready to receive a ball that would never arrive.

Bye, champ . . .

'You know, life sometimes isn't as easy as it seems,' he said.

'I told you it's fine. You don't need to explain.'

They looked at each other.

'It must have been hard for you too, Jordan.'

Jordan shrugged. 'It's hard for everyone.'

He picked up his helmet and got to his feet. Burroni did the same. He was shorter than Jordan but sturdier. All the same, without his perennial black hat on his head, he seemed strangely exposed and fragile.

'So long, James.'

A few minutes later, as he got on his bike and looked through his visor at the figure of James Burroni standing in the doorway of his house, Jordan told himself that coming here had been the right thing to do.

What he had said was true.

It *had* been hard. It was hard for everyone. For Burroni, for Christopher, for him.

But if they didn't work fast, it would be even harder for a woman they didn't know but who was out there somewhere, a target for a man who thought of her as Lucy.

CHAPTER 15

Chandelle Stuart leaped to her feet, her face distorted with anger, her smooth black hair moving to partly hide it. The elegant dark Versace dress she was wearing rode up her long, thin legs, showing the two men sitting on the couch a strip of bare skin above her stockings.

'What the fuck are you talking about?'

The tone of voice held all the arrogance of one accustomed to command without having earned the right. She stood facing the two men for a moment, then turned and snatched up a pack of cigarettes from a shelf behind her, lighting one as if she was hoping to set fire to the world. She then marched to the large window that led to a balcony overlooking Central Park and stood there with her back to them, puffing greedily at her cigarette.

In the sky above the city, summer stormclouds were massing.

Jason McIvory turned to Robert Orlik, the other 50 per cent of McIvory, Orlik & Partners, a law firm specializing in managing estates, based in an elegant building downtown. The two men exchanged a knowing glance. For too long, they had been exposed to this woman's whims, not to mention her coarse language.

And they were tired of putting up with it.

But for the moment they simply made themselves more comfortable on the couch and waited for this umpteenth fit of rage to subside.

McIvory crossed his legs. If Chandelle Stuart had turned at that moment, she would have caught a slight smile on his face with its slicked-back white hair and well-tended moustache. When he considered he had given the woman enough time to recover, he continued the speech this hysterical attack had interrupted.

'I think you know precisely what we're talking about, Miss Stuart. You don't have any money left. Or hardly any.'

Again Chandelle turned like a fury, and again her black hair whipped around her head like a pirate flag in the wind. 'How's that even possible, you dickheads?'

McIvory pointed to the leather briefcase on the floor by his feet, propped against a low glass table that had cost several hundred dollars an inch. 'The accounts are all here. All the papers were signed by you. In some cases, if you remember, we even requested a waiver of responsibility for certain investments of yours that weren't – how shall I put this? – entirely orthodox from a financial point of view.'

Chandelle Stuart extinguished her cigarette in the ashtray with a ferocity she would have happily applied to the faces of the two men. 'How do I know you two haven't been cheating me all these years?' she hissed.

Robert Orlik, who had been silent so far, now spoke up. His voice was strangely similar to his partner's, as if all those years of working together had made them one and the same.

'Miss Stuart, out of respect for your late father, I'll pretend I didn't hear that. For years I've been willing to tolerate your behaviour, not to mention your colourful language, but I'm not – or rather, *we* are not – willing to tolerate any aspersion on our honesty and professionalism. Having said that, in order to make sure we understand each other perfectly, I'd like to take a step back and summarize the facts. When your father, Avedon Lee Stuart, died seven years ago, he left you a personal fortune, in property, stocks and shares, and cash, amounting in total to about five billion dollars.'

'We had tens of billions,' she cut in, 'and that son of a bitch frittered it away on all kinds of crap.'

'I'm afraid that's where I must contradict you. There was only five billion and that money wasn't "frittered away", as you put it. Your father bequeathed most of the family fortune to a series of charitable foundations, so that the Stuart name should leave a lasting legacy.'

'And you two just happened to be appointed trustees of that fortune.'

Orlik looked at her coldly, like an experienced gambler seeing a novice approach his table. 'Our role as trustees is neither here nor there,' he said. 'Nor is the reason your father left you only part of the inheritance, which is linked to matters of which we are unaware and are unable to judge.'

'All that crap about charity and the Stuart name is just that: crap. That megalomaniac only did it because he hated me. The bastard always hated me.'

How right he was! I'm only surprised he didn't strangle you at birth, you stupid bitch!

Robert Orlik's face revealed nothing of this thought. Her last comment had been all too typical of her character, and in particular her relations with their firm. Managing both the dead man's estate and Chandelle Stuart's personal activities represented a great many hours, all fully invoiced, which counted for a great deal in the annual balance sheet of McIvory, Orlik & Partners. Now that her stock had been wiped out, their willingness to support her had sharply decreased.

'If leaving a daughter five hundred million dollars means hating her, I wish my father had felt the same way about me.'

He leaned forward and took a fairly bulky file from the briefcase. He placed it delicately on the table-top as if the weight of what it contained had the power to smash the glass.

'Anyway, here's the detailed account of all your activities over the years and the consequences of some of your choices.'

'It's all your fault. You should have advised me.'

'We did, but you didn't listen to us. Your activities as a film and theatre producer, for example . . .'

Now that the white heat of her anger had abated, the grim reality facing Chandelle Stuart had given a grey tinge to the usual pallor of her face. Her skin was like an old woman's. Not that this lessened her arrogance and disdain.

'I studied directing – I know about the cinema. What's wrong with producing movies?'

'There's nothing wrong with investing in film production. But there's one thing you have to remember. If the films make a reasonable profit, it becomes a job. If they don't, it remains a very expensive hobby. In your case, too expensive, I'd say.'

'Where do you get off, talking about things like that? What do *you* know about art?'

'Not much, I admit. But I do know about figures.'

He took the file from the low table, placed it on his knees and started leafing through it. When he found the page he was looking for, he took a pair of gold-rimmed spectacles from the breast pocket of his jacket and arranged them on his nose.

'Here we are. Let's take the novel by that man Levine. You paid four million dollars just to snatch the rights from

Universal. It was all a trick on the part of the author's agent, who made you pay a fortune for something you could have had for two hundred thousand dollars. If you recall, we advised you to sit tight and wait. Instead of which, you plunged straight in.'

'It was a terrific novel. I couldn't let it get away.'

'And indeed it didn't. Except that for that price you could have bought Scott Levine's entire output for the rest of his life. And then there was the film you made of the book. Shall we talk about that?'

'It was a great movie. The premiere in Los Angeles was packed.'

'But then it died a death at the box office. You spent a hundred and fifty million dollars on a film that barely made back eighteen, if I'm not mistaken. And shall we talk about *Clowns*, the musical that was supposed to be the new *Cats*? A production costing tens of millions that didn't even have one performance. Written and directed by you with music by a lounge bar pianist you met on a cruise ship.'

'The man was a genius!'

Orlik made a dismissive gesture. 'If he is, you're the only one who thinks so. The rest of the world seems happy to leave him on his ship.' He closed the file and put it back on the low table. 'I don't see any point in continuing. There are plenty of other examples. All too many, in fact. It's all here in black and white. If you want a second opinion, any other lawyer you choose can take a look at it.'

For a moment, Chandelle seemed disoriented, which briefly gave her the semblance of a human being. Her shoulders drooped and she looked defeated, humiliated, aware of the consequences of her decisions.

'How much do I have left?'

McIvory now took up the reins again. 'We have to settle your tax arrears and the last debts to the banks. If all the works of art here are sold, you might be able to keep hold of this apartment and . . . let's say . . . two hundred thousand dollars. Though personally, I think you should let the apartment go.'

Chandelle Stuart's nerves finally snapped. 'This is my home!' she screamed, her face purple with rage. 'This is the Stuart Building, my family's building! I can't leave it! I'll never go, do you understand? Never!'

McIvory feared for a moment that her vocal cords would crack. Her hysterical screaming became so shrill as to verge on the supersonic. To avoid sustaining the gaze of those bloodshot eyes, he raised his arm and looked at the time on his elegant Rolex Stelline.

'Unfortunately we do have to go. I think you need to be alone for a while, to think about what we've told you. Good evening, Miss Stuart.'

The two lawyers stood up. For years they had harboured the desire to give this conceited girl a good slapping, but now that it had happened, it had a bitter aftertaste. They didn't feel responsible for their client's financial ruin – by ignoring their advice, she had brought it all on herself – but they did feel dismayed by the total vacuity of her response, even now that it was staring her in the face that her life, as she had always lived it, was over for good.

Jason McIvory and Robert Orlik turned and walked towards the elevator, which opened directly onto the living room. Seeing them going, Chandelle felt lost. For the first time in her life, she was no longer in control of her own destiny.

She quickly ran and placed herself between the lawyers and the elevator, grabbing Orlik by the arm to stop him. The

126

two men had never thought they would hear Chandelle Stuart address them in such imploring tones.

'Wait. Maybe we can talk. I'll come to your office tomorrow and I think we can manage to sort things out. If we sell the house in Aspen and maybe the ranch . . .'

Despite the habit of indifference that years of work had given him, Robert Orlik was tempted for a moment to feel a touch of compassion for this spoiled child, who had had the luck to be born in an earthly paradise and the stupidity to destroy it with her own hands.

'Miss Stuart, you don't have a house in Aspen, or a ranch. They were both sold, on your instructions, to finance a film or some other scatterbrained enterprise. I don't know any other way to put this, Chandelle. You don't have anything left.'

The anger returned, like a storm after a brief lull. 'It's all your fault, you fucking thieves. I'll make you pay for this, cocksuckers. You and all the faggots in your fucking practice. Do you understand what I'm saying? I'll have you disbarred. You'll all end up in jail.'

This new outburst of anger put paid to any lingering compassion the two lawyers might have felt. The door of the elevator finally slid open in front of them. As Orlik entered, McIvory lingered for a moment on the threshold and turned to confront Chandelle, who was watching them with her face distorted by impotent rage.

'There's something I've been wanting to say to you for years. You're not a little girl any more and so you'll allow me, for a moment, to adopt your language.'

His smile was polite and professional, his tone almost gentle.

'We hate your ass, Miss Stuart. And if I have to be honest, it isn't even a nice ass.'

Chandelle Stuart was speechless for a moment. Her mouth formed a perfect O of surprise and her eyes opened wide as if in search of the words her voice could not find.

From inside the elevator, the last thing Jason McIvory and Robert Orlik saw, before the doors slid shut, was the figure of a woman rushing like a harpy towards the grand piano behind her, in a desperate search for something to hurl at them.

As they started their descent, the two men were silent, although both were wondering how much the Chinese vase they had just heard smashing against the walnut doors of the elevator might be worth.

CHAPTER 16

Chandelle Stuart found herself alone with her rage.

With her Prada shoes, she kicked at the fragments of the Chinese vase, unaware of its value, just as she had been unaware of the value of the life she had so systematically thrown away.

The anger seemed to have increased her strength. Frantic and blind in her fury, she literally tore off her dress and flung the shreds at the wall.

She was now wearing only a bra and a pair of black lace panties, as well as the stockings. Young as she was, her thin, unnaturally pale body had the slightly sagging skin of someone who has lived too long in the fast lane.

She started walking through the apartment, wringing her hands.

All she could think of, the one image she had branded on her eyes, was the fossilized expressions of those two so-called lawyers.

She started mumbling to herself, almost without moving her lips, which were reduced to a purplish-blue slash by the expensive lipstick, murmuring a rosary – not of prayer but of curses.

Jason McIvory and Robert Orlik, two motherfucking bastards. She had always hated them, ever since she had first seen them at the reading of her father's will. She had loathed their unctuous smiles when she had learned from the attorney that she had been practically disinherited. Black and funereal, like two vultures, they perched on their chairs, waiting to pick clean with hooked beaks the still-warm carcass of that other bastard, her father.

She could still see him, with his money and his pathetic pretensions to be a father figure, and all the shrinks with their Freud and their Jung and their fake-soothing voices that she had been forced to endure for years, while he fucked all the whores within range.

May he rot in hell.

Chandelle looked up at the ceiling, as if he hovered there, and began a shouted dialogue with the air – a piece of acting which, if it had been in a play or a film, would have been the best performance of her life.

'Are you listening to me, Avedon Lee Stuart? I hope you can hear me even from the hell where I sent you. I also hope you realize it was me – *me* – who let you die! I want that so much, I feel like killing myself just to come and tell you in person. But you won't get that satisfaction from me. Do you understand? Burn happily in hell while you can, you cunt, because when I get there it'll seem like paradise.'

Lost in this hysterical delirium, Chandelle had moved through the apartment, continuing to undress frenziedly until she had nothing on but her stockings. She finally reached her bedroom – a room which, like all the rest of the apartment, reeked of casual money and a dissipated life. Her nudity, as it appeared in the big mirror in front of her, was not enough to calm her: she saw a bony woman, with small, somewhat withered breasts, her pubic hair completely shaved. There was an unnatural innocence in that naked body, a fragility belied by her wild-eyed gaze and the traces of saliva at the corners of her thin mouth.

'You wanted me to live up to the family name, didn't you? You asked me to live . . . how did you put it?'

She spread her legs, placed her hands on her sides and pushed out her pelvis. She tried to change her shrill voice into a deeper one, and her nakedness became a grotesque attempt to imitate a male figure.

'Oh, yes . . . to live according to the principles that have always been the foundations of the Stuart public image.'

She laughed hysterically.

'Do you know what I did instead? I got myself laid by everyone, everyone I wanted, everyone I liked. Do you hear me, Mr Stuart? I hope that look you threw me before you died was because you understood I was the one who sent you to that lake of shit where you're swimming now. Yes, your daughter's a whore. And yes, your daughter killed you.'

This final cry faded away, as if the energy summoned up by her nervous crisis was suddenly exhausted. She collapsed back on the bed with her arms and legs open.

The contact with the cool surface of the satin bedspread made her shiver, and she felt her nipples wrinkle. She reached out a hand, lifted a corner of the bedspread and wrapped herself in it. Then she closed her eyes and started to remember what she had done to her father, seven years earlier.

When her mother, Elisabeth, had died in an automobile accident near their house in the mountains, the reaction of Chandelle's father had been to have a stroke. Not because of the grief of his loss, but because in the twisted wreck of the car they had found, as well as her body, the body of a young ski instructor from Aspen, sitting in the driver's seat with his pants down. It was blindingly obvious that the car had come off the road because the passenger at that moment had been giving the driver a blowjob. And the journalist who had been first on the scene was neither blind nor a moron. He had written an article that had made his fortune and nearly killed the last male representative of the Stuart dynasty. Everyone in New York's financial circles had laughed behind Avedon Lee Stuart's back, remembering the oft-invoked principles that had always been the basis of the family's public image.

He had been admitted to Emergency and saved at the last moment, although almost the entire right-hand side of his body was paralyzed. When he had been pronounced out of danger, he had decided to spend his convalescence in their apartment, tended by an army of omnipresent, overpaid nurses.

Chandelle had greeted her mother's death with total indifference, even though at the funeral she had managed to wear the expression required of a grieving daughter. But her father's illness had filled her with revulsion. He lay in bed, fed through a drip because his mouth, being bent to one side, prevented him from eating anything, and there was a constant thread of drool trickling down his chin.

She had never loved her father, but now the creature into which he had been transformed literally disgusted her, and it was out of that disgust that the idea had been born. She hadn't had the slightest qualm. In fact, she had welcomed it as the only course of action that could solve her problems once and for all.

All at once she had turned into a devoted and concerned daughter.

With the excuse that she wanted to personally attend her

father, she had often taken over from the nurses, who were much more attached to their paycheques than their duties anyway. She had discovered that Vitamin K could greatly increase the coagulation of the blood. Every time she had been alone with him, she had taken advantage of the moments when he dozed off to inject massive quantities of the vitamin into his drip.

Chandelle had a very clear memory of the night when, after yet another dose, her father had opened his eyes wide and seen her standing by the bed with a syringe in her hand. For a moment, it was as if he had seen the end and realized that he couldn't do anything but accept it. Then his eyes had glazed over again.

Chandelle had watched, spellbound, as the line representing his heartbeat on the monitor beside his bed had gradually gone flat. Then she had left the room, closing the door delicately behind her.

'Asleep,' she had whispered to the nurse sitting outside with a magazine in her hand.

The woman had taken her smile for that of a loving daughter, instead of someone who at last feels free.

Even now, lying on the bed, thinking again about that evening, that same smile appeared on her face.

The memory had completely calmed her. She felt relaxed, full of a languor that needed to be satisfied. In her own way.

Still wrapped in the cover, she turned on her side, picked up the telephone on the night-table and dialled a number.

When she heard the voice answer, she didn't even bother to say her name.

'Hello, Randall? I want to have a bit of fun tonight – to do something exciting. Can you bring a car, around midnight? Nothing too flashy.'

133

She didn't wait for confirmation, nor did she expect any objections, not that she would have listened to any, not from Randall. She paid him a decent enough salary, and sometimes, when she felt like it, she gave him something a little more satisfying as a reward.

She opened a drawer just below the phone, put her hand inside and moved it around until she felt a small bag taped to the underside of the table-top.

Carefully removing the tape, she took out a small plastic wrapper full of white powder. She opened it, stuck her fingers in and took a pinch. She lifted it directly to her nostrils and snorted strongly, first into one, then the other. She put the bag down on the night-table. There was no point in putting it back. She was going to need it tonight, a lot of it . . .

She smiled up at a ceiling as white as the powder.

She waited for the rush of the cocaine, so similar to the perfect orgasm of pain. The drug had always had an erotic effect on her, and thinking of the evening that awaited her made her feel even more languid.

She slipped a hand under the covers, opened her legs and ran her fingers from her breasts to her navel and then further down until they reached the shaved slit between her legs.

She opened it with her fingers and found it already wet. She closed her eyes, imagined a stranger, and quivered with pleasure.

CHAPTER 17

When she looked again at the time, she saw it was almost nine. Far from draining her, that little treat she had allowed herself had given her new energy. She decided she was hungry and had a craving for Japanese food. She got out of bed and, putting her hands on her back, arched her thin body and looked at herself smugly in the mirror. She had completely recovered from her earlier attack. She was herself again, cool-headed, in control.

That asshole who'd called himself her father had understood, despite himself.

Those two bloodsuckers who called themselves her lawyers would understand, too.

She would show them who Chandelle Stuart was.

For now, she would take a hot shower and then call Randall Haze and ask him to pick her up earlier. Maybe he could also book her a table at Nobu. Then, before she carried out her plans, she might go hear some music in a club in the Bowery, or whatever else came to mind.

She went in the bathroom and slipped into the multi-function tub with its shiatsu hydromassage shower. As she greeted the beneficial pressure of the water on her skin, it struck her that she needed to be as beautiful as possible tonight. She needed to appear like an unattainable vision to the strangers she would meet. She wanted to see the incredulity on their faces, and then the desire, and then the pleasure that only comes from a dream coming true.

She dried her smooth, glossy hair, applied a deodorant stick to her shaved armpits, and sprinkled her body in the right places with an aromatic essence created specially for her by a traditional perfumery on Canal Street.

After making herself up in a slightly more eye-catching way than usual, she went from the bathroom to the walk-in closet. Here she put on black underwear and self-supporting stockings, which she particularly liked for the effect they had on the male imagination, but even more because they were very comfortable and practical.

Very useful for taking advantage, wherever she was, of any sudden, unexpected itch she got for sex.

From the clothes hanging in the closet she chose a fairly short black dress she thought would emphasize her slender figure and long legs.

She had just put on the dress and was taking a second snort of cocaine before calling Randall when she heard the entryphone buzzing.

She wondered who it could be at this hour.

The security guards had a direct line to the apartment, and early that afternoon she had given the rest of the day off to the staff in order to have privacy when she was talking to her lawyers.

She approached the little video screen in the bedroom. When she pressed the button, the face of the person who had rung appeared on the screen, framed by the camera positioned over the door of her private elevator in the left wing of the huge shiny marble entrance to the Stuart Building.

Chandelle was surprised to see *him* there, especially

dressed like that, with a hood over his head that seemed, from the slightly blurry image, to be part of a tracksuit. They hadn't seen each other for quite a while and she didn't really feel in the mood to see him tonight, despite the feelings she had once had for him.

His voice emerged slightly muffled from the small speaker. 'Hi. Is that you, Chandelle?'

'Yes, this is she. What do you want?'

Her unfriendly tone did not seem to affect him. He smiled at her from the screen. 'Can I come up? I need to have a word with you.'

'Now? I was just on my way out.'

'It won't take long. I have some news you might find interesting.'

'All right. I'll send down the elevator. You don't need to do anything, I control it from here.'

As she walked through her vast apartment to the living room, onto which the elevator door opened, Chandelle continued to wonder what he could possibly have to tell her that was so important he'd show up at this hour.

Especially after all this time.

Given the way he was dressed, maybe he'd been running in Central Park, and had passed her building and decided to drop in.

She activated the code that opened the elevator doors in the lobby. The elevator served only her apartment, and she could operate it from there using a code known only to her.

As she waited, she hoped she could get rid of him quickly. But then she realized that was a lie she was trying to peddle to herself. She made an effort to stay calm, even though the man who was on his way up continued to give her a kind of perverse, sadistic thrill. She had felt it as soon as she met him, and then again every time she was in his presence.

If only he knew . . .

For a moment she was tempted to rush to her bedroom and do another line of coke.

The whoosh of the doors opening stopped her in the middle of the room. There he was, standing in the elevator, in the light pouring down from above. He was wearing a tracksuit with the hood up so that his smile was in shadow, and he had his hands deep in his pockets.

He stepped out, and for the first time she realized how cold a smile could be.

'Hello, Chandelle. Sorry to bother you at home. But as I said, this won't take long.'

With perfect timing, the clouds that had watched over New York all afternoon broke at that moment. There was a flash of lightning, a roll of thunder, and then the rain came pouring down, so hard that it bounced off the tiles of the balcony onto the window sills.

The man continued walking in her direction. As he came level with her, he took his right hand out of his pocket. Chandelle thought he wanted to shake her hand, instead of which she realized with a shudder that he was holding a gun.

She was so busy looking at the black hole of the barrel, she did not notice that the smile had vanished from the man's face, nor was she aware of the mocking tone in his words.

'It won't take long, although I have the impression that for you it may feel that way.' He paused. His voice became as soft as velvet. 'My sweet Lucy . . .'

Chandelle Stuart raised her head abruptly. She would never

know that the look in her eyes was exactly the same as the one her father had thrown her from his deathbed.

There was another flash of lightning beyond the windows, and it cast her shadow on the wall, the shadow of a useless woman who was about to die.

CHAPTER 18

Outside, in the darkness, it was pouring with rain.

From his window overlooking 16th Street, Jordan watched the drops falling straight from the sky, enshrouding the lights and wonders of New York.

He had once seen an old film with Elliott Gould, called *Getting Straight*. During the credits, thanks to a trick of the camera, the main character was shown walking along a crowded street, advancing normally, while the cars and the people were going backwards.

That was exactly how he felt now.

Jordan didn't know if the way he was doing things was right or not, but he was certain that he and the people around him weren't going in the same direction.

Moving over to the couch, he picked up the remote and switched on the TV, turning to the Eyewitness Channel. They were showing an item recorded that afternoon. In close-up was a reporter whose name he couldn't remember, with a microphone in his hand. Behind him could be seen planes and a bright patch of rain on the runway of an airport.

'A large number of people were at the airport today to greet the coffin containing the body of Connor Slave, the singer kidnapped in Rome a week ago with his girlfriend Maureen Martini, an officer in the Italian police, and savagely murdered. His fans will be able to pay their last respects over the next few days in a specially arranged chapel. The funeral will take place—'

Jordan switched off the sound, leaving only the images on the screen and the rain beating against the window-panes. Another young man who would never grow old, he thought.

The telephone started ringing, and Jordan stood there looking at it, uncertain whether or not to answer. His doubts were resolved by the figure of Lysa emerging from the corridor in her robe and handing him the cordless.

'It's for you.'

Jordan put the phone, still warm from Lysa's skin, against his ear.

'Jordan, it's Burroni. I think it's happened.'

'What's happened?'

'I'm afraid we have our Lucy.'

'Shit. Who is it?'

'Chandelle Stuart. They found her in her apartment this morning.'

'Where?'

'The Stuart Building, on Central Park West.'

Jordan's hands felt clammy, as if the dampness of the rain falling blindly on the windowpanes had somehow entered the room. 'I was hoping that bastard would leave us a little more time.'

'I'm on my way there now. Want me to pick you up?'

'Sure. In this rain, I don't think it'd be a good idea to use the bike.'

'OK. I'm on my way. I'll be there in five minutes.'

Standing in the middle of the room, Lysa watched him as he put on his leather jacket.

'I'm sorry you got woken up, Lysa. I don't know why they didn't call me on my cellphone.'

'It doesn't matter, I wasn't asleep. Trouble?'

'Yes. Someone else has been killed, and it looks like there may be a connection with the murder of my nephew.'

'I'm sorry.'

'Me, too. I only hope that this time we find something that helps us catch this madman.'

They stood facing each other in an apartment that didn't belong to either of them.

'Jordan, I'm not sure what to say in situations like this.'

'You don't have to say anything. It's OK, Lysa. I hope you get some sleep. Good night.'

He walked out, closing the door behind him and deciding to go downstairs on foot rather than call the elevator. From the apartment below came the sound of music. Connor Slave, of course.

He got to the front door just as a Ford with Burroni at the wheel pulled up at the kerb across the street. Jordan ran out into the rain and, as he dashed across the road, he saw Burroni lean over to open the door on his side. He got in. The car smelled of damp carpet and imitation leather.

Through the windscreen, swept by the wipers, he looked up at the bright rectangle where, behind the glass, the figure of Lysa stood motionless against the light. A presence and an absence.

Burroni had followed the direction of his gaze to the lighted window. 'Your apartment?'

'Yes.'

Burroni didn't ask any questions, and Jordan didn't choose to say any more. As they moved away from the kerb, Jordan remembered waking up on the morning after the evening he and Lysa had met.

He had opened his eyes, and immediately smelled something he wasn't used to smelling, at least in his own home: the aroma of coffee he hadn't made himself. He had got up and put on jeans and a T-shirt. Before going to the living room, he had checked his appearance in the bathroom mirror. His face looked exactly the way he had expected it to look. The face of a man who had taken a few blows the previous night.

He had washed his face, left the bathroom and walked to the living room, and there she was.

Or there *he* was.

Thinking about that now, he felt as embarrassed as he had that morning. But Lysa's face had borne no trace of the previous evening's conversation.

Only a smile.

'Good morning, Jordan. How are your eye and nose? I can see them, but how do they feel?'

'I'm hardly aware of them.'

'Good. Want a coffee?'

He had sat down at the table, which was laid for two. 'This is quite a privilege. What have I done to deserve it?'

'It's the first day of my first time in New York. I also deserve it. How do you like your eggs?'

'Do I get eggs, too?'

'Sure. What kind of bed and breakfast would this be without eggs?'

Lysa had brought the plates to the table and they had eaten breakfast almost in silence, each absorbed in their own thoughts. But then Lysa had put an end to that little moment of peace and opened the door to the outside world.

'They just talked about your nephew on TV.'

'I can imagine. This case is going to create quite a stir.'

'And what will you do now?'

'Before anything else, find a place to stay. I don't want to go to my brother in Gracie Mansion. Everyone would be watching me. I prefer to keep as low a profile as possible. There's a hotel on Thirty-Eighth that—'

'Listen, I have a proposition. Seeing as how my husband isn't a problem any more . . .'

It was like a punch to the stomach. Jordan had hoped his reaction didn't show on his face.

Lysa had continued as if everything was normal. 'I've only just arrived in the city and I want to do a bit of sightseeing before I start looking for a job. In other words, I'll be out most of the time. As for you, this business will surely be over sooner or later and you'll be free to go. In the meantime, you can stay here, if you want.'

She paused and tilted her head to one side, with an amused, almost defiant gleam in her golden eyes.

'Unless that's a problem for you?'

'Of course not,' Jordan had replied, a bit too hastily, and immediately felt like a fool.

Lysa had stood up and started clearing the table. 'Time to get going.'

'Want a hand?'

'God, no. I think you have more important things to do.'

Jordan had looked at his watch. 'Yes. I'll take a quick shower and then be on my way.' He had started for his room but Lysa's voice had stopped him.

'Jordan . . .'

He waited.

'They talked about you in that news item I saw on TV.

They said you were one of the best police officers New York has ever had.'

'They say all kinds of things.'

'They also said why you're not a police officer any more.'

'. . . tonight by her bodyguard.'

Burroni's voice brought him back to that rain-washed car and the streetlights and the reflections on the wet asphalt.

'Sorry, James, I was miles away. Do you mind repeating that?'

'I said she was discovered tonight by her bodyguard. He called Headquarters and I was the one who spoke to him. From what he told me, especially about the way the body was arranged, this could be it.'

'Does my brother know?'

'Of course. He was told immediately, just like he asked. He said to inform him if things really are the way they look.'

'We should know soon enough.'

They said nothing more for the rest of the ride, each deep in thoughts they would have preferred to leave at home.

Jordan knew the Stuart Building, a slightly sinister edifice, some sixty storeys high, adorned on its upper levels with gargoyles reminiscent of those on the Chrysler Building. It occupied the entire block between 92nd and 93rd Streets on Central Park West, looking out on Central Park and the Jacqueline Kennedy Onassis Reservoir. The name Stuart meant money, real money, lots of it. Old Arnold J. Stuart had ruthlessly amassed a huge fortune from steel in the days of the Fricks and the Carnegies. Subsequently the family's interests had expanded into almost every field. When Chandelle Stuart's parents had died in quick succession a few years earlier, she had found herself sole heir to a vast fortune.

145

When they got to the location, Burroni parked the car immediately behind the Crime Scene team's van. He switched off the engine but made no move to get out.

'Jordan, there's something I think you should know, especially after what you told me today.'

Jordan waited in silence. He didn't know what Burroni was about to tell him, but he sensed it was something that wasn't easy for him to say.

'You know, about this Internal Affairs business. I did take that money. I needed it. My son Kenny has—'

Jordan raised his hand. 'It's all right, James. I guess things have been hard for you, too.'

They looked at each other for a moment, their faces made spectral by the orange light of the streetlamps and the reflections of the raindrops on the car windows.

Then Jordan said, 'Come on, let's take a look at this shit.'

They opened their doors almost simultaneously, got out, and ran towards the entrance of the building in the rain.

CHAPTER 19

The first thing the two men saw as they entered the apartment was the motionless female figure sitting by the piano – a shiny black Steinway grand that must have cost a fortune. She was sitting on a bar stool high enough to support her back against the curve of the instrument. Her elbows rested on the lacquered top, her hands dangling over the edge. Her face was turned towards the keyboard, as if she was listening spellbound to music only she could hear.

Her black dress was low-cut but sober, and they couldn't make out her features, which were concealed by the long smooth hair that covered her face. Her legs were crossed, giving a glimpse of her bare thighs, and from her knees a shiny substance had run down her calf and smeared the material of her stockings.

Without realizing it, Jordan found himself speaking in a lower voice than he would normally have used, as if the malign spell of that silent concert was not to be broken. 'Just like Lucy with Schroeder.'

'Who's Schroeder?'

'Another character from *Peanuts*, a musical prodigy who's crazy about Beethoven. Charles Schulz always draws him sitting at his toy piano. Lucy's in love with him and she always sits in this position when she listens to him playing.'

They slowly approached the body. Burroni pointed out that the elbows had been stuck to the surface of the piano with a mass of glue. Glue had also been used to stick her dress to the back of the stool. The crossed legs had been kept in position in the same way, but so much adhesive had been used that it had dripped down.

'She's glued, just like your nephew. But this time our cartoonist really went to town.'

'Who'd like to bet it's the same brand? Ice Glue.'

Jordan put on the latex gloves that Burroni handed him, then lifted the victim's hair to uncover her face.

'Holy Christ.'

The victim's eyes, staring at the keyboard, were held open by the same glue that her killer had used on the rest of the body. Jordan pointed out the bruises around her neck.

'She was strangled, too.'

Jordan let the hair go and it fell like a curtain over those unnaturally staring eyes. He walked to the other side of the piano to see the body from a different angle. What he saw brought him up short. The lid of the piano was raised, and on the little flap where the music usually rested was a white sheet of paper with some handwritten words on it:

It was a dark and stormy night . . .

A chill went through him. He knew all too well what those words meant. It was a famous line from *Peanuts* but, at the same time, it was a death sentence for somebody. Burroni came up behind him and looked over his shoulder.

'What the fuck is that?'

'It's another warning. If we don't find this son of a bitch in a hurry, we'll soon be dealing with another poor dead bastard got up to look like Snoopy.'

Jordan walked away from the piano and at last took a look

around. When the elevator doors had opened, he and Burroni had been drawn immediately to the chilling spectacle of the corpse. Now he was able to get a better idea of their surroundings. The apartment was furnished, at least the part of it they could see, in a minimalist style, with furniture in wenge and anodized aluminium, and couches and drapes in pale colours ranging from sand to tobacco. Everything around them spoke of wealth. There were paintings and art objects that told the long history of the Stuart family. The wall to his right was entirely occupied by a painting, and there was nothing to suggest that it wasn't an original. It was a preparatory study for Géricault's *The Raft of the Medusa*, the same size as the finished painting in the Louvre.

The presence here of that particular painting, it struck Jordan, was like an ironic twist of fate.

Géricault. Jerry Ko.

Two painters with similar-sounding names, their work united by the same violent despair. Each in his way had depicted life as a hopeless journey towards death. And now Chandelle Stuart's soul was also adrift on that fragile raft.

As he walked towards the painting, he noticed a couple of things he had not spotted before. Strewn on the floor near the elevator were fragments of a vase that seemed to have been thrown against the door, to judge by the marks on the panelling. And around the living room were torn shreds of what appeared to have been an item of clothing.

Just then, the Medical Examiner appeared from beyond the wall occupied by the painting. When he came level with Jordan and Burroni, he replied immediately to the question he read in their eyes.

'For now, I can't tell you very much, except that the victim was strangled and that death probably occurred some time between nine and eleven.'

Jordan pointed to the fragments near the elevator and the pieces of material on the floor. 'These would seem to suggest a struggle, even though there doesn't appear to be any sign of it on the victim.'

The ME waved towards the corpse without looking at it. 'Well, I can't really do a proper examination of the body yet, not with the way it is. In fact, I'm wondering how we're even going to get it out of here. God forgive me, but if we weren't dealing with a death, I'd think we were in an episode of *Mr Bean*.'

Although the ME had seen almost all the variations that death could offer during the course of his career, even he seemed bemused by the circumstances of this one.

'Let us know the results of the post mortem as soon as possible,' Burroni sighed.

'Of course. From what I gather, I'm likely to get a phone call quite soon telling me this case is top priority.'

He left them to join the men who had come to remove the body, and who were standing by the piano with bewildered expressions on their faces.

'What do you think, Jordan?' Burroni asked.

'Frankly, I'm not yet sure what to think. And that worries me a little.'

'Do you reckon we're dealing with a serial killer?'

'Everything seems to point to it, but I'm not entirely convinced. We're clearly dealing with someone who's not right in the head, someone with his own private symbolism, but it all seems a bit too elaborate, too complicated . . . Serial killers, at the moment of contact with their victims, are usually wilder, more frenzied, less concentrated. I don't know. I think we should have a word with the bodyguard.'

Burroni made a sign to the officer who had greeted them in the lobby and brought them up to the apartment, a sturdy black man with a moustache, who was still standing by the door of the elevator. He left his post and joined them.

'Where's the man who found the body?'

'Follow me.'

They made their way past the members of the Crime Scene team, who were just finishing off their work, and through the apartment – a walk that confirmed to them its vast size and luxury – until they came to a large room that was clearly some kind of study. On the walls were high bookcases full of books that could be reached with the use of metal ladders running on rails. A large pair of French doors facing the entrance led to a balcony that was probably the continuation of the one outside the living room.

Behind a desk partly occupied by a computer, a man was sitting. He got to his feet when he saw them come in. He was tall and athletic-looking, with grey hair, angular features, and a small scar near the right ear.

'I'm Detective Burroni and this is Jordan Marsalis, a police consultant.'

Jordan might once have smiled at a term like that, which meant everything and nothing. Now it just made him feel like an intruder, more anxious than ever to keep in the background and let Burroni be the official face of the investigation.

'I assume I spoke to you on the phone, Mr . . .?'

'Haze. Randall Haze. Yes, it was me who called you when I discovered what had happened.'

The man came out from behind the desk and Burroni and Jordan shook hands with him in turn. He was a strong man: you could sense it not only from his grip but by the way he moved. It was the kind of strength that came from the experience of the streets, not from fake martial arts schools or gyms where people were pumped full of steroids.

'Before we go on, there's something I want to say,' he told them. 'I guess you're lifting prints from all over the apartment . . .'

'Of course.'

'And of course you'll find mine, too. So I'll tell you this before you discover it for yourselves. I've done time. Five years for assault and attempted murder. I'm not justifying myself, just explaining. I was a rough kid, I made a mistake and I paid for it. Since then, I've gone straight.'

'OK, noted. Please sit down, Mr Haze.'

Before he sat down again in one of the two armchairs in front of the desk, Haze arranged the crease in the pants of his elegant dark-grey suit. Burroni walked to the French doors and stood there for a moment, staring out at the darkness.

'How long have you been working for Miss Stuart?'

'About five years, give or take a month.'

'In what capacity?'

'Bodyguard and private secretary.'

'How private, exactly?'

'My job was to accompany Miss Stuart in personal situations she preferred not to . . . how shall I put it? . . . not to make public.'

For the moment, Burroni chose not to pursue that subject. 'So tell us what happened.'

'This evening Chand . . . Miss Stuart called me.'

'What time was this?'

'Around eight thirty, I think. In any case she called me on her cellphone. You should be able to check the time from the phone company's records.'

Burroni turned, with the fleeting expression on his face of someone who doesn't like being taught how to do his job. 'All right, we will if we have to. And what did she want?'

'She told me to be here by midnight because she was planning to go out. I got here at a quarter of twelve, came up to the apartment and found the body. I immediately grabbed the phone and called you.'

'Was it normal for her to go out at that hour?'

'In some cases, yes. Miss Stuart was . . .' Randall Haze broke off, bowed his head and looked at the floor as if a chasm had suddenly opened up between his shiny shoes.

At this point, Jordan decided to intervene and went and sat down on the chair facing him.

'Mr Haze, listen to me. There's something here I don't understand and when that happens I feel stupid. Unless it's the person I'm talking to who's stupid. And I don't think that's the case here. So, is there something we should know?'

Haze let out a sigh. 'Miss Stuart was sick.'

'What do you mean by "sick"?'

'I don't know what else to call it. She was sick in the head. She had very dangerous tastes and the biggest part of my work was to protect her whenever she satisfied them.'

'Can you be more spectifc?'

'Chandelle Stuart was a nymphomaniac who liked being raped.'

Jordan and Burroni looked at each other. They were both thinking the same thing: this could mean big complications.

Haze continued his story without need for further prompting. 'I went with her to protect her in situations that most women would have thought of as their worst nightmares. Some nights, Chandelle had sex with ten, even twelve men at a time. Homeless people, vagrants, people of all races. And

153

it was completely risky sex, without any kind of precautions. At other times, I had to stay hidden here in the apartment in case one of the sadists she'd invited home went a bit too far and did her real harm. And then there were the films.'

'What films?'

'The ones I made. Everthing she got up to, either here or outside, I had to film with a digital camera. Then it was all transferred to DVD and she'd watch it later. It gave her a kick, watching herself in those kinds of situations. The discs should be here somewhere.'

Burroni and Jordan looked at each other again.

'I assume Miss Stuart paid you well for these services of yours,' Jordan said.

'Oh yes. When it came to money Chandelle Stuart was very generous. When she wanted, she could be generous in all kinds of ways . . .' Randall Haze bowed his head again.

'A few more questions and you'll be free to go. Does anything seem to be missing from the apartment?'

It was just a routine question: both Burroni and Jordan knew perfectly well that robbery was extremely unlikely as a motive for this homicide.

'At first sight, I'd say no. Seems to me everything's normal.'

'And have you noticed anything or anyone suspicious lately? Anything unusual, I mean.'

'No, everything she ever did was unusual.'

'Do you know if Miss Stuart ever saw or knew a man named Gerald Marsalis? He was also known as Jerry Ko.'

'You mean the Mayor's son, the guy who was killed a while ago? I saw his picture in the papers. As far as I know, she didn't. Though come to think of it, one time when I was with her at a disco called Pangya, he was there. They passed each other and waved their hands. So maybe they did know each other, but in all the time I've worked for her, I never heard her mention his name, and I certainly don't think they ever saw each other.'

Jordan gave an almost imperceptible nod to Burroni. The detective put his hand in his pocket, took out a business card, and gave it to Haze.

'All right, Mr Haze, I think we're done for now. I'd like to continue our conversation this afternoon, at Headquarters. When you get there, ask for me.'

Haze took the card and slipped it into the pocket of his jacket, then stood up and said goodbye.

They waited for Chandelle Stuart's now unemployed bodyguard to leave the room, then Burroni took his walkie-talkie from his belt.

'Burroni here. A man's on his way down. Grey hair and dark suit. His name is Randall Haze. Put someone on his tail, twenty-four-seven. And make sure it's discreet. This guy knows his job.'

In silence, they left the study and walked back the way they had come. By the time they reached the living room, the body had been removed. There were still traces of glue on the shiny lacquer of the piano, as well as marks left by the crime scene team to indicate where the elbows had been.

'What do you think, Jordan?'

'I think we're in deep shit. We have two victims. Two extremely dubious individuals, both from very high-profile families. And the same MO linking them. So far we've managed to keep a pretty tight lid on things, but how long do you think it's going to take now for the whole story to come out, including my involvement in the investigation?'

'I think this means we have to work damn fast.'

'Right. For a whole lot of reasons. The most important being that, if we don't, we'll soon have three victims instead of two.'

'And what do you think of Randall Haze?'

'You were right to put someone on his trail, but I don't think it'll lead us anywhere, any more than it has with LaFayette Johnson.'

'Christ, what a story. The things people do for money.'

Jordan shook his head, staring at the piano. 'It's not only a matter of money. In fact, I'd say that in this case money has nothing to do with it. You may think this is crazy after what he told us, but I'm convinced that Randall Haze was in love with Chandelle Stuart.'

Burroni turned to look at Jordan.

He was standing in the middle of the room, gazing intently at the enormous painting on the wall, as if he had just become aware that there was a new passenger on board the raft of the Medusa.

CHAPTER 20

The walkie-talkie on Burroni's belt emitted the two beeps that meant a call. The detective lifted it to his ear.

'Detective Burroni . . . All right, we're on our way down.' He turned to Jordan. 'The Security Manager for the Stuart Building has just arrived. You want to talk to him?'

'No, you go, for now. If you don't mind, I'd like to stay here for a few minutes alone.'

Burroni nodded. He did not yet fully understand Jordan Marsalis's investigatory methods, but he had accepted them, instinctively knowing that it wasn't just a question of experience or inclination, but of genuine talent. The man's fame was fully justified. He stepped into the elevator and the doors closed noiselessly on the image of Jordan, motionless in the middle of the living room.

Jordan stood there, waiting for the apartment to speak to him. There was always something that hovered in the air at a murder scene, some invisible sign you couldn't pick up with fingerprint powder or Luminol or any of the other methods available to the investigators. Jordan had often sensed it, and every time he had felt goose bumps on his skin. It was as if Death wanted one last round of applause and was going to wait there until it came.

Calmly, he walked back in the direction of the study where

they had questioned Randall Haze. On the way, he went inside all the rooms he had previously only glanced in, and listened to what the apartment was telling him. It was a story of wealth and boredom and sickness, of money spent – in vain – trying to defeat the boredom and the sickness.

At last he came to the study. He knew something had struck him while he was talking to Haze, but he couldn't remember what it was. That was why he was here again, alone, waiting for an answer only he could hear. He sat down in the armchair he had occupied during the questioning and let his eyes wander around the room.

Behind him were bookshelves filled with volumes. To his left, the French windows, leading to the balcony and the lights of the city. Facing him, on the wall behind the desk, a Mondrian with its lines and squares and perfectly balanced colours. On either side of the desk, two more areas of shelving similar to that on the wall behind him.

On a shelf to the left of the desk there were . . .

That was what it was! Jordan stood up and went to take a closer look at the four volumes with dark red bindings lined up side by side on a shelf at eye level. On the cover of the one closest to him was a logo and below it, in gold lettering, the words:

Vassar College
Poughkeepsie

He knew Vassar. At one time, it had been reserved for women, and along with six other women's colleges had formed part of a group called 'The Seven Sisters'. It was considered very exclusive, with fees of about a hundred thousand dollars a year. At the end of the 1960s, a glance at the balance sheet had persuaded the board to open Vassar College to men. The college specialized in the creative fields, like art, writing and drama.

Jordan took out one of the volumes and opened it. It was a yearbook containing the photographs of all the pupils on a course of Theatre and Film Directing. He continued leafing through the pages until he found the photograph he was looking for.

Chandelle Stuart, much younger and much less well groomed, looked out at him, unsmiling, from the glossy page. Her dark, slightly frowning eyes fully revealed her difficult character, partly concealed by a pair of glasses that might have been there with the express purpose of giving her an intellectual air. Jordan couldn't help comparing that image with the one he still had in his mind: the same eyes held open by a layer of glue, staring as if blinded by the sudden flash of death.

Then he was struck by a detail.

Pinned to Chandelle's chest was a brooch. It was only a cheap thing made of tin, the kind that had been popular in the mid-1970s. There were black lines on a white background, lines immediately recognizable as the graphic style of Charles Schulz, and those lines depicted a face.

Lucy.

Jordan felt the kind of exhilaration he had not experienced for some time. It was as if a hole had been made in the wall of a dark room to let in a ray of light.

He had never confessed it to anyone, but he was firmly convinced that every investigator setting out to track down a criminal was really doing it for himself, that justice was merely a pretext, and that what he was really looking for was that exhilaration, a high as strong as any you could get from drugs.

He had often wondered if murderers had the same high at the moment they committed their crimes. And if he himself was anything other than a potential criminal who had somehow ended up in a uniform.

He took out his cellphone and dialled his brother's private number at Gracie Mansion. Christopher replied immediately, which meant that he was already awake. Or maybe still awake.

'Hello?'

'Chris, it's Jordan.'

'At last. How's it going?'

'Badly. I'm at Chandelle Stuart's apartment.'

'I know. What can you tell me?'

'It's him. Same killer as Gerald. The victim was stuck to a piano in a way that recalls Lucy, the *Peanuts* character.'

'Shit.'

'Precisely. And for the moment, no lead worthy of the name. We're waiting for the post-mortem report and the Forensics results.'

'I've already given orders for everything to be done as quickly as possible. We should have the first results soon.'

'Listen, there's something I'd like to ask you.'

'Go ahead.'

'Gerald went to college for a couple of years, didn't he?'

'Yes.'

'He didn't go to Vassar, by any chance?'

'Yes, he did. Why?'

'I think you should make a call to the President of Vassar and tell him I'll be going there to ask him some questions soon. And I'd like to go alone.'

'No problem. I'll get on it right away. Is this an actual lead?'

'Maybe yes and maybe no. I have a kind of idea, but I want to be sure before I talk about it.'

160

'All right. Keep me informed. Anything you need, you've got. This was all we needed, another maniac at loose in the city.'

'OK, talk to you later.' Jordan hung up and put the phone in his pocket.

At that moment, preceded by a slight squeak of new shoes on a wooden floor, an officer materialized in the doorway.

'Detective Burroni asks if you could go down. There's something he wants you to see.'

Jordan followed the officer. In silence, they stepped into the elevator and travelled down to the lobby. The main entrance of the Stuart Building was T-shaped, with the widest part facing the street. The ceiling was very high, giving a sense of space, and the floors were of marble. In the middle, opposite the two revolving doors, and beneath the inevitable American flag, was the Security and Information desk. At the moment, a man in a black uniform was sitting there. He watched them pass with a slightly stunned expression on his face, as if bemused by the night's agitation.

They went in through a door behind the Security desk and climbed two flights of stairs, until they reached a large room with a balcony that gave a view of the entire entrance. In front of a bank of TV screens, another man in a black uniform was sitting with his back to them. Beside him was Burroni and a tall middle-aged man with a receding hairline, whom Jordan knew well. His name was Harmon Fowley and he was also an ex-cop. When he had retired from the police, he had become a consultant for Codex Security, a company for which Jordan had also occasionally worked after he had quit the Department.

If Fowley was surprised to see him, he didn't show it. He held out his hand. 'Hi, Jordan. Pleased to see you.'

'Me too, Harmon. How're you doing?'

'Surviving. These days, that's a luxury.'

For a moment, Jordan read on Fowley's face the same dissatisfaction he himself felt.

'I was sorry to hear about your nephew,' the man went on. 'A nasty business. And if I understand correctly, what happened here tonight has something to do with that?'

Jordan looked to Burroni for support. Burroni nodded: Fowley could be trusted to be discreet.

'Yes. We think the two things are connected. We don't yet know how, but we have to work fast, otherwise there's going to be another victim.'

'And fast means fast,' Burroni confirmed. 'Do you mind if we take another look at what we saw earlier?'

They all stood together behind the man sitting in front of the screens, while Fowley explained the system.

'As you can see, the entrance is filmed day and night on closed circuit TV. The recordings are made directly onto rewritable DVDs. We keep them for a month and then recycle them. There are lots of stores, offices and restaurants in the lower part of the building. The apartments are all on the upper floors and are served by a series of elevators on both sides of the lobby. The one exception is Miss Stuart's apartment. That has a private elevator, which is controlled from inside the apartment and comes equipped with its own code and video entryphone.'

'Does the entryphone camera on that elevator take recordings?'

'No. It wasn't considered necessary since the area is already covered by the other cameras.'

Burroni pointed to the series of screens. 'And look what they picked up this evening.'

Fowley placed a hand on the seated man's shoulder. 'Go ahead, Barton.'

The man pressed a button and on the central screen, which was larger than the others, the images started appearing. They had been taken from a camera directly facing the entrance. At the beginning, they saw the figure of a man in a jacket and tie walk past the window on the left and approach the revolving door. As he was about to enter, a figure ran across the street and came up behind him. He was wearing a tracksuit with the hood up and his head bowed so that his face was concealed.

Jordan gripped the edge of the desk. For a fleeting moment, he had the absurd idea that inside that hood wasn't a living face, but the grinning skull and empty eye-sockets of Death.

On the screen, the man stepped into the revolving door, and as it turned he moved in such a way as to make sure the person who had entered before him was between him and the cameras for as long as possible. In spite of this and in spite of the blurred nature of the image, it was clear that he had a limp in his right leg. When the two men were in the lobby, the man in the tracksuit started walking fairly quickly and disappeared from the frame on the right of the screen.

The angle changed. They were now watching the images from another camera.

Again, the man was seen from the back. They saw him limp to Chandelle Stuart's private elevator and press the button, not with a finger, but with the sleeve of his tracksuit, clearly trying to avoid leaving prints on the button. From the movements of his head they could tell that he was talking to someone, presumably Chandelle. Soon afterwards the elevator doors opened and the man stepped inside. As the doors closed, he still had his back to the camera.

'What time was this?' Jordan asked.

Fowley indicated the time-code on the screen. 'Ten before ten.'

Jordan moved to the side of the officer who was working the DVD player. He could sense the unease in the room. Although films and novels were full of highly improbable killers, flesh and blood murderers were generally fairly predictable and made lots of mistakes, out of stupidity, or conceit, or inexperience, or because they got carried away by the emotion of the moment. This man, though, seemed much colder, much more determined, and above all much more intelligent, than the norm.

'The son of a bitch knew there were cameras,' Jordan said. 'He waited for someone to go in and used him as a screen. And he kept his back to the camera all the time.'

'There's another thing,' Fowley said. 'We're just opposite Central Park and most people who live here regularly go jogging there at all times of the day or night. If I show you other recordings, you'll see dozens of people looking exactly like that one. The security guard certainly didn't notice anything suspicious about him.'

Burroni leaned on the desk. 'Barton,' he said to the seated man, 'what's your first name?'

'Woody.'

'All right, Woody, I'm going to ask you for two favours. The first is to make us a copy of this recording. The second, and this would really be a great help, is to keep as quiet as you can about what you've seen and heard tonight. Other people's lives may depend on it.'

Barton, who gave the impression that he was a man of few words, confirmed with a nod that he understood the situation perfectly.

'There's no problem about that,' Fowley said. 'I can vouch for Barton.'

Jordan started feeling a little restless. Ever since he had arrived, he had done nothing but store data, and now he felt the need to go somewhere quiet and process it. Burroni must have felt the same need, because he now held his hand out to Fowley.

'Thank you. You've been a great help.'

'My pleasure. Good luck, Jordan.'

'You too. Good night, Harmon.'

They went downstairs, crossed the lobby, and found themselves back on the street. The air was cool, and the rain had almost stopped. They walked to the car. Burroni was the first to say what they were both thinking.

'LaFayette Johnson said he saw somebody just like that as he entered your nephew's building.'

'Yes. Which means two things, maybe three.'

'Shall I say it or will you?'

Jordan nodded at Burroni. 'Go ahead.'

'The first is that the person who killed Gerald Marsalis also killed Chandelle Stuart. The second is that she knew her killer personally, or she wouldn't have let him in. The third is that it's quite likely the first victim also knew him.'

'Precisely. But there's another thing.'

Burroni raised his eyebrows in a silent question.

'In all probability,' Jordan said, 'the person who's been indicated to us as the third victim also knows the person who's planning to kill him. And we have to discover who both of them are, before we find Snoopy dead as well, maybe glued to his doghouse.'

CHAPTER 21

By the time Jordan opened the door to the apartment, the sun was coming up. The rainclouds had gone, and now a bright red light was descending the walls of the skyscrapers to chase the shadows from the streets.

He was greeted by the slight fragrance of vanilla that had hovered persistently in the air ever since Lysa had first appeared in that apartment and in his life. In the deserted living room he found the TV on, with the sound turned way down. He took a few steps into the middle of the room and saw her. She was lying asleep on the couch facing the TV, breathing gently, a light plaid thrown over her. As he looked at her lying there, alone and defenceless, Jordan could not help feeling like an intruder.

He switched off the TV set. For a moment, Lysa stirred in her sleep and opened her eyes. They were iridescent in the morning light, and Jordan, looking down at her, felt as if he was seeing something, not only that he had never seen before, but that he had never even known it was possible to dream about. Then he immediately felt stupid for thinking such things.

Lysa closed her eyes again and turned lazily on her side, smiling like someone who at last feels safe.

'Oh, good,' she said sleepily. 'You're home.'

The naturalness and familiarity of those few words seemed to break through the shell Jordan had always placed around himself. He was a man who had spent all his life alone and, whenever he had heard a voice inside him asking why, he had preferred to ignore it. There had been people whose lives had crossed his, men with whom he'd exchanged words and gestures of affection and trust, women who had come to him with the promise of something he had taken for love. Ultimately, he had not let any of them linger for long.

Lysa opened her eyes again and looked at Jordan as if seeing him for the first time. She sat up on the couch.

'What time is it?'

'Six-thirty.'

'What happened last night?'

'Someone else died.'

Lysa did not ask for any further details, and Jordan was grateful to her for that.

'I was watching television to see if they talked about it and I fell asleep.'

'We actually managed to keep the media off the scent this time. For now, at least.'

Lysa got up and went into the kitchen. He heard the refrigerator door opening. 'Would you like a coffee?' she called out.

'No thanks, I already had breakfast in the diner opposite. All I need now is a shower to make me feel like a human being again.'

Jordan went to the guest room and undressed, throwing his clothes haphazardly on the bed. He stepped into the bathroom and looked at his image in the mirror. He looked the same as ever, and yet he knew he wasn't the same person who, only recently, had walked through this apartment with a helmet in his hand, ready to embark on a journey to an unknown destination.

Things had changed.

The desire to escape was still there, but now he was scared to think about what he was escaping from.

He turned on the faucet and stepped into the shower. He washed himself all over, trying to get the sickly smell of glue out of his nostrils and the sense of clamminess from his skin: the clamminess he always felt after being at a crime scene.

He started his usual game with the watermixer.

Hot. Cold.

Gerald. Chandelle.

Hot. Cold.

Linus. Lucy.

Hot. Cold.

The blanket. The piano.

And Lysa . . .

Hot. Cold.

With an irritable gesure he pressed the lever and stopped the jet of water. He came out, dripping on the rug, dried himself and quickly shaved. He put a few drops in his eyes, which were red from lack of sleep, and again checked his image in the mirror. For a second, he caught himself trying to see it through Lysa's eyes.

The ringing of the cellphone jolted him out of these thoughts. He went and picked it up from the bed, starting to get dressed as he answered.

'Hello?'

'Hello, Marsalis, Medical Examiner Stealer here.'

'That's quick.'

'I was right, I got that call I was expecting. Maybe I should have been a clairvoyant instead of a pathologist. Anyway, the post mortem isn't finished yet, but there are a couple of things you may like to know.'

'I'm listening.'

'Apart from the confirmation that death was the result of strangulation, the first is that the victim had had sexual relations. And it looks like she had them *after* she was killed.'

'You mean the killer strangled her first and then raped her?'

'Precisely. We found traces of lubricant from a condom.' Stealer paused. 'The kind of condom that has a retardant effect on the man and a stimulant effect on the woman.'

'Holy Christ, what kind of sick bastard are we dealing with?'

'With a very unfortunate sick bastard. The condom he used was faulty.'

'And?'

'A small amount of his semen remained in Chandelle Stuart's vagina. Small, but enough to carry out a DNA test on. I've already requested it.'

Jordan wedged the phone between his face and his shoulder and sat down on the bed to put on his socks. 'That's a piece of luck.'

'Yes. Murderers don't always leave calling cards.'

'Right. A pity we can't read his name and address on it.'

'That, I'm afraid, is your problem.'

'Unfortunately, yes. Marks on the body?'

'Traces of glue on the wrists. Plus traces of adhesive tape.'

Just as Jordan had thought.

'Anything else?'

'Apart from the bruises on the neck, nothing. Despite appearances, there's no sign of struggle. The only curious detail is that we found tiny fragments of fibre under the nails.

169

The Crime Scene team has ascertained that it's identical to the torn dress found on the floor.'

'Almost as if she'd torn the garment off herself.'

'Precisely. For the rest there are some scattered bruises, but they pre-date last night.'

From what Randall Haze had told them, Jordan did not have much difficulty in imagining how Chandelle Stuart had got them.

'One last thing, though I don't know how much help it might be.'

'At this point, anything can help. Go ahead.'

'On the groin, there's a scar from a small plastic surgery operation. The removal of a tattoo, I'd guess. For the moment that's all I can tell you.'

'You've told me more than enough. Thanks, Stealer.'

'Have a good day.'

'If it turns out to be one, it'll be thanks to you.'

Jordan hung up and threw the cellphone on the bed. Then he opened the closet and chose a clean shirt. As he finished dressing, he felt a sense of optimism growing inside him. He put on his watch and looked at the time. It was almost seven, and in spite of his sleepless night he felt quite bright. The rush of adrenaline from his excitement over these new clues had effectively replaced the hours he would otherwise have spent tossing and turning in bed, searching desperately for a flash of intuition.

He grabbed his helmet and leather jacket. This would be a perfect day for a ride on the bike, he had decided. A ride to Poughkeepsie, for example. It was more or less halfway between New York and Albany, and with the Ducati he would be there in no time at all. He went back in the living room. By now, Lysa had also changed and was standing by

170

the window. Beyond the roofs, the late-spring sky was wonderfully blue.

When she heard his steps on the wooden floor she turned. What she said when she saw him enter the room seemed more like a thought spoken out loud than an actual observation.

'Your eyes are the same colour.'

'As what?'

'The sky.'

They were both silent for a moment. Then Lysa noticed the helmet and jacket. 'Going out?'

'Yes. There's something I have to do.'

Jordan was pleased the subject had been changed: he always felt embarrassed by compliments on his physical appearance.

Lysa continued staring at the full-face helmet. 'What's it like, riding a bike?'

'There's danger. And speed, if you want it. But most of all, there's freedom, if you're capable of it.'

Lysa kept looking at him in silence. Jordan had learned to know those moments of hers, when she smiled ironically out of one side of her mouth and her eyes had the sly expression of a bored cat.

When she spoke, the innocence of her voice masked the provocation of her words. 'Do you think I am?'

'There's only one way to find out,' Jordan replied without thinking. 'The place I'm going isn't too far from here. Would you like to come with me?'

She let the meaning of this sink in, then said, 'I don't have a helmet.'

'No problem. Across the street, on Sixth, there's an accessories store where I usually buy things for my bike. When we go down, we can get one for you.'

'It won't be open yet.'

'The owner's a friend of mine and sleeps on the premises. He won't be happy but he'll wake up.'

'OK. Give me a second.'

Lysa disappeared into the corridor. She soon reappeared wearing a pair of jeans, a padded leather jacket and vaguely country-style boots. She had tied her hair in a pony tail, and to Jordan she appeared more luminous than the daylight they would find outside.

'Ready.'

Jordan was not at all sure he could say the same. But as he was only a man, at that moment he did the only thing he could: he lied.

'So am I.'

As they went downstairs, however, Jordan felt better than he had done for a long, long time. Like most people, he expended more imagination on finding excuses than on actually living. So he preferred to attribute this new feeling to the excitement of the investigation rather than admit it was due to the prospect of spending a day with Lysa.

CHAPTER 22

A motorbike meant riding without the need for words.

Jordan remembered that at a certain point in his life it had been neither easy nor hard to reject the comfort of a car roof over his head or the hypnotic dance of the windshield wipers. It had simply been natural. A motorbike meant waiting under a bridge for the rain to ease off. A motorbike meant that cyclops eye cutting through the darkness. A motorbike meant speed when necessary but, above all, as he had said to Lysa, it meant freedom – and you could never have enough of that.

At Amazing Race, the store opposite his apartment, he had bought a full-face helmet for Lysa. Jordan had watched as her eyes disappeared behind the dark plastic of the lowered visor and had immediately missed them.

Now he could feel her behind him, moving in perfect time to the demands of the road, which require us not to escape our fears, but rather to throw ourselves into them and conquer them if we want to feel safe. Lysa seemed to have grasped that on a motorbike the right thing to do was what came least naturally.

She was the perfect travelling companion.

Jordan felt the thrust of the engine and the sense of compressed gravity as he accelerated. He had the road in front of him, under him and behind him, and despite everything Lysa was still there, docile and yielding at the bends, present and absent, still clinging to him to remind him that she existed – even though now the scent of vanilla was lost on the wind.

Leaving New York, they had taken the West Side Highway leading north, and then Jordan had chosen Route 9, which for some stretches ran alongside the banks of the Hudson River. They passed West Point, hanging sheer over the river, as rigid as its rules. They passed Sing Sing, cut in two by the railroad, where the prisoners could hear the freedom of the train whistle beyond the walls. They were greeted with open arms by the iridescent green of the late-spring vegetation.

They passed houses, little harbours with boats riding at anchor in the sun, ready to ply the river during the summer. Jordan was at peace, not thinking of anything. He would have liked this journey to last forever.

But eventually they reached Poughkeepsie. They passed the station, a redbrick building where at that moment a single taxi slumbered, and entered the town, which seemed to Jordan an archetypal little provincial place. They rode down one of the many Raymond Avenues in America, past churches and veterans' associations and an untold number of traffic-lights and restaurants. After an intersection, they came to a low perimeter wall. An imposing-looking building could be glimpsed in the distance, surrounded by tall trees and wide lawns.

Jordan did not need any further indication that they had reached Vassar.

He turned right, following the signs, and as they rode for a long stretch down a street that ran alongside the campus, he realized that the area over which it extended must be vast.

The wall was higher now, in a vaguely medieval style that Jordan couldn't quite place. They finally came to three arches, the widest of which was the main entrance to the college. Jordan stopped and removed his helmet. A security guard with very short hair and a ruddy face approached.

'Good morning. I'm Jordan Marsalis. I have an appointment with President Hoogan.'

Christopher knew Travis Hoogan, the President of Vassar College, personally. The guard's reaction confirmed to him that the call he had requested of his brother had been made and had had the required effect.

'Good morning, Mr Marsalis. I was told you were coming. I think the President is on the golf course. You could wait in the cafeteria while I beep him.' He pointed up the path ahead of them. 'Go along the avenue to the end then turn right. There are signposts with all the directions. The golf course is on the right. The cafeteria is just facing it. You can park your bike nearby.'

Jordan rode the Ducati at a moderate speed along the broad wooded avenue lined with flowerbeds and an impressive English lawn.

Up ahead of them was the main block of Vassar College, a severe-looking building in dark brick, with big white windows, consisting of a central part and two wings to right and left that seemed to have been added slightly later. At the highest point of the roof, fixed to a white pole, an American flag fluttered.

Following the guard's directions, they turned right. They passed other buildings: a theatre, a swimming pool, a gym, a tennis court. The fact that there was even a golf course forced Jordan to admit that the hundred-thousand-dollar-a-year fee might be worth it, after all.

They reached the parking lot and Jordan turned off the engine.

As soon as they got off, Lysa removed her helmet and leaned forward to let her dark hair free, mussed it with her hand until it had found its shape again, then lifted her head sharply so that the hair cascaded back onto her shoulders, glossy in the light. For a moment, Jordan had the absurd idea that when she turned to him, he would have to look at her face in a mirror in order not to be turned to stone. But when she did, her smile and her eyes were so bright, they would have turned even Medusa to stone.

Lysa looked around happily. 'It's beautiful.'

'What is?'

'Everything. The day, the sun, the journey, the bike. This incredible place. And to think it's a school! I know people who would be happy just to spend a week's vacation here.'

'Well, we have to be content with one day. Apart from anything else, it's free.'

They walked in silence towards the cafeteria, a low building a few dozen yards away, hidden from them by a tall hedge of mixed vegetation, tended in such a way as to give the impression of being untamed.

A girl passed them, walking fast. She had coloured leggings and a green T-shirt, with a pair of jogging shoes tied together and thrown over her shoulder. On her feet, she wore a pair of Japanese-style thongs. Her red-dyed hair seemed strewn over her head at random. Taken out of that context, she would have looked like a young homeless woman trying to figure out how and where to get through the day. Here, she was only an oddball from a good family attending a college that charged exorbitant fees. Jordan found himself thinking of his nephew here, just as much of an oddball, a few years earlier.

Maybe, in her way, that girl really was homeless.

They followed her up a small flight of steps and through a glass door into the cafeteria, a large hall with yellow-painted walls. Some young people were working in the service area, others were sitting at tables, talking among themselves.

There was an understated air about the place, although an ATM cash machine was in full view on the wall to the left. The red-headed girl went straight to it and slipped her card into the slot. Jordan smiled to himself. Some of these kids might adopt a casual, bohemian style, but they were happy to use the credit cards provided by their parents.

On their entrance, all male heads had turned in perfect unison to look at Lysa, and the hum of conversation had died down. If Jordan hadn't been so busy noticing this, he would have noticed that many of the girls were looking at him in the same way.

At that moment, a man came through the glass door beside them, carrying a golf bag over his shoulder. He was about sixty, as tall as Jordan, with somewhat sparse hair of an indefinable colour, worn slightly longer than average. His eyes were hidden behind a pair of unrimmed spectacles. He gave the impression of being a calm person, someone who had had everything he wanted out of life.

He approached them with a smile. 'Jordan Marsalis, I assume. I'm Travis Hoogan, the President of this godforsaken place.'

Jordan shook the hand held out to him. 'Pleased to meet you. This is Lysa Guerrero.'

Hoogan's eyes lit up with contained mischief as he held Lysa's hand a moment longer than necessary. 'Miss Guerrero, what a delight to meet you. Your presence on this earth tells us common mortals that miracles do happen.

Which is why I shan't lose hope that I can yet improve on my golf handicap.'

Lysa threw her head back and laughed. 'If you're as good on the golf course as you are at making compliments, I think we'll soon be seeing you at the Masters.'

The President gave a little shrug. 'Oscar Wilde said that the problem isn't that we grow old on the outside, but that we stay young inside. Believe me, knowing that doesn't help. Thanks, anyway.'

Jordan had not told Lysa why they had come to Vassar. After these pleasantries, Lysa showed her usual tact by saying, 'I think you two have something to talk about. While you do, I hope you don't mind if I take a look around.'

Hoogan made a gesture, as if granting her a hypothetical key to the college. 'If I did mind, I fear the male members of the board would ask for my resignation.'

Lysa headed for the door and went out. Two young men on their way in stood aside to let her through, stood for a moment in the doorway, looked at each other, then turned back to follow her.

Hoogan smiled as he watched her go. 'She may not be a pure miracle, but she's something very close to one. You're a lucky man, Mr Marsalis.' Then his tone changed abruptly. 'When Christopher rang to tell me you were coming, he told me you've both been in a bad state since Gerald's death. I was really sorry to hear about the boy, and I hope you find something while you're here that may help you discover who killed him.'

'I hope so, too.'

'Shall we go to my office? I think we can talk there without being disturbed.'

As he followed Hoogan out of the cafeteria, Jordan looked

through the windows and saw Lysa standing under a tree, helmet in one hand, gesturing with the other to a squirrel that was looking at her curiously from the top of a branch.

She was smiling, and Jordan thought she looked very happy.

CHAPTER 23

The office of the President of Vassar was exactly as Jordan had imagined it. It smelled of leather and wood, with a faint hint of pipe tobacco. The room was straight out of an illustration in the *Saturday Evening Post*. The furniture would have made the fortune of any dealer in modern antiques. The only odd note was provided by the computer on the desk.

On the way in, Hoogan had asked his secretary, a bright-looking girl with a sly smile, to hold his calls. The girl had made a note of this, and before they disappeared through the door had found the time to give Jordan an interested once-over.

Hoogan went to the window, which looked out on the avenue that Jordan and Lysa had ridden along a while earlier, and drew the curtains to avoid the light shining in Jordan's face. Then he sat down behind the desk.

Jordan wondered how many times young people had found themselves on the chair where he was sitting now, waiting to be lectured to by the President of Vassar. Maybe his nephew Gerald had been one of them.

'The answer is yes.'

'I'm sorry?'

'You were wondering if your nephew was ever in this office. The answer is yes, more than once.'

Hoogan took advantage of Jordan's surprise to remove his glasses and clean them with a napkin he had taken from a drawer. As he put them on again, Jordan noticed that he had grey eyes.

'His father, though, almost never.'

He said this not as an accusation, but as a statement of fact. But there was a definite note of regret in his voice. He leaned back in his chair.

'You see, Mr Marsalis, among the young people who come here to study, only a few really deserve to do so, because they really want to. That's a civilized way of saying that most of our students have been . . . how shall I put it? . . . dumped here by their families. Sometimes by tacit agreement. "You keep out of my way, and I'll keep out of yours".'

'And which category did Gerald belong to?'

'Your nephew was probably insane, Mr Marsalis. Or if he wasn't, he was playing his part very well.'

Jordan was forced to admit that this terse description seemed to fit Gerald – and Jerry Ko – perfectly.

'Vassar College focuses on a number of artistic fields,' Hoogan went on. 'Fine art, creative writing, directing. They're fields in which talent can't be bought, but where it is possible to postpone the realization that it isn't there. Gerald, on the other hand, did have talent. A great deal of talent. But he was convinced that it had to go hand-in-hand with certain extreme life choices. I don't know what triggered this idea in him, but I can tell you he professed it like a dogma. And there's something else. He scrupulously avoided any visit from his father. I got the impression that he hated him, and I suspect that's one of the reasons why he behaved in that way.'

'Did Gerald have friends when he was here?'

'He could have had dozens. In his own weird way, he was

181

a kind of idol. But he was too busy demonstrating that he didn't need anyone. Not even us.' Hoogan placed his elbows on the desk and leaned forward slightly. 'I followed his career after he left here. You may think I'm being cynical, but trust me when I say I was very saddened by his violent death, but not surprised.'

Nor was I, unfortunately.

More than anything else, Jordan had listened to Hoogan talking at length about Gerald as a way of judging the man's character. Now that he was sure he was up to the mark, it seemed the right moment to explain the reason for his trip to Poughkeepsie.

'There's one thing you may not know, Mr Hoogan. Have you heard the latest news?'

'No, I've been on the golf course all the time.'

'Last night, Chandelle Stuart was murdered at her home in New York. She also studied here in Vassar. Around about the same time as Gerald.'

Hoogan took off his glasses and cleaned them again, even though they didn't really need it.

'Chandelle Stuart. I remember her very well. How did it happen?'

'Mr Hoogan—'

The President stopped him with a gesture of his hand. 'Call me Travis, please.'

Jordan was pleased at this openness, because it gave greater weight to what he was about to say. 'All right, Travis. What I'm about to tell you is strictly confidential. So far we've managed by a miracle not to let any of this get out and we'd like to keep it that way. The circumstances of Chandelle Stuart's death are such as to suggest a connection with the murder of my nephew.'

'What kind of connection, if you don't mind my asking?'

Despite everything, Jordan felt slightly uncomfortable revealing the circumstances of the crimes to Hoogan.

'You may find this incredible, but the person who killed them arranged their bodies to resemble two characters from *Peanuts*.'

'You mean Charlie Brown and so on?'

'Precisely. Gerald was sitting against a wall with a blanket stuck to his ear, and Chandelle was at the piano. Linus and Lucy.'

As Travis did not ask him for clarification, it was obvious that he was familiar with the strips.

'And in Chandelle Stuart's apartment we found something that leads us to believe that the next victim will be Snoopy.'

Travis Hoogan, the President of Vassar College, a man whose life had revolved around words, seemed to be struggling to find a single one. 'My God. That's crazy.'

'I think that's the right word. Can you think of anything that might link the two of them with *Peanuts*?'

'None at all. Not only that, I can't think of anything to link them with each other. This is a small world and we know everything about everybody. Especially where two such unusual personalities are concerned. But I don't remember ever hearing of a connection between your nephew and Chandelle.'

'What do you remember about her?'

'Rich. Unbearable. And probably sick. The fact that she's dead doesn't change the memory I have of her.'

'Did she have friends?'

'I'd say the same about her as about your nephew, although with her it was slightly different. Gerald didn't want anybody,

183

and nobody wanted Chandelle. The only person she was at all friendly with was Sarah Dermott, I think.'

'Who was Sarah Dermott?'

Hoogan turned to the computer and tapped on the keyboard for a few moments.

'Here she is. Sarah Dermott, from Boston. She was here on a scholarship. She was part of that small percentage I mentioned before, the ones who really want to be here. She was intelligent, gifted – and very ambitious.'

Jordan noticed the slight stress on the word 'very'.

'She and Chandelle attended the same Directing course. I think Sarah tolerated her for a short period because she was convinced that a member of the Stuart family might be useful to her, but after a while she was forced to throw in the towel. Chandelle was too much even for someone as ambitious as her.'

'Where can I find this Sarah Dermott?'

'Los Angeles. She's directing in Hollywood – I think she has a contract with Columbia. She was here recently at a reunion of ex-students.'

'I think it might be useful for me to speak to her.'

'No problem.' Hoogan picked up a phone from the desk and pressed a key. 'Miss Spice, could you get hold of Sarah Dermott in Los Angeles for me, please? Put her right through.'

Less than a minute later, the telephone rang. Hoogan lifted it to his ear.

'Sarah, this is Travis Hoogan, calling from Vassar . . . Very well, thanks. I have someone here with me who needs to speak to you about an important matter.'

Jordan leaned across and took the cordless from Hoogan. 'Hello, Miss Dermott. I'm Jordan Marsalis, New York Police Department.'

Basically, he thought, it wasn't a lie but only a half-truth.

'What can I do for you?' The voice was bright, precise, the voice of someone with not much time to spare, but friendly enough.

'I'm sorry to bother you, but I thought you ought to know that Chandelle Stuart has been murdered.'

There was a moment's silence, then: 'Oh my God, when?'

'Last night. Now, I need to point out that what I'm about to tell you is in the strictest confidence.'

As he said these words, Jordan wondered how much longer it would be before the whole story was widely known, if he continued to tell everyone like this.

'We have every reason to believe that the person who committed the crime is the same person who recently killed Gerald Marsalis. I don't know if you heard about his death?'

'Yes, of course. Wait a moment, are you a relative of his?'

'Gerald was my nephew.'

'I'm so sorry. Gerald was a difficult kid, but I'm sorry he ended up like that.'

'Did you know him?'

The response was immediate. 'Nobody really knew him. We could sense he had talent but he was always on the edge. Closed, introverted, rebellious, sometimes violent. And alone.'

'How about Chandelle Stuart?'

'She was pretty much the same, except she didn't have any talent to back it up. I think I was the only person she opened up to a little bit. She wasn't really close to anyone at Vassar, though there were reliable rumours that outside the campus she led a fairly colourful life. If you're investigating her, I guess you know what I mean.'

'Perfectly. What can you tell me about their relationship?'

There was a moment's pause. 'Well, they knew each other. But as far as I remember, everyone was out for himself. Gerald was too hostile and Chandelle too rich to really connect.'

'I'm going to ask you a question that may seem strange, but please think about it carefully before you answer.'

'Go on.'

'Did you ever hear either Chandelle or Gerald refer to the characters in the *Peanuts* comic strip? Linus, Lucy, anything like that.'

'I don't think so . . . No, hold on, now that I come to think of it, there was something once.'

Jordan's heart skipped a beat.

'One day I went into Chandelle's room while she was taking a shower. As I was waiting for her to come out I went to the desk, and on it there was a handwritten note.'

'Do you remember what it said?'

'Yes. The exact words were: *It's for tomorrow. Pig Pen.*'

'Do you have any idea who this person was, who called himself Pig Pen?'

'No.'

'And what happened then?'

'Chandelle came out of the bathroom, and when she saw me looking at the note, she took it from the desk and tore it up. Then she went back in the bathroom. I think she threw the pieces in the toilet because immediately afterwards I heard the sound of flushing.'

'Didn't you think that was strange behaviour?'

'With Chandelle Stuart, everything was strange.'

'Can you think of anything else? Any other detail?'

'No. But I'll give it some thought.'

She had started to sound excited. Jordan remembered he

186

was talking to someone involved in the film world, constantly on the lookout for ideas.

If you're thinking to turn this into a movie, Sarah Dermott, let us know in advance how it's going to end.

'Anything else you remember is sure to be of use. I'll get your telephone number from President Hoogan and call you again.'

'Feel free. And good luck.'

'Thanks.'

He hung up and handed the cordless back to Hoogan. Then he stood up, as he always did when he needed to think.

'Something new?'

'Another *Peanuts* character. Pig Pen.'

'I don't know that one.'

'He was a minor character, who was more or less dropped after a while. He's a little boy who attracts dust. He's always so dirty that the one time he shows up at a party looking neat and tidy they won't let him in because they don't recognize him.'

'Now you mention him, he does sounds familiar. Did Sarah bring him up?'

'Yes. And instead of clearing things up, it just makes them more complicated.'

'Well, I'm not sure there's anything else I can do to help you.'

'You've been an enormous help. I'll say to you what I just said to Sarah Dermott. Anything at all that you think of, get in touch.'

'Of course.'

At that point Hoogan did the only thing he could. He stood up and looked at his watch. 'I think it's lunchtime. Officially, I'd like to invite you, but if you want my advice, refuse politely but firmly. The Vassar cafeteria isn't too bad but your companion deserves better. And some of our teachers are deadly boring. Are you going back to New York now?'

'Yes.'

'I can recommend a very good restaurant a few miles from here. You won't even have to make too much of a detour. It's an old tugboat moored at the river bank. Very evocative. It's the place I'd go if I were with someone like Lysa.'

Jordan picked up his helmet from the chair.

Hoogan came out from behind the desk. 'That girl has the most incredible eyes I've ever seen. Nobody with eyes like that can be a bad person.' He smiled and held out his hand. 'I wish you luck, Lieutenant Marsalis. You're a good man but I think you're going to need it.'

'So do I. Goodbye, Travis. You don't need to see me out. I remember the way.'

Jordan left the President's office and retraced his steps to the cafeteria. When he got there, the place was full. Some young men and women were standing in line, while others were already sitting at the tables, eating. He just had to follow the direction of some of their eyes to know where Lysa was.

She was standing just outside the glass door, leaning against the low wall next to the steps, and looking with a rapt expression at the trees in the grounds. He came up to her without her noticing.

'Here I am.'

Lysa turned her head towards him. 'Everything all right? Did you find what you expected to?'

He tried to be positive. 'A few small things. It seems to me I'll have to work a lot harder to get the big picture. In the meantime, I think we both deserve a decent lunch.'

'Where?'

Jordan adopted a slightly mysterious tone. 'I've just been recommended somewhere near here.'

A moment or two later, as Lysa's eyes again disappeared behind the visor of the helmet, he couldn't help recalling Hoogan's words.

Nobody with eyes like that . . .

CHAPTER 24

The restaurant recommended by Travis Hoogan was a beautifully renovated tugboat, moored at a concrete landing-stage that extended into the Hudson. In the tranquillity of its shelter, between elegant streamlined small yachts, this short, squat craft that had once pulled huge steamships gave the impression of an aging lion benevolently watching over its young.

When Jordan stopped the bike and saw what the place was called, he was pleased he could hide his grimace behind the visor of his helmet.

Steamboat Willie.

It was the title of one of Walt Disney's first cartoons. Right now, cartoon characters seemed to be everywhere. Maybe his own life was slowly turning into a cartoon – *his* life and that of every person involved in this absurd story.

They got off the Ducati and Jordan again watched the ritual of Lysa's hair emerging from the helmet, and again it aroused complicated feelings in him, feelings he preferred to attribute to the nervous state in which the investigation had put him.

They walked across the short wooden footbridge and entered the dimly lit restaurant, which smelled of wax polish and, perhaps through the power of suggestion, the sea. The furnishings were in strictly nautical style, with shiny brass fittings and tables covered with rough canvas tablecloths as blue as the colour of the hull.

A youngish waiter immediately came towards them with a gait that remined Jordan of the movements of a spring. He had a friendly demeanour and a tanned face that made him seem more like the cabin boy of a sailing ship than the waiter of a restaurant on an old tugboat chained to the bank of a river.

'Hello. Do you prefer to eat inside or, as it's such a nice day, do you want to sit at a table on deck?' He immediately switched to a conspiratorial tone. 'If I can give you a piece of advice, there's a better view outside and you'll be more private.'

Jordan left it to Lysa to choose.

'I think outside sounds perfect.'

They followed the waiter to a table in the shade of a wooden pergola near the stern. The waiter placed two menus with oilcloth covers on the table and left them alone to choose.

Jordan took one of the menus and opened it. As he stared at the words describing the food, he thought again about the conversations with Travis Hoogan and Sarah Dermott. According to the rules, he should have called Burroni and told him about Sarah Dermott's revelation, but he preferred to wait until he had absorbed it himself.

What was the role of this fourth *Peanuts* character, after Linus, Lucy and Snoopy? The first two had revealed their identity when they had died. Snoopy, whoever he was, was running the same risk, if he wasn't at this moment receiving a visit from a man with his hood up and a limp in his right leg.

It's for tomorrow. Pig Pen.

191

What was supposed to happen tomorrow? Who was Pig Pen?

'If you tell me where you are, I can try to get to you, or at least call you.'

Lysa's voice brought him back to the here and now. Jordan put the menu on the table and looked up at Lysa's ironic smile and the waiter standing there expectantly with a pen and notebook in his hand.

'I'm sorry. I was thinking. Have you already chosen?'

'A few minutes ago.'

'Then, to speed things up, I'll have whatever you're having.'

The waiter nodded, scribbled something in his notebook, and said, 'OK, fried snake for both.' He responded to Jordan's look of surprise with a disarming smile. 'Oh, don't worry, sir, it's a speciality of the house. The chef cooks it so well, even the rattle is tender.'

He turned and walked away along the deck with his strange, elastic walk. Jordan turned to look at Lysa.

Nobody with eyes like that . . .

Jordan realized he didn't know anything about her. He didn't know anything about her life or why she was in New York. He couldn't decide if the reason he hadn't asked was because he was afraid of being indiscreet or because he was afraid of what she might say.

During the brief time they had spent under the same roof, they had seen little of each other. Jordan had been busy with the case, and whatever Lysa was busy with, she seemed to be in possession of an enviable resource: a sunny but determined character, an optimistic irony with which to confront any small unpleasantness she might find in her path.

There had been just one night when he had come back very

192

late and, as he tiptoed past her room, had thought he heard her crying. But when they had seen each other in the morning, there had been no trace of those tears on her face.

'How come there's such a big difference in age between you and Christopher?'

'Oh, it's a very simple story,' Jordan replied, trying to keep his voice as light as possible. 'My father was a good-looking young man without a penny who played tennis very well. Christopher's mother was a good-looking and very rich young woman who played tennis very badly. They met and fell in love. There was just one small problem. He was a young man with qualities that in some circles are considered faults, she was a young woman born and brought up in one of those circles. Before the wedding, her parents made my father sign a prenuptial agreement as big as a phone book. Things were fine for a while but then the inevitable happened. My father gradually realized that his wife was growing closer to her circle and leaving him more and more on the outside. When he asked her to follow him and make a life of their own, he was rejected in no uncertain terms. His father-in-law was of course only too ready to show him the door. My father left that house as he had entered it, without a cent in his pocket. And it was made harder and harder for him to see his son. Then he met my mother, and twelve years after Christopher, I was born. The first time Chris and I met, he was already launched on his political career and I'd just left the Police Academy. Through no fault of our own, we were two brothers with no brotherly feelings towards each other. And that's how things have always stayed.'

At this point, the waiter arrived, carrying two plates.

The food Lysa had ordered wasn't fried snake, but an excellent fish dish cooked in a delicate basil and coconut milk sauce. As they started eating, Jordan made up his mind to tackle the subject he had avoided up until now.

'I don't think my life has been all that interesting, when you come down to it. But you haven't yet told me anything about yourself.'

Lysa made a gesture with her hand that did not chime with the shadow that had passed for a moment across her eyes. She hid behind a smile that was still not sufficient to conceal her bitterness.

'Oh, well, it's quite simple. All I need to tell you is that nothing has been simple for me.' She paused briefly but significantly. 'Ever.'

She seemed to be talking as much to herself as to him.

'I was born in the middle of nowhere. If I told you the name of the place, it wouldn't mean anything to you. It was the kind of place where everyone knows everything about everyone else. My father was a Methodist pastor and my mother was the kind of woman who could only have been the wife of a man like that. Devoted, silent, accommodating. Can you imagine how it must have been for a man obsessed by God, proudly watching his only son grow up and then realizing that by the age of fourteen he's sprouting breasts? I was hidden, like a punishment for his sins, and for the world's sins, until his love of God prevailed over his love for his child, male or female. At sixteen, when I left home, without even touching the door, I saw it close behind me.'

Jordan was not sure he wanted to hear any more. All his life he had lived in a black and white world that excluded shades of grey. The things that had been happening to him lately had changed all that, and so had the people he had been meeting – including Lysa.

He had finally understood the attraction she exerted over

him. Beautiful people didn't usually have much character, because they had never suffered, never had to work hard for anything, always found lots of other people willing to give them everything on a plate. Lysa was beautiful, but in her case nothing had been simple.

Ever.

'After that, I moved from one place to another. It was the usual story everywhere I went. Running away from the people who were interested in me, when they discovered what I am. The people I was interested in running away from me for the same reason.'

'Hasn't there ever been anyone?'

'Oh, yes. As in any self-respecting story of disillusion, there was a moment of illusion. There was a man in the first place I stayed. A nice man, lively, friendly. He was an actor. I should have known that when you spend your life pretending, it comes easily. But when we were together he made me laugh till I cried.'

'And then what happened?'

'What always happens. The laughter ended and only the tears remained.'

Lysa suddenly changed expression, adopting a light tone, out of modesty or out of fear that she had already given too much away. She became again what she always was, cheerful but hidden.

'So, here I am. Do you know the joke about the dreamer, the madman and the psychiatrist?'

'No.'

'The dreamer builds castles in the air, the madman lives in them, and the psychiatrist collects the rent. That's the reason I came to New York. I'm tired of building and living, now I'd like to collect some rent.'

Jordan realized all at once that he had to talk clearly to this woman. And he didn't like what he intended to say, because he knew she wouldn't like it either.

'There's something I have to tell you.'

Lysa picked with her knife at part of the fish she had on her plate. 'I'm listening.'

'I think I ought to look for somewhere else to stay.'

'I understand.' Curt, brief, almost indifferent.

Jordan shook his head. 'No, I don't think you do.'

He put his knife and fork down on the plate. He did not want to distract Lysa or be distracted by anything himself.

'When I was a child, I lived with my parents in Queens. Next door lived another little boy, named Andy Masterson. Obviously, we often played together. One day his parents gave him a little electric car. I remember him going around, sitting in that little red plastic car with his eyes glowing with joy. I knew I couldn't have one and I kept watching him, hoping that at least he'd let me have a little ride in it, but it never happened.'

'Your friend Andy wasn't a generous child.'

'I don't think he was. But that's not the point.' Jordan looked straight in Lysa's eyes. 'I remember the way I wanted that little red car. I wanted it desperately, with all the imagination I possessed. I wanted it with the force and intensity and sadness that only a child can have.'

'That must have been a big problem.'

Jordan took a deep breath and lowered his eyes. 'No. That was a small problem. The big problem is that, right now, I want you much more than I ever wanted that car.'

When he looked up again, he saw Lysa's eyes on him. For a moment her expression did not change. Then her face hardened and she got up from the table.

She spoke without looking at him, with the tiredness of déjà vu in her voice. 'I think you're right. Maybe it is better if you look for somewhere else to live. I don't think I'm hungry any more. If you'll excuse me, I'll wait for you by the bike.'

She walked away, her hair dancing in the breeze from the river. Jordan felt more alone than he had ever been in his life, alone with his little regrets and his little shames, which made him feel a little man.

He waited a few moments and then called the waiter and paid the bill. The waiter understood from his expression that something had changed between the two of them. He accepted the tip and thanked him, but without his former ebullience.

Jordan walked across the gangway. There was the Ducati, and there was Lysa, standing next to it, her face already hidden behind the helmet. As had happened before, he immediately felt nostalgia for her face, but knew there was no smile beneath the dark visor. For him or anyone.

Without saying a word, Jordan took refuge in his own helmet, got on the bike and waited for him to join her.

When he felt her get on behind him, he started the engine, and they set off on their silent journey back to New York.

CHAPTER 25

Maureen Martini woke with a strong feeling of itching in her eyes. Gently, she passed her fingers over the bandages, as if that small gesture could in some way alleviate the discomfort. She had been warned that it would happen – irritating that tingling.

After the operation, the small scars left by the intervention had healed with a speed that had surprised even Professor Roscoe, the surgeon who had performed the transplant. Such an accelerated recovery time had accentuated the generally optimistic mood. And today was the day she would find out if they were right or wrong. At exactly eleven o'clock the bandages were to be removed and they would leave her alone to face the future.

Torn between optimism and pessimism, she hadn't slept well during the night. In one of the few moments when she had slipped into a kind of half-sleep, she had found herself immersed in a strange dream, which had struck her by the extraordinary clarity of its images and even now, after waking, had left a stronger memory than most dreams.

The setting of the dream was a child's room. Not the room she'd had as a child in Rome: she didn't recognize the furniture, and vegetation and a riverbank could be seen through the window. She had been sitting at a desk and she could see her own hands drawing something. The drawing showed a man and a woman. The woman was leaning against a table and the man was standing behind her. Childish as it was, the drawing was very precise and it was clear that the two were making love. Then a door to her left had opened and a man with a moustache had come in. She had shown him the drawing with the pride and innocence that only a child could feel. The man had looked at it and then lost his temper. His lips had moved, though she couldn't hear what he was saying, and his face had turned red. He had waved the drawing in front of her eyes then torn it up. Then he had grabbed her by the hand, dragged her to a closet, and bundled her into it. Maureen remembered the man's face vanishing as the door closed and the darkness devoured her.

She had woken clammy with sweat.

She was in Manhattan, in her mother's apartment on the top floor of a brownstone building at 80 Park Avenue, not far from Grand Central Station. Maureen would have preferred to stay in the apartment her father owned downtown but it was obvious, given her condition, that during her convalescence she would need a woman's care.

So, after the operation, she had reluctantly agreed to spend that time in Mary Ann Levallier's apartment. Despite her mother's natural concern about what had happened to her, Maureen was under no great illusion about the nature of their relationship. There was a kind of atavistic affection between them, but anything resembling friendship didn't seem to be on the cards.

Muffled by the double glazing, the noise of the New York traffic reached her from below. This was the city she knew best, after Rome. She had always been suspended between two different worlds: she was part of both and yet did not really belong to either. Only one person had ever formed a bridge between the two worlds for her.

One person.

And now . . .

Ever since she had woken at the Gemelli Hospital, her life had been a rapid succession of monochrome sensations. The darkness had forced her other senses to form some vague idea of what was happening around her. Even the journey from Rome to New York had been a series of fragmented emotions.

And in all that time, in that darkness, Arben Gallani's earring had never stopped swaying and Connor's blood-drenched body had never stopped falling in the dust, and Maureen had never stopped screaming.

The voice of Professor William Roscoe, the surgeon who was going to operate on her, had been just one more voice that had superimposed itself for a while on her long, silent scream. A deep baritone, with a soft accent she couldn't quite identify but which wasn't the dry, sharp accent of New York. She remembered sensing his presence by the bed. He had smelled of clean shirts and aftershave.

'Miss Martini,' he had said, 'the operation you're going to have is relatively straightforward, and has a fairly short post-operative period. Two new corneas will be implanted and I'll use stem cells to avoid any problem of rejection linked to your genetic peculiarity. I think we'll be able to remove the dressings in a few days, and I can practically guarantee that you will see again. The only complication is that you'll subsequently have to undergo a couple of very minor operations, using more stem cells, to stabilize the new corneas. In addition, I'm afraid you'll have to wear dark glasses for a while, but that'll merely add a touch of mystery to your usual charms. Have I been thorough enough, or is there something you'd like me to clarify?'

'No, you've been extremely clear.'

'Don't worry. As I said, in a week at the outside you'll see again.'

'Of course I'll see again,' she had replied calmly.

Of course I'll see again. Not because of what I want to see but because of what I must *see. A face looking down the barrel of a gun . . .*

The operation had been the squeaky wheels of a gurney, more disinfectant smells, voices in an operating room full of lights of which she could sense only the heat, the prick of a needle in her arm, and then nothingness. The anaesthetic had been a simple leap into a deeper darkness, during which she had been able to allow herself the luxury of not thinking.

When she had come round, she had been greeted by the voices and hands of her father and mother. And her mother's perfume, discreet and exclusive. Maureen had tried to picture her, sitting by the bed, elegant despite everything. A mixture of class and self-control. At other moments she would have called it coldness, but now she preferred to give her mother the benefit of the doubt.

By now, the itching in her eyes had worn off, and she needed to go to the bathroom, a banal physical need that made her feel alive. She did not want to call her mother, nor did she want to submit to the attentions of Estrella, the Hipsanic housekeeper. Even that obstinate little gesture towards self-sufficency pleased her. She got up from the bed and groped her way cautiously towards the bathroom, narrowly avoiding a cabinet and an armchair. Reaching the wall, she ran her hand over the cold, smooth surface until it felt the glossier surface of the bathroom door. She found the handle and turned it until she felt it give. She pushed open the door, took one uncertain step inside the room and suddenly . . .

. . . there's light and a woman's face covered in blue paint under me. We're lying on the floor and around us everything is white, with splashes of colour, and I'm on top of her body and part of me I didn't even know I had is moving in and out of her and she's warm and moist and I see her face turning pale as the colour gradually drains away. I see her but can't hear her as she reaches orgasm – and then suddenly I'm standing. Now I can see my penis and I grab it and shake it, drops of sperm spattering all around me as I fall into the bottomless pit of a pleasure I've never known before. Now I'm on the ground and . . .

. . . I'm standing in front of a mirror and my face looks at me, a face as red as if covered with the blood of a thousand wounds. It looks out at me through that bright rectangle from another world, a world that seems to have made madness its basic rule. My lips move as I aim a finger at my image like a gun and . . .

. . . I'm walking towards the door at the far end of this huge room that's filled with light and I open it and in the darkness of the landing there's a motionless figure and then the figure steps forward . . .

Maureen was kneeling on the floor with her hands on her temples, again engulfed by the darkness. She felt exhausted, as if after a nightmare or an orgasm, especially the latter. She was drained as if the pleasure she had just felt had been real, even though she had experienced it as a man. The hand she had felt moving over the penis had been hers, and so was the sperm that had spurted out, and so was that part of the body she shouldn't have, couldn't have.

She bent slowly forward until her hot forehead touched the cold marble floor, cooling her fever.

It isn't possible. It isn't possible . . .

She was on the verge of panic when the door opened.

'*Madre de Dios*, what's happening, miss? Wait, I'll help you.'

It was Estrella. Maureen heard her steps coming closer. At the same time, she heard the clack of her mother's heels approaching from another part of the apartment. She felt the comfort of two strong hands.

'Come, miss, lean on me. I'll take you back to bed.'

Estrella helped her to her feet and guided her through the bedroom, supporting her with her sturdy body. Halfway to the bed, Maureen heard her mother's voice.

'What happened, dear? Did you feel sick?'

'It's nothing, Mother. I slipped and fell.'

'How is this possible, Estrella? I thought I made myself very clear. Miss Maureen was not to be left alone for a moment.'

Maureen shook her head. 'It's nothing to do with Estrella. It's entirely my fault. I wanted to go to the bathroom by myself and I slipped. I'm fine now.'

'I'm surprised that in your condition,' her mother said, irritation now replacing concern, 'you still want to show off with such acts of bravado. I can't believe it. What sense is there in that?'

Maureen didn't think it was worthwhile trying to explain. Instead, she changed the subject. 'What's the time?'

'Nine-thirty. Time you got ready. Don't forget, our appointment with Professor Roscoe is at eleven.'

How could I forget? I've been counting the hours and the minutes.

'All right, I'll get dressed.'

'Perfect. I'll order a cab for ten-thirty. Estrella, you stay here, and this time be careful what you're doing.'

When her mother had gone, Maureen let Estella guide her back to the bathroom and help her to undress.

'What a lovely body you have, miss. Not an ounce of fat. Just like a movie star.'

Maureen remained silent, picturing Estrella's plump figure and middle-aged face, which must once have been beautiful. She turned on the faucet and let the warm water pour over her. She forced herself to talk in order not to think about what had happened and what was about to happen.

She dried herself and got dressed in clothes she had learned to recognize by touch, letting her hair be combed by hands not her own and accepting the judgement of eyes not her own.

'There now, miss. Trust me. You look beautiful.'

Estrella's words reminded her, strangely, of Duilio, the manager of the garage where she kept her car in Rome. God alone knew if he was still alive. God alone knew if Rome still existed. Or the world.

God alone knows if I'm still alive . . .

When her mother came to tell her that the cab was waiting in the street, she followed her out, hoping for an answer to that question.

CHAPTER 26

As soon as they got out of the cab, Maureen and her mother were greeted by a male nurse, and now another unknown man with toothpaste breath was pushing her in a wheelchair along the corridors of Holy Faith Hospital, the institution where she had had her operation. She knew New York well enough to remember that Holy Faith was on the Lower East Side, just below Tompkins Square Park. Several times during her brief stay she had wondered if you could see the tops of the trees from the window. And every time it had occurred to her that she might never see trees again.

Maureen had been silent during the taxi ride, letting her mother guide the driver, who spoke English with a strong Russian accent.

She had tried to imagine what he looked like.

His guttural accent had reminded her of another voice, inescapably connected to the image of a cross-shaped earring with a little diamond in the middle. She strove to think about something else, but the only thing that came into her mind was that strange experience she had had in the bathroom – the memory of it scared her. She wasn't sure whether or not to mention it to Professor Roscoe, but in the end had decided against it. She imagined the surgeon telling her, in an embarrassed tone, that she might benefit from some psychological support. And the last thing she needed right now was people suspecting that what she had been through had affected her mind.

Holy Faith was a small hospital, focusing entirely on the field of ophthalmology. And in that field, Professor William Roscoe was one of the greatest specialists in the world. Although he was still relatively young, some said that his research into stem cells could well earn him the Nobel Prize before too long.

And, if everything had gone as he'd predicted, he would soon find a place of honour in Maureen Martini's private pantheon.

Whoever was pushing her wheelchair made a right turn. There was the sound of a door opening and the wheelchair was pushed into a room – and then she felt her father's hand brushing her cheek and heard his voice.

'Hello, darling.'

'Hello, Daddy.'

'Everything's going to be fine, you'll see.'

'I second that, Miss Martini.' The voice of Professor Roscoe. 'How are you feeling?'

'Quite well.'

'I don't suppose you got much sleep last night?'

'No, I didn't.'

'It's normal to feel nervous. Nurse Wilson, pehaps you'd give Miss Martini a tranquillizer.'

'Actually, I'd prefer to do without.'

'Please, Maureen.' Her mother's voice. 'Do what the Professor tells you.'

She heard footsteps approaching. The nurse gave her a plastic cup containing a pill and another cup with water, and helped her to get them both down.

'Good,' Roscoe said. 'Nurse Wilson, would you be so kind as to lower the blinds and switch on the little lamp on my desk?'

Maureen heard the noise of a stool that the doctor was moving in order to sit next to her.

'Excellent. Now let's see how we're doing.'

A slight pressure under the chin to lift her head, and then two expert hands carefully removing the Band Aids.

First one . . .

oh God please please God

. . . then the other

please God please please

There was the touch of cool air on her closed eyelids. Time seemed to be standing still, and so was her breath. It felt to her as if everybody in the world was outside the window, looking in at the drama being played out in that room.

'Now, Miss Martini, I want you to slowly open your eyes.'

Maureen did as she was told . . .

please God please God please!

. . . and saw only more darkness.

She felt her heart explode in her chest, as if it had wanted to give one last noisy sign of its presence before it stopped beating forever.

Then out of that darkness there came a sudden light and she saw a figure of a man leaning over her with his hands raised towards her face.

A moment later, pitch blackness again.

Maureen heard her own voice emerge almost breathless from her dry mouth. 'I can't see.'

'Just wait,' Professor Roscoe said calmly. 'It's perfectly normal. You have to give your eyes time to get used to the light.'

Maureen closed her eyes again. There was a slight burning sensation in them, as if they had been sprinkled with sand.

When she opened them again she saw the most beautiful dawn in the world. She saw a soft pink light rise over the office and a man with the same face as before leaning over her in a white coat and some colourful paintings on the bright walls and a small lighted lamp like a beacon on the desk and a red-headed nurse at the back of the room and her mother in a blue suit and her father with a hopeful expression on his face and the usual regimental tie around his neck and she finally managed to allow herself, after all that had happened, the luxury of unbridled tears of joy.

The man in the white coat smiled and spoke to her, and at last Professor Roscoe had a face as well as a voice.

'How do you feel now, Miss Martini?'

She was silent for a moment, then she, too, smiled. 'Professor, has anyone ever told you you're a very handsome man?'

William Roscoe stood up, took a step back, and grinned. 'Yes, they have, Maureen. But this is the first time a woman has said it after being treated by me. Usually, as soon as they get a good look at me they stop saying it.'

Mary Ann Levallier and Carlo Martini had been silent, as if not quite sure what was happening. Now they ran to hug their daughter, without realizing that they were also hugging each other.

'Now, then, after this understandable outburst, may I continue with my work?' Roscoe held out a hand to Maureen. 'Let me take a proper look. I'd like you to get up slowly. You might feel slightly dizzy, after all this time without sight.'

He helped her to the other end of the room, where he sat

her down on a stool in front of what looked like a complex piece of machinery and placed her chin on a rest.

'Don't worry. It looks worse than it is.'

Roscoe sat down facing her and started a careful examination. There were flashing blue lights and instruments that tickled her eyeballs and made her eyes water.

'Good, very good.'

Roscoe stood up and helped her to her feet.

'As I said, you'll have to wear dark glasses for a while longer. The sense of discomfort will gradually ease. Nurse Wilson will give you an antibiotic to be taken in drop form. I'd also like to prescribe a collyrium – which is a special eye-wash. Don't use computers, avoid television as much as possible, try not to tire yourself, get as much sleep as you can, and come back and see me in a week for a check-up. Depending on how well you're recovering, we'll decide then when to insert the second lot of cells. Well, that's it. As far as I'm concerned, you can go.'

As they exchanged the ritual farewells, Maureen took a moment to fix Professor William F. Roscoe in her memory. He was three or four inches taller than her, not exactly a handsome man but certainly attractive, with his greying temples, healthy, outdoor complexion and slim build, not to mention his contagious smile and natural ability to communicate.

As she was wheeled back to the main door of Holy Faith Hospital, Maureen looked around her with wonder. The pale green tiles on the walls were like a Roman mosaic, the sun waiting for them outside like the light off the Bay of Naples.

She gave her father a farewell hug. He could now go back to Rome in a very different frame of mind from the one in which he had travelled to New York.

The ride back to Park Avenue was another feast for the eyes. Mary Ann Levallier was silent while her daughter savoured the colours and the images. She felt as if she could actually *see* the noise of the traffic and *smell* the odours of the city. The electronic clock next to the Virgin Store on Union Square was a work of art, not just a monument to the passage of time, and Grand Central Station was a magical place where trains set off for all kinds of wonderful destinations.

When they entered the apartment they were greeted joyfully by Estrella, who followed Maureen apprehensively to her room, as if she still needed a guide. Maureen asked to be left alone, only requesting Estrella to lower the blinds before she went out.

The release of tension suddenly sent her tumbling into a pit of exhaustion. She sat down on the bed and started taking off her shoes, then lay down and decided to commit a brief transgression, a treat after all the time she'd spent listening to faceless voices on the radio.

She picked up the remote, switched on the TV, and hopped to the Eyewitness Channel.

'Investigations continue into the mysterious death of Chandelle Stuart, sole heir to the Stuart steel fortune, found dead two days ago in her apartment in the Stuart Building on Central Park West . . .'

The image of a dark-haired, thin-faced young woman appeared on the screen.

'Although the authorities have been keeping many details of the case confidential, reliable sources are linking this homicide to that of Gerald Marsalis, better known as Jerry Ko, the Mayor's painter son, found killed in his studio three weeks ago. It's believed that a press conference . . .'

210

Maureen had stopped listening to the words. A man's face had come up on the screen.

A face Maureen knew.

She had seen it that very morning, during what she had taken for a hallucination.

It was the man who had smiled at her from a mirror, with a face as red as if it was covered with the blood of a thousand wounds.

CHAPTER 27

The taxi stopped at the end of Carl Schurz Park, near Gracie Mansion. After paying the turbanned driver, Maureen got out and set off along the slightly sloping asphalt path that led to the official residence of the Mayor of New York. From the right came the cries of children in the playground. Below was the little square with the statue of Peter Pan.

Maureen came to a bench and sat down. She had the strange feeling that she was being led against her will to play a role someone else had assigned her, in a story she didn't understand.

Anyone looking at her would have simply seen an attractive young woman, resting in a park for a moment before resuming her day. And that was exactly what she would have liked to be right now. A normal person with a normal life, without memories, especially without memories that weren't hers. The discovery she had made the previous day had left her shaken. The violent images that had come to her out of the blue had turned out be messages from a place where a murder had been committed.

Maureen took off her dark glasses and put them down beside her on the bench.

When she had seen the image of that murdered young man on television, and had discovered who he was and what had happened to him, it had taken her several minutes to recover her composure. Then she had picked up the telephone and called Professor Roscoe at Holy Faith Hospital.

'Hello, Maureen. Is something wrong? Are you feeling all right?'

'No, I'm fine. No physical problems, if that's what you mean. I just wanted to ask you something.'

'Go ahead.'

'Do you know the identity of the donor? Do you know whose corneas you gave me?'

There was a pause at the other end. Maureen wasn't sure how to interpret it. Maybe Roscoe would say he didn't know, or maybe that he knew but couldn't tell her.

'No. We're informed that organs are available, and we're told the genetic type of the donor, but not his or her identity. The organs are removed elsewhere and for reasons I'm sure you can understand, the whole thing is completely confidential.' He paused. 'Maureen, I know how you're feeling. It's quite understandable, especially when you've been through such a terrible ordeal. But you have to think about yourself now and nobody else.'

Maureen had again been tempted to tell him about the things she had been seeing, but she suspected that if she did, she would just be going from one cage to another, gawped at by people who thought her deluded.

No, this was something she would have to deal with by herself for the moment.

'I suppose you're right.'

'I *know* I am. Not because I'm conceited, but because I've had a lot of experience of these things. Just go with the flow, take what life has to offer. And if you don't like what life has to offer, I'm sure you'll find the strength within yourself to change it.'

She had said goodbye to Professor William Roscoe, the man who, in saving her from one nightmare, had unwittingly landed her in another. She had put the phone down and looked around the room, wondering whose eyes she was seeing it with. And then she had found herself in the same state of mind as the day before, when she was still waiting to know if she would regain her sight or not.

With one difference.

This time she had actually been able to see night turn to dawn after all those sleepless hours spent trying to find a way out of the impenetrable forest of her thoughts.

In the end, she had clung to the only rational thing she still had left. She was a police officer and she might be able to help solve a murder. How, she didn't yet know.

She was still afraid of the reactions she would get from her family and colleagues, but that was a risk she had to take. And that was why she now found herself sitting on a green-painted bench in the park beside Gracie Mansion. She was aware that Mayor Marsalis knew her mother well, and she hoped that this, as well as evidence of her impressive service record in Italy, would somehow mitigate the enormity of what she was planning to tell him.

But now that she was about to do it, her courage failed her for a moment. She wondered if a guilty person felt the same way before turning themselves in. Picking up her dark glasses and putting them on to give herself at least the semblance of shelter, she stood up, took a deep breath and walked towards the gate.

CHAPTER 28

'How is it possible you don't have a single fucking lead?'

Christopher Marsalis stood up from the chair behind his desk. He had rolled up his shirtsleeves and loosened his tie, and his dark jacket was thrown over the back of the chair.

He then ran his hand through his white hair, looked at the two men sitting in silence facing him, and sat down again.

'I'm sorry. I'm just a bit nervous.'

Jordan had never before heard his brother apologize for anything.

'Mr Mayor,' Detective James Burroni said, 'I assure you we're following every avenue. We have men interviewing all the teaching staff who were at Vassar College at the time Chandelle Stuart was there. We're talking to United Features Syndicate, who publish *Peanuts*. We've even contacted the heirs of Charles Schulz to see if there's anything that might prove useful in the notes and papers in their possession.'

Christopher moved his chair away from the desk, trying to find a more comfortable position. There were dark circles under his eyes. Looking at him, Jordan guessed that he hadn't slept much since this whole thing had started.

'Detective, I'm sure you're doing all you can. What I can't stand is knowing that we're in here twiddling our thumbs while a serial killer is out there planning another homicide.'

Jordan got up out of his chair. 'I'm not convinced about that. A serial killer usually loves publicity. He wants his actions to be known to the media – that's how he gets his kicks. In this case, he hasn't made the slightest attempt to break the blackout we've managed to maintain so far regarding his MO.'

'That may be true, but I can't think of a better name for someone who goes around killing people using a comic strip as inspiration.'

'That comic strip has to be the key to everything. But I can't yet see how.'

Jordan started walking around the room, once again thinking aloud in a way that Burroni had by now learned to recognize and respect. He listened in silence to his cold analysis of the facts, as impersonal as if one of the victims wasn't his nephew and he wasn't in the presence of the victim's father.

'Let's think. We have a person who carries out murders inspired by comic strips. The first victim is an important figure, not only a famous painter, but also the son of the Mayor of New York. The second victim – a woman this time – also belongs to a very high-profile New York family. And this new homicide also points in the same direction: a world-famous comic strip called *Peanuts*.'

Jordan paused, as if an idea had flashed into his mind for a moment and immediately vanished again.

'On both occasions, we find a clue to the next victim, but a different kind of clue each time. The body of the first victim is arranged to look like Linus, with his security blanket stuck to his ear and his thumb in his mouth. A man in a tracksuit with a slight limp in his right leg is seen near the scene of the crime. The second victim is arranged to look like Linus's sister, Lucy, who has a crush on Schroeder, the musical prodigy. The same man with the limp is seen here, too. We discover that both victims studied in the same place and probably both knew their killer. What we don't know is if the third and future victim, who we already know is going to be made to look like Snoopy, was also a student at Vassar, or if he or she knows a man with a slight limp in his right leg. And let's not forget one important thing. We have a DNA sample.'

Jordan looked at Burroni and Christopher, as if only just realizing that they were in the room.

'And let's also not forget that we now have a further very small advantage over the killer.'

'What advantage?' Christopher asked.

'We have a name. Pig Pen. Another character from *Peanuts*. And the person we're looking for doesn't know we have it.'

Silence fell for a few moments, while Christopher and Burroni absorbed what Jordan had been saying.

Burroni was the first to react. 'Mr Mayor,' he said, standing up, 'in the light of what we've been saying, I'd like to go back to Headquarters to check my men's reports from Vassar and see if there's anything new.'

Christopher held out his hand. 'Thank you, Detective. I know you're doing a good job and I won't forget you when the time comes.'

As Burroni shook the Mayor's hand, Jordan turned his head to the window to hide his expression. He, of all people, knew how short lived his brother's memory could be.

Burroni left the room and gently closed the door behind him. Jordan and Christopher were alone. However, they did not have time to say a word before the door opened again and Ruben Dawson, the Mayor's right-hand man, appeared.

'What is it, Ruben?'

Jordan was surprised to detect a touch of indecisiveness in Dawson's demeanour.

'The guard at the gate has just called me,' he said. 'He says there's a woman asking to speak with you. She claims to be an officer in the Italian police.'

'What does she want?'

'She says she may have some information about the murder of your son.'

CHAPTER 29

Maureen was waiting by the gate.

Through the bars, she could see a few dark sedan cars parked in the small forecourt, and next to the cars a bright red motorcycle propped on its kickstand. An Italian bike, she thought.

Thing had happened the way she had imagined. When she had approached the gate, the guard on duty, a square-jawed man with a gait that seemed appropriate to some hot Southern climate, had left the sentry box and come towards her.

'Hello, miss. How can I help you?'

'Hello, Officer. My name's Maureen Martini and I'm a Chief Inspector in the Italian police. I'm also an American citizen. I need to speak to the Mayor urgently.'

She had handed the guard her passport and badge. Out of politeness, he had taken the documents but had not even looked at them.

'I'm afraid this isn't the best time to talk with the Mayor.'

Maureen had expected this reaction. She had taken off her sunglasses and looked the man straight in the eyes. 'Why don't we let him decide that? Just tell him I have information about his son's murder.'

The guard's glacial expression changed. 'Wait here a moment.'

He went back to the sentry box, and through the glass Maureen saw him simultaneously pick up the telephone and check the passport and badge, then nod as he listened to the answer.

Soon afterwards, he came back and handed over the documents. 'You can go in, Inspector Martini. Someone will come out to meet you.'

Maureen went through the gate and crossed the little forecourt. As she climbed the steps to the main entrance, the door opened and a very Anglo-Saxon butler appeared.

'Follow me, madam, the Mayor is expecting you.'

Maureen was so tense, she paid scarcely any attention to her surroundings, thus she almost missed a man in a suede jacket and a round black hat throwing her a curious glance as he walked past her. At the end of a corridor, the butler stopped outside a door. He knocked lightly and, without waiting for a signal from inside, opened the door and stood aside.

'Please go in, madam.'

Maureen took a couple of steps into the room, which looked like a small study. The door closed noiselessly behind her.

There were two people in the room.

Standing between her and the window was a tall man with salt and pepper hair. He had the most incredible blue eyes she had ever seen and the kind of face and attitude that instantly made you think he was a man you'd like to have beside you in a crisis. The other man, who was quite a bit older, was sitting at the desk. He had the confident body language that power carries with it, as well as the visible signs of the stress that power also brings. His were the same blue eyes as the other man – but they were weary eyes, and his heavy body told a tale of too many official dinners and too little exercise.

He stood up as she came in, and held out a thin hand. 'Hello. I'm Christopher Marsalis. And this is my brother Jordan.'

The tall man did not move or say anything, simply nodded.

'Hello, Mr Mayor. I'm sorry to burst in on you like this. I'm a Chief Inspector with the Italian police.'

'You speak English very well – and your face looks familiar. Have we ever met before?'

Maureen smiled politely. 'You may know my mother. She's a criminal lawyer, here in New York. Her name is Mary Ann Levallier. Everyone says we look very much alike. My name is Maureen Martini.'

When she said her name, the man who had been introduced to her as Jordan Marsalis took a step towards her.

'I'm sorry if this is an unpleasant question,' he said. 'Are you the late Connor Slave's girlfriend?'

Maureen was grateful to him for using the present tense. 'Yes, I am.'

The Mayor clearly also knew her story, because he now said, 'I'm sorry for your loss.'

Silence fell for a moment. The two men were both looking at her. She realized that the moment had come.

'I'll get straight to the point. I see you both know what happened to Connor and myself. As a result of that experience, I suffered lesions to my eyes that necessitated a cornea transplant. Because of a problem of genetic incompatibility, there were very few donors available. Despite that, one was found.' Maureen looked into Christopher Marsalis's blue eyes. 'I have reason to believe that donor was your son Gerald Marsalis.'

'It's possible,' Christopher told her. 'I myself authorized

221

his organs to be used when I found out he had a donor card. If that's the case, I'm pleased it helped you regain your sight. But what does any of that have to do with the investigation into his death?'

Maureen took off her sunglasses. The light from the window was like a blade in her eyes.

'I know what I'm about to tell you will seem impossible to you. In fact, I feel the same way. It's crazy, but . . . I keep having recurring visions of your son's life.'

The moment she had finished speaking, Maureen felt the silence of pity fall over the room. The mayor looked at his brother, then back at her, and when he spoke, it was in a deliberately calm voice, as he tried his best to look her in the eyes without flinching.

'Miss Martini, what you have just been through was traumatic. I know how difficult it is to accept certain things, and I say that from personal experience. Your mother is a good woman and a good friend. I think you should allow me to go home to her and rest until you have healed.'

Maureen had come into the room knowing that, when she told them what was happening to her, this would be the only possible response. She couldn't blame them. She herself would have done the same in these circumstances.

'Mr Mayor, with all due respect, I would never have come here if I didn't have a reasonable certainty that what I'm saying is true. I accept that the word "reasonable" may seem a bit incongruous in this case. I'm a police officer and I was trained to go by the facts, not far-fetched speculation. Believe me when I say I thought long and hard before coming here, but now that I am here I wouldn't change my story even if challenged by a whole panel of psychiatrists.'

She stood up, feeling naked and defenceless in front of

these two men, put her dark glasses back on and said the rest of what she had to say without looking at either of them in particular.

'I'll be staying with my mother a while longer. If you think I'm crazy, call her. If you want to give me the benefit of the doubt, call me. I'm sorry to have disturbed you.'

She turned and headed for the door, leaving behind her a silence she knew was a mixture of surprise, embarrassment and compassion.

As she was about to touch the handle, her eyes fell on a photograph in a wooden frame next to the door. In it, two men were shaking hands and smiling at the camera. One she knew very well: President Ronald Reagan. The other was Christopher Marsalis, looking much younger than he was now, with dark hair and a moustache. She had not recognized him immediately because he had changed so much, but his blue eyes were unmistakable. Maureen realized in a flash that she had seen him before – not as he looked now, but as he looked in the photograph.

It was the same man who had entered the child's room in her dream and torn up the drawing.

She spoke without turning around, afraid of the reaction on the faces of the two men.

'A long time ago, your son was making a drawing. It was a childish but quite accurate sketch of a man and a woman making love against a table. You came into his room and he showed it to you. You got very, very angry. You tore up the paper and as a punishment shut your son in a closet.'

Only then did Maureen turn. She saw Christopher Marsalis stand up without speaking, go to the window and look out. To Maureen, his silence was more eloquent than words could ever be. When at last he spoke, his voice seemed frayed by

223

time and memory.

'It's true. It happened many years ago. Gerald was a child. At that time my wife was still alive, although she'd already started going in and out of hospital. I was much younger then, of course, and because of her illness she and I had not had sexual relations for more than a year. There was this very pretty maid working in the house and I . . .'

He paused, as Maureen had expected: the usual pause before a confession.

'It happened in the kitchen. It was an instinctive thing, and it was only that once. Gerald must have seen us without our noticing. When he showed me the drawing, he was very proud. Obviously, he hadn't understood what we were doing. He was just delighted with his little artwork. I was afraid he might show the drawing to someone else, so I tore it up. Then I made him swear he wouldn't tell anyone – and to make it clear to him that he'd done something wrong, I shut him in that closet. He was only a child, but I have the feeling he never forgave me.'

Maureen saw again the door closing on his anger-reddened face, and imagined the child plunged into darkness.

Jordan Marsalis came to help his brother in his moment of weakness. 'Miss Martini, as you said before, you're a police officer, with all that entails. I used to be a police officer too, so we both know what we're talking about. You must admit there are unusual elements in this situation. If anything like this was used by either of us in court, we'd be forced to go for pyschiatric counselling twice a week. But I guess I have to take what you've told us seriously. You said there were other . . .'

Maureen realized he was struggling to give a name to something she herself could barely express in words.

'Are you asking me if I saw anything else?'

'Yes.'

Maureen felt a sense of liberation, as if she was at last emerging from the solitude into which all these experiences had plunged her. She started telling them about all the images that had come to her: the woman with the blue face beneath her, Gerald's red face in the mirror, the threatening figure on the landing . . .

She was so absorbed in her story that she was barely aware of the effect of her words on the two men. When she had finished, it was the Mayor who spoke first.

'This is crazy.'

Jordan seemed less shaken.

'I think we ought to decide on a line of action,' he said. 'We have two victims. The MOs make us think the murders are linked by a number of elements we can't yet define. The one link we've so far found between Gerald Marsalis and Chandelle Stuart is that both of them studied at the same college.'

He took some coloured photographs that were lying on the desk and pushed them towards Maureen.

'Vassar.'

Maureen came over, sat down, picked up one of the photographs and . . .

. . . I'm walking along an avenue that cuts across a large lawn. As I walk, I pass young men and women who look at me without greeting me: I don't greet them either. In front of me there's a big austere building, full of windows, and I raise my arm to look at my watch. Suddenly I start walking faster and then begin to run towards the entrance and . . .

225

. . . I'm in a room and my field of vision is restricted, as if the images are coming to me through holes, and apart from me there are two other people in the room, a man and a woman dressed in dark clothes and wearing plastic masks with the faces of characters from Peanuts. *The woman is Lucy and the man is Snoopy. My heart is pounding and I turn my head to see what the other two are looking at . . .*

. . . and there's a man with his back to me leaning over a table where a body is lying, apparently a child, and suddenly the man lifts his arms and in his right hand he's holding a knife that's all red with blood and there's more blood dripping from his hands and staining the sleeves of his jacket, and even though I can't hear him I know the man is screaming and I . . .

. . . I'm still with the man and woman in dark clothes and Lucy and Snoopy masks but we're somewhere else and the man is leaning against the wall and he takes off his mask and his face is young and tanned and streaked with tears and then he hides it in his hands and he slides down the wall until he's sitting on the ground and the woman . . .

Maureen was kneeling on the ground, looking at a knot in the wooden floor between two sports shoes. The shoes and the strong arms helping her up and into a chair belonged to Jordan Marsalis.

The voice was Jordan's too, but it seemed to come from a million miles away.

'What's the matter, Miss Martini?'

Maureen heard another voice, from equally far away. Somehow, she realized it was her own.

'A murder. There was a murder.'

'What do you mean? What murder?'

She did not hear the last question. Her body gave way and she fainted. The darkness was like a lifebelt thrown by a merciful hand, before another hand – the icy hand of terror – could grab her.

CHAPTER 30

When Maureen regained consciousness, she was lying on the floor, a hand supporting her head. The light hit her immediately, once more like sand in her eyes. She quickly closed them again.

'I need my glasses.'

She reached out a hand and felt the shiny surface of the wooden floor beneath her palm, groping for her glasses, assuming they had fallen beside her when she had pitched forward. She heard a movement behind her, felt the arms of the glasses being slid delicately over her ears, and then the blessed coolness of the dark lenses. She opened her eyes and was glad the others could not see her as she did so because they were glistening with tears. She tried to recover her normal breathing and heartbeat.

'Are you all right?' The voice was Jordan's.

'Yes,' she said.

No, she thought. *I'm not all right at all. If this is the price I have to pay in order to see, I'd prefer to go back to the old darkness and the images of my own nightmares – and not witness someone else's nightmares as a powerless spectator.*

'Do you want a drink?'

Maureen shook her head. The images of what she had seen were fading. Only the fear remained, like a knife in her stomach. She tried to sit up and saw Jordan's face in front of her and smelled his breath. It smelled good and healthy, with only a slight hint of tobacco. Obviously it had been he who had supported her and laid her on the floor before she could fall headlong.

'Help me up, please.'

Jordan put his hands under her armpits and gently lifted her back into the chair where she had been sitting when . . .

'Are you OK?'

'Yes, I'm fine now. It's gone.'

'What happened?'

Maureen passed a hand over her forehead. Despite what she had told the two men earlier, she could not help feeling a sense of shame for this new . . .

this new . . . what?

Maureen decided to call it an 'episode'. She certainly didn't want to use the word 'attack', not even to herself.

'I saw something,' she said.

Christopher Marsalis sat down behind the desk, facing her. 'What?'

Maureen pointed to the photographs strewn on the table. 'I saw Vassar. Not as it is now, but as it was some time ago.'

'How do you know that?'

Maureen indicated the trees lining the avenue leading to the big building in the background of one of the photographs. 'These trees were smaller when I saw them.'

'Go on.'

'I was there, running along that avenue in the photograph. Then suddenly I was in another place entirely. With Lucy and Snoopy.'

Still absorbed in what she had seen, Maureen did not notice

229

the start that Christopher Marsalis gave or the glance he threw his brother.

'Lucy and Snoopy?' the two men said almost simultaneously.

Maureen did not catch the anxiety in their voices, only the surprise. 'I'm not out of my head,' she hastened to say. 'I mean, I was with two people wearing *Peanuts* masks, specifically the characters of Lucy and Snoopy. I was wearing a mask, too.'

Jordan sat down in front of her and took her hands. 'Maureen, sorry to interrupt . . .'

Maureen was pleased to hear him use her first name. It was familiar, it was protective, it was . . . human.

'There's something I haven't told you,' he went on. 'Are you familiar with *Peanuts*?'

'Who isn't?'

'Well, whoever killed Gerald and Chandelle left the bodies in positions similar to two of those characters. My nephew had a blanket stuck to his ear and a finger in his mouth like Linus. Chandelle Stuart was leaning on a piano like Lucy when she listens to Schroeder playing. And the killer gave us a clue that suggests his next victim will be Snoopy.'

Jordan's voice was calm and radiated trust, and Maureen admired him for the way he managed to conceal what he must really be feeling.

'You mentioned a murder,' he prompted quietly.

'Yes. In the room where we were, there was someone standing in front of a table. On it was a body – a child, I think. I couldn't see very well because the man had his back to me and was standing between me and the table. Then he lifted his arms and in his right hand there was a knife with blood on it.'

'And then?'

'Then all of a sudden I was somewhere else. And the two people in the masks were there again and the person in the Snoopy mask took it off and was crying.'

'Did you see his face?'

'Yes.'

'Would you be able to recognize it?'

'I think so.'

Jordan leaped to his feet, as if galvanized. He turned to his brother, who had been listening to them in silence.

'Christopher, call President Hoogan. Tell him we need to get into the Vassar database urgently. Ask him for the password.'

Christopher immediately grabbed the telephone.

Jordan turned back to Maureen. 'The only thing we feel fairly confident about is that this Snoopy was also a Vassar student. If that's the case, we can try to locate him on the college database and place him under police protection, if we're still in time.'

'Travis,' came Christopher Marsalis's excited voice, 'I'm telling you this is a matter of life and death. I don't give a flying fuck about privacy. You want warrants, I can have a ton of warrants for you in fifteen minutes. But right now I need what I asked. And I need it *immediately*!'

He waited a few moments and then hung up. The heat of the conversation had caused two small red patches to appear on his cheeks.

'I gave Hoogan my private email address. In a minute he's going to send us the link to the database, with the password.'

'Good. Maureen, how are your IT skills?'

'I did an intensive course on computer crime. I'm not quite at the level of a hacker, but I'm not bad.'

'Excellent.'

231

They moved to another study at the opposite end of the residence, a larger room full of electronic equipment. There were computers with plasma screens, printers, scanners, fax machines and photocopiers.

Ruben Dawson, as impeccable and laconic as ever, was sitting at one of the computers. His expression did not change when they came in. Even Christopher's urgency did not make a dent on his impassive surface.

'Ruben, open my email. There should be a message from Vassar College in Poughkeepsie.'

Dawson did as he was told, and immediately a whole series of unread messages appeared on the screen. He stood up and gave his chair to Maureen without a word.

Maureen took off her glasses and sat down in front of the keyboard. She clicked on the message from Vassar and followed the link. Then she typed in the user name and password the President had provided.

This gave her access to a sequence of dates corresponding to academic years. The list seemed interminable.

'And now?'

'Christopher, what years was Gerald at Vassar?' Jordan asked his brother.

'Ninety-two and three, I think.'

That *I think* said a great deal about the relationship between father and son.

'Try the period between ninety-two and four. Is there a way of distinguishing the men from the women?'

'Doesn't look like it,' Maureen said. 'It's the database of a college, not a police file. If we knew the name, we could find the record, not the other way around.'

Jordan placed his hands on her shoulders, in a gesture of solidarity. 'Then I think we're going to have a look to a whole lot of faces. Let's hope the one we're looking for is among them.'

Despite the itching in her eyes, that coating of fine sand as she gazed at the screen, Mauren forced herself not to think too much, and to concentrate on that interminable succession of faces, that endless litany of Alans and Margarets and Jamies and Roberts and Allisons and Scarletts and Lorens and . . .

'There he is! It's him!'

A young man with reddish-brown hair and delicate features looked out at them with a shy smile. Maureen shuddered at the thought that right now, the adult version of that image was somewhere out there, unaware that they were fighting against time to save his life.

'Alex J. Campbell,' Jordan said, behind her. 'Born in Philadelphia on—'

'Of course!' Christopher cut in. 'He's the son of Arthur "Eagle" Campbell, the champion golfer. His father is English but has lived in the United States for years. I think he's a US citizen now. He lives in Florida and plays on the senior circuit.'

'Alex Campbell is also a writer,' Maureen said. 'A couple of years ago he was on the bestseller list with a novel that caused a bit of a stir. I actually read it. *Solace for a Disappointed Man*. I think it was published by Holland and Castle.'

It was Jordan who said aloud what they were all thinking. 'The phrase I found on the piano in Chandelle Stuart's apartment refers to Snoopy's ambition to be a writer.'

There was a moment when they were all still – like the pause between the flash of lightning and the roll of thunder. Then Jordan took his cellphone from his pocket and dialled a number.

'Burroni, this is Jordan. Listen carefully. We have another name. He's an ex-student of Vassar College named Alex Campbell. He's a writer, and his books are published by Holland and Castle. His father is Arthur Campbell, a golfer who lives in Florida. He may be Snoopy. Have you got all that? . . . Good. Try to track him down. Do it discreetly, we don't want to cause any alarm. We have to find him before our man does.'

Jordan put the cellphone back in his pocket. Nobody spoke. Now all they could do was wait.

Maureen rose from her chair and turned to Jordan. Instinctively, she had considered him from the start as her only point of reference, like an animal recognizing the scent of its fellow. Perhaps Jordan felt the same thing. His eyes met hers and he seemed to read her thoughts.

'The link between the victims could well be what you "saw",' he told her. 'They were all witnesses to a murder. And if we don't find Alex Campbell in time, we may never know what murder that was.'

Maureen did not reply, but simply put her dark glasses back on. It wasn't just that her eyes were smarting, it was also that she felt uncomfortable at being the centre of attention like this. She finally had the answer to a question she had always wanted to ask Connor: now she knew how cold and alone it must sometimes feel, being up there on the stage responding to the applause of the crowd.

CHAPTER 31

'West Village, corner of Bedford and Commerce.'

After giving the cab driver his home address, Alex Campbell sat back in his seat, a seat that had known better days and newer springs. The driver pulled away from the terminal at JFK airport where Alex's plane had just landed and his cab became one more in the long line of vehicles headed for the city.

It was not dark yet, but the lights in the buildings were on. After all the time Alex had spent in his house on Saint Croix, in the Virgin Islands, being back in the vibrancy of New York scared and startled him, as always, although there were compensations. Alex Campbell was a man and also a writer. But he was not a brave man, and that made him insecure as a writer. And like all insecure people, he needed constant reassurance. This city seemed to be the only source of that reassurance. When the praise and flattery dried up, and the anxiety returned, he knew it was time to get back to his island.

The cellphone in his pocket started ringing. He put a stop to the ringing without even looking at the display. He had programmed the phone to signal to him the times for the different pills he had to take in the course of a day. He unzipped the travelling bag he had with him and took out a small plastic box from which he removed an Amiodarone tablet. For some time now, his heart had shown a tendency to develop an irregular rhythm, and Amiodarone was the only drug that could keep it under control.

He put the tablet in his mouth and, as was his habit, managed to swallow it without need of water.

He had had a weak heart ever since he had been a skinny boy who tired easily. There had been a time when the doctors had feared he was suffering from dilated cardiomyopathy, a degenerative condition that leads the heart to become enlarged until it is almost unable to pump blood, necessitating a transplant.

When his father – the great 'Eagle' Campbell, the man who had performed some of the most spectacular shots in the history of golf – had realized that his son would never be a champion, in golf or any other sport, he had lost interest in him. In any case, he had been so busy cultivating his own legend, he had little time left to care about the people around him, even his own son.

His mother Hillary had behaved in exactly the opposite way, and had caused even more damage, if possible. She had taken him under her suffocating wing and taught him fear and evasion.

From that moment on, Alex had been scared of everything, and had spent his life running away.

The cellphone rang again. On the little display screen he saw the name and photograph of Ray Migdala, his literary agent.

'Hello?'

'Hi, Alex. Where are you?'

'I just got in. Right now I'm in a cab on my way home.'

'Good.'

'Did you read the material I sent you?'

236

'Of course. In fact, I finished it this afternoon.'

'What do you think?'

There was a moment's silence that set alarm bells ringing in Alex's mind.

'I think we need to talk.'

'Shit, Ray, why all this mystery? Did you like it or not?'

'That's what I want to talk to you about, when we meet. How about tomorrow morning, or are you too tired after your journey?'

'No, let's talk right now. And talk clearly, for once, if you can.'

'All right, if that's what you want. I read your new novel, and I think it's crap. Was that clear enough?'

'What are you talking about? Did you read it properly? I think it's great.'

'Then it's best you should know you're the only one who thinks that. I had a long talk with Haggerty, your Editor at Holland and Castle, and he's of the same opinion as me.'

At this point, Ray may have remembered Alex's state of health and realized he had been too harsh, because his tone changed.

'Alex, I'm saying all this for your own good. If you publish this book, the critics will slaughter you.'

'You know what the critics are like, Ray. They don't matter when it comes to sales.'

'I wouldn't be so sure of that. And I have to tell you that Ben Ayeroff, the Editorial Director, has no intention of finding out.'

The distant stirrings of panic. Now the approaching city no longer seemed a haven where he would get all the praise and flattery he needed, but a threatening place where failure was always in wait and always severely punished. The

Queens-Midtown Tunnel, which they would soon be entering, loomed like a bottomless pit.

'What do you mean?' Alex asked, trying to keep his voice firm.

'I mean, quite simply, that they have no intention of publishing your book. They're even prepared to write off the advance they gave you.'

'I don't give a damn. There are other publishers in the world. Knopf, Simon and Schuster—'

'I know, but I won't be taking it to them. I don't want to kill you with my own hands.'

Immediately, Alex Campbell's heart started thumping in his chest. Reading between the lines, it was obvious that Ray was much more concerned about his own reputation right now than his client's.

'Maybe we should take a step back, Alex. I'm sorry to be blunt. Holland and Castle published your first novel because your father reluctantly agreed to let them have his autobiography. Frankly, the novel was very weak and nobody bought it, but the publisher more than covered his expenses with the sales of your father's book. You are aware of all that?'

Alex was all too aware of it. He remembered the humiliation when his mother had informed him of the arrangement and had convinced him that it was necessary in order to get himself known.

'Of course I am, but what's that got to do with it? The first book was an apprentice work and that's how it should be seen.'

'That's true. And that's why you managed to get the second one read. When you showed up with *Solace for a Disappointed Man*, you hit the jackpot, critically and

238

commercially. Quite rightly: it was a masterpiece. I don't know how to say this. This third novel of yours doesn't even seem to be written by the same person who wrote *Solace*.'

It was lucky that Ray couldn't see Alex's expression. If they had been face to face, his agent might have seen just how much truth there was in what he had said.

It doesn't even seem to be written by the same person . . .

If he'd been capable of it at that moment, Alex Campbell would have laughed.

In the big house in Vermont where he had lived with his mother, there was an odd-job man they had inherited from the previous owner. His name was Wyman Sorensen and he lived in an outbuilding at the far end of the grounds. For as long as Alex could remember, he had always been the same: a tall, thin, white-haired man, who seemed to have been born inside clothes that were always one size too large for him.

But he had a calm voice and the most serene smile and eyes you could imagine.

To Alex, with an increasingly absent father and a mother who had isolated him from everyone, Wyman had become the one true anchor. Wyman was the only person who didn't treat him like an invalid but like a normal child.

The man had taught him everything he knew. They were like two fugitives from the world, a world Alex was forbidden to enter and in which Wyman wasn't interested at all. Wyman was like a character out of a novel by Steinbeck, a man who had built for himself a comfortable home in his own personal Tortilla Flat.

From him, Alex had learned a love of books and reading, discovering an alternative universe into which he could escape without moving an inch from the chair on the front porch of the little house at the far end of the grounds. Thanks to Wyman, he had understood the importance of words and imagination, even though he had never had much experience of either. Thanks to him, he had had the idea of one day applying to Vassar, with a view to a career in writing, and that had been the first real decision he had taken independently of his mother.

The old man had died peacefully in his bed when Alex was fourteen. He was not permitted to attend his funeral because, according to Hillary Campbell, the emotion of it might be too strong for her son's fragile constitution to bear. That morning, he had wandered through the grounds, feeling really alone for the first time. Coming to the house where his friend had lived, he had found the door open and gone inside, feeling slightly ill at ease, as if he was violating the privacy and trust of a person who could no longer defend himself. Despite everything, he had started to look through Wyman's things, wondering where all this stuff would end up, given that the old man didn't have any relatives.

Then he had opened a drawer and found a heavy folder with a black cover tied at the front with red string. On the black cover was a white sticky label bearing a handwritten title: *Solace for a Disappointed Man*.

He had taken it out and opened it. Inside were hundreds of numbered sheets covered in small, nervous handwriting. Alex could scarcely believe that, in this day and age, someone could have had the patience and devotion to write that mass of pages by hand.

Alex had taken the folder to his room and kept it hidden among his most private possessions. He eventually read the whole manuscript, a novel that Wyman had written over the years without ever telling anybody. Alex hadn't understood it completely but had kept it as a memento of his greatest friendship, and later as a kind of treasure to be spent in the future.

And spent it he had.

After his first novel had met with public and critical indifference, he had decided to publish *Solace* under his own name, making just a few small modifications to adapt the story to modern tastes and his own way of expressing himself.

There had been no signal while they were driving through the Midtown Tunnel, and so that awful conversation with his agent had been suspended. But as soon as they came out into the open, he pressed *call*, and Ray replied at the first ring.

'I'm sorry,' Alex said. 'I was in the tunnel, there was no network.'

'I was just saying there's no need to worry. Ayeroff was harsh, but I think if I go to work on them, they may be willing to give you the time you need to get the book the way it should be, the way only you know how to write it.'

No, I don't know how to write it. The person who might have known has been dead for a long time.

He would have liked to scream these words until he cracked his vocal cords, instead of which he kept silent, hiding his true thoughts, as he had almost always done in his life.

'We'll work it out, you'll see,' Ray went on. 'There are worse things in the world. Have you heard what's been happening here in New York?'

'No, you know I cut myself off completely when I'm on Saint Croix.'

'The Mayor's son was murdered. You know, the painter. And Chandelle Stuart, too.'

Alex Campbell started feeling palpitations in his chest, and he broke out in a cold sweat. The hand holding the cellphone grew clammy.

He asked a question to which he already knew the answer. 'Chandelle Stuart the steel heiress?'

'That's the one. They're not saying much about it, but it looks like it's the same killer both times. Could be a good idea for a thriller.'

Alex Campbell's mouth was so dry, he could barely speak.

'Are you still there?'

'Yes, I'm here. How did it happen?'

'Nobody knows. Like I said, they're not giving anything away. Only what I just told you. Understandable, given that it's the son of Christopher Marsalis . . . What's the matter, Alex, are you all right?'

'Sorry, I'm just a little tired. Don't worry, I'm fine.'

But he wasn't fine at all.

The sour taste of fear had returned, and as so often in the past, his first impulse was to run away. He would have liked to tell the cab driver to turn around and go back to the airport. He wanted to be back in the peace and quiet of his island. Only the fact that there wouldn't be any planes to take him there until the next day stopped him.

'OK,' Ray said. 'Let's talk tomorrow. We can decide what to do then.'

'All right.'

He hung up as the cab turned from First Avenue onto 34th Street. From that moment on, the ride home was a series of out-of-focus images of neon signs and moving cars through the dirty windows.

His temples were throbbing. Even though it wasn't the right time, he searched in his bag for the plastic box and

242

swallowed a Ramipril, the pill he took to keep his blood pressure down.

Two names continued to echo in his head.

Gerald and Chandelle.

And one word.

Murdered.

He didn't have time to indulge in memories. The cab stopped outside his building almost without his having noticed the distance they had travelled. He paid and got out. As he looked for his keys, he walked towards the low, welcoming building, with the three steps leading up to the walnut front door and the brass knocker.

Bedford Street was a short, narrow street close to the Hudson, and at that hour was quiet and dimly lit. The only light came from an old-fashioned tailor's shop on the corner with Commerce Street, just opposite his building. The fact that the light was on was a sign that someone was still working there, but Alex Campbell was so lost in thought that he barely noticed. Nor did he notice a rundown old car parked 100 yards further back that set off as his taxi entered the street and drove up behind him with its headlamps off. He did not hear the car stop or see the man who got out, leaving his car door open, and came towards him. The man was wearing a tracksuit with the hood up and limping slightly with his right leg. Alex Campbell had just climbed the steps and was inserting the key in the lock when he saw an arm enter his field of vision. Immediately he felt a damp cloth pressed to his nose and mouth. He tried to struggle free, but his attacker was holding him in a suffocating vice, with his other arm around his neck.

He tried to breathe, but a sharp smell of chloroform filled his nostrils. He felt a slight burning sensation in his eyes, his sight grew blurred, and his legs gradually gave way. His slender body collapsed into the arms of his attacker, who held him up without any difficulty.

A few moments later, he was slumped in the back seat of a beat-up Dodge Nova. The hooded man sat down in the driving seat and, without switching on the headlamps, moved away from the kerb and unhurriedly joined the lights and chaos of the traffic.

CHAPTER 32

Alex Campbell was naked and terrified.

He lay there, freezing cold, ribs jolted by the poor suspension, in the dark, foul-smelling trunk of a fast-moving car.

After the attack outside his front door, he had not fainted completely but had remained sunk in a strange torpor that had left his body as heavy as if his bones had suddenly turned to lead. The first corners the driver had taken had sent him slipping little by little from the worn seat to the floor of the car. He had lain there as they had driven along a street that had seemed interminable, with the dusty smell of the carpet under his nose, seeing the lights of the city from a low angle. After a time, they had stopped in a deserted, dimly lit area, with a yellow light flashing intermittently in the distance: a lighthouse, maybe, or an air traffic control tower.

He had heard the click of the back door opening and cold air had rushed in. The air smelled of rust and seaweed, and for the first time in his dazed state he had had a lucid thought. He had realized that they must be somewhere near water.

A man had entered his field of vision, dressed in a cheap tracksuit, his face covered in a ski mask, with openings through which only the eyes and mouth could be glimpsed. He had grabbed Alex with black-gloved hands, pulled him up as easily as if he was a weightless bundle, and sat him up again on the back seat with his legs protruding out of the car, dangling in the air like a puppet at the mercy of a puppetmaster.

He had seen his abductor take a roll of adhesive tape and a large utility knife from his pocket. The blade had glittered menacingly in the semi-darkness as, with a few rapid, precise gestures, the man cut a strip of tape and placed it over Alex's mouth and another which he placed around his wrists.

He had then taken him out and, supporting him effortlessly, had dragged him to the back of the car. There, he had propped him against the bodywork, keeping him in that position by putting one arm around his waist, while opening the lock of the trunk with his free hand.

The man had hoisted Alex roughly inside, lifting his legs to cram them in, and trained a torch at his face. Alex had seen the blade of the knife enter the beam of light just in front of his eyes. His heart pounding crazily, he had lost control of his body and had urinated and defecated at the same time.

He had emitted a desperate whimper, which the man had ignored completely, just as he had ignored the dark stain spreading over Alex's pants. Calmly but skilfully, the man had started systematically cutting off his prisoner's clothes. Alex had shuddered every time the blade had come into contact with his skin.

Tears continued streaming from his eyes. Bit by bit, he had been stripped bare, until he lay surrounded by torn shreds of clothing stinking of piss and shit and fear. The lid of the trunk had been closed, plunging him into darkness and leaving him alone with his terror and his stench.

In the silence, there were more sounds of doors closing, and then the engine started up, telling him that this had been only a halt and not their final destination.

Now he lay there in the trunk, thinking frantically.

Who was this man?

What did he want from him?

He remembered what Ray had told him not so long ago –
an hour? a century?

– Gerald Marsalis and Chandelle Stuart were dead.

The two people he had once known as Linus and Lucy had
been murdered. And now he was bound naked in the trunk of
a car, perhaps travelling to the same fate.

He could feel his teeth chattering uncontrollably with fear
beneath the tape that covered his mouth. And with the fear,
as predictably as those signals from his cellphone telling him
when to take his pills, came the remorse – guilt and sorrow
for something that had happened a long, long time ago.

For years he had wanted to tell that story, but had never
had the courage. In a way he had tried to tell it in his books,
through the medium of words on paper, hiding his confession
in metaphors, even though he knew these attempts would
never bring absolution.

After a while –
an hour? a century?

– Alex felt the car stop with a jolt, as if it had mounted the
sidewalk.

While the engine purred, he heard a door opening.
Immediately afterwards came a sharp metallic noise, and then
another like an anchor chain being pulled and the squeal of a
gate opening on badly oiled hinges.

Again the door closing and again the movement, as they
drove slowly down a street that seemed to be full of
holes. Then the car stopped for good and the engine was
switched off.

Alex again heard the creak of the door opening and then

the noise of footsteps on the gravel, and at every step his heart thudded. The lid of the trunk was opened and the light of the torch aimed downwards, allowing him to glimpse the outline of the man, who was clutching a long pair of wire-cutters in his right hand, holding it across his shoulder to balance the weight. He gave a brief glance at his passenger, lighting the interior of the trunk for a moment, and then, as if satisfied by what he had seen, closed the lid again, leaving a yellow blotch in Alex's eyes as his only memory of the light.

All the noises from outside reached Alex through the filter of the throbbing he felt in his ears. After what seemed an endless series of palpitations, the thumping in his heart suddenly became a paroxysm of irregular beats, a phenomenon he had learned over time to recognize and dread. He was finding it harder and harder to breathe, as if the oxygen was not getting to his lungs.

In normal circumstances, he would have started breathing through his mouth, sucking greedily at the air he needed to survive, but right now, with the tape preventing him from doing that, he had only his nostrils to rely on. The dust and the stench of his own excrement were like a film gradually clogging the narrow passageways through which the air reached his ribcage.

His heartbeat was now a succession of short, desperate contractions.

pa-tuc pa-tuc pa-tuc pa-tuc pa-tuc pa-tuc

Acid sweat was running down his forehead and into his eyes, burning them. He tried to raise his arms to wipe his face, but the position he was in and the tape on his wrists made that impossible.

From outside came a new noise, sharp and metallic, like that of a padlock being cut, then the screech of a sliding door, then footsteps approaching on a gravel surface.

pa-tuc pa-tuc pa-tuc pa-tuc pa-tuc pa-tuc

The lock of the trunk snapped open. As a sliver of light came in, Alex heard a muffled cry and saw his attacker raise his left arm to support his right as if, as he had opened it, the lid of the trunk had somehow injured him.

By the light of the torch, which he had placed on the roof of the car to have his hands free, the man, with an instinctive gesture, rolled up the right sleeve of his tracksuit to check the injury. There was blood on his skin, all the way from his wrist to . . .

Alex's eyes opened wide in surprise.

On his abductor's right forearm was a big, colourful tattoo depicting a demon with the body of a man and thin butterfly wings.

Alex knew that tattoo, and knew who wore it. He knew when it had been done, where it had been done and who had one just like it.

And he also knew that the person who had one just like it was dead.

The effect of the chloroform had by now completely worn off. He started whimpering and tugging and kicking in a fit of hysteria while his heart

pa-tuc pa-tuc pa-tuc pa-tuc pa-tuc pa-tuc

pounded uninterruptedly in his throat and chest.

As if surprised by his own gesture, the man hurriedly rolled down the sleeve of his tracksuit and partly closed the trunk, leaning his body on it. Through the crack, Alex saw him bend double, clutching his arm as if the pain was very strong. A bloodstain was spreading over his sleeve.

At that moment, from some vague point in the darkness, came a voice.

'Hey, what's going on? Who are you? How did you get in here?'

The weight on the trunk eased and the lid, freed from the man's body, went up slightly. The suspension gave a jolt, and the torch fell from the roof of the car and went out.

Alex heard steps rapidly approaching, then the sound of other steps on gravel as his abductor moved away from the car.

'Hey, you! Stop where you are!'

There was the sound of running feet coming past the car, and he surmised that his abductor had run away and the newcomer was running after him. The echo of the two men's steps faded in the distance.

Silence.

Alex raised his head and pushed the half-closed lid up with his forehead until it opened completely and he was at last able to see where he was. It was a large, dimly lit open space. To his left, in the distance, perhaps on the other side of the river, were the familiar lights of New York. To his right, on the edge of his field of vision, were streetlamps and buildings and a road running alongside a metal fence.

Those lights and those buildings meant that there were cars, people, help.

Life.

Pressing his legs against the wall of the trunk, he managed with difficulty to turn and sit up. With equal difficulty, he raised his bound hands to his mouth and pulled off the tape. He sucked at the damp night air as if it was his mother's breast. His heart was still pounding in his chest. He felt as if it might explode at any moment and transform his naked body into a shower of bloody fragments.

pa-tuc pa-tuc pa-tuc pa-tuc pa-tuc pa-tuc

Trying not to hit his head on the lid that swayed over him, Alex awkwardly turned and got on his knees. Supporting himself with his hands on the edge of the trunk, he managed to climb out, leaving his soiled and torn clothes behind.

He took a few hesitant steps towards the distant lights, heedless that he was walking on the rough surface of an unpaved street. He did not even glance at the warehouse outside which the car had parked. All that mattered were the lights he could see ahead of him, which right now represented his only hope of survival.

In a flash, he remembered the bloody tattoo he had glimpsed in the torchlight. Alex knew who the man was, and he knew what he would be capable of doing to him if he came back, even though he didn't know why.

This thought added terror to terror and gave his brain the nervous energy he needed to order his numbed legs to move.

In panic, he started running towards those lights, a dull pain still throbbing in his ears and chest

pa-tuc pa-tuc pa-tuc pa-tuc pa-tuc pa-tuc

not even noticing that his bare feet were leaving bloody prints on the rough ground.

CHAPTER 33

The police car, a blue and white Ford Corona, slowly descended the ramp from the Williamsburg Bridge and turned right. This area was mainly inhabited by Orthodox Jews, with their hats, beards and long side-locks, but at this hour there was almost nobody about. The lights in the kosher butchers' shops and supermarkets were off and the shutters down.

Manhattan with all its colours was far enough away to make this area seem like a different world entirely. There were only a few cars passing. Officer Serena Hitchin, a pretty twenty-nine-year-old black woman, was at the wheel and Lukas Furst, her partner, was sitting beside her, smiling and beating a somewhat unsteady rhythm with his hands on the plastic dashboard.

'Is this how it's supposed to go?' he asked.

Serena had for some time been in a relationship with a member of the cast of *Stomp*, the musical that had been playing for a number of years at the Orpheum, a theatre on Second Avenue. Lukas knew how important the relationship was to her but never lost an opportunity to tease her good-naturedly about it.

Serena laughed. 'You really don't have any ear for music, Luke.'

Lukas leaned back in his seat, a smug expression on his face. 'Is that so? You may like to know I was in the church choir when I was a kid.'

'That must have been before God appeared during the service, pointed to you and said, "Either he goes or I do".'

Lukas turned towards her with his index fingers crossed, as if Serena were a vampire. 'Silence, blasphemer. If that had really happened, the Almighty would have pointed me out to everybody and said, "This is My masterpiece. One day this man will be great".'

Serena chuckled, showing white, regular teeth. 'You're really crazy, you know. Still think that, huh?'

'Of course I think it. It'll happen sooner or later, you'll see. My name in lights on Broadway, and then I'll show up at the precinct in a car that'll turn you all green with envy. Look what happened to Captain Schimmer . . .'

Lukas Furst was a handsome young man, who looked especially good in uniform. He had indulged his passion for showbusiness – and a certain talent – by attending a whole series of acting classes, and every now and again played walk-on parts in movies or TV shows. At the precinct, everyone still remembered the pride with which he had announced that he was appearing in a Woody Allen film. He had dragged them all to the movie theatre, and when the scene had finally arrived they had seen him from the back for about two seconds. The teasing had continued for days.

Lukas opened a window to light a cigarette. By a tacit agreement with his partner, that was the only way he was allowed to smoke.

'Yes,' he said, 'the captain made it. He got the break.'

The Captain Schimmer he was talking about had become a police consultant on movies and, when he had retired, still

253

quite young, had delved further into that world and now often appeared on screen playing cop roles in movies and TV shows.

'Your break was to join the police, Luke,' Serena said. 'I don't think you'd ever leave this job. You like it too much.'

Lukas took a last puff and threw his cigarette out the window. Then he turned to Serena. 'Of course -- I was born to be a police officer. But I also like the idea that I was born to win an Oscar one day. And when I do, I'll thank my ex-partner Serena Hitchin, who with her faith in me and her support helped me to achieve my goal.'

It was a quiet night, they got along well, they were pleased with their lives and their work, and there was no valid reason not to joke between themselves.

But as always happens, the valid reason soon presented itself.

The radio started crackling and immediately afterwards a voice emerged.

'Calling all cars. Maximum alert from Headquarters. A male Caucasian named Alex Campbell has been abducted, and it's possible that the man who abducted him is the killer of Gerald Marsalis and Chandelle Stuart. Alex Campbell is about thirty years old, six feet tall, with thin brown hair. The abductor is driving a very old Dodge Nova with marks of filler on the bodywork. I repeat, maximum alert.'

Lukas let out a whistle. 'Jeeze. With all the secrecy there's been about this case, putting out a message like that on the normal frequency must mean they're shit-scared.'

'So would you be if you were the Mayor of New York and your son had been killed like that.'

'I guess so.'

As they spoke, they had turned right at the beginning of

Roebling Street onto the street that led down to the East River. They crossed White Avenue and found themselves at the end of Clymer Street, facing the sign of the Brooklyn Navy Yard.

Beyond the rust-coloured perimeter fence that marked off the area, the outlines of old subway cars could be glimpsed, heaped up and waiting to be turned to scrap. In the darkness, a few tall dark brick buildings, many of them dilapidated and abandoned, loomed over the street.

Serena turned left and drove at moderate speed along Kent Avenue, heading south towards Brooklyn Heights. They passed the pound where confiscated cars were kept, to be auctioned after a fixed period. For a moment, Lukas allowed his attention to wander as he looked at all those vehicles waiting for new owners. Then:

'Holy shit! Who the fuck's that?'

Hearing Serena's alarmed voice, Furst turned his head abruptly towards the street.

In the dim light cast by the streetlamps, a man had come out through an open gate in the perimeter fence and was running towards them with his hands up. Apart from a few scraps of clothing around his shoulders, he was stark naked and was moving as if every step cost him a huge effort. When he realized that theirs was a police car, he stopped, lifted his hands to his chest, slid slowly to his knees, and remained in that position, motionless, in the middle of the roadway.

Serena stopped the car and she and Lukas got out, leaving the doors open. As they approached, Serena noted out of the corner of her eye that her partner had taken his gun from his holster.

They reached the kneeling man, who was breathing with difficulty and looking at them with incredulous tears rolling

255

from his eyes, as if he was witnessing a miracle. In the light of the headlamps, they finally managed to make out his features.

'Serena, the description matches the one we just heard.'

'OK, keep your eyes peeled, Luke.'

While Lukas remained standing, with his gun at the ready, Serena kneeled next to the man, who was looking at them in silence, both his hands pressed to his chest. His breath was a kind of wheezing, and there was a strong smell of excrement about him.

'Are you Alex Campbell?' Serena asked.

The man nodded wearily, then closed his eyes and keeled over. Ignoring her revulsion at the stench, Serena quickly moved to support his head and stop it hitting the ground.

She placed her fingers on his neck and found the pulse.

'His heart's beating like crazy. I think he's having an attack. We need an ambulance.'

Still keeping his eyes on the surrounding area, Lukas started retreating towards the car. A moment or two later Serena heard his voice contacting Headquarters and asking for medical assistance and backup.

She turned her attention back to the wretched heap of fear and shame and pain into which someone had transformed Alex Campbell.

The man looked up. His voice was a mere breath emerging with difficulty from his body. Serena heard him whisper some words too soft to be heard.

'What did you say? I didn't understand.'

Alex Campbell lifted his head an inch, a movement that seemed the result of an enormous effort. Serena slipped a hand under his head to support it and moved her ear closer to his mouth, but his feeble words were almost lost in the noise of Lukas's footsteps as he came running back.

'The ambulance will be here s—'

Serena looked up and said urgently, 'Shut up a minute!' She again leaned towards the man, but darkness was gradually invading his eyes. The words that emerged from his half-open mouth were his last.

Serena could immediately see that help was pointless. Under her fingers, the fragmented heartbeats slowed down, grew weaker, then disappeared entirely.

Serena Hitchin felt a sense of loss, the same she always felt when she was forced to be present at the extinction of a life. She didn't think it would ever get any easier, even after many years of service. Gently, she raised a hand and closed the dead man's eyes.

CHAPTER 34

The real struggle was against time.

Sitting in the passenger seat as they drove through the streets of New York, Jordan looked straight ahead of him. The lights and the shadows flashed by as if they, rather than the vehicle in which he was travelling, were in movement. He felt as if he was in one of those primitive special effects from the days of silent movies, when the actors kept still and a painted panorama revolved behind them.

And maybe that was how it was.

Every person involved in this case thought he was moving forward, whereas the world was rushing past them, mocking their paralysis.

Jordan knew why he was feeling this way: he was certain that he had failed.

In the back seat was Maureen Martini, silent and alone. Jordan admired the woman's strength of mind, torn as she was between rationality and something that *had* no rational explanation. Few people would have been able to accept what was happening to her, but she was sustained by an unshakeable belief that she was not crazy.

Thanks to her, they had identified Snoopy. When it had happened, they had all been in too much of a hurry to stop and wonder how she had done it. They had called Alex Campbell but nobody replied. His cellphone was off. A quick internet search had yielded the name of his literary agent, Ray Migdala, who told them Campbell had just landed at JFK and was on his way home. Jordan had informed Burroni and immediately afterwards he and Maureen had rushed in the police car from Gracie Mansion towards the address that Migdala had given them.

It was during the ride that the news had come in.

The radio had started crackling and the driver had picked up.

'Officer Lowell.'

'I'm Detective Burroni. Is Jordan Marsalis there with you?'

Jordan had taken the microphone from Lowell.

'Hello, James. What's going on?'

'I got to the scene and found a patrol car there. It was there because a while ago, a guy who owns a tailor's shop opposite Campbell's building called 911 to report a kidnapping.'

Jordan had felt a shiver down his spine. He had preferred not to continue the conversation by radio.

'I'll be right there. We can talk then.'

When they reached the corner of Bedford and Commerce, they immediately saw the patrol car and Burroni's service automobile parked outside Alex Campbell's address.

Burroni was on the sidewalk opposite talking to a tall, dark-haired, middle-aged man with an olive complexion.

As they got out of the car, Burroni looked at Maureen in surprise and then threw an inquisitive glance at Jordan.

'It's OK, James. This is Maureen Martini, from the Italian police. I'll explain later.'

Burroni merely nodded at Maureen and turned again to the tall man.

'Mr Sylva, can you repeat what you saw, please.'

The man started his story in an accent Maureen recognized as Brazilian. He pointed to the lighted window behind him. 'I was in my shop, working. A taxi pulled up and Alex got out.'

'By Alex you mean Alex Campbell?'

'Yes. I've known him for years.'

'Go on.'

'He paid the driver and walked to the front door. A car drew up behind him and this guy opened the door—'

'Can you describe him?' Burroni cut in, throwing Jordan a significant look.

Even before Mr Sylva spoke, Jordan already knew what he would say.

'I didn't see his face because he was wearing a tracksuit with the hood up. What I can tell you is that he was slightly above average height and had a bit of a limp in his right leg.'

'And then what happened?'

'He got out of the car, came up behind Alex and attacked him. He put an arm around his neck as if he wanted to strangle him. Alex must have fainted, because this other guy held him up and bundled him into the back seat of the car. Then he got in behind the wheel and drove off.'

'Did you get the licence number?'

'I didn't have time. As you see, there's not a lot of light here and he had his headlamps off. But the car I remember well. It was a Dodge Nova, very beat-up. Couldn't tell you what colour it was. The bodywork was all patched up with filler.'

A call immediately went out about the abduction. Not long afterwards, a report came in from a patrol car in Williamsburg that Alex Campbell had been found.

Dead.

*

Burroni's car turned left onto Kent Avenue and drove towards the intermittent lights that could be glimpsed beyond the barriers. The street had been cordoned off. Over their heads they could hear the noise of a helicopter's blades but could not tell if it was a police helicopter or one that belonged to a TV channel.

Almost all the buildings on Kent Avenue had their windows open, and people were leaning out to see what was going on.

When they reached the cordon, a police officer signalled to two of his colleagues and the barriers were moved aside to let the car through.

They continued slowly and stopped behind a police car parked in the middle of the street. Just in front of the car, lying on the asphalt in the light of the headlamps, was a white sheet beneath which could be made out the outline of a body.

The crude light of the headlamps and the blue reflection on the sheet reminded Maureen of other cars, other headlamps, a scene that had happened thousands of miles away.

Nasty business, isn't it?

A young, athletic-looking officer was standing near the patrol car. When he saw them get out of their car, he came towards them.

'I'm Officer Furst. I was on patrol with Officer Hitchin. We were the ones who called this in.'

'Detective Burroni. I'm in charge of this case.' Burroni didn't bother to introduce Maureen or Jordan. Partly because it wasn't necessary, but mainly because he wasn't quite sure how he'd explain their presence at a crime scene.

'Was he already dead when you found him?'

The officer shook his head. 'No. He came out of that gate

261

and ran towards us. He was stark naked and seemed terrified. When he saw us, he fell on his knees. We figured he might be the guy we'd just been notified about, so we asked him and he nodded. Then I think he had a heart attack.'

Jordan had stepped away from the group and was looking around as if he wasn't interested in this account. Burroni had learned to know him, however, and knew that none of what the officer was saying had escaped him.

'Did he say anything before he died?'

'I don't know. Just before that happened, I'd gone back to the car to ask for an ambulance. My partner was with him when he died.'

Jordan approached. 'Where is your partner now?'

Officer Furst gestured towards the flashing lights beyond the barrier. 'Over there by the warehouse, where they found the car used in the abduction.'

Jordan moved over to where the body lay. He crouched down and lifted a corner of the sheet. Officer Furst, Maureen and Burroni came up behind him.

Maureen kneeled beside Jordan. She reached out her hand and lifted the sheet until she had uncovered almost all the body.

'Poor guy.'

There was compassion in her voice, but it was steady. Jordan had to admit to himself that his admiration for this woman was increasing by the minute.

'Yes. To have got this far and then have a heart attack . . . He must have been really scared. I think we need to take a look at the car.'

They got back in their car, leaving Officer Furst to guard the body until the Medical Examiner and Crime Scene team arrived, and headed for the warehouse.

It was on the left of a large open space, next to a construction site. There was a big sliding door that was open, and inside it was dark. Outside, two police cars were parked next to the Nova that Sylva had described as the vehicle in which Alex Campbell's abductor had driven away. The trunk was open and a police officer was inspecting it with a torch. When Burroni, Maureen and Jordan came up behind him, he stood aside to let them see what he had been looking at, and also to get away from the stench.

'Found anything?'

'Just a few rags that stink to high heaven. The trunk was already open when we got here. We haven't looked in the car yet because we were waiting for you.'

'Good.' Burroni took a pair of latex gloves out of his pocket and handed them to Jordan. 'I think this is your call.'

Jordan thanked him with a nod of the head. He put on the gloves, asked the officer for his torch, and opened the rear door of the car with a creak. The interior was of imitation leather, which time and the men who had sat there had reduced to a kind of spider's web. There was a smell of damp and dust in the car.

Jordan let the beam of light play over the interior until, on the floor behind the passenger seat, he saw a small transparent plastic bag with something in it. He leaned in, grabbed it with his left hand and straightened up.

He gave the torch to Burroni, then put a hand in the bag and took out a red cloth wrapped around a curious old pair of glasses, with frayed elastic instead of arms, and an old-fashioned-looking padded leather cap. He looked at them for a moment as they lay there on the cloth, which he now saw was a woollen scarf.

'What's in the warehouse?'

263

The answer came from another officer who had just come up behind them. 'We haven't gone in yet. The light switches aren't working. I sent Officer Hitchin to get the light connected.'

As if in immediate testimony to Officer Hitchin's excellence, a series of dim fluorescent tubes came on in hesitant succession inside the building. Those present went to the entrance to look in, and were stunned by what they saw.

The warehouse was full of the wrecks of vintage planes, presumably kept there waiting to be restored. There were two Hurricanes, a Spitfire, a Messerschmitt with the Luftwaffe insignia, a Japanese Zero with the sign of the Rising Sun. At the back, half hidden by the more recent machines, was an old biplane Jordan thought might be a Savoia Marchetti.

'The son of a bitch.'

When Burroni and Maureen looked round, he pointed to the biplane and at the same time waved the objects in his hand. 'This is an old aviator's cap, and these are flying goggles from the same period. And then there's the scarf. That bastard wanted to put Alex Campbell in a plane, got up to look like Snoopy when he plays at being a World War One flying ace.'

'But why naked?' Burroni asked.

Jordan gave a disgusted smile. 'I think this is our man's latest refinement, James. Snoopy is a dog, and apart from a few distinctive accessories like these, he never wears clothes.'

At that moment, a pretty black woman officer appeared and came towards them, saying, 'I heard you were looking for me.'

'Are you Officer Hitchin?' Burroni asked.

'Yes, sir.'

'You assisted Alex Campbell when you found him?'

'Yes.'

'Did he say anything before he died?'

'Yes, he murmured a few words.'

'What did he say?'

'He mentioned a name. Julius Wong.'

'Just that? Nothing else?'

Officer Hitchin threw an anxious glance at her colleagues, as if what she was about to say might be a subject for jokes for some time to come. 'I don't know, maybe I misunderstood, because it doesn't make any sense.'

'Officer, let us be the judges of that. Just tell us what you heard.'

'Before he died, Alex Campbell said something else . . .'

She paused.

'Immediately after that name, he said the words "Pig Pen".'

CHAPTER 35

Time had again become the opponent to beat.

Sirens blaring, Burroni's car raced across the street map of New York. Officer Hitchin's revelation about Alex Campbell's last words had opened a new door: they knew perfectly well who Julius Wong was – but they didn't know why Julius Wong was Pig Pen.

And they were going to his home to find out.

The cellphone in Jordan's pocket rang. It was his brother.

'Any news?'

'Yes, and it's not good. Alex Campbell is dead.'

There was a moment's silence.

'Same perpetrator?'

'Apparently, yes, but this time something went wrong for our man and somehow, Campbell managed to escape. The poor guy must have had a weak heart though, because the emotion brought on an attack that killed him. Before dying, he managed to give us a clue.'

'What was it?'

'It seems from his last words as if the next victim is to be Julius Wong. We're on our way to his place now.'

'Julius Wong? Holy Christ, Jordan. You know who his father is?'

'Of course. And I also know who he is.'

'All right. But take care. Let Burroni go in first.'

'Got it. I'll keep you posted.'

Jordan hung up and put the phone back in his pocket.

Christopher's anxiety was more than justified. It was not for nothing that he had advised him to keep one step behind Burroni. His legitimate fear was that, as Jordan didn't have an official position, they might end up getting caught out on a legal technicality.

Julius Wong was the only son of Cesar Wong, and that made him officially a member of the New York jet set. He was also a psychopathic pervert who had escaped prison many times thanks to money, his father's power and a series of very expensive lawyers. Among other charges, a couple of girls had accused him of rape and assault, an accusation that had been quickly retracted before the trial. It was assumed that someone had got to them, offering money, or threats, or whatever. And that someone was most likely Mr Wong senior.

Cesar Wong's front was that of a wealthy businessman involved in various sectors of the economy, with a particular interest in retail and property. The reality, even though nobody had ever been able to prove it, was that he had a finger in some much less savoury pies, such as drugs and arms trafficking. He had laid the foundations of his huge fortune when he was still a young man with a lot of imagination and scarcely any scruples, thanks to the brilliant stratagem of laundering dirty money through the Chinese stores on Canal Street. That fortune had grown in the same confident way until he had reached a position of absolute, impregnable power. It was said that he had an untold number of senators on his payroll. All that, of course, was speculation. The one sure thing was that you wouldn't want to step on his feet. And if anything happened to his son, the person responsible would pay dearly.

Burroni's car pulled up in front of a three-storey building on West 14th Street, amid the fashionable boutiques and renovated buildings of the newly gentrified Meatpacking District. They were followed by the patrol car with Lukas Furst and Serena Hitchin in it, and another patrol car with two officers they had picked up in Williamsburg.

Maureen, Jordan and Burroni got quickly out of the car and walked to the front door of the building. It was a light structure in anodized aluminium and unbreakable glass. The small lobby they could see through the windows was almost completely occupied by elevator doors and a huge dragon tree.

On the wall by the front door was a line of bells equipped with a video entryphone. After a rapid glance, Jordan pressed the button marked with a J.

Nobody replied.

Jordan rang again – but again the entryphone remained blind and mute. He tried a third time, holding the button down for a long time. Finally they heard the crackle of the microphone, followed by a hostile voice.

'Who's that?'

Burroni moved his badge close to the camera and then placed himself so that he was framed as clearly as possible.

'Police. I'm Detective Burroni. Are you Julius Wong?'

'Yes. What the fuck do you want?'

'If you let us in we'll tell you.'

'Do you have a warrant?'

'No.'

'Then fuck off.'

Burroni's jaw hardened, but he forced himself to remain calm. 'Mr Wong, we don't need a warrant. We aren't here to arrest you or search your home.'

'Then I repeat the question, in case you've got wax in your ears. What the fuck do you want?'

Jordan gently moved Burroni aside and placed himself in front of the cold eye of the camera.

'Mr Wong, we have serious reason to believe that someone is planning to kill you. Would you like us to come in and talk about it, or would you prefer us to leave you alone so you can ask your killer the same question when he shows up with a gun in his hand?'

There was a moment's silence. Even though he didn't think it likely, Jordan hoped Julius Wong was shitting in his pants right now like that poor wretch Alex Campbell.

Then finally the lock clicked and Burroni opened the door. Jordan put a hand on his arm.

'James, it might be better if Maureen and I keep out of this.'

Burroni had not heard Christopher's words, but immediately grasped the meaning of Jordan's. 'Yes, it might.'

He turned to the officers behind him and pointed at Lukas Furst and Serena Hitchin.

'You two, come with me. You other two take a look around, and keep your eyes open.'

Furst and Hitchin followed Burroni inside and up the stairs. The other two separated to check the surroundings.

Jordan and Maureen were left alone outside the building. On the other side of the street, near the corner with Eleventh Avenue, grey-suited bouncers stood on the sidewalk outside High Noon, a famous disco frequented by models and other people in the fashion business.

Jordan looked at Maureen's face and saw that she was tired, with rings under her eyes.

'I don't understand what's happening,' she told him. 'Too many things in too little time. And to be honest, I'm scared. Damn scared.'

Jordan saw her bow her head, as if ashamed of that moment of weakness. He lifted her chin with his hand. 'I'd be scared too, if I were in your place.'

'But at least you know what your role is, in all this. I'm not sure of anything any more.'

Jordan smiled resignedly. 'Believe me when I say, I'm not sure what my role is either. Now that you're part of it too, I realize how difficult it must be for you to accept the reason why. But you're a fantastic woman and I'm sure that you've been an excellent police officer, and will be again.'

Maureen looked into his incredible blue eyes but said nothing.

She had only known this man for a few hours but felt she could trust him. Somehow she sensed that he had been through similar experiences, and this would account for the instinctive rapport that had sprung up between them.

She stood up on tiptoe, a shimmer of tears reflected in her eyes, and Jordan felt the moist warmth of her lips on his cheek. Not even for a moment did he think there was the slightest sexual connotation to that kiss. It was only a silent way of saying *you've understood me and I've understood you*.

'It's going to be all right, Maureen,' he said.

He put his arms around her slim body and let her lay her head against his chest, and they stood there, motionless, in the rectangle of light projected on the sidewalk through the glass door.

When Jordan looked up, he saw Lysa on the other side of the street, standing beside a big BMW sedan, looking at him.

Nobody with eyes like that . . .

Since their trip to Vassar and their conversation in the restaurant on the river, Jordan had moved with his few things to a hotel on 38th Street and they had not communicated or met. When Lysa realized that Jordan had seen her, she turned her head abruptly towards a group of people, men and women who had just come out of the disco and were joining her. They came level with her and, laughing, got into the BMWs and Porsche Cayennes parked along the kerb. Lysa took her seat in the big sedan, next to the driver.

The car set off and as it moved away she kept her eyes fixed straight ahead, leaving in Jordan's mind the image of her silent profile.

He had no time to think because, almost simultaneously, the door of the elevator in the lobby of the building opened to reveal three figures.

One was Officer Lukas Furst.

The second was Burroni.

The third person was a man of about thirty, almost as tall as the detective, with a slim physique and smooth shiny hair, his regular features given an extra charm by his remote Asian origins. Only his mouth, thin and cruel, spoiled the perfection of that face.

He was wearing a white shirt and dark jeans, and his wrists were handcuffed in front of him.

Burroni put a hand on his elbow and pushed him out of the elevator. Julius Wong wriggled free as if the detective was unclean.

'Don't touch me, pig. I can do it myself.'

'OK, go ahead.'

With Burroni's eyes on him, Wong opened the glass door and followed the direction the detective indicated. Once outside, he looked defiantly at the world around him for a moment. In spite of his anger, his eyes were murky, bearing the mark of vice and depravity.

As Burroni and his prisoner walked to the car, Jordan noticed that Julius Wong had a very pronounced limp in his right leg.

CHAPTER 36

Lysa Guerrero took off the long T-shirt she had worn during the night and stood naked in front of the bathroom mirror. The silvery surface sent her back her own image, cut off at the waist by the cabinet with the white marble top. The reflection of the stone contrasted sensually with her olive Latin skin, but right now Lysa was in no mood to take pleasure in that. She raised her arms, mussed her long dark hair with a casual gesture and then let her hands descend until they were touching the brown nipples on her firm, high breasts, which were the perfect size to be contained in the palm of a man's hand. Her sigh created a small damp halo on the glass of the mirror. If she had been a dreamer, she might have imagined that Jordan Marsalis would open the door behind her at any moment, with his shirt red with blood and astonishment on his face at seeing her there.

And it would start all over again.

But that was and would remain only a fantasy.

It was a long time since Lysa Guerrero had been able to afford the luxury of dreams.

She moved closer to the mirror and looked deep into her own eyes. They were tired and red from the almost sleepless night she had just spent.

When she had got back the previous night, she had

undressed, climbed into bed and turned out the light, hoping she could blot out the reality around her. She had lain there in the darkness, her eyes open, with only a thin sheet to protect her from her fear and bitterness. Through the open window, from the floor below, music had risen in slow wreaths as if to mock her, the usual song played by the unknown fan of Connor Slave.

> *There's n grindstone known to man*
> *Can crush this rock inside my heart.*

Listening to the soft music and absorbing the meaning of the lyrics, she had continued to see Jordan embracing that woman, the two of them motionless in a shared moment. And by an irony of fate, right in front of the building where . . .

When she had left the disco with a group of people who didn't mean anything to her, heading for another place that didn't interest her, she had walked blithely towards the parked cars, trying to delude herself that the world was smiling at her, that everything around her was hers or could easily be hers.

Then she had seen them, that image of normality.

A man born a man embracing a woman born a woman.

She moved away from the mirror, stepped into the shower and opened the faucet. She let the water engulf her, without even waiting for it to become hot, anxious for it to wash away her tears.

This time it wasn't the world that had rejected her, she had done it herself.

She had fallen in love with Jordan in a single second, maybe the very moment he had appeared at the bathroom door with his nose all bloody and his incredible blue eyes wide open with astonishment at the sight of her naked body.

She had offered Jordan the chance to continue living in her apartment. She had done it instinctively, wanting nothing but to stay close to him, knowing perfectly well that it was wrong. And she had done that other thing, hiding behind all the alibis she had managed to find for her decision, knowing all the same, deep inside, that this, too, was a wrong choice.

She remembered her determination when she had arrived in New York, that lunch of oysters and champagne during which she had been importuned by a stupid man named Harry and the way she had treated him – as she had decided to treat everyone from now on. When she had left, she had seen, stretched out in front of her, a land to be conquered in all its splendour, whereas now she had come to the desolate conclusion that in reality there was nothing here worth conquering.

All her life she had asked for nothing but to hide, to keep close to the walls, avoid the limelight. She had wanted that with all her heart, just as she had craved a kind person who would want her and accept her for what she was. She had simply wanted what everyone else had.

She had dreamed of it and tried to get it, but in vain.

Because of her physical appearance, all the men she met desired her, ran after her – but when they discovered who and what she was, they turned their backs on her. But then they'd phone her at two in the morning, their words blurred by alcohol, saying they happened to be in the vicinity and asking if they could come up for a while and have a drink, and promising that if she let them do what they wanted, she wouldn't regret it.

That was how she had learned that the world, when it was able to escape the conventions, did want people like her, after all. On the sly, in secret, maybe, but it did want them. There was a whole host of enthusiasts – deviants, if you preferred to call them that – who asked nothing better than to spend a few hours with a girl like her, rewarding her generously, after which they would return to their normal life, with a woman as a wife and boys for sons and girls for daughters.

And so she had continued on her way, gritting her teeth and holding back the tears.

Then, one day she had received an envelope. And inside it was that crazy, perverse – but very lucrative – proposal . . .

She had surrendered, told herself that if that was what they wanted from her, that was what they would get. A hundred thousand dollars seemed a fair price to pay.

But before anything happened, Jordan had appeared. She had felt him getting ever closer to her day after day, attracted to her despite himself like a moth to a flame. Then, at the restaurant on the river, he had said those beautiful words.

As always, she had run away. She had dismissed him because she was scared that this was yet another illusion, her decision made even more painful by her feelings for the man, feelings that she had never experienced before with such intensity.

And now she was alone again, with shame as her only companion.

She turned off the water, stepped out of the shower, put on her robe, and started drying her hair. Once it was done, she walked into the bedroom, slipped into jeans and a T-shirt, and then took out her suitcase and threw it on the bed. Removing her clothes from the closet, she started packing – swiftly but with great precision.

Lysa was good at packing. It was something she had done many times.

Taking the remote from the night-table, she aimed it at the TV set. She hopped to NY1, to have company as she packed. On the screen, she saw a TV studio with two anchor-people, a man and a woman Lysa didn't know, sitting behind a desk.

'. . . we're waiting for further information, which we'll let you have if it comes in during the show. In the meantime, there appear to be important developments in the case of Gerald Marsalis, the Mayor's painter son, better known as Jerry Ko. Let's go over to Peter Luzdick at Police Plaza. Are you there, Peter?'

A reporter holding a microphone was shown in front of the unmistakable red abstract sculpture outside Police Headquarters.

'Yes, Damon. I'm here and I can confirm that Julius Wong, who was taken in by police last night, has now been charged with the murder of Gerald Marsalis. I understand that there is also evidence linking him to the murder of Chandelle Stuart and to last night's kidnapping of writer Alex Campbell, in the course of which, as we know, he died of a heart attack.'

Lysa felt a wave of cold hit her stomach and spread through her veins, turning her blood to ice. She gasped and sat down on the bed before her legs could give way, her face as pale as the marble in the bathroom.

On the screen, the reporter continued, 'From what I understand, the investigators are waiting for the results of a DNA test, to determine the source of semen found in Chandelle Stuart's body. Right now we have no other details. We expect there to be a press conference very soon.'

A coloured photograph appeared, with the speaker's voice over it.

'Julius Wong, the son of Cesar Wong, is no stranger to the police or the courts. Some years ago . . .'

Lysa turned off the volume but continued staring at the screen.

The image of Julius Wong stared back at her, cold and silent.

CHAPTER 37

Jordan raised his arms from the table and leaned back in his chair, to allow the dark-jacketed waiter to put the plate down in front of him. As the man walked discreetly away, Jordan looked at the dish with a puzzled air.

'What the hell's this?'

Maureen smiled across the table with its crystal glasses and elegant white linen tablecloth. She had the same colourful dish on her plate.

'Breast of pigeon cooked in cocoa and grape sauce.'

Jordan moved his chair closer to the table and picked up his knife and fork. 'If the food's as impressive as its name, it should be good.'

'My father always says that cooking is like literature. It has no limits except the imagination. He's convinced that food should satisfy as many senses as possible. Taste, smell, sight.'

Jordan cut a small piece of the pigeon, lifted it to his mouth and started chewing it slowly. An ecstatic expression spread across his face. 'Fantastic. I have to say, Martini's deserves its reputation.'

Maureen laughed.

'You did it!' said Jordan.

'What?'

279

'You laughed. That's the first time I've seen you laugh. You should spend more time here.'

'Or more time with you.'

Maureen had invited him to dinner at her father's restaurant, an elegant two-storey period building on 46th Street, between Eighth and Ninth Avenues, not far from the lights of Times Square and the Broadway theatres. It was only when she had said that she was the daughter of one of the best-known restaurateurs in New York that the penny had finally dropped, and Jordan had accepted the invitation gladly.

On the face of it, they were celebrating the happy ending of an investigation in which neither of them had officially participated and in which neither of them had really wanted to participate. In fact, the real reason for being here together was the formless but solid thing that had connected them from the start, a thing to which neither of them could give a name.

Maureen continued watching Jordan as he ate. For the first time, she noticed that he had beautiful hands. There was something in him that reminded her of Connor, even though the two men were so different, both in personality and physical appearance.

Connor was creativity, a magician casting the spell of music. Jordan was strength and silence. Connor had beautiful long hands that quivered like the strings of a violin. Jordan had masculine hands which, it seemed to her, would never have held a gun if there wasn't a need.

She wondered if, at another time or in another place, something might have developed between her and Jordan. But it was a pointless question, and any answer would be equally pointless. She continued looking at him every now and again, enjoying the pleasant sense of relaxation his presence gave her.

Jordan's calm voice surprised her as she was thinking this. 'Have I passed the test?'

Maureen could have kicked herself. She should have known that her excessive attention would not escape Jordan.

She smiled apologetically. 'I'm sorry. There is no test. If there were, you'd have passed it long ago.'

At that moment, fortunately for him, Jordan felt his cellphone vibrate in his pants pocket. He had put it on vibrate so as not to disturb the other customers, but in agreement with Maureen, he hadn't switched it off. Since the arrest of Julius Wong, they had been kept out of things, for obvious reasons. It would have been difficult to explain Jordan's role, let alone Maureen's, now that the media were fully involved. They were forced to follow the story from a distance, unable to participate in the interrogations or keep up to date with new developments. They had to rely on whatever came from Burroni or Christopher.

Maybe it was one of them calling now.

Jordan saw there was no number on the display screen. He pressed the key, ignoring a few heads that had turned towards their table with an air of disapproval.

'Hello?'

'Jordan, it's James.'

Jordan looked across at Maureen and nodded. 'What's up?'

'It's him, Jordan. They did the DNA test – a perfect match. Plus, he hasn't been able to provide a scrap of an alibi for any of the days when the murders were committed. And that includes yesterday. He says he was at home all evening. I don't think there's any doubt it's him, though we can't get a word out of him.'

Jordan mutely absorbed this information.

'Jordan,' Burroni continued, 'I don't know what you did to get us where we are now. And I haven't a clue how the Italian woman fits in. There are a whole lot of things I just don't understand.'

Jordan could hardly blame him. In agreement with Christopher, he had decided to keep Burroni in the dark about what Maureen had brought to the investigation. And especially about the way she had found out what she knew.

'If it's any consolation, I'm in the same position as you are.'

'There's something else I wanted to say, Jordan. I really liked working with you. And I'm not just saying that because of my personal thing and the way it got sorted out. I'm saying it because it's true. You're a great cop, and I think it's a scandal what happened to you.'

'It's all right, James. Don't worry. Keep me informed, and say hello to your son for me.'

Jordan hung up and turned to Maureen. 'It's him. The DNA test nailed him. The game's over for Julius Wong.'

They were both silent for a moment. Then Jordan said what they were both thinking. 'You know it isn't over for *us*, though, don't you?'

'Yes, I do,' Maureen replied in a low voice.

'You saw something that led us to Julius Wong. I haven't the faintest idea how it's even possible, but you and I both know it's true. Which means the murder you say you saw when those people were wearing *Peanuts* masks must be true, too. Do you think Wong was the person you saw with a knife in his hand?'

'I don't know, Jordan. I only saw him for a moment, with his back to me. Now that I've seen him in person, I think it's possible. The build is similar.'

Maureen made a sign to the waiter who was approaching to clear the table. He understood, turned around and walked back the way he had come, leaving them alone.

'We need to find out what happened in that room,' Jordan went on, 'even though we don't know where, when or why. It could provide the motive for the murders, but at the same time we can't talk to anyone because they all, Burroni included, would laugh in our faces or call in the nearest psychiatric unit.'

Maureen felt a sense of panic. 'I don't know if I can do it again, Jordan.'

He reached out a hand and placed it on hers. Maureen found it incredible how such a small gesture could be so reassuring.

'Yes, you can. You're a strong woman and you're not alone now. And above all, you're not crazy. I know that, and I believe you. Sooner or later all this will be over.'

Maureen did not have time to reply, because at that moment a slim man in a beautifully tailored dark suit approached the table and addressed Jordan.

'Sir, if this delightful creature you have in front of you is telling you you're very handsome, don't believe her. She says the same thing to every man she meets.'

Jordan was puzzled, but then he saw a smile appear on Maureen's mouth. 'Jordan, this is Professor Roscoe, the surgeon who operated on me. It's thanks to him that I can see now. William, this is Jordan Marsalis, a very dear friend.'

Roscoe held out his hand to Jordan and shook it with a firm grip, the grip of a sincere, self-confident man.

'Sorry if I disturbed you, but the fact is, we doctors are a bit like prima donnas. We like to savour our successes. It may not always be appropriate, but we're only human.'

Roscoe turned his attention to Maureen. 'How are your eyes, Miss Martini?'

'They're fine. I still don't know how to thank you.'

The surgeon did not notice how false Maureen's enthusiasm was, nor did he see the shadow that passed over her face as she uttered those words. Jordan wondered how Roscoe would have reacted, had he been told about the side-effects of the operation.

'My dear, I think your operation was one of the best things I've ever done in my life. Apart from the professional satisfaction it gave me, it's also flung wide for me the doors of this Holy of Holies of New York cuisine. I've discovered that your father has opened an almost unlimited line of credit for me here, which I'm not embarrassed to take advantage of . . .' he gave a disarming smile '. . . though I'm limiting myself to alternate days.'

Jordan pointed to the empty chair next to his. 'We've nearly finished, but if you'd like to join us . . .'

William Roscoe indicated with a glance a table behind him where two elegant, slightly stiff-looking men were sitting. 'Those two barons of medical research at the table over there would never forgive me. It's incredible how lacking in a sense of humour some scientists are.'

He moved away from the table with a conspiratorial air. Maybe he had misconstrued the meaning of their presence here together, but neither Jordan nor Maureen saw fit to enlighten him.

'I'll leave you to it,' he called pleasantly. 'Have a good evening.'

He turned, and walked with an elegant gait back to the table where his colleagues were waiting for him, their faces buried in big leather-bound menus.

Jordan and Maureen did not have time to talk about Professor Roscoe, because the cellphone Jordan had put down on the table started vibrating again.

This time the number appeared on the display and Jordan recognized it immediately. It was the landline in his apartment, and he knew who was at the other end. For a moment, he was tempted to reject the call. He looked around, ill at ease.

Maureen understood his embarrassment and pointed to the phone. 'Answer it, it might be important.'

You don't know how important. And you don't know how afraid I am that it might be.

He took the call and immediately heard the voice he desired and feared.

'Jordan, it's Lysa.'

He had not forgotten the look on her face when she had seen him embracing Maureen the previous night. He couldn't forget it, because he hadn't forgotten what he himself had felt on seeing her. He kept his reply curt, not because he didn't have the words, but because he was afraid to utter them.

'Go on.'

'I need to talk to you. About something important.'

'OK. I'll call you tomorrow morn—'

'No, Jordan. Maybe I didn't make myself clear. It's very important and very urgent. I need to talk to you now. I won't have the courage tomorrow.'

Jordan looked at Maureen. She understood and nodded her head.

He glanced at his watch, mentally calculating the time it would take him to get to 16th Street on his bike.

'OK. I'll be there in twenty minutes.'

'Problem?' Maureen asked.

'Not at all. A personal matter, nothing to do with the case.'

'Then go. Don't worry about me. I'm at home here. I'll take advantage of my father being away to boss everyone around.'

Jordan stood up. He was tall and strong, but right now Maureen thought he looked like a lost little boy.

'We'll talk tomorrow. Maybe we can meet and work out a strategy.'

'All right. Now go – three of your twenty minutes have already gone.'

As she watched him walking to the cloakroom to pick up his leather jacket and helmet, Maureen told herself that when a man has that expression on his face, it's almost always because of an affair of the heart. So it wasn't hard to believe that it was a matter that had nothing to do with the case.

Neither she nor Jordan knew just how wrong this last supposition was.

CHAPTER 38

Jordan stopped the Ducati in front of the building, switched off the engine and propped the bike on the kickstand. He removed his helmet and waited there for a moment, looking at the glass in the main door, as if he could somehow read his future by magic on the shiny surface. He did not have his key with him and besides, even if he had had it, he wouldn't have wanted to go straight up and open the door as if nothing between him and Lysa had changed.

He got off the bike and approached the door, with his helmet hanging from his hand.

It was here, not so long ago, and pretty much at this hour, that he had used it as a weapon to defend himself from the attack of Lord and his friends. After which, he had gone up to the apartment with a black eye and blood dripping from his shirt. And found Lysa, half naked in the bathroom, and her ironic reaction to his surprise at finding her there.

Do you always have a nose bleed when you're embarrassed?

He remembered her words, her face, her eyes, and what was beneath the robe when she had opened it, and he would have preferred none of this to have happened.

But it had.

Jordan was a man who had seen death, who had killed. And

287

yet now, he felt defenceless in the face of all the things he had not understood about Lysa, and especially all the things he had not understood or accepted about himself.

He made up his mind and pressed the button. Maybe she had seen him from the window, because the answer came almost instantaneously.

'I'm on my way down.'

In spite of himself, Jordan felt relieved. He heard the click of the lock and soon afterwards Lysa appeared, the way he had always seen her.

Beautiful and sensual.

'Hi,' she said simply.

'Hi,' he replied.

Jordan saw that Lysa was avoiding meeting his eyes. She looked tired, as if she had been thinking too much and sleeping too little.

'Have you already eaten?' she asked.

'Yes, I was having dinner when you called.'

Having dinner with her? Lysa would have liked to ask, but she held back.

'Sorry I disturbed you,' was all she said.

'It's OK. We'd already finished.'

Lysa nodded towards the lighted windows of the diner across the street. 'How about a coffee?'

Jordan was pleased with the suggestion. In the apartment they would have felt alone – among people they could have the illusion that they were together. 'A coffee would be great.'

They crossed side by side, in the semi-darkness, Jordan with the weight of the helmet in his hand and Lysa with the weight of what she was carrying inside, whatever it was.

Then everything happened quickly.

There was the roar of a motorbike and a blue and white

Honda raced around the corner of the building, carrying two people wearing full-face helmets.

The driver braked sharply, and the passenger lifted an arm in their direction.

As the first shot rang out, Jordan grabbed Lysa and pushed her to the ground, then lay down on top of her to cover her with his body.

There were two more shots in rapid succession.

Jordan felt something whistling over his head, and brick dust falling on them from where the bullets had hit a wall.

The Honda accelerated violently, its tyres screeching on the asphalt as the bike slithered round in a U-turn that caused a couple of cars coming in the other direction to slam on their brakes.

Jordan lifted his head. There was an eerie silence after the noise of the gunshots. His shirt felt damp and sticky on the right side of his chest. He rolled onto his side to let Lysa breathe.

'Are you all right?'

Lysa raised her head off the ground as best she could, trying to see a particular point on her body. Jordan followed the direction of her gaze and saw a red stain spreading on the left side of her chest.

'Jordan, I . . .'

In a moment he was kneeling beside her, trying to reassure her as best he could. 'Be quiet, don't speak. Everything's all right.'

Jordan opened her blouse and saw that the bullet had struck the lower part of her shoulder, just above the heart. He moved his face closer to hers.

'Lysa, can you hear me? It's not serious, you can make it. Hold on. An ambulance will be here soon.'

Lysa couldn't speak but blinked to show that she had understood.

Just then, Annette came running out of the diner with a table napkin in her hand. He grabbed the napkin from her, rolled it into a ball and pressed it to Lysa's wound. Lysa grimaced with pain.

'Annette, come here, just keep doing what I'm doing. We have to stop the bleeding.'

Jordan stood up, took the cellphone from his pocket and put it in the pocket of her green apron. 'Call 911 and tell them what happened. I'll call you as soon as I can.'

Jordan picked up his helmet, put it on without fastening it, and ran to the Ducati. He kick-started the engine, put it in gear, and set off at top speed, the rear wheel skidding. He shot across the intersection like a missile, narrowly avoiding a green minibus with the logo of a catering company, whose driver was forced to swerve sharply towards the sidewalk.

Jordan then joined the flow of traffic, trying to think as he continued to accelerate.

It was fairly unlikely that the two men on the Honda had taken any of the crosstown streets heading east, which would have meant endless intersections and traffic-lights. Going through a red light or riding down those streets at high speed would bring a police car on your trail before long.

It was more likely that they had continued southwards along Eleventh Avenue, where the traffic flow was easier and the speed-limit a lot more lenient. The two men had a significant head start on him, but Jordan could not let that deter him.

He hit the avenue from 14th Street, where only the previous evening he had put an end to a series of deaths with the arrest of Julius Wong.

The Ducati was running at 95 mph, weaving between the cars with the agility of a bullfighter's cape. Jordan was filled with anxiety and anger. The sight of the red stain spreading over Lysa's blouse had shaken him. He didn't know who the attackers were, but it was quite clear that they'd been gunning for him and had hit Lysa by mistake.

There were works in progress near Pier 40, signalled by warning signs and a row of yellow plastic road humps, causing a bottleneck to form. As Jordan approached, he saw the tail-light of a motorbike moving in and out of the lines of cars.

In all probability, the driver of the bike, after keeping in the left lane, had been forced by cars to join the right-hand lane. If Jordan had taken the same route, he would have been slowed down in the same way.

In an instant he took a decision.

He braked with no warning, earning curses from the motorists behind him, then swerved resolutely to the right and suddenly accelerated until he got the bike up onto the sidewalk, moving his body in such a way as to avoid too much skidding.

The anger of the engine echoing Jordan's own rage, he launched himself at top speed along the walkway beside the river, praying that the rear tyre would not be damaged from the impact as it had hit the sidewalk.

Thanks to his greater speed, he soon caught up with the bike, which had now moved clear of the bottleneck. He hadn't been 100 per cent sure it was them, but when he saw the blue and white of the Honda in the yellowish light of the streetlamps, he could not help letting out a cry of elation.

'Got you, you bastards!'

He accelerated even more.

An evening jogger running towards him jumped up on the parapet to avoid him, his eyes wide in fright.

Jordan wasn't afraid. The adrenaline of the chase was working on him like a drug. All he wanted was to make those two men pay for Lysa's bloodstained blouse.

The driver of the Honda became aware out of the corner of his eye of the scarlet flash of the Ducati racing along the sidewalk to his right, turned and saw Jordan, and put on a burst of speed.

Now the two bikes were racing each other.

Jordan saw the passenger raise his right arm in his direction and this time he clearly made out the gun. With perfect timing, he swerved to the left at the exact moment the man squeezed the trigger. He saw the flash but the sound of the shot was covered by the engine noise.

Taking advantage of a driveway, Jordan managed to get back down on the asphalt and follow the Honda, keeping to the left, making it hard for the man sitting on the passenger seat, who had the gun in his right hand, to take aim.

Despite this, Jordan was forced again to swerve violently when the man moved the gun over to his left hand and fired two shots towards him almost blindly.

Jordan had not been able to see what kind of gun was being used, so he didn't know how many bullets the man had left. There had been three shots outside the diner, and now another three. If it was an average automatic, it would have nine or ten bullets, which meant he must have at least three left.

In the meantime, the two bikes were still going at a mad speed, almost side by side, swaying between the cars like crazy balls in a pinball machine.

The river had disappeared from view and now they were travelling past the Financial District, with the Merrill Lynch and American Express buildings on the right and the lights of Ground Zero on the left.

Jordan saw a patrol car coming in the opposite direction with its lights flashing, do a rapid U-turn at Albany Street and set off in pursuit of them. He wasn't surprised. Two motorbikes shooting along the avenue, with the passenger on one continuing to fire wildly at the driver of the other, was more than enough to alert the police.

Jordan did not care. He kept going, his eyes fixed on the bike ahead of him. Only the Honda bike was distinct: everything else was a chaos of light and colour and noise.

The driver of that bike, too, must have noticed that they now had a police escort, because at the end of the long avenue, he headed straight for Battery Park, where the paths were narrow. He was an excellent driver, and no doubt trusted to his skill to shake off his pursuers. The police car would not be able to manoeuvre well in the park, and the driver probably thought he'd be able to give Jordan the slip, too.

They skirted Castle Clinton, the driver of the Honda performing a perfectly controlled skid.

Jordan told himself that he had to find a way to stop the other bike. He himself was a good biker, but this other guy was in a different league. If he fell, or if the other man put on enough speed to get out of the park at the other end, he would never catch up with them again.

As he was thinking this, the Honda swerved to the right and headed towards the ferry terminal for Ellis Island, narrowly avoiding the souvenir stands, which were closed at this hour.

Jordan saw the man aim the front of his bike in the direction of the water and accelerate violently. He realized immediately what the guy was planning to do. It was a reckless manoeuvre. The park was separated from the sea by a walkway that led to the Staten Island ferry terminal. The driver of the Honda was planning to jump the flight of steps leading down to the walkway.

It was an extremely difficult feat to pull off, because it had to be done diagonally, otherwise, given the narrowness of the walkway, you would hit the parapet on the other side. If the guy succeeded, Jordan would never be able to catch up with him, because he himself didn't feel at all confident of being able to perform the same manoeuvre.

He saw the Honda rise on its rear wheel, the driver clearly trying to avoid the weight of the engine tipping the bike forward during the jump. A moment later, its engine screaming, the bike was in the air.

It was the passenger who jeopardized the manoeuvre. Maybe out of fear, maybe out of inexperience, he did not move in time with the driver, and his weight made the bike skid as it hit the ground. The passenger was flung from the saddle and fell on his back on the thick metal bar that ran along the top of the parapet. Jordan saw his body bend at an unnatural angle, before his legs went up and he fell straight down into the sea with a perfect overturn. In the meantime, the driver, trapped beneath the Honda, was crushed by its weight against the concrete base of the parapet.

Jordan had braked in time, stopping his bike a few inches from the top of the steps. He opened the kickstand, got off, and ran down the steps towards the point of impact.

By the dim light of the streetlamps he saw the man lying under the crumpled bike, and from the position of the head in relation to the body realized he would never again shoot anybody. Jordan did not even need to check the pulse on his throat to know that the man was dead.

He removed his helmet, put it down on the ground and bent over the man.

At that moment, he heard a noise of running steps behind him, and a torch was aimed at his back, immediately followed by a voice he knew.

'Hey, you, get up with your hands behind your head – now! Then turn around slowly, lie down on the ground and stay there.'

Jordan imagined the scene. One of the two cops aiming the beam of light at him and the other near him, with his gun levelled, ready to shoot at the slightest sign of a reaction.

He stood up, holding his hands behind his neck. It was the first time he had been on the receiving end of this procedure.

'I'm not armed.'

'Do as I say, asshole,' the voice he knew said. 'We've got you covered. One false move and I shoot.'

Jordan turned and allowed the torch to play over his face. He addressed the voice hidden in the darkness, just behind the beam of light.

'If anyone had to arrest me, I'm glad it's you, Rodriguez.'

The light lingered a moment longer on Jordan's face, then the beam descended to take in the bike against the parapet and what could be seen of the body wedged under it.

'Shit. Lieutenant Marsalis.'

I'm not a lieutenant any more, Rodriguez . . .

This time, Jordan didn't bother to say it.

'Can I put my hands down?'

The two cops put their guns away and came towards him.

'Of course. But what happened? They reported two bikes having a kind of race along—'

'Rodriguez,' Jordan cut in, 'please, lend me your cellphone. Just let me make a quick call, and then I'll tell you everything you want to know.'

When they came level with him, Rodriguez handed him the phone. Jordan dialled the number as if the keys were red hot. The cellphone he had slipped into Annette's pocket started ringing and she picked up immediately.

'Jordan here. Where are you?'

'At Saint Vincent's Hospital, on Seventh Avenue and Twelfth.'

'Yes, I know it. How is she?'

'The ambulance arrived immediately. She's still in the OR.'

'What are the doctors saying?'

'Nothing, so far.'

Jordan was glad that the poor lighting concealed the fact that his eyes had suddenly become watery.

'I'm a bit tied up right now. I'll be there as soon as I can.'

'Don't worry. There isn't much more you could do than I'm doing.'

'If there's any news, call this number.'

'OK.'

'Thanks, Annette. I'll find a way to pay you back.'

'That's what I'm doing right now, Jordan. And I'm sorry it has to be like this.'

Jordan hung up and handed the phone back to Rodriguez. The other police officer – Rodriguez introduced him as Officer Bozman – had knelt by the bike, his torch trained on two sightless eyes in a dark-skinned face visible below the lifted visor of the helmet.

'He's gone,' he said, standing up again.

'You need to call the River Police,' Jordan told him. 'There was another guy who was thrown off the bike and ended up in the water. From the way he hit the rail, I'd guess he isn't in much better shape than this one.'

Rodriguez walked off to ask for the backup he needed and Bozman leaned over the parapet and shone his torch down at the dark waters lapping against the pier.

Jordan crouched again by the body of the man under the bike. Out of habit, and seizing the opportunity since nobody was paying any attention to him, he quickly searched him. There was nothing in the pockets. He unzipped the leather jacket and in the inside pocket found a white envelope, with no address or anything else written on it.

Without thinking, he slipped it into the breast pocket of his shirt.

He then unfastened the dead man's helmet, slipped it off, and wasn't especially surprised to discover Lord's wide-open eyes staring up at the dark sky.

Son of a bitch.

He had promised it and he had done it.

And because of his partner's bad aim, Lysa had taken the bullet meant for Jordan.

As they waited for the requested backup, Jordan told Rodriguez and his partner what had happened. The frogmen arrived, and the body of the passenger was soon fished out of the sea. They had found him directly under the parapet, anchored to the bottom by the weight of his helmet, which had filled with water. His back was broken, and with the water dripping off him he looked like a rag doll a child had dropped in the sea. As for Lord, Jordan's last image of him was his face disappearing under the zipper of a body bag as they put him in the ambulance. His eyes were staring into nothingness, and not even one officer had bothered to close them. Jordan hoped none of them ever did, so that the bastard could continue to look at the lid of his coffin for all eternity.

CHAPTER 39

Sitting on a padded chair in a hospital room, Jordan waited.

When he had stopped the Ducati outside the entrance to Emergency, he had found himself under a white, blue and gold sign announcing that this was the St Vincent Catholic Medical Center.

Jordan had instinctively grimaced.

In the same place, the powerlessness of men and the power of God.

Jordan had thought about Cesar Wong and Christopher Marsalis, two men who, despite all their wealth and influence, had not been able to prevent their sons killing or being killed.

As for the power of God . . .

Jordan had parked his bike on the street, even though he was almost sure he wouldn't find it when he got back. The glass entrance door had opened automatically in front of him and he moved through, taking off his helmet.

A Chinese nun had passed him, as white as the walls. Jordan watched her hurry by as he tried to orientate himself, and it was only when the immaculate figure was out of sight that he had seen Annette sitting on a chair over to his right, still dressed in her waitress uniform.

She rose and came to him. He didn't need to speak, as she

could read the question in his eyes, and told him, 'Still nothing.'

Jordan forced himself to recall the cliché philosophy that no news is good news. 'Thanks, Annette. You can go if you want. I'm here now.'

She pointed towards Reception, where a woman in a blue suit was sitting behind the desk next to a computer. 'There are some formalities to get through. They asked me a lot of questions I couldn't answer.'

'Don't worry, I'll deal with it.' Jordan lowered his voice and his eyes. 'Did they tell you she's a man?'

His words had no effect on Annette, who had long ceased to be surprised by anything. 'No, they didn't tell me. But if she is, all I can say is that, for a man, she's the most beautiful woman I've ever seen.' Then she had put a hand in the pocket of her apron and gave him back his cellphone. 'Did you get them? The guys who shot her, I mean.'

'Yes. And I can tell you, they'll never shoot anyone again.'

'Amen to that.' Annette glanced at her watch. 'Well, I think it's time I got out of here.'

Jordan took out some money. 'At least let me give you the cab fare.'

'Jordan, I wouldn't take your money if I had to walk from here to Brooklyn. Don't worry, I'll catch the subway.'

She started towards the door, but then turned with a wicked grin: the first time Jordan had ever seen an expression like that on her face.

'What I wouldn't mind, though – if you ever have a moment – is for you to take me for a ride on that lovely bike of yours.'

Jordan replied with a surprised smile.

'You men,' Annette said, shaking her head ironically. 'Let me tell you something. At my age I'm out of the running, that's why I can say it. And I suspect you're so much above all that, you don't even know it . . .'

'What?'

'You're one of the handsomest men I've ever met. Good luck to you and that poor girl.'

And with that, she waved goodbye and left. Jordan stood there watching her until the glass door had closed behind her.

Then he went to Reception. The woman at the desk was a kindly lady identified by the badge on her dark jacket as Mrs Franzisca Jarid. He gave her the details Annette had not been able to provide, and noted that Mrs Jarid had not given any sign of caring too much about the discrepancy between the physical appearance and true gender of Alexander Guerrero known as Lysa.

Jordan didn't know if Lysa had private insurance or not. He promised to go to her apartment the next day to look for it, and for the moment showed his own credit card.

Franzisca Jarid looked at the card for a moment, then looked him in the face and indicated the row of chairs to her left, deserted at that hour. She had asked him to sit there and wait, assuring him that he would be informed as soon as there was any news.

And here he was, still waiting.

Right now, the case seemed as remote as the furthest star from the earth. All Jordan could think about was Lysa's bewildered eyes as she lay on the asphalt, and the surprise and fear in them when she had sought his.

He realized that the two of them had never talked. The only time they had done so, they had told each other nothing but tame fragments of themselves: he had been too involved in the case and she too unreachable, too secretive. They had never discussed a book, never commented on a play on the way out of a theatre, never listened to music, apart from the Connor Slave songs endlessly played by their downstairs neighbour.

I want you much more than I ever wanted that car . . .

The words he had said to her that day at the restaurant on the river had made her run away. It was only now that Jordan understood: she hadn't run away from *him*, but from his fear of her.

There was a noise in the corridor to his right, and his heart skipped a beat. But it was only two young nurses who came through the doors, walked past him and crossed the lobby, chattering away about personal things. They disappeared, leaving Jordan to his wait. He would never know what the taller of the two was going to do with Robert that weekend, or what was written on the birthday card he had sent her.

By an association of ideas, these words reminded him of something.

He passed a hand over his chest and felt in the pocket of his shirt for the envelope he had taken, without even knowing why, from Lord's jacket. He took it out and examined it. It was a simple white envelope without anything written on it, and at first he thought it was empty.

He opened it and found inside a little slip of coloured paper. He was surprised to see that it was a cheque for twenty-five thousand dollars, issued by the Chase Manhattan Bank – or rather, half a cheque, as somebody had cut it in half, diagonally. Part of the name was missing, but there was enough of it for Jordan to know the identity of the person it was made out to.

. . . ay Lonard

DeRay Lonard, better known as Lord, who at that moment was being slid into a freezer at the morgue.

Jordan sat there on his chair, with his elbows on his knees, looking at that piece of coloured paper, without understanding how and why.

Two green plastic shoes appeared on the floor in front of him, the kind surgeons wear in the operating room.

'Excuse me, are you Jordan Marsalis?'

Jordan looked up and saw a doctor still wearing his white coat and cap from the OR. He was quite young, and slightly built, but his dark eyes conveyed efficiency and calm.

Jordan stood up. 'Yes.'

'My name's Melvin Leko and I'm the surgeon who just finished operating on your friend.'

'How is she?'

'The bullet went in and out without damaging any vital organs. She's lost a lot of blood and it'll take a day before we can make a real prognosis, but the patient is in excellent health and I think I can say with reasonable certainty that she'll pull through.'

Jordan heaved a sigh of relief. 'Can I see her?' he said, trying not to be too obvious in his impatience.

'For the moment it's better if you don't. She's in post-op and only just coming around from the anaesthetic. I think we should keep her sedated in intensive care until tomorrow morning. Trust me, there's nothing you can do here right now. You might as well go home. She's getting the best of care.'

'Thanks,' Jordan said, holding out his hand.

'It's my job,' Dr Leko said, shaking it.

The doctor walked away and Jordan picked up his helmet

from the chair and left the hospital – to discover the second miracle of the night: his bike was still there. He took it as a good omen.

As he put on his helmet, he wondered how the medical staff would solve the problem of whether Lysa should be admitted to a women's ward or a men's.

CHAPTER 40

Maureen woke up feeling even more tired than when she had gone to bed. Although she had taken a sleeping pill, she'd had a restless night, dozing fitfully and having bad dreams, not even sure that the images welling up from her sub-conscious were completely hers.

The digital clock on the grey marble surface of the night-table indicated that it was almost noon.

Throwing off the crumpled sheet, she got out of bed, put on her dark glasses and opened the curtains, letting in the sunlight. She looked down at Park Avenue, and found herself envying all those people driving cars, marching along the sidewalks, moving through the city, all of them surrounded exclusively by the *here and now*, not plagued by messages from some other unknown dimension.

After discovering that her visions related to the life of Gerald Marsalis, she had felt an obligation to go and see the work of Jerry Ko in a retrospective organized by a gallery in Soho. She had walked through the rooms alone, calmly, with no sense that she had seen any of the paintings before. She had expected a new 'episode' at any moment, but nothing had happened. And yet gradually, a sense of unease had overcome her: inside and behind those canvases, she had seen darkness and destruction, the pain of a mind devoured by nightmares.

Jerry Ko, like Connor Slave, was an artist who had died young, probably at the height of his creativity. But it seemed to Maureen that Gerald had already died, long before his physical death.

She moved away from the window and the curtains fell back, blocking out the world outside. As she pulled on her tracksuit pants, she heard the phone ring faintly somewhere in the apartment. In order not to disturb her rest, her mother had removed the ringing mechanism from the phone in the room in which she slept. After a moment, the door opened noiselessly and Estrella put her head in.

'Ah, miss, you're awake. Pick up the telephone, there's a call for you from Italy.'

Maureen approached the night-table and picked up the receiver, wondering who it could be. 'Yes?'

She was surprised to hear the reassuring voice of Franco Roberto, her friend and lawyer.

'How's the most beautiful Chief Inspector in the Italian police?'

'Hi, Franco, don't tell me you're still working at this late hour.'

'Of course I'm still working. I will probably be at it most of the night, preparing for an important hearing tomorrow. A man has to earn a crust, you know.'

'If I remember your fees, that's quite some crust.'

'Listen, I've been in touch with your father. I understand the operation was completely successful.'

You have no idea how successful . . .

'Anyway, I wanted to give you some more good news. The proceedings over what happened between you and Avenir Gallani will be a mere formality. On the basis of your testimony, half the police in Rome got down to work. They did a thorough search of Manziana Forest and found a bullet lodged in a tree which, according to Ballistics, is the same as those taken from Connor's body. It confirms your version of events a hundred per cent.'

Maureen was silent for a moment.

'What's the matter? Aren't you happy?'

'Of course. It's very good news.'

Or at least, it should have been. Not so long ago, in that situation, she would have got on the first plane that would take her to Connor, so that she could hug him and share that joy with him. But how could she be happy now, if this result had been obtained at the price of his death?

Franco seemed to guess what she was thinking, because his tone of voice became as sensitive and comforting as only he knew how.

'Anyway, everyone here is longing to see you. I'm not so dumb as to think that everything can be the way it was before, or to try and make you believe that. But if you'll allow me a rather hackneyed remark, trust in time and the people who love you. It won't change anything, but it helps to bear it. You know I'm always here for you.'

'I know, Franco, and I'm really grateful. Good luck with your hearing.'

Maureen put the telephone down. She knew how much truth there was in Franco's words.

She was young.

Some people said she was beautiful.

Some even said she was beautiful and intelligent.

Yet only once had the presence of another person made her feel the most beautiful, intelligent and desired woman in the world.

And now he was gone and she was alone.

Maureen decided that a cup of coffee couldn't make the day any more bitter than it already was. Just a bit hotter. Estrella would have been happy to bring her one if she had asked her, but she preferred to leave the room and go and make one for herself.

As she walked barefoot along the corridor towards the kitchen, she heard voices from the other side of the large apartment. One was definitely her mother's. She found that strange, because at this hour Mary Ann Levallier was usually in her office, which occupied half a floor in Trump Tower.

She came out into the entrance hall and saw her mother in the company of two men she appeared to be showing out.

One was a tall muscular man with crew-cut hair, his neck barely contained within the collar of his shirt, which he wore open, without a tie. He was wearing a black suit and Maureen could not see the colour of his eyes because they were hidden behind a pair of dark glasses.

The other man was about sixty, shorter and much thinner, looking spruce in a dark, impeccably tailored double-breasted suit. His slicked-back hair was streaked with white, and his eyes were slightly narrow, hinting at an Oriental ancestry. The man's glossy skin reminded Maureen strangely of a waxwork.

His voice was curiously deep, in marked contrast with his slender build.

'Miss Levallier, I don't know how to thank you for agreeing to receive me in your home rather than in your office. For reasons of my own, I thought it best to talk to you somewhere less . . . how shall I put it? . . . official.'

'That's quite all right. I shall get down to the case immediately.'

She noticed Maureen and took a step towards her.

'Oh, Maureen, there you are. Mr Wong, this is my daughter Maureen.'

The man smiled, and as he did so his eyes narrowed. There was something frozen about that smile, despite the warmth he tried to put in his voice.

'You're a lucky woman and your daughter is a lucky woman for the same reason.'

He held out his hand. As she shook it, Maureen was surprised to find that his skin was not scaly, like a snake's.

'Pleased to meet you. My name is Cesar Wong and this is Mr Hocto. He's a man of few words, but then I don't employ him for his oratory. Your mother agreed to see me and help me with a matter very close to my heart.'

Maureen threw a rapid glance at Mary Ann and saw her stiffen. She looked back at Cesar Wong's waxen face and gave him her best smile. 'I'm sure you have everything my mother will need to help you resolve your problem.'

Cesar Wong pretended not to notice Mary Ann's unconscious gesture of annoyance. He made a little bow with his head.

'And I'm sure you're right. I bid you good day, Miss Levallier. And good luck to you, Maureen. I assume that, like everyone, you will need it.'

During all that time, Hocto had been a silent presence behind them. When he realized that the conversation was over, he moved to open the door for Cesar Wong. Maureen was convinced that he would just as casually have broken the necks of the two women in front of him, if his employer had asked him to. The two men went out. When they closed the door behind them, it seemed to Maureen that all at once the temperature in the room had gone up a few degrees.

Mary Ann Levallier took her by the arm and drew her to the kitchen. Anger flashing in her eyes, she spoke in a low voice, as if afraid the two men could still hear her.

'Are you crazy?'

'Why? I don't think I said anything that isn't true. He's a rich man, his son killed three people and you're a lawyer.'

Mary Ann had regained all her self-control, that cool-headedness that had made her one of the best criminal lawyers in New York State.

'You know, Maureen, there's one major difference between the two of us.'

'Only one?'

Mary Ann carried on as if she had not heard. 'As you so rightly said, I'm a lawyer. As far as I'm concerned, a person is innocent until proved guilty. You're a police officer, so of course you think exactly the opposite.'

Maureen could almost have laughed. Her mother, hired to defend the man she had helped to get arrested! For a moment she felt like telling her everything, to see how Mary Ann Levallier's logical, pragmatic brain would react if she told her of her part in the case, especially the way she had become involved in the first place.

She limited herself to smiling and shaking her head.

'Do you think this is a laughing matter?'

'Laughing, no. Smiling, definitely. Though even if you lived a hundred years, you'd never believe the reason.'

'Is that all you can say?'

'No. Except that I was going to make myself a coffee. But now I'll think I'll go out for it.'

Maureen turned her back on her mother, leaving her standing in the middle of the room, beautiful, elegant and distant, to watch her as she walked away along the corridor.

310

As she opened the door to her bedroom, she realized 'it' was about to happen again. Another episode was on its way.

By now, she had learned to recognize that long shudder down her spine. Before the dizzy spell that always occurred before one of her episodes, she managed to get to the bed.

She had just sat down on the edge of the mattress, forcing herself not to scream, when . . .

. . . I'm sitting by a large window at the table of what seems to be a college cafeteria, and around me are young men and women – and one of the girls is sitting on the other side of the room looking at me, and with a slight nod of her head signals to me to follow her when she gets up from the table and goes towards the exit and I . . .

. . . I'm in another place and I can feel the pressure on my cheeks of the hard edges of a plastic mask, and through the eyeholes I see people with their hands in the air, looking at me terrified. They're crying out words but I can't hear them, and in my hand there's the weight of a gun and I wave it towards these people, who lie down on the floor and . . .

. . . a figure dressed in dark clothes and a Pig Pen mask, carrying a pump-action rifle and a canvas bag, comes to me and grabs me by the shoulder, and from the vein standing out on his throat I can tell he's yelling something and . . .

. . . there's a beautiful young black woman with short hair sitting on a chair in the middle of a room, and her huge dark eyes are wide with fear and there's adhesive tape over her mouth, and her arms are tied to the chair. Behind her there's a figure dressed in dark clothes

wearing a Lucy mask who's finishing tying her up and . . .

Maureen suddenly found herself back in the present, lying on her bed, with the neck and armpits of her T-shirt soaked in sweat, and feeling that sense of bewildered exhaustion this thing always left in her body and mind. She would have liked to turn over, grab the pillow and start crying until her life was given back to her.

Instead, she reached out, picked up the telephone and dialled the number she had learned by heart.

'Jordan, it's Maureen. It happened again.'

'Has it passed? Are you all right now?' There was such genuine concern in his voice that she immediately felt less alone, less desperate.

'Yes, I'm fine.'

'Did you see something new?'

'Yes.'

'Then if you're up to it, I think we should meet.'

'Yes, I'm up to it. Where?'

'If you like, I can come over there. Or we could meet in my apartment.'

Maureen immediately thought how hard it would be to justify to her mother Jordan Marsalis's presence in her apartment.

'I'll come to you. Give me the address.'

'Fifty-four West Sixteenth Street, between Fifth and Sixth.'

'Great. Just give me time to get there.'

Maureen put the phone down, got up from the bed and walked, still slightly unsteadily, to the bathroom to take a shower.

CHAPTER 41

Maureen's call had come just after Jordan had closed the door of his apartment behind him. He put the cellphone back in his pocket and looked around. Lysa must have hired furniture to replace the pieces he had put in storage. The apartment looked more complete now, more lived-in, with colourful posters on the walls. It bore the marks of her taste, insofar as taste could be expressed with rented furniture.

A half-empty coffee cup stood abandoned on the table, a T-shirt was draped over the back of a chair, and her vanilla scent hung in the air. It was as if she would be back any minute, instead of lying in a hospital bed, attached to a monitor, with tubes in her veins.

Jordan had come up to the apartment to look for the health insurance policy, if Lysa had ever had one. This had been his home not so long ago, but now he felt like an intruder.

When he was in the police, he had made dozens of searches, but they had always been justified by the needs of an investigation. Not even for a moment had he ever felt he was violating someone's privacy, but now he did. Especially someone like Lysa, who guarded her privacy so fiercely.

He decided to start his search in the bedroom. Even here, where there were no major changes, the touch of a delicate hand could be felt. The new blue bedspread, raffia mats, also blue, on the floor, the newly cleaned lampshade of the bedside lamp: the room gave off a sense of light and peace.

Usually, when he had conducted police searches, he had been looking for things people had tried their best to hide. In this case it was quite likely that the most obvious place was also the right one.

He opened the wall closet opposite the bed and was immediately lucky.

On the highest shelf, to the left, next to a pile of T-shirts, was a thick leather document holder. He sat down on the bed and opened it.

It was full of papers and documents neatly arranged, as might be expected of a woman like Lysa. In his thoughts, Jordan realized he had instinctively used the word 'woman'.

Good luck to you and that poor girl . . .

He remembered the way Annette, as she left St Vincent's, had continued talking about her as a girl, even after learning the truth. Well, if that was what Lysa felt that she was, then it was only right for him and everyone else to think of her that way.

Jordan started to go through the documents one by one, without taking them out. Between two birthday cards, he found a slightly faded colour photograph. Despite his scruples, he slid it out and held it carefully between his fingers, as if a brusque movement could somehow hurt the people in it. A very beautiful little boy stood, smiling shyly, between an austerely dressed man and woman, who were glowering at the camera. In the background a white wooden building could be seen, probably a church.

He checked inside the document holder but there was no other photograph. The whole of Lysa's past was encapsulated in that single image, its colours already starting to fade. He recalled again what she had told him about her family, at the restaurant on the river.

When I left home, without even touching the door, I saw it closing behind me . . .

He put the photo back where he had found it and continued going through the documents. Finally, in a transparent plastic folder, he found her Social Security card and insurance policy.

As he took them out of the folder, an envelope fell onto the bedspread. It was unsealed, with the flap simply tucked inside.

Jordan took it and turned it over. It was a simple white envelope, with nothing written on it, but Jordan was scared of what he might find inside.

He lifted the flap and, holding the envelope by the edges, emptied the contents on the bed.

They consisted of four slips of paper, each divided in half by a sharp diagonal cut, which someone had put together again with adhesive tape. His hands slightly unsteady, he laid them out side by side. There were four cheques, each for twenty-five thousand dollars, issued by the Chase Manhattan Bank, similar in every way to the fragment he had found in the pocket of the late DeRay Lonard, also known as Lord.

Except that these were made out to Alexander Guerrero.

Without realizing it, Jordan got to his feet and took a step back. He stood there, staring, dazed, at those rectangles of coloured paper. Then he put his hand in his pocket, took out his cellphone, and speed-dialled Burroni.

The detective replied at the second ring.

'James, Jordan here.'

315

'Hi. I heard you put on quite a firework display last night.'

'Yes. A son of a bitch I sent to the can decided to have his revenge. Unfortunately, someone entirely innocent got caught in the crossfire.'

'I heard. I'm sorry. How is she?'

'Stable. The doctors are holding off on a prognosis for now. James, listen, the reason I'm calling you is that I need a favour.'

'Anything you like.'

'I'll shortly be sending you a fax with a photocopy of part of a cashier's cheque issued by the Chase Manhattan Bank. The name of the payee is partly missing, but it's DeRay Lonard, the guy who shot at me last night. See if you can find out who requested the issue.'

For the moment, Jordan preferred not to talk about the cheques made out to Lysa that he had found in the apartment.

'Got it. Anything else?'

'Not for the moment.'

'Then let me tell you the latest about Julius Wong. There are things coming out about him you wouldn't believe. Your nephew may have been some kind of mad genius, but this guy's a real nutjob. He's still refusing to say a word, but we've discovered a couple of things that are strange, to say the least, from the point of view of coincidence.'

'Such as?'

'On 14 September 1993, in Troy, a town near Albany, in the branch of a local bank – the Troy Savings Bank – there was a robbery carried out by four masked people, who got away with almost thirty thousand dollars. And guess what kind of masks they were wearing?'

'Plastic masks depicting characters from *Peanuts*. Linus, Lucy, Snoopy and Pig Pen, to be precise.'

316

Burroni was speechless for a moment.

'Jordan, I don't know how you do it, but your talents are wasted. But that's not all.'

'Surprise me.'

'I'll try. Among other things, we combed the area around Poughkeepsie, to a radius of about five or six miles. The owner of a bar recognized Julius Wong from the photographs he was shown. He claims that about ten days after the robbery in Troy, he overheard a heated discussion in his bar between Wong and three other people, two men and a woman, that didn't degenerate into a fight only because the bar owner chased them out with a baseball bat. And he added that one of those three people was definitely your nephew.'

'Maybe this'll lead us to the motive, which is the one thing we don't have. You've done a great job, James.'

As he was talking to Burroni, Jordan had moved to the living room, where reception was better. From the window he saw a taxi pull up at the sidewalk. Maureen got out, paid the driver, and immediately looked up at the building through dark glasses. Jordan leaned out and made a sign with his fingers to press the button for the third floor. Then he went to the entryphone to open the front door.

'James, there's something I need to do right now. Keep in touch.'

'OK, speak to you soon.'

Jordan hung up and opened the door to the landing. He could hear the noise of the elevator coming up. A few moments later, Maureen stepped out and came towards him.

Jordan stood aside to let her in. She was walking with her back slightly stooped, and even with her glasses on he could sense that her eyes were tired of seeing what they were forced to see.

317

Jordan smiled at her, encouragingly. 'Hello, Maureen. I'd like to say good afternoon, but I'm not sure it is.' He pointed to the couch. 'Sit down. Let's talk.'

He realized that Maureen wanted nothing more than to get things off her chest, things she had carried alone until now. As soon as she had sat down, she immediately started telling him about the latest episode.

She spoke with her eyes down, so that she did not see the reaction she was provoking in Jordan as he stood listening to her.

When she had finished, he sat down next to her and took her hand. 'Maureen, I just had a call from Burroni that tallies perfectly with what you've just told me. The thing you saw was a robbery my nephew, Julius Wong, Chandelle Stuart and Alex Campbell all took part in. The only thing we have to discover is the identity of the woman. If they were dressed in the same way, she must be linked to the murder you say you saw the other time. And if Julius Wong is responsible for that, we can add it to the list of his crimes.'

Maureen took off her glasses to look at him, even though he knew how much the light hurt her eyes. 'That's only going to make things worse for me.'

'How do you mean?'

'Mary Ann Levallier has just been hired by Cesar Wong as his son's defence attorney. In case you've forgotten, Mary Ann Levallier is my mother.'

Jordan smiled again, and again it was meant to be supportive. 'When my brother hears about that, it may make things difficult for him, too – although I'm sure he already knows. In any case, we'll soon find out.'

'What do you intend to do?'

Jordan stood up and held out his hand to help her up. 'My brother is at Gracie Mansion right now. And that's where we're going.'

CHAPTER 42

Jordan and Maureen got out of the cab and set off along the path that led to the front gate of Gracie Mansion. Jordan had preferred to get to Carl Schurz Park that way, rather than force Maureen to sit on the back seat of a motorbike. It would have proved dangerous if she had had one of her episodes during the ride.

For most of the journey they had both been silent, with Maureen looking out of the window, as if mesmerized by what she could see of the city through her dark glasses, and Jordan sneaking glances at her from time to time. Maybe, in the light of what was happening to her, she was thinking that there was another world somewhere, a real world, whereas everything around her was merely illusion – and nothing was true except what she saw, sometimes, through her eyes.

After a while she had said, without turning to look at him, 'There's something there, Jordan.'

'What do you mean?'

'There's something inside me – something I feel I ought to know, but can't pin down. It's as if I'm looking at someone behind a shower curtain. I know he's there, but I can't see his face.'

Maureen had removed her glasses for a moment and

immediately put them back on again, adjusting them with excessive care on her nose.

'The best thing to do is not to think about it,' Jordan said gently. 'It'll come by itself.'

'That's precisely what I'm afraid of.'

Maureen had fallen silent again and Jordan took the opportunity to call St Vincent's and ask to speak to Dr Melvin Leko. The surgeon recognized his voice immediately.

'Good afternoon, Mr Marsalis.'

'Good afternoon. How is Miss Guerrero?'

'In excellent shape, considering what happened to her. She's still quite groggy, but the prognosis is good.'

'Is there anything I can do?'

'Not for the moment, no.'

'Thank you. If it's not too much bother, please keep me informed of any developments.'

'Of course.'

Jordan had hung up just as the taxi drew into the kerb at the end of their ride.

And now they were passing the bench where Maureen had sat, the day she had gone to Gracie Mansion, trying to summon up the courage to appear in front of strangers and ask them to accept something that she herself could hardly believe.

Everything around her seemed a replay of that day: the trees, the patches of sunlight on the grass, the cries of children from the playground, the bronze statue of Peter Pan in the little square below them.

Even the security officer on duty was the same. He allowed them to pass through without hesitation.

The butler who greeted them at the door of Gracie Mansion informed them that the Mayor was busy at the moment, having a meeting with two representatives of his party.

Thanking him, the pair made their own way to the room where Ruben Dawson was sitting at the computer, as impeccable and impassive as ever, in the company of a technician.

'Ruben, we need to get on the internet . . .' Jordan left the phrase hanging and glanced at the other person present in the room, a sturdy man of about thirty who was sitting at another computer with his back to them.

'Martin,' Ruben said, 'would you mind excusing us for a moment?'

'Of course not, Mr Dawson.'

While waiting for Martin to get up and leave the room, Jordan went to the photocopier and, shielding what he was doing with his body, took from his jacket pocket the cheque he had found on Lord. He made a copy, put it in the fax machine and sent it to Burroni.

Then he turned and said to Dawson, who was still sitting in front of the computer, 'Ruben, do you think the town of Troy has a local newspaper?'

'I don't know, but we can soon find out.' After a rapid search, he leaned back in his chair and pointed to the screen. 'Here it is. The *Troy Record*.'

'Could you phone them and ask if their archives have been digitized and are accessible online? I don't think they'll refuse if the request comes from the New York Mayor's office. Please say it's very important.'

Ruben stood up and went to the phone. Before dialling he turned to them for a moment.

'Remember we're dealing with a newspaper. If there's something you're trying to keep secret, that's hardly the best way to go about it.'

Jordan was forced to admit that Christopher, in choosing Ruben Dawson as a colleague, had not misplaced his trust.

'Right now,' he said, 'I don't really care.'

Ruben dialled the number and asked to be put through to the editor. As he spoke, Maureen sat down at the desk and went on the *Troy Record* website. Jordan came up behind her and put his hands on the back of the chair.

Ruben said what he had to say and put the phone down. 'Done. The archive is partly computerized and goes back twelve years.'

He gave them the password. Maureen clicked on *Archive* and typed it in. Under the logo of the newspaper appeared an internal search engine.

She heard the voice of Jordan behind her.

'The robbery took place on 14 September 1993, so it makes sense to check the 15 September edition.'

Maureen typed in the date, and the relevant edition appeared on the screen. The item they were looking for was on the city section and took up the whole page. It was written by a journalist named Rory Cardenas.

DOLLARS AND PEANUTS
Charlie Brown Robs a Bank

A robbery took place yesterday at the East Greenbush branch of Troy Savings Bank, on the Columbia Turnpike. Three people wearing masks depicting characters from the comic strip Peanuts *entered the bank, threatened customers and staff with pistols and a pump-action rifle, and seized the bank's entire holdings, amounting to thirty thousand dollars. Linus, Lucy and Pig Pen drove away in a white Ford that was waiting outside with the engine on, driven by a person wearing a Snoopy mask. The Ford was later found abandoned about six miles south of Troy, having apparently broken down, but the robbers vanished without trace. Nobody was hurt during the robbery, but a 72-year-old woman, Mary Hallbrooks, was taken ill and was promptly admitted to Samaritan Hospital, where she is still under observation. Doctors say her condition is stable. It is the first time a branch of Troy Savings Bank has been targeted by . . .*

The article was accompanied by a photograph of the manager and images of police officers searching the premises of the bank. Maureen felt the pressure of Jordan's hands loosen on the back of the chair.

'Well, we already knew all that. But the other thing you saw is likely to have happened at about the same time as the robbery. If that's the case, the news should be in the same edition.'

And indeed, two pages further on, in the bottom right-hand corner, was the article they were looking for.

Maureen zoomed in to enlarge it. There were two photographs to accompany it. One showed an attractive, light-skinned black woman with short hair, smiling calmly. The other, a child with dark eyes and even lighter skin than his mother's. He looked bright, and gazed out at them with an amused expression.

Although the circumstances in which she had first seen the woman were very different, Maureen recognized her immediately. Without a word, she put a hand on Jordan's wrist and gave it a little squeeze.

NURSE'S SKILLS NOT ENOUGH TO SAVE HER SON'S LIFE

Thelma Ross, a professional nurse at Samaritan Hospital in Troy, yesterday fell victim to a tragic sequence of events that resulted in the death of her son, Lewis, aged five. Playing in the garden, the child was stung by a large number of hornets. The violent anaphylactic shock that followed caused a laryngeal oedema that soon completely blocked his respiratory tract. His mother, who has had extensive experience as an operating-room nurse, performed an emergency tracheotomy on young Lewis, but not even this could save his life. By the time the paramedics arrived, the child was dead. On behalf of a community to which she has given so much, we would like to express our sincerest condolences to Thelma Ross on her terrible loss.

Jordan placed a hand on Maureen's shoulder in his excitement. 'There's something not quite right here. The news as reported doesn't really correspond to what—'

He broke off. Even though Ruben had no idea what they were referring to, Maureen knew why.

'Find me the number of Samaritan Hospital in Troy,' Jordan told her.

Maureen opened *Yellow Pages*, and within a few moments the telephone numbers and address of the hospital appeared on the screen. Jordan immediately grabbed the telephone and dialled the number.

The operator replied almost at once.

'Samaritan Hospital, how can I help you?'

'Could you put me through to Human Resources?'

'One moment, please.'

After a few moments of the usual switchboard music, a resolute-sounding voice came on the line.

'Michael Stills.'

'Good afternoon, Mr Stills.My name's Jordan Marsalis and I'm calling on behalf of the Mayor of New York.'

'Of course you are. Sorry if I kept you waiting, but I had the President of the United States on the line.'

Jordan admired the man's quick reflexes and did not take it badly. He had expected a reaction like that, even if not such an ironic one.

'Mr Stills, I understand your surprise. I'd have come in person but this is a very urgent matter. Maybe your switchboard could get you the number of Gracie Mansion and you could ask for me. I'm the Mayor's brother.'

'That won't be necessary. You've managed to convince me. Carry on.'

'I'd like some information about an employee of yours, a nurse named Thelma Ross. I need to know if she's still working there and if so, whether I can speak to her.'

At the other end, there was a sigh and a slight pause. 'Ah, Thelma. The poor woman . . .'

'I know what happened to her and her son. What I'd like to know is where I can find her now.'

'Everybody here liked her,' Stills went on, as if lost in his own memories. 'She was a very sweet person and a wonderful nurse. She never really got over that death. She fell into a depression that got worse until she ended up in a semi-catatonic state. Currently she's in a psychiatric hospital.'

'Do you remember what it's called?'

'I'm not sure, but I think the name is The Cedars or The Oaks, something like that. I know from colleagues who visit her that it's just outside Saratoga Springs, to the north of here. I believe it's the only hospital of its kind in the area.'

'Could I speak to her husband?'

'Thelma isn't married. I guess she was once, but by the time she arrived here she was a single parent.'

'Thank you, Mr Stills. You've been extremely helpful.'

Jordan hung up and was silent for a moment, trying to absorb what he had just heard.

'Thelma Ross is in a mental hospital near Saratoga Springs. I don't know how much help she could be, but I think we really need to pay her a visit.'

From Jordan's tone, Maureen understood that their visit to Gracie Mansion was over. Christopher was still busy, and the idea of leaving without seeing him and having to explain the reason for their presence didn't bother either of them.

They said goodbye to Ruben, opened the door and walked in silence down the corridor to the main door.

Dawson stood in the doorway, watching them walk away until they had disappeared around a corner. Then he went back in the room, took his cellphone from his pocket and dialled the number of a charitable association.

When someone picked up at the other end, he did not even bother to say his name. Despite his proverbial self-possession, he could not help slightly lowering his voice in deference.

'Tell Mr Wong I have some news that might be of interest to him . . .'

CHAPTER 43

The helicopter was flying north over the Hudson, at a height of 2,000 feet. From his seat by the window, Jordan watched its shadow glide over the surface of the river. At Jordan's request, and without asking too many questions, Christopher had put his own helicopter at their disposal – an Augusta-Bell AB139 that had taken off from the Downtown Manhattan Heliport, headed for Saratoga Springs. He had already contacted The Oaks, the hospital where Thelma Ross was a patient. After talking to the director, Colin Norwich, Jordan had opted for a helicopter when he had heard that the hospital had a landing strip.

Now he and Maureen were sitting side by side behind the pilot. Although the cockpit was soundproofed, they had followed his advice and put on Peltor headsets, so that they could talk during the flight without being disturbed by the noise of the blades.

Jordan pressed the button that excluded the pilot from their conversation and turned to Maureen, who was sitting with her head tilted slightly back, as if she had dozed off behind her dark glasses.

'There's something I don't understand,' he said.

Her reply showed him that she was awake and, like him,

thinking hard. 'Let's see if it's the same thing I've been wondering.'

'Given what's gone before, there's nothing to suggest that what you saw isn't true. But if that's the case, and if Julius Wong killed Thelma Ross's son – why did she never inform the police?'

'Yes, that is what I was thinking.'

'Let's hope she can tell us something, although the doctor I spoke to seemed a bit vague about that.'

Maureen again turned to the landscape on her side as the helicopter veered round. 'Right now,' she said, 'all I want is to understand.'

Perhaps because he was not in love with her, Jordan felt closer to her than he had ever felt to almost anyone before. What had happened to him two days earlier had brought him even closer to her. When he had seen Lysa lying on the ground, with that red bloodstain spreading over her blouse, draining the colour from her face, he had understood what Maureen must have felt when Connor Slave had been killed.

Lysa . . .

The previous evening, after his visit to Gracie Mansion, Jordan had gone to St Vincent's to see Lysa, even though he had already spoken to Dr Leko. When they had allowed him to creep into her room for a moment, he had found her asleep, with her hair spread on the pillow, as pale and beautiful as if, instead of being in a hospital bed, she was on the set of a photo call. Her heartbeat, represented by a green line moving across a monitor, was regular, much more so than his.

As he stood beside the bed, Lysa had opened her eyes and looked at him, her gaze still blurry from the drugs. It had seemed to Jordan that a slight smile had hovered over her lips for a moment, but then she had drifted back to that painless place where the drugs allowed her to find refuge. Jordan had left the room as he had entered it, in perfect silence, leaving Lysa in the kind of deep sleep that he had sought in vain all night.

The pilot lifted his right hand and pointed downwards at the glittering surface of Saratoga Lake beneath them.

'That's the lake. The place we're looking for is at the north tip.'

The helicopter turned again and lost height. As they came in to land, Jordan saw two buildings, surrounded by pleasant grounds. One of the buildings was smaller than the other, and lay just beyond the landing strip. The second, to its right, was much larger and had a broad forecourt that led to a flower garden.

The pilot switched off the engines. Jordan and Maureen disembarked, stooping to avoid the blades, then walked along a path lined by a hedge of holly bushes. A man was moving in their direction.

Jordan held out his hand. 'Hello. I'm Jordan Marsalis and this is Maureen Martini, who works for the police in Italy.'

As he shook their hands, the man, almost as tall as Jordan, with longish chestnut hair and a brisk air, introduced himself.

'Welcome. I'm Colin Norwich, Director of The Oaks. We spoke on the phone.'

'Thank you for agreeing to see us and let us meet with your patient.'

As they walked towards the large building, Norwich said, 'You told me this is a very important matter. I don't know what you're expecting from Mrs Ross, but I fear she's unlikely to be of much help to you.'

'Why is that?'

'Two main reasons. The first is that, because of the trauma

she suffered, Thelma – to put it in layman's terms – has created a barrier around herself beyond which she almost never goes. We had to work long and hard to help her find some kind of balance. Now she alternates agitated periods with whole days when she doesn't speak. When she first came here, all she could do was scream.'

'And the second reason?'

Dr Norwich stopped and looked gravely, first at Jordan and then at Maureen. 'Although it may not seem like it at first glance, this is a hospital. I'm a doctor and Mrs Ross is my patient. I'm responsible for her. If your being here upsets her in any way, I'll have to ask you to cut short your visit immediately.'

While speaking, they had reached the semicircular fore-court in front of the building. Norwich pointed to an extremely well-tended garden beyond a low redbrick perimeter wall. A few women were strolling freely along the paths, alone or in groups. Others were being pushed in wheelchairs by nurses in white uniforms.

'Those are some of our patients. As you can see, this is a women-only institution.'

Jordan made a gesture with his arm, taking in everything around them. 'Dr Norwich, I get the impression this place is reserved for people able to afford some rather high fees.'

'I wouldn't put it quite so crudely, but yes, you're right.'

'Mrs Ross was a nurse. How can she possibly afford to stay in a place like this?'

'From what I understand, she had a personal fortune of almost a million and a half dollars. I know it's managed by a bank and yields enough to cover her expenses.'

'Doesn't it strike you as strange that a simple nurse should have so much money?'

'Mr Marsalis, I'm a psychiatrist, I don't work for the IRS. What I find strange is what's in my patients' heads, not in their bank accounts.'

The arrival of a somewhat overweight but pretty blond nurse saved Jordan from the embarrassment of finding an appropriate reply to this. The woman stopped beside them, irreproachable in her white uniform but looking at Jordan with eyes that expressed pure gluttony. Maureen smiled to herself: she could well imagine the nurse looking in the same way at a double portion of strawberries and cream.

Norwich explained to her the reason for the presence of these two strangers at The Oaks. 'Carolyn, take Mr Marsalis and Miss Martini to Thelma. Make sure everything goes OK.'

It didn't escape Jordan's notice that Norwich had slightly lowered his voice for these last words. The nurse finally took her eyes off Jordan.

'Yes, Doctor.'

'You can go with Carolyn. If you'll excuse me, someone's waiting for me in my office. I'll come and see you before you leave.'

Norwich turned and walked resolutely towards the entrance to the building. Maureen and Jordan followed the nurse, who moved in a surprisingly agile way in spite of her far from sylphlike figure. Carolyn led them along the paths of a garden full of colours so unusual that Maureen felt as if she had entered a Monet painting. The patients they passed all had the gentle, surprised air of people living in worlds of their own.

Thelma Ross was sitting motionless on a stone bench in a gazebo completely covered in climbing roses. She was wearing a grey skirt and a somewhat old-fashioned pink twin-set that made a pleasant contrast with her dark skin. She was older than her photograph in the newspaper but her skin was smooth and unlined. She was still a beautiful woman, as if fate, content with having affected her mind, had decided to show mercy to her body.

Alerted by the sound of their arrival, she looked up. Maureen gave a slight shudder, despite the heat. The woman's eyes were black and tranquil, but it was obvious that reason had long since fled from them.

It was the first time that Maureen had found herself in close contact with a person she had seen in one of her hallucinations. If any doubt still remained, she only had to reach out her hand and touch Thelma Ross's shoulder to know that those images were real enough.

The nurse approached the woman. 'Thelma,' she said gently, 'we have a little surprise for you. These people have come to see you.'

The woman looked first at her and then at Jordan as if they did not exist. Finally her eyes came to rest on Maureen. 'Are you a friend of Lewis?' She had an incredibly soft voice and gave a strong aura of innocence.

Maureen crouched in front of her. 'Yes, I'm a friend of Lewis.'

Thelma lifted a hand and touched her hair. Maureen again saw her gagged, her eyes wide with terror, as a stupid girl wearing a Lucy mask tied her to a chair.

The woman gave a big smile. 'You're so good looking. My Lewis is good looking too. He's at school now. He's going to be a vet one day. I'd have preferred him to choose medicine, but he just loves animals.'

Maureen lifted her head and met Jordan's eyes. They were both almost certain by now that they had made a pointless journey. Nevertheless she gently took the hands the woman held in her lap.

'Mrs Ross, do you remember what happened to Lewis when he was stung by hornets?'

The question did not reach the place where the woman's mind had taken refuge. 'Lewis is very good at basketball. He's the best in the team and runs very fast. The coach says he'll become a great playmaker.'

Jordan took the photographs of Julius Wong and his victims from his pocket and handed them to Maureen.

'Thelma, do you know any of these people?'

Maureen showed her the photographs one by one. Her expression did not change as she looked at the faces of the people who had forced her to sit on that stone bench and build in her head a future for a child who would never grow old.

Jordan put his hand in the inside pocket of his jacket and took out some folded sheets of paper. When he opened them and passed them to her, Maureen saw that the figure of Snoopy was drawn on the first of them.

Maureen placed the first sheet on Thelma's lap. 'Mrs Ross, have you ever seen this character?'

Thelma Ross took the page in her hand and looked at it with the same absent eyes with which she had greeted their questions and examined the previous photographs.

Then, all at once, her breathing grew more rapid.

As Maureen held out the images of Linus, Lucy and Pig Pen, Thelma Ross's eyes gradually opened wider while she shook her head with brief hysterical movements, breathing in through her open mouth all the air she could get. For a moment everything remained motionless – and then from her throat came such a piercing scream that Maureen instinctively stood up.

The nurse moved quickly. She took a pager from her pocket and pressed a button. Then she pushed aside Maureen and Jordan and approached the woman, who was still screaming.

'Thelma, calm down, everything's fine.'

She put her arms around the woman's shoulders in an attempt to immobilize her. Thelma, meanwhile, was grabbing and tugging at her cardigan, trying to pull it off herself as if it had suddenly become scorching hot.

'Get away from here, you two.'

Jordan and Maureen left the gazebo just in time to see Dr Norwich come running, followed by two nurses, also fairly hefty. One of the two was holding a syringe. Norwich rushed over to the bench and, helped by the nurses, rolled up the sleeve of the cardigan and plunged the needle into Thelma Ross's arm.

Then Norwich took Jordan by the elbow and spun him around. He was furious. 'And to think I gave you permission to see her! I assume you're proud of what you've done. As far as I'm concerned, you're no longer welcome here. You've already done enough damage for today.'

Turning his back on them, he rejoined the nurses. Thanks to the injection, Thelma was starting to calm down.

Jordan and Maureen walked back to the landing-strip without having the courage to look each other in the face.

Sitting side by side, in silence, in the helicopter taking them back to New York, Jordan couldn't stop thinking about what had just happened, the look of horror on Thelma Ross's face and that scream which would echo in his ears for a long, long time to come.

The woman's reaction to the *Peanuts* characters was clear confirmation that the newspaper article had not told the whole story, and that there was a connection between what had happened all those years ago and what Maureen had seen.

335

He wondered why, when confronted with two people who wanted to communicate with her, Thelma had instinctively chosen to speak to Maureen.

He turned his head for a moment to look at her profile against the light from the window and remembered what he had thought the day before, during the brief cab journey to Gracie Mansion.

Maybe that was the reason.

For Thelma, as for Maureen, nothing around her was true except what her own eyes had seen.

CHAPTER 44

When the door of the room opened, Lysa had her eyes closed but she was awake.

Her brown hair, pulled back and tied in a ponytail, brought out the perfection of her features. Her eyes opened as softly as the door through which Jordan had come. She still had a drip attached to her vein but the monitor next to the bed had been switched off.

'Hello, Jordan.'

'Hello, Lysa.'

This was a moment they had both waited for and feared at the same time. Lysa was beautiful and pale, and Jordan felt awkward and self-conscious.

'Are you all right here? Do you have everything you need?'

He made a gesture to indicate the room, which was so comfortable, it did not even seem like a hospital room. The bed was facing the door and on the left was a large window with the curtains open, through which the sun drew a rectangle on the floor, like a little carpet of light.

'Oh yes. The staff are fantastic. That woman, Annette, came and brought me my things. She's a very good person.'

Jordan nodded. It was yet another favour he had asked of his friend: to go to the apartment and choose all the things a woman might need in a situation like that. He felt less embarrassed asking her to do it than to do it himself.

'I'm sorry. I know it isn't pleasant having strangers going through your things, but I had no idea what . . .'

'You had one idea. A very good one, I'd say.'

Lysa pointed to the table by the window, on which stood a big bunch of flowers, arranged by the nurses in a vase. When Jordan had sent them from a shop on the Hudson, he had thought for a long time about what to write on the accompanying card. Whatever came into his mind had seemed inappropriate or childish. In the end he had made up his mind and put a simple *J* in the middle of the card, hoping Lysa might guess from that everything he was unable to say.

'They're lovely and they gave me a great deal of pleasure. I'm very grateful.'

'That's all right. But how are you feeling?'

Lysa gave a wan smile. 'I don't know. They say I'm fine. I haven't taken many bullets in my life though, so I have nothing to compare it with.'

'You don't know how sorry I am, Lysa.'

'Why? You saved my life.'

'If it wasn't for me, your life would never have been in danger in the first place. That bullet you took was meant for me.'

He told Lysa all about his previous history with Lord, the man he had once arrested and who had tried to take his revenge. He didn't tell her the two men were dead, let alone about the half-cheque he had found in a pocket when he had searched Lord's body, or the cheques he had found in her apartment.

Lysa interrupted him, surprising him by completely changing the subject, as if her mind had been elsewhere.

'She's beautiful.'

'Who?'

'The girl I saw you with the other night. She's beautiful and I'm sure she's what she seems. A woman.'

'Lysa, Maureen's just—'

'It doesn't matter, Jordan, believe me.' She gave a drawn smile, then turned towards the window. 'The problem isn't who I saw you with, but *where* I saw you.'

Lysa indicated an aluminium chair against the wall to the left of the bed, facing the window.

'Sit down, Jordan. I need to tell you why I called you the other night. Sit down and listen, and please don't look at me as I speak, or I won't have the courage to do it.'

As Jordan sat down, his gaze fell on the bouquet of flowers, and he remembered the words his mother used to recite while they tended the little flowerbeds together outside their house.

. . . a scarlet rose for passion . . .

'What I'm about to tell you isn't a justification, but only an explanation. You see, I didn't come to New York by chance, but for a specific purpose. All my life I'd tried to be a normal person, with a normal life, who didn't feel like a freak of Nature every time she looked in a mirror. I only wanted the same things everyone has. I wanted to belong, to wake up in the morning and go to bed at night after a day filled with ordinary things, just like the previous one. That may sound like a boring life, but I envied the women who had it. Instead of which, I was surrounded by men who avoided me by day and who I had to avoid at night. Maybe my father was right when he said that my beauty was a gift from Satan. Then one day, in the place where I used to live before I moved here, that damned letter came . . .

. . . a yellow tulip for jealousy . . .

'It was a message asking me if I would like to earn a hundred thousand dollars. I threw it in the garbage, thinking it was a sick joke. The day after, another one came, and the next day, yet another. Every single one assured me that this wasn't a joke and, if I agreed to do what they wanted, I was to put an ad in the *New York Times* saying simply *LG OK*. Well, I did it. Two days after the ad went in, I got another letter, containing four cheques of twenty-five thousand dollars each, issued by the Chase Manhattan Bank and made out to me, or rather, four half-cheques, because they'd been cut in half with scissors. Together with the cheques there were instructions about what I had to do in order to receive the other halves. That put paid to any scruples I might still have had.'

Lysa paused. Jordan realized she was crying but continued to keep his eyes fixed on the flowers.

. . . a ring of daisies for love . . .

'When I realized what was involved, I said to myself: why not? After all, that was all the world seemed to want from me – a body and a bit of time. A hundred thousand dollars seemed a good reward for throwing all my scruples away.

. . . a white anemone for pain . . .

'I arrived in New York determined that from that moment on, I would be what I was asked to be. A well-paid toy. I carried out my mission, put what I had to hand over into a Post Office Box in Pennsylvania Station, and two days later found in the letter box of your apartment a white envelope with the other halves of the cheques inside. My mysterious benefactor had kept his word. In all this there were two things I hadn't reckoned on. The first was that, wherever you go, your conscience always follows you.

. . . and a violet for treachery . . .

'The second is that I would meet you. I tried to ignore you, I kept on with what I had to do, thinking you would be only the latest illusion and the latest disappointment. But that didn't happen. Every day, as I discovered the person you are, and also the person you don't know you are, I realized I couldn't do without either. I was in love with you, but unfortunately by this time I was no longer the same person you caught naked in the bathroom. Through my own actions, I'd become someone else, someone who'd never feel clean again, no matter how many showers she took. That was why I threw you out when I realized you were getting closer to me.'

Jordan knew how much these words were costing her. He knew it from her tone of voice, and the tears that ran from her eyes. And at the same time he was terrified, because he did not know how much it would cost him.

'When I saw that item on TV about your nephew's murder and the DNA test that nailed Julius Wong, I understood just what I had done, and in what kind of madness I'd become involved. I'd taken a hundred thousand dollars to have sex with a man and then hand over a condom containing his semen. And that man was Julius Wong.'

Jordan was rooted to the spot, so spellbound by that stupid bunch of flowers

. . . and a violet for treachery

that he almost did not hear Lysa's final words.

'Now please, just get up out of that chair and go. Go to do whatever you have to do, but go without looking at me, please.'

Jordan stood up and walked to the door without turning around. He opened the door and closed it again gently behind him. As soon as he was away from the hypnotic influence that Lysa, for good or ill, exerted over him, his mind formulated a thought.

He immediately took the cellphone from his pocket, but realizing that there was no network on this floor, he went to the elevator and, as he pressed the button, continued to turn over that thought, like a nail piercing his brain.

No sooner did he leave the elevator than he dialled Burroni's number.

'James, it's Jordan again.'

'What can I do for you?'

'I wanted to know if you had any news about that search I asked you for the other day.'

'Oh, yes. Hold on a moment.'

Jordan heard the sound of paper rustling, as if Burroni was looking for a note lost somewhere amid the jumble of his desk.

'Here we go. The cheque was issued by the branch of Chase Manhattan Bank on the corner of Broadway and Spring. The request wasn't made on a current account. The amount of the cheque was paid in cash.'

'Did you manage to find out the name of the person?'

'The request was in the name of a John Rydley Evenge, but the clerk who handled the transaction doesn't remember him. That branch of Chase Manhattan is huge and they issue hundreds of cheques like that every day.'

'But aren't they obliged to report cash transactions, because of money laundering?'

'Only for large sums. In this case, the amount was relatively small. Plus, the name of the payee was on the cheque. It would have been another matter if it had been made out to the bearer.'

'Great work, James. But I need to ask you another favour.'

'Go on.'

'I need you to do a couple of things for me, legally but not officially, if you get my meaning.'

'Sure.'

'Do you have two or three bright girls on your team who can provide protection for someone when they're off duty?'

'If I say it's for you, I'll find plenty. It seems you left quite an impression around here. Where is this person?'

'Room 307, Saint Vincent's Hospital, on Seventh Avenue.'

'I know it. When do you need it for?'

'Half an hour ago.'

'Roger. You said a couple of things. What's the other?'

'Do we have any journalists we can trust?'

'There are a few who owe me favours.'

'Then maybe you could ask them to write about the shoot-out I was involved in the other night. Tell them to report that Miss L.G. was hit by mistake and that she died as a result of the wounds she sustained. Do you think that's possible?'

'There shouldn't be any problems. I'll let you know.'

After hanging up, Jordan stood there in the middle of the lobby, thinking about what Burroni had just told him, but above all about what he hadn't told Burroni.

He hadn't told him about the cheques in Lysa's apartment, even though they were just like the one James had investigated. For the moment, he preferred not to involve him in that story. To do so would mean throwing Lysa to the wolves.

There was something much more important that had emerged from Lysa's confession. Or rather, two things.

One was that, in all probability, Julius Wong was innocent of the murders of Gerald and Stuart and the abduction of Campbell.

343

The other was that Lord's passenger had *not* fired at the wrong target.

The bullet hadn't been meant for him, but for Lysa.

CHAPTER 45

The yellow cab that had brought Maureen from the East River Heliport dropped her outside 80 Park Avenue. She paid the fare, got out, and was about to enter the lobby when she came smack up against the massive figure of Mr Hocto. She had been thinking about Thelma Ross's terrified reaction at Saratoga Springs, and hadn't noticed him.

Hocto, his bodybuilder's physique contained in the usual dark suit, addressed her in a soft, kindly voice. He had a foreign accent that Maureen could not quite place.

'Excuse me, Miss Martini. Mr Wong would like to have a word with you.' He indicated a big dark sedan waiting at the kerb with the door open. 'Please, come this way.'

Without a word, Maureen followed Hocto to the car. Her first instinct had been to refuse the invitation, but her curiosity as to what Wong wanted of her gained the upper hand.

As she slipped into the leather seat next to Cesar Wong, Hocto closed the door after her then went around to the front and got in behind the wheel.

Wong was in a sober made-to-measure suit, his smile like a blade in his waxy face.

'Good evening, Miss Martini. I'm infinitely grateful to you for agreeing to talk to me. I know you don't have a very high opinion of me.'

He made a little gesture with his hand to forestall any reaction from Maureen.

'I shan't attempt to justify myself. I know perfectly well what I am and what I can expect from people. Since I was young I've always tried to be more feared than loved. That may have been my mistake. Especially with Julius . . .'

This statement did not require any comment and Maureen did not make one.

'You don't have children, Miss Martini. I know it's a cliché but I assure you it's true: when you have children, your outlook on life changes, no matter how hard you try to stop that happening.'

There was no trace of emotion in Cesar Wong's voice, but he was staring straight ahead of him in an exaggeratedly meaningful way. In the meantime, the car had pulled away from the kerb and joined the evening traffic. Wong had presumably asked Hocto to drive around the block while the conversation lasted.

Wong turned to look at Maureen. 'My son is innocent,' he said, with an unusual amount of urgency in his voice.

'Aren't all children?'

Wong gave a slight smile. 'Don't let what I've just said deceive you. I've done many questionable things in my life, but I like to think that whatever I've done, I've always kept my wits about me. The fact that Julius is my son has never blinded me to his failings.'

He took an immaculate handkerchief from his jacket pocket and dabbed at the corners of his mouth.

'I know he's sick. He has serious personality disorders that have caused us a certain amount of trouble in the past. I managed to keep him out of prison by a miracle on a couple of occasions, but I never thought he could ever go so far as to

346

murder someone. Besides, that's why I hired Mr Hocto. It was his job to keep an eye on Julius and make sure he didn't get in too deep. On the evenings when the murders were committed, Julius was at home. He might have evaded Hocto once, but three times? I find that very unlikely.'

'Why don't you make Hocto testify at the trial, then?'

Wong's expression was that of a man forced to explain something to a child. 'Miss Martini, I am what I am and Mr Hocto has a past he's not proud of. And among the sins of his youth is a sentence for perjury. Plus, he's my employee. It wouldn't take a DA to demolish his testimony – the cleaner in your mother's office could do it.'

Maureen did not understand where he was going with all this. 'You've already hired one of the best lawyers around to defend your son. Where do I fit in?'

'That's precisely what I was about to ask you. I know almost everything about you, Chief Inspector Martini. I know what happened in Italy and I know why you came to America. I also know you were involved in the investigation that led to the arrest of my son, although I'm not sure exactly how . . .'

His words made her feel exposed, as if she was naked in the middle of a crowd of strangers. At that moment, the car pulled up again outside 80 Park Avenue, and Cesar Wong aimed his frozen, inky eyes at Maureen.

'What exactly can I do for you?' she asked without averting her gaze.

'Just as you helped to get my son arrested, in the light of what I've told you, I'd like you to help prove his innocence.'

'You may be overestimating me, Mr Wong.'

'No, I think you may be underestimating yourself, Maureen. I know people's weaknesses. I've built my fortune

347

on that knowledge. And I don't see many in you.' His voice grew softer. 'Help me, Miss Martini. I won't offend you with the lure of money, because I know you don't care about money. I assure you, though, that in some way I'll be able to repay you. I don't yet know how, but I assure you I will.'

The door opened on her side. Hocto was standing outside, on the dark sidewalk, holding the door for her.

Maureen put one foot out. 'I'm perfectly prepared to believe that, Mr Wong, although I can't quite see what I can do to earn your gratitude. I'm not even sure I want to. I don't have anything against your son but, by nature and by training, I'm a person who tries to get at the truth, even if it's not always the simplest or most comfortable thing. I'll think about what you've told me. Have a good evening, Mr Wong.'

Maureen got out of the car and walked to the door of her building. Without logic and perhaps without reason, she was assessing positively what Cesar Wong had said.

On the way up in the elevator, she continued to think about this curious encounter. She did not wonder where Wong had got his information from. Knowing not only the facts, but the background to the facts, was vital to someone in his line of work. And the world was full of people who were very sensitive, as he himself had said, to the lure of money.

She entered the apartment, to find it deserted. Her mother was out, and as she didn't like having live-in staff, Estrella had finished her work at seven and left.

Maureen stood for a moment in the entrance, where she had seen Cesar Wong for the first time. Then, after a moment's reflection, she headed for her mother's study.

Once there, she went straight to the elegant wooden desk in the middle of the room.

On the malachite surface she immediately found what she

348

was looking for: a big folder with the name *Julius Wong* on the heavy green plastic cover. Maureen opened it. As she had anticipated, it contained all the documentation her mother was using to prepare her defence.

Maureen sat down at the desk and went through the material. There were copies of the statements, medical reports, lab tests. After about an hour, she had examined everything.

If her mother, like all lawyers, was a good tightrope walker, this time she would have to perform amazing feats of acrobatics to avoid a death sentence for her client. All the evidence pointed to him. The presence on the various crime scenes of a man with a limp in his right leg – Julius had had an operation on his cartilage and ligaments recently. The robbery committed, along with the other victims. The MO of the homicides, perfectly in keeping with the psychological profile of Julius Wong, who had been accused on several occasions of sexual violence, assault and paedophilia, not to mention excessive use of alcohol and narcotics.

His DNA matched the semen found in Chandelle Stuart's vagina. Even the warehouse where he had tried to turn Alex Campbell into a grotesque parody of Snoopy belonged to his father: the planes it contained had been bought by Cesar with a view to donating them to the city after restoration.

The only thing still unclear was the motive. The investigators speculated that it was an old grudge dating back to the robbery, maybe over how the money had been divided, a grudge that Julius Wong had harboured for years until it had finally exploded.

And yet . . .

My son is innocent . . .

She could still hear Cesar Wong's voice, monolithic in its

certainty. She felt an instinctive revulsion for people like his son, but one of the main tenets of the job she had chosen was that you should never be swayed by personal bias but keep as far as possible to the facts.

My son is innocent . . .

There was one possibility in a hundred that it was true, and a thousand possibilities that Cesar Wong had lied. She remembered her mother's words –*As far as I'm concerned, a person is innocent until proved guilty* – and with a sigh got up from the desk and left the study.

She hesitated for a moment by the kitchen. Not only did she have no desire to eat – above all, she had no desire to eat alone. For a moment she thought of calling Jordan, telling him about her encounter with Cesar Wong, and maybe suggesting they discuss it over dinner. But as soon as the helicopter had landed, Jordan had seemed anxious to dash away on his bike. She remembered all too well his furtive behaviour the evening they had dined together at Martini's, when that phone call had come. As a woman, Maureen had understood immediately that behind his embarrassment there must be something that meant a great deal to him, emotionally speaking. Basically, Maureen knew nothing about him, did not know if he had a wife or girlfriend. She liked the man, she regarded him as a friend, and did not want to create any embarrassment in his private life with ill-timed phone calls.

She went to her bedroom, took off her shoes and lay down on the bed, savouring this moment of idleness. She even put off the pleasure of a shower until later.

As she lay there on the piqué bedspread, looking up at the ceiling, she felt strangely calm, without that sense of anxiety that had been with her like a crow perched on her shoulder ever since she had become aware of the terrible gift she had inherited.

She was calm and alert.

One by one, she thought about all the images that had come to her from the wretched life of Gerald Marsalis. The red-painted body, the demon's face in the mirror, then the face of the blue woman distorted with pleasure, the curious sensation of having a penis, a child's innocent drawing, Christopher Marsalis's anger, Thelma Ross's horrified face, the man with the bloodstained knife, the robbery and the *Peanuts* masks . . . and that menacing figure in the half-light of the landing, which faded just before he emerged into the light and revealed his identity . . .

Lying under that blue ceiling, which was part of the real world like everything else around her, at last and without warning, the flash arrived. She found herself sitting up on the bed, with the sensation that the mattress beneath her had unexpectedly sent up a huge burst of heat.

It was as if she had been carrying a fragmented image inside her – an image she had so far been unable to complete. Now, suddenly, the full picture was there, as clear as could be. Maureen felt like an idiot for not having seen it before.

Although she still didn't understand why, she knew who had killed Gerald Marsalis and Chandelle Stuart, and caused the death of Alex Campbell.

CHAPTER 46

The darkness and the waiting were the same colour.

Sitting in the dark, Maureen had had enough of both to be scared of them. She had learned the hard way that sometimes sight isn't exclusively physical, it's also mental. Beyond the curtains in the place where she waited, beyond the windows, in the yellow glare of 1,000 lights, the dazzle of 1,000 neon signs, lay the madness they called New York.

On the low table next to her chair, there was a Beretta 92 SBM – a gun with a slightly smaller handle than usual, expressly designed for women.

It belonged to her mother.

She knew her mother had one, and had taken it from the drawer where it was kept, just before leaving the apartment.

She had cocked it before putting it down on the glass table-top, and the noise of the bolt had echoed in the silence of the room like the sound of a bone cracking.

Gradually, her eyes had become accustomed to the darkness and she had gained some idea of the place where she was, even with the lights off. She was staring at the wall in front of her, sensing rather than seeing, the dark patch of a door.

Once, at school, she had learned that when you look intensely at a coloured surface and then take your eyes away, there remains imprinted on your pupils a bright patch of colour exactly complementary to the one you have just been staring at.

This cannot happen in the dark, however, since darkness generates only more darkness.

When the person she was waiting for arrived, light would suddenly flood the room.

After an apparently endless road travelled, after a long journey down a tunnel where only a few paltry lamps showed the way, two people would finally emerge into the light. The only two people in possession of the truth.

A woman scared by the knowledge that she had it.

And the man she was waiting for.

The killer.

As soon as she had realized who he was, Maureen had called Jordan but his cellphone was off. Jordan was the only person to whom she could have explained how she had got to the truth. The only other person who knew what was happening to her was his brother, but Mayor Christopher Marsalis was too anxious for revenge on his son's killer to accept a far-fetched theory that might refute the overwhelming evidence against Julius Wong.

Any other person involved in the case, starting with Burroni, would have told her not to worry and to stay where she was, and then have shown up with nurses and a straitjacket.

She had looked in the phone book for a name and had found a telephone number and an address in Brooklyn Heights. She had called, let it ring for a long time, then hung up.

As she was leaving the apartment, her mother had come in, looking as beautiful and impeccable at the end of the day

353

as if she had only just left home. Maureen embraced her, taking care not to let Mary Ann feel the solid bulk of the gun in the belt of her jeans, then kissed her on the cheek and looked her in the eyes. 'You were right, Mother.'

A moment later, she had already closed the door behind her, leaving Mary Ann Levallier standing in the entrance, looking after her daughter as if she was possessed by an alien will.

Throughout the taxi ride, Maureen continued without success to call Jordan. Finally she made up her mind to leave him a message, explaining what had happened, where she was going, and what she was planning to do.

The driver dropped her at the address she had given him, on the corner of Henry and Pierrepont Streets. As soon as she got out of the taxi, Maureen had tried to take stock of the situation. Henry Street was lit for most of its length by round streetlamps with a soft, creamy light, but along the last stretch, for some reason, they were out. The first lamp on Pierrepont Street was about thirty feet from the corner, and the traffic at that hour was practically non-existent.

Good.

She couldn't have arranged it better herself.

She had stood there for a while, protected by the cocoon of the dark, looking at the front of the large two-storey redbrick house, made gloomy by the darkness and its heavy imitation Gothic architecture. At any other moment, Maureen would have thought it excessive. Now, the external appearance of the building seemed wholly in line with this whole succession of absurd events.

The entrance was situated beneath a rectangular canopy, sufficiently wide to offer shelter from even the most violent storm. A small flight of steps led up to the wooden door, the upper part of which was a rectangle of frosted glass with stained-glass inserts.

Moving her hands over it, Maureen discovered that it had a purely aesthetic function and was not shatterproof. This greatly simplified things. The door presumably opened on a hall that led to the rest of the house. It was rather unlikely that it was protected by an alarm, because any idiot throwing a stone at the glass as a joke would have set it off.

Maureen had taken a leather case from the back pocket of her jeans. It was a gift from Alfredo Martini, a distinguished-looking elderly gentleman with unusually long fingers, who had nothing in common with her apart from the surname and the fact that they periodically met at the police station, after he had been caught entering apartments where he had not been invited. When he was dying of cancer, Maureen had made sure he didn't get sent to prison for the umpteenth time. As a mark of gratitude, he had given her his tools and taught her how to use them.

She usually kept them in a pocket in the lid of her dressing-case, but by a stroke of luck, when she had left Italy, the person who had packed her bags had unwittingly left them there.

Taking out the tools she needed, she carefully picked the lock of the front door, which was much stronger to look at than it turned out to be. She kept telling herself that what she was doing was neither logical nor legal. But she didn't care: all that mattered, now that she knew *who*, was to find out *why*. She had held her breath as she opened the door but, as she had predicted, no alarm had been set off.

She found herself in a fairly large, high-ceilinged, soberly furnished entrance hall. There were a few ornamental plants, and some paintings on the walls, which she could barely

355

make out in the darkness. On the wall facing the door she glimpsed a low table between two chairs, and immediately next to it a curtain of indeterminate colour. In the walls to right and left, two solid-looking doors led to the rest of the house.

She went over to the chair and sat down to wait. She had with her all the weapons she needed: the gun, the element of surprise, and the truth.

The only thing missing now was him.

Time passed.

Announced by a glow in the glass in front of her, a car pulled up on the street just outside. There came the noise of a door slamming, followed by the light of the headlamps moving away, and then the sound of feet climbing the steps to the front door. She heard a key being inserted in the keyhole, then the click of the lock. By chance, another car passed at that moment, and through the frosted glass Maureen saw a man's figure silhouetted against the light. That was how she had always seen him in her imagination – a vague shape to which she had been unable to give a face or a name until the door in her mind had opened.

Calmly, she reached out her hand and picked up the gun from the low table, stiffening her arm muscles to support the weight. Having the weapon reassured her: it was only an inert piece of metal, it was neither good nor bad, but it was something tangible, which was what she needed at that moment, after all her forced journeys into the unreal.

Another car passed in the street just as the glass door opened noiselessly, drawing the shadow of a man in the square of light projected on the floor by the headlamps. The light lapped at Maureen's feet like a wave, then receded as the man came in and closed the door behind him.

He did not switch on the light straight away, and when he did, he had his back to her and did not immediately notice the woman sitting on the chair against the wall facing the door. Maureen was glad of that momentary gap, which allowed her eyes to become accustomed to the change in light.

When the man turned and saw her sitting facing him with a gun in her hand, for a second or two the surprise of it froze him. But then Maureen saw his face and body relax, as if this was a moment he had somehow expected and for which he was prepared.

He was a killer, yet Maureen could not help but admire his sangfroid. That simple reaction was enough to confirm to her that her suppositions had been correct.

The man nodded towards the gun and said one incredulous word. 'Why?'

Maureen, with the same simplicity and in the same calm voice, replied, 'That's what I came to ask *you*.'

'I don't understand.'

'Gerald Marsalis, Chandelle Stuart, Alex Campbell.'

The man made a series of brief nods with his head to confirm that he had understood. Then he shrugged. 'What does it matter now?'

'It matters to me.'

'What does any of this have to do with you anyway?'

'You'd never believe it.'

The man smiled. His eyes were on her but Maureen sensed that he was not seeing her. 'You have no idea of the things I'm willing to believe . . .'

Maureen also sensed that he had said these last words more for himself than for her. Then, whatever image the man had had in his mind vanished as quickly as it had come and he was back in the room, facing her.

'Where would you like me to begin?'

'It's usually best to begin at the beginning.'

'All right. Let's go over there. We'll be more comfortable.'

Still aiming her gun at him, Maureen stood up – and felt an episode about to begin. There came the long shudder she knew well, and then that familiar sensation of something coming at her, rolling fast towards her from a distance, and she heard the noise of the gun falling to the floor and . . .

. . . I'm standing in the middle of a large room full of light coming from high windows, and I'm walking towards the wall at the back and looking down at my feet, which are red against the clear tiles on the floor – and in the meantime I'm moving closer to the door that leads to the stairs and . . .

. . . I'm in a bedroom where Julius is lying on top of Chandelle and slapping her as he fucks her, and there's Alex with his pants down waiting his turn and jerking off, and I'm also masturbating and . . .

. . . I'm outside another door that opens slightly and there's the beautiful, incredulous face of Thelma Ross appearing in the crack and immediately afterwards she's pushed inside and falls on the floor screaming, and a hand holding a gun enters my field of vision and . . .

. . . I'm again in front of the half-open door of this light-filled room and I open it and there's a figure in the shadow of the landing who advances towards me. He's wearing a tracksuit and I finally manage to see his face and I realize he's speaking to me although I can't take my eyes off the gun he's holding. He's smiling and . . .

Maureen found herself lying on the floor, her strength gone, just like all the other times that the personal ghosts of Gerald Marsalis had assailed her. Gasping for breath, she pressed down on her arms and lifted herself until she was on all fours on the floor. She stayed in that position for a moment, head bowed, hair falling like weeping willows at the sides of her face, trying to get her heartbeat, which she could hear throbbing in her ears, back to a normal rhythm.

In that final vision, Maureen had at last seen the face of the person who had killed Jerry Ko, at the exact moment he had entered his loft, aiming a gun at him.

Maureen slowly raised her head.

There in front of her was the same man, standing looking at her with his head tilted slightly to one side and a puzzled expression on his face. He was dressed differently but, just as in that vision, he was holding a gun, aimed directly at her.

CHAPTER 47

Harmon Fowley of Codex Security was standing in front of the main entrance of the Stuart Building, waiting for Jordan. When Harmon realized that Jordan was the man on the saddle of the red motorbike that was pulling up at the sidewalk, he waited for him to put it on the kick-stand and switch off the engine.

He looked admiringly at the Ducati as Jordan got off. 'Italian, eh? Nice machine.'

Jordan removed his helmet, and shook the hand Fowley held out to him. 'Yes. A very nice machine.'

'How fast does she go?'

'Fast enough to stop the traffic cops getting the number.'

'Don't tell me Lieutenant Marsalis breaks the law.'

Jordan remembered Officer Rodriguez. 'You sound like someone I know. Do I need to remind you I'm not a lieutenant any more?'

'Maybe not officially, but I think you still keep your hand in. From what I hear, you caught the guy they were looking for.'

'Apparently, yes.'

'Only apparently?'

'I need to check something and I can only do that through you. Thanks for waiting for me. You're doing me a very big favour.'

Fowley shrugged. 'Don't mention it. Since my divorce, I've had a lot of time on my hands.'

'You know what they say? When the cat's away, the mice . . .'

Fowley returned a mirthless smile. 'Seems like right now the cat's having more fun.'

'Do you miss her?'

'I don't know . . . I spent the last three years dreaming of freedom, and now that it's here I don't feel any satisfaction coming home late with a few more beers in my body. The fact I don't have to wipe the lipstick marks from my shirt-collar kind of takes away the sense of adventure.'

By now they had gone through the revolving doors into the Stuart Building.

The pleasantries were over. Now it was down to business.

'From your call, I got the impression this was quite urgent. What can I do for you?'

'Harmon, I need to take another look at that evening's DVDs. Do you think it's possible?'

'No problem. And you're in luck – Barton's on duty tonight. You remember him from last time? He's one of my men and we won't have any problems with him.'

As they climbed the stairs leading to the control room, Jordan remembered the night of Chandelle Stuart's murder. When they had seen the limping figure crossing the lobby of the Stuart Building, they had allowed themselves to be blinded by that apparition and had neglected other possibilities.

One above all, which Jordan couldn't forgive himself for not considering.

He had seen him come in, but he hadn't seen him go out.

They came to the desk where Barton was sitting, his face lit by the reflections from the bank of screens.

'Barton,' Fowley said, 'my friend here would like to examine the DVDs of the night the Stuart girl was killed. Is that possible?'

'Sure. Come with me.'

Barton got up from the leather armchair and led them into an office to the left. Inside, on the wall facing the door, were shelves on which all the used discs were arranged in chronological order. In the middle of the room was a desk with a computer linked to a DVD player.

'This is the office where we keep the discs and format them to use again.'

Barton approached the shelves and took out two black plastic cases, which he placed on the desk.

'Here we are. That night's recordings from the cameras at both the entrances.'

Jordan moved a chair from the wall towards the desk. 'Good. I think I can manage by myself now. I'm not asking you to stay here with me – this might take a long time and I know you're busy.'

Barton pointed to the computer. 'Do you know how this kind of program works?'

'I think so, yes.'

'To play the discs, it's pretty much like a regular home DVD player.'

Jordan sat down and switched on the computer. 'I think I'll get by.'

Barton nodded and left the office. Fowley had realized that Jordan was following his own thought processes and wasn't with them any more. He put a hand on his shoulder.

'OK, Jordan, I'm going. Whatever you're looking for, I hope you find it – or not, whichever you think is better.'

'Thanks, Harmon. You're a friend.'

'Don't mention it. I'll tell Barton, whatever you need, he should let you have it.'

Jordan watched him go out and close the door behind him. Then he turned and picked up the first case, took out the disc and inserted it in the player. On the computer screen he clicked on the icon *DVD Player* and started watching.

Thanks to a lot of judicious fast-forwarding, it took him little more than an hour to go through both discs.

It had been both grotesque and tragic seeing again the killer's limping figure, made ridiculous by the speeded-up motion, on his way to accomplish his fatal mission.

He had watched until his eyes smarted the constant view of those entrances over a period of twelve hours, deserted for the most part, apart from some rare nightbird coming home after a night on the town. According to the hour marked on the time-code, only towards morning did the scene start to become more animated: early-morning joggers headed for Central Park, men in grey suits holding briefcases, a couple with suitcases who looked as if they were leaving on vacation.

As the hour approached when the stores and offices opened, the number of people coming in and out increased, until he was faced with the usual hustle and bustle of a place like the Stuart Building.

Jordan found no trace of what he was looking for. No limping figure, even half hidden by the others, trying to slip away unobserved by one of the cameras.

According to what he had seen, the man had entered the building but hadn't left it.

Unless . . .

Jordan forced himself to start all over again from the beginning. He began replaying the first disc, watching even more carefully, and at a certain point his gaze was attracted by something that made him quickly press the *Stop* button.

He went back a little and replayed the recording at normal speed. He checked the time-code on the screen. The images he was seeing corresponded to seven-thirty in the morning.

A man in a dark suit was crossing the lobby towards the exit, taking care to always keep his back to the camera. Even though he was almost hidden by the people who were starting to crowd into the lobby, Jordan had spotted him precisely because of the illogical way in which he was forced to move in order to preserve that position.

And at a certain point something happened.

A bald, well-built man who was coming in the opposite direction, distracted because he was talking to someone next to him, knocked into the man in the dark suit as he headed for the revolving doors. The impact spun him around and for a moment he had his face to the camera.

Jordan immediately paused and reversed the image frame by frame until he had the man in the middle of the screen.

It took him a moment to find the zoom function on the toolbar and enlarge the figure. And although the image became grainier as he did so, he soon found himself looking at a face he knew.

Jordan's heart skipped a beat.

If things were as he suspected, this man had waited all night on the stairs in order to leave unobserved by mingling with the morning crowd.

To be absolutely sure, there was still one thing he needed to check, and to do that he had to go up to Chandelle Stuart's apartment.

He left the office and walked to the bank of screens showing images similar to those he had just finished watching.

'Burton, are there still seals on Chandelle Stuart's apartment?'

'No, they were removed a couple of days ago.'

'Do you have the code?'

'Yes.'

'I need to take a look around. If you don't trust me, send someone up with me. I don't want to get you in trouble.'

Burton took a yellow Post-it from the desk in front of him, quickly wrote down a number and handed it to him. 'Mr Fowley said anything you want.'

'Thanks, Barton. You're a good man.'

A minute or two later, he was stepping out of the elevator into Chandelle Stuart's apartment. There in front of him was the white outline drawn by the Crime Scene team to mark the position of the body.

He took a look around. The apartment had remained the same but now there was no sense of expectation in the air. Only a slight layer of dust on the furniture.

He passed the Gericault painting without so much as a glance and walked towards the study and the bedrooms.

This time, too, what he was looking for was so normal that nobody would have bothered hiding it away. In fact, they would have taken care to have it as close to hand as possible. He started with the bathrooms, then moved to the bedrooms, examining any piece of furniture that had drawers.

Nothing.

And in looking for what he did not find, he found what he was not looking for.

In a drawer in the study was a series of medical records. He glanced at them for a moment, then took them out and placed them on the table. He read through them one by one. They were mainly reports of tests and periodic check-ups, but to his surprise he discovered something that might explain a lot.

He had remembered a while earlier that, in the photograph in the Vassar College yearbook, Chandelle Stuart had been wearing a pair of glasses – quite thick ones, from the look of them. Yet in the apartment, right now, there was no trace of spectacles or contact-lens cases, or bottles of saline solution to wash them, which was what he had been looking for.

But what he *had* found was a report recording the success of a laser operation to reduce her short-sightedness, performed at Holy Faith Hospital.

To clarify his ideas, Jordan needed to have a few words with the person he had seen on the DVD, leaving the Stuart Building the morning after the death of Chandelle Stuart. Maybe it was only a coincidence and there were a number of possible explanations, but he was curious to know what that person was doing in that place, at that time, and on that particular day.

It was a question that could only be answered by the man himself, the elegant and ironic Professor William Roscoe, who in all probability was also the person who had requested a series of cheques from Chase Manhattan Bank in the name of John Rydley Evenge. Chance maybe, but if you replaced the middle name with an initial, it became John R. Evenge.

Revenge.

CHAPTER 48

'Revenge,' William Roscoe said. 'That's the only reason. You of all people should be able to understand that.'

Maureen said nothing, trying not to be mesmerized by the black eye of the gun pointing at her.

'Tell me one thing, Maureen. When that man killed Connor Slave right there in front of you – once past the initial grief, didn't you feel a fierce hate and an obsessive desire for revenge? Don't you feel right now the desire to have him in front of you so that you can make him pay in person for all the suffering you've felt and will have to feel for the rest of your life?'

Yes, with all my strength, she thought.

'Yes, but that's not up to me,' she said out loud.

Roscoe smiled. 'You're not a good liar, Maureen. The light of hate is in your eyes. I recognize it, because I know all about hate, and *I* gave you those eyes.'

For some moments after finding Maureen at his mercy for a reason he could not grasp, William Roscoe had felt stunned, unsure what to do next.

'Are you all right?' he had asked as she got up off the floor, with even now, despite the situation, a doctor's professional concern in his voice.

Maureen had replied with a terse nod of the head, unable to speak.

Pointing with the barrel of his gun to the curtain behind her, Roscoe said, 'Through there.'

Moving the curtain aside, Maureen discovered that beyond it lay a narrow corridor which led to the rear of the house. With the barrel of the gun thrust into her back, she moved slowly forward. In the dim light, she could just see the outline of a glass door leading to a porch at the other end. However, before they got there, Roscoe ordered her to stop in front of another door, a heavily armoured one, in the wall on the left.

The surgeon went up to a device attached to the wall next to the door, and placed his open palm on it. The door opened inwards, and a light inside came on automatically, revealing a steep staircase leading downwards.

'Go down.'

Maureen had preceded him down two flights of steps and finally they had come out into a huge room completely tiled in white, which took up the entire basement area of the house. Standing on the small railed gallery just inside the door, she was impressed. Illumined by overhead lights, there in front of her was a real research laboratory, filled to bursting with machines and instruments whose purpose she did not know but which gave the impression of being very expensive and state of the art. Against the wall to the right was a long workbench on which stood a number of computers and a huge electronic microscope linked to monitors by fibre-optic cables. In the middle of the room, like an island, was another workbench, this one occupied by a whole series of machines equipped with articulated arms for working in a sterile environment. Half the wall to the left was taken up by a large window, beyond which could be glimpsed a refrigeration chamber lit with bluish fluorescent light.

'My private lab,' Roscoe declared, as they descended the steps. 'Nice, don't you think? It's in places like this that we try to revolutionize science. Though I admit it's sometimes all smoke and mirrors.'

He had pointed to the window, beyond which even the fluorescent light seemed frozen.

'What you see there is nothing but a sophisticated refrigerator, fed with liquid nitrogen, where I keep embryos, frozen at about minus two hundred degrees Celsius. At that temperature, a rose would break like glass and a human being breathing in a mouthful of air would die before he could breathe out.'

Beside the refrigeration chamber, Maureen had noticed a row of pressurized cylinders surmounted by pressure gauges. From them, thick, dark pipes led through the wall into the chamber, presumably helping to maintain a constant temperature. As he spoke, Roscoe had forced her to walk across the lab and sit down on a swivel chair in front of a computer. He then disappeared from her field of vision, before asking her to put her arms behind the back of the chair, where he bound her wrists with adhesive tape.

Roscoe's expression now was one of commiseration at the pettiness of the world. 'All us scientists make the same mistake. We pursue knowledge, hoping that one day, it will make us like God. How foolish.'

Roscoe looked her in the eyes, and for the first time Maureen saw the gleam of madness in them.

'Every new acquisition of knowledge merely confronts us with a new ignorance. It's a vicious circle. The only thing that can make us really superior to God is justice.'

'Unfortunately, men's justice is all we have,' she said quietly.

'No, the only thing we have is the law. And applying the law doesn't always bring justice.'

He was leaning nonchalantly on the tiled workbench behind him, holding the gun in his right hand and looking at it as if it were a strange ornament rather than a weapon.

It was then that Maureen had at last asked him the reason for these absurd deaths, and the answer had emerged – precise and to the point.

Revenge.

And now the time had come for them both to lay their cards on the table and get the answers they were seeking.

Maureen only wanted to know *why* and Roscoe only wanted to know *how*.

He was the first to speak – distractedly, almost indifferently. 'Who knows you're here?'

'Nobody.'

'Why should I trust you?'

'Because of the way I discovered it was you who killed Gerald Marsalis.'

'What do you mean?'

Maureen was counting on the fact that, sooner or later, Jordan would hear her message and come running. Roscoe was a killer but he was still a doctor and above all a scientist. There was only one way to gain time: to arouse his curiosity by telling him about the strange experiences she had had since he had operated on her.

'It may seem incredible to you, but I saw you kill him.'

Roscoe looked at her for a long moment as if she had suddenly gone mad, then burst out laughing. 'You saw . . .? Please, don't make me laugh.'

'I told you you wouldn't believe me. Do you remember when I phoned you to ask if you knew the identity of the donor?'

'Yes, I remember very well.'

'I think the corneas you used on me were taken from Gerald Marsalis.'

'What makes you think that?'

'The fact that since I opened my eyes I've been tormented – and that's the correct word – by images of his past life.'

'Are you pulling my leg? Do you think you're in an episode of *The X Files*?'

'Unfortunately not. If I were, I could just switch off the TV to make all this go away. But it's not that simple.'

'Well, let me tell you: as a scientist I'm obliged to believe only what I touch with my own hands and see with my own eyes.'

'This time you'll have to believe what I saw with someone else's eyes. I'm here and that seems sufficient proof. Just now, when I fell down in front of you, I had one of those episodes – and I saw you again. The front door was ajar. You were wearing a tracksuit with a hood and, when Gerald opened the door, you emerged from the shadow of the landing with a gun in your hand. And he was painted all in red.'

Roscoe was speechless for a few seconds. Then: 'That's incredible . . .'

'Incredible's the right word, William. That's the reason why I didn't tell anyone that I'm here. How do you think any normal, everyday cop would have taken it, if I'd told him I'd seen a murder though the eyes of the victim?'

Maureen hoped her argument was sufficiently convincing. Unfortunately, she was forced to provide an abridged version of events and not mention any other image that had come to her, especially those concerning Thelma Ross. Doing so would have meant revealing that other people knew about her visions and might be aware that she was here. Best case scenario, Roscoe might leave her tied to the chair and escape.

Worst case scenario . . .

As a scientist, he was now completely engrossed in what he had just heard: it was clearly a new and fascinating area to explore.

'There must be an inherent message in the cells, a kind of imprinting, a neuronal link that's somehow preserved by the individual. This is fantastic! We can explore it together, we can—'

'Together?' Maureen cut in.

'Of course. With research like this, I have to have you at my disposal for the tests I'll need to do.'

'What makes you think I'll cooperate with you?'

Roscoe suddenly seemed to remember who they were and why they were in this position: a police officer tied to a chair and a killer holding a gun aimed at her head.

Nevertheless, as in their previous encounters, he managed to put a tinge of irony in his words.

'Because I'm the only person who knows the whereabouts of the stem cells needed to continue your therapy. Report me to the police and I'll never tell you where they are. You'll be back in the state in which I first met you. The moment Julius Wong is set free, you'll lose your sight.'

CHAPTER 49

Jordan drove his Ducati under the trees and the yellow lamps of Henry Street until he reached the building he was looking for.

He had switched on his phone immediately after leaving the Stuart Building and heard Maureen's message. Although she could know nothing of the progress he had made, the brief recording told him that she had reached the same conclusions as he had – and that she was paying Roscoe a visit.

The message had dispelled any lingering doubts on Jordan's part, but a chill went through him when he learned that Maureen was planning to go alone to the man's house. He cursed himself for having switched off his phone. He should have known he was Maureen's one point of reference, the only person in whom she could confide her visions.

Being unable to locate him, she had decided to go it alone.

In a way, Jordan could understand her, but that didn't make him any the less anxious. He had jumped on his bike and roared off to the address Maureen had left him in her message at the highest speed the Ducati and the rules of the road allowed him.

Once there, he stopped the bike, got off and walked to the opposite side of the street to examine the massive two-storey building on the corner of Pierrepont. That stretch of Henry Street was completely in darkness and, in the shadows cast by the distant lights of the cross street, Jordan found the house disturbing, almost malign.

From outside, it seemed deserted.

The windows were dark rectangles in the walls and, apart from the orange glare through the glass of the front door, there was no other light that might suggest someone was inside.

He left the front of the house and went to take a look in back. There was a high wall there, built of the same red bricks as the house itself. From the trees of various kinds peering out over the top, Jordan assumed that the area between the wall and the house was occupied by a garden. After a quick estimate of the height, he realized he could not reach the top of the wall even if he used the bike to climb on.

At the end of that brick wall, adjacent to Roscoe's property was a three-storey building currently being renovated. Jordan looked up at the scaffolding. He made up his mind. Without too much difficulty he slipped in through a hole in the fence. The work was clearly at an early stage, and nobody was making too much effort yet to prevent possible intrusions. The ground floor of the building was almost completely devoid of walls.

There was a smell of bricks and lime in the air. Jordan located the stairs – rough concrete steps without a handrail – and climbed one floor. As he reached the landing, he tripped over a black plastic container, almost invisible in the semi-darkness, which someone had left on the ground. It was filled with tools, and it overturned with a metallic noise that echoed in the silence.

He held his breath for a moment, afraid that he might have

attracted someone's attention, his tibia bone smarting where it had hit the container.

No sign of life.

Jordan relaxed. From the landing he looked out at the garden of the next house, insofar as the wall and the branches of the trees allowed him to do so. Then he looked around the landing where he stood. To his left was a stack of long wooden planks, which would probably be used to extend the scaffolding to the upper floors.

He went and lifted one and, holding on to the tubular rail of the platform to balance the weight, slid it out until it reached the edge of the wall. He made sure it was well supported, then chose another and slid this one too in such a way as to lay it over the first one, hoping that it was the right length for what he was planning to do.

Among the tools he had accidentally scattered on the floor, he found what he was looking for: a crowbar, which he slipped into the belt of his pants.

He then went back to that improvised bridge suspended precariously over the darkness between the scaffolding and the wall of Roscoe's house. Stretching out a foot, he placed it on the plank, supporting himself on the pipe. Then he let go and took his first step across.

Jordan had never suffered from vertigo and hoped he wasn't going to start now.

Keeping his eyes fixed straight ahead, moving one foot in front of the other like a tightrope-walker, with sand and sacks of cement as a safety net, he got to the other end of the bridge, where he let out a long sigh of relief. Sitting down astride the wall, he slid one of the planks back down until it touched the ground. The effort of doing this without making a noise and at the same time ensuring that it did not slip, made the blood throb violently in his temples, and he had to stop for a second to catch his breath and get over a touch of dizziness.

When he had recovered, he checked that the plank was solidly supported by the wall on which he was sitting. Jordan's intention was to use it as a slide, moving down it until he touched the ground.

Unfortunately, when he tried to put his plan into action, things went wrong. As soon as he got on the plank, the end pointing to the ground slid forward abruptly. Jordan instinctively grabbed the edge of the wall, but his left hand lost its grip on the mossy bricks and he ended up hanging by one hand. At the same time, his body twisted and he distinctly heard the crack of the shoulder-joint being knocked out of place. The violent spasm made him lose his grip. His fall was cushioned by a cheesewood bush, but at the same time he rolled forward, and again his dislocated shoulder was hit by a series of stabbing pains. Jordan found himself lying on his side on the ground, panting for breath. He waited until the pain reached an acceptable level, then tried to sit up.

The tops of the trees and the perimeter wall blocked the light from the streetlamps, and he had to accustom his eyes to the semi-darkness. When he had a better sense of his surroundings, he stood up and walked to the trunk of a tree. It was a maple, with rough bark. Leaning against it for support, he gave a sharp tug to his arm to get his shoulder back in place. The pain nearly made him faint. With his good hand, he felt around the shoulder. It was likely that the ligaments had been weakened the night he had been attacked by Lord. It still hurt a lot and the shoulder hadn't set well, almost completely impairing the mobility of his arm.

Jordan forced himself not to think about it. Maureen might

well be in danger and there was no time to lose. He turned his attention back to his surroundings.

Moving cautiously over the soft ground, he came to a large glass-enclosed porch, forming a kind of inner garden. In the dim light, Jordan saw the outlines of plants and what he thought were rattan armchairs. The porch was connected to the inside of the house via a French door. Beyond it, Jordan saw a long corridor, lit by a rectangle of light.

Jordan took out the crowbar and, with some difficulty, thanks to his unusable right arm, he forced open the porch door. There was a sharp click, not too loud, and he slipped inside.

Creeping across the porch, narrowly avoiding a low table, he came to the French door. Before using the crowbar again, he tried turning the handle – and much to his surprise the door opened.

He started along the corridor and soon came to the source of the light he had seen from outside – a door open on a narrow staircase, leading down. Noticing that the door was armoured and that there was a fingerprint-reader next to it, Jordan told himself that whatever was down there must be something really important.

As he descended the first step, he heard a cracking noise beneath his shoe. He lifted his foot, and saw beneath it a pair of dark glasses on the rough surface of the step. He bent down to pick them up, causing another spasm in his shoulder, and recognized them immediately, despite the broken lenses.

They belonged to Maureen.

In the silence, he thought he heard voices coming from below.

He descended cautiously, keeping slightly to the side and

supporting his right arm with the good one to avoid painful knocks. He came to a first landing, where there was a right turn leading to another flight of steps. The voices were louder now, although he still could not make out any words.

Never before had Jordan so regretted the lack of a gun.

He started down the second flight. With every step he took, the volume of the voices increased, and by the time he reached the bottom, he could hear that there were two of them.

One was Maureen's, the other he had only heard once but recognized anyway.

The voices were coming through a wide-open door, accessed by a narrow gallery which Jordan reached by turning left and descending two or three more steps.

From where he was standing, he could see apparatus and instruments that suggested the basement was some kind of laboratory. He leaned against the wall and peered through the door. He didn't like what he saw. He didn't like it at all.

On the opposite side of the huge room, beyond a workbench that occupied much of the central space, was Maureen, sitting on a chair with her arms tied behind her back, her face turned towards the door where Jordan was now hiding.

With his back to him stood the figure of a man Jordan had seen not long before in a video recording, cautiously crossing the lobby of the Stuart Building after killing Chandelle Stuart.

There was just one difference. Now he was present in flesh and blood, and was holding a big gun aimed at Maureen's head.

CHAPTER 50

Maureen had just received that hissed threat from William Roscoe when over his shoulder she saw Jordan appear beyond the door up on the gallery. She immediately looked down. When she looked up again, she forced herself to look straight into her jailer's eyes, to avoid betraying Jordan's presence.

But she had to find some way to show Jordan that she knew he was there to help her. She therefore said something that Roscoe could take as a response to what he had just said, but pitching her voice in such a way that Jordan could hear her.

'Now that you know I saw you, I think I'm entitled to an explanation, don't you?'

Jordan had understood. He leaned out, gave her a thumbs-up sign, then moved his hand in a circular gesture, indicating that she should keep Roscoe talking.

The doctor had not noticed a thing, but by chance he now moved to the side, in such a way as to keep both Maureen and the door into the lab within his field of vision. That made it completely impossible for Jordan to try to sneak in and take him from behind.

Roscoe looked condescendingly at Maureen. 'I think that's only fair,' he concluded. 'A little while ago you asked me to begin at the beginning. Well, that is where I have to start, if you're going to understand.'

He paused for a moment, as if he had to prepare himself mentally before confronting yet again the wreckage of his life.

'Many years ago, at a seminar I gave in a hospital in Boston, I met a nurse. She was black and her name was Thelma Ross. It was love at first sight, as if we had been put on earth solely for that purpose. It was the most beautiful, the purest thing I had ever felt in my life. Do you know what it means to meet somebody and realize that from that moment on, nobody else will ever matter as much to you as they do?'

Maureen felt her eyes grow moist.

Yes, you bastard, of course I know.

Roscoe seemed to read her mind. 'Yes, I see you do know. You understand what I'm talking about.'

He continued in a different tone of voice, as if that knowledge had created a kind of complicity between them.

'At the time I was at a delicate stage in my career. I was the pupil and chief assistant of Professor Joel Thornton, who was then the world's greatest expert in my field. Everyone, including him, regarded me as his rightful heir, the rising star of ocular microsurgery and ophthalmological research. In addition to which, he was also my father-in-law, because I'd just married his elder daughter, Greta. Thelma knew all about my situation and she had no intention of doing anything that might endanger my career. She told me that if I was forced to choose her, over time I would come to resent her. The fact was, Thornton could easily have ruined me. Having someone like that against me would have meant the end of my career.'

Roscoe allowed himself a little excursion into sarcasm.

'America isn't quite the democratic country we try to export as a model. A white man leaving the WASP daughter of a famous surgeon for a coloured girl . . .'

He did not finish the sentence, leaving Maureen to draw her own conclusions.

'Thelma and I continued meeting in secret. Then she fell pregnant. We agreed to keep the child, and that's how Lewis came into the world. I'd found Thelma a job as Chief Surgical Nurse at Samaritan Hospital in Troy, a town not far from Albany. It was the perfect place. Close enough to allow me to see her and the child when I could, and far enough not to be too exposed. In any case, we were very discreet, so much so that none of her friends ever saw me or even knew of my existence. To everyone, Thelma was a young divorcée, survivor of an unpleasant marriage she didn't like to talk about. To Lewis, I was a kind of uncle who loved both of them and always showed up with lots of toys. I'd found an isolated house for them and when I went to see them we stayed there. There was no risk of Thelma and me being seen together. Five years passed. Thornton died and things between Greta and myself deteriorated to the point that she asked for a divorce. I agreed to it with violins playing in my head, and that same day, that cursed day, I went up to Troy to tell Thelma that I'd be free soon and we'd be able to live together.'

From his rapt expression, Maureen could see that Roscoe was reliving in his mind the images evoked by his story.

'Lewis was playing in the garden and Thelma and I were in the house. As I was telling her what was going to happen, I heard Lewis scream and then he came running into the house, crying and holding his arm out to me. I could see he had been stung several times, and from the size of the punctures I guessed they were hornet stings. I knew that simultaneous stings from a number of insects of that kind can cause serious anaphylactic shock. I told Thelma to get out the car and take him straight to the Emergency Room at Samaritan. She'd just gone back inside, when we heard the doorbell ring. Thelma opened the door and there they were.'

Maureen saw Roscoe's jaws contract and hate – pure hate – distort his features.

'Four people in sweatshirts and dark pants – three men and a woman, wearing masks of various characters from *Peanuts*. Linus, Lucy, Snoopy and Pig Pen, to be precise. One of them, I don't know who, pushed Thelma violently back inside. She fell to the floor and they came in with guns aimed at us. They gathered all three of us in the same room and ordered us not to move. We guessed what was going to happen, because not long after that, a police car stopped in front of the house and two officers came and rang the doorbell. The one who seemed to be the leader – the one with the Pig Pen mask – aimed a gun at Lewis's head and ordered Thelma to go to the door and get rid of the police.'

Roscoe looked up at the white ceiling and took a deep breath, as if that was the only way he could continue.

'I don't know how Thelma managed to be convincing in that situation, but somehow the officers were persuaded that nothing unusual was going on. They went back to their car and drove away. In the meantime Lewis was getting worse. He was finding it hard to breathe. I knew what was happening. The hornets' stings had provoked a laryngeal spasm that was gradually blocking his respiratory tract. I begged them to let us go, saying I was a doctor. I explained what was happening to Lewis, and that he needed help. I swore with tears in my eyes that I wouldn't go to the police – I even kneeled in front of the one with the Pig Pen mask. It was no use. I still remember the indifference in his voice as he said, "You're a doctor, you deal with it." He left me free in my movements, but to avoid my doing anything to try and escape or fight back he ordered Lucy and Snoopy to take Thelma into another room while I took care of my son. By this point, Lewis had fainted and couldn't breathe. To avoid asphyxia, with two guns pointing at me, I took a scalpel from my bag and there, without anaesthetic, without instruments, like a butcher, I was forced to perform an emergency tracheotomy on my son and try to give him air by inserting the holder of a ballpoint pen in his throat.'

Tears of rage and grief fell from Roscoe's eyes. Maureen knew from personal experience how difficult it was to tell which burned the more.

'It was pointless. I couldn't save him. When I heard that his heart had stopped beating, I raised my arms and started screaming. I could feel my son's blood running down from my hands.'

Maureen suddenly connected those grainy images in her visions.

It was him I saw with his back to me, not Julius. What I took for a knife was actually a scalpel.

'Then someone, I don't know who, hit me on the head and knocked me unconscious. When I came to, they'd gone. They'd taken our car and escaped, leaving behind them the body of my son lying like an animal on the table and Thelma tied to a chair in the other room. When I untied her and she saw what had happened, she rushed to the table and hugged the body of Lewis so hard, it seemed as if she wanted to absorb him into her own body and give him back his life. It's a sight I've never forgotten, one that's sustained me like a drug all these years: the tears of my woman mixed with the blood of our son.'

'Why did you never go to the police?'

'That was Thelma's decision. She was the one who persuaded me to leave. She didn't want me to be found there. After the grief, she'd suddenly become as cold as ice. She told me what she wanted me to do. Even if those four were caught, she said, they'd do a bit of time in prison, and then they'd be free to do more harm. She made me swear I would find them and kill them with my own hands. If that meant never seeing each other again, that was a price she would gladly pay. That was why we decided she'd say she had performed the tracheotomy herself.'

Out of nervousness, Roscoe continued rhythmically opening and closing the hand that was not holding the gun, as if trying to rid himself of a cramp.

'I lived with revenge as my one purpose in life, while I watched Thelma gradually lose her mind and sink into the limbo where her mind had taken refuge from suffering. She's in a psychiatric hospital now. I haven't seen her in years . . .'

His voice had dropped in volume. For a moment, Maureen felt compassion for this man who had sacrificed his present and future to a revenge that could never wipe out the past.

'After almost ten years of effort, time and money, I'd still not managed to track them down. The bastards seemed to have vanished into thin air, as if they'd never existed. Then, one day, chance smiled on me. Chandelle Stuart, on the advice of her family doctor, came to me asking for a laser operation to cure myopia. It's an almost routine operation but, being the kind of person she was, she said it had to be done by the best there was. During the check-up, she made a mistake . . .'

He paused, staring into space.

'What mistake?' Maureen asked.

Roscoe turned his head abruptly towards her, as if Maureen's voice had woken him from a trance.

'She asked me if I knew a good plastic surgeon who could remove a tattoo on her groin. She told me it was a memento of a person who had meant a lot to her but who she now wanted to wipe out of her life. She unzipped her pants and when I saw the tattoo I was struck dumb. The day Lewis died, in a moment of nervousness, Pig Pen had rolled up the sleeve of the black sweatshirt he was wearing. It had only been for a moment, but long enough for me to see that he had a big tattoo on his forearm – a demon with butterfly wings. What Chandelle Stuart was showing me was exactly the same tattoo. She couldn't know I had seen it, because at that moment she was in the other room with Snoopy and Thelma. And without noticing what was going through my head, thinking because of the expression on my face that I was turned on by her, that whore Chandelle Stuart, standing in front of me with her pants down, had the nerve to take my hand and rub her crotch with it.'

Roscoe's jaws were tight, his face ashen with scorn. His hand was a clenched fist, the knuckles white with the tension.

'From that day on, my life changed. I lived in a frenzied state, as if hundreds of voices were talking in my ears simultaneously. I had a lead, so small as to be almost non-existent, but still it was something. All my free time was devoted to my investigations, all the money I made was spent on it. I hired private detectives, paying them exorbitant sums. I went back to the time of the events and discovered that at that time Chandelle was studying at Vassar. One by one I identified Gerald Marsalis and Alex Campbell. Julius Wong, who was the worst of them all, was more difficult, because he hadn't attended the college, but I somehow managed to give him a face and a name too.'

Roscoe was smiling now. Perhaps he was reliving the

385

thrilling moment that every researcher lives for – when he finally makes his breakthrough.

'When I found out that Julius Wong was Pig Pen, I wanted to go straight to him, ring his doorbell and put a bullet in that depraved face. But then I calmed down and forced myself to think. Eventually I made my mind up. I was going to kill them, one by one, but in such a way that blame fell on Julius Wong. Chandelle Stuart, Gerald Marsalis and Alex Campbell would be allowed to die, but not him. He had to pay more than all the others, he had to spend the rest of his days on Death Row, knowing that every day that passed was bringing him closer to the moment when someone would administer the fatal injection.'

Maureen decided to act, insofar as it was in her power. Taking advantage of the fact that Roscoe was distracted by the emotion of his story, she put her feet on the ground and started cautiously to move the swivel chair to which she was tied, in such a way as to force him, if he wanted to look her in the face, to turn his back to the door behind which Jordan was hidden.

'I started to get organized. The luck that had for so long turned its back on me now seemed to be working in my favour. Julius Wong had undergone surgery on his cartilage and ligaments, and for a while went around on crutches. When he gave them up, he still limped a bit. It wouldn't last long, but that short time was enough for me.'

An inch.

Another.

Then another.

'I had noticed that Julius and I had pretty much the same build. So I first killed Linus – in other words, Gerald Marsalis. When I got to his place, he recognized me immediately. I forced him to sit on a chair, then I put adhesive tape around his wrists and calves and strangled him, making sure he suffered as much as possible. And as he was dying I asked him if he now understood what my son had felt as the air stopped getting to his lungs. Once he was dead, I glued him to the wall with a blanket against his ear, just as Schulz draws Linus in the strips, and wrote that stupid message on the wall. I knew the police would decipher it immediately, but I needed it to give the impression that the murder was the work of a psychopath. I intended to be seen leaving with a limp, but as I was hiding on the stairs, a girl came out of Gerald's apartment and left the door ajar. From the landing I'd heard him phoning someone and asking them to come there. That meant I had less time than I'd anticipated, but it was a great opportunity to leave a clue. When the person arrived and rang the bell downstairs, I took the elevator and passed him at the entrance. I bumped into him in such a way that he'd notice me but wouldn't see my face.'

'But didn't it occur to you that the others, once they knew how Gerald had been killed, would become suspicious?'

Roscoe shrugged. 'Gerald was the Mayor's son, and that meant it was very likely the details would be kept under wraps – which was, in fact, the case. I had decided to use *Peanuts* because I knew that sooner or later they'd trace it all back to the robbery all those years ago. It might have provided a motive – Julius wanting to take revenge for a slight he'd suffered, or something like that.'

Another inch, taking advantage of the fact that Roscoe was looking down for a moment.

When he looked up again, Maureen caught a sharp, self-satisfied expression on his face.

'Then it was Chandelle's turn. And I'm not ashamed to say

that killing that useless creature was a real pleasure. I crossed the lobby of the Stuart Building wearing the same tracksuit and walking with the same limp as before. I tried to be as furtive as possible, and always be hidden by someone else, but in reality I was making sure I was caught by the cameras. I knew that would be the first thing the police checked. I told Chandelle I had some news about her operation and she let me come up. How surprised that whore was when she saw me in front of her with a gun in my hand! With Linus I'd had to be quick, but with Chandelle I had much more time at my disposal. I forced her to talk, making her think I would spare her if she did. I discovered a whole lot of things. She confessed to me that she'd had an affair with that sex maniac Julius, and also how he'd gradually involved the other two in the robbery – Gerald because he was crazy, and Alex Campbell because he was weak and psychologically dependent on Julius. Finally she revealed the reason all this had happened. The bastards had committed the robbery for kicks, just to do something different, feel something different. Do you understand what I'm saying? My son had died because these people, out of boredom, had decided to "try something different". And what's more, that bitch told me she had recognized me as soon as she entered my office the first time. She had enjoyed the sick sensation of knowing what I didn't know, maybe actually becoming aroused at the thought of what she had done to me. When I went to her and put my hands around her neck and she begged me not to kill her I whispered in her ears, echoing Julius, "I'm a doctor, I know what I'm doing." Then I glued her to the piano, to make her look like Lucy, wrote the note pointing to the next victim, and left.'

At last, Roscoe changed position. With an almost

distracted movement, he turned and rested against the bench, as if he was tired of standing and needed a support. The gun, though, was still in his hand, and the barrel was still aimed at Maureen's head.

'First, though, I left a new clue, the crucial one. I made it seem as though the killer had raped Chandelle after killing her. And just think, to do that, I used a dildo I found in one of her drawers. I put it in a condom filled with Julius Wong's semen. I chose the kind that slows down the man's pleasure and stimulates the woman's, firstly because it leaves a more obvious chemical residue and secondly because using a condom on a corpse was perfectly in line with the psychological profile of a psychopath. I made a hole in it so that it would leave a small residue of sperm, and it would look as though the condom was faulty.'

'And how did you get hold of it?'

'That was the hardest part. Julius Wong had been interested in sex and violence since he was young, but had become very choosy. Straight sex with women didn't interest him any more, he needed something stronger, more extreme. The alcohol, the drugs and his sick brain had made him . . . how shall I put it? . . . a man of refined tastes. I remembered someone I had met some time ago.'

Jordan came out into the open and started to creep down the short staircase. Maureen saw that his right arm was hanging at his side in a strange way, as if it was broken.

One step.

Two steps.

Three steps.

Maureen was following Jordan's descent and Roscoe's story with the same bated breath.

'Every now and again I would tour the county giving

seminars. In a hospital near Syracuse I met a nurse. She was an extremely beautiful woman, maybe one of the most beautiful I've ever seen. There was something distinctive about her, she had a sensuality you could almost touch. Her name was Lysa and she had one fairly unusual characteristic, which was that she was actually a man. We became friends and she started to confide in me. She was a gentle, melancholy, reserved person. And above all honest – nothing like those mercenary transsexuals you find on the internet. We stayed in touch, even when she stopped working at the hospital. It struck me that a pervert like Julius Wong wouldn't be able to resist the excitement of having relations with a sexual curiosity like that. I played on Lysa's weakness, her weariness at fighting a battle she considered lost from the start. I contacted her anonymously and offered her a hundred thousand dollars to have sex with Julius Wong and hand over a condom filled with his sperm.'

'And didn't it occur to you that this Lysa might report you to the police when she discovered what Julius Wong had been accused of? Especially knowing that what nailed him conclusively was the DNA test.'

'Of course, there was always that possibility. But that was another problem I solved. Without knowing I was in any way involved, she herself had written to tell me she was moving to New York, and to give me the address of the apartment she had rented. And you want to know something funny? It was the apartment of Jordan Marsalis, the Mayor's brother, Gerald's uncle . . .'

For a moment, Roscoe seemed to be reflecting on the mocking way that fate managed the affairs of men. Then he dismissed that thought with a gesture of his hand, as if waving away a troublesome fly. 'In any case, as I said, it's no longer a problem. I read in the newspaper that she's had an accident . . .'

Maureen was horror-struck by the chilling significance of those words. 'You're crazy.'

'That's possible. Maybe you have to be crazy to do what I did. But I succeeded.'

'Not entirely. Things didn't go too well with Alex Campbell, did they? He managed to get away from you.'

William Roscoe gave Maureen a devilish smile. 'Do you really think so?'

Maureen looked at him, stunned.

'Congratulations, Maureen, I see you've understood. It was all planned. I made sure he got away because I needed him alive, he had to be the person with the final clue that would identify Julius Wong. I chose him because he was actually the least guilty of them. That day, he was the only one who begged the others to leave us alone.'

In the meantime, Jordan had reached the opposite side of the central bench and ducked down beneath it. Maureen assumed he was planning to creep around it until he was behind Roscoe, then take him by surprise. Unaware of his presence, Roscoe continued his macabre account of his actions.

'I knew he'd gone to his house on Saint Croix. Luckily, thanks to my work, I've developed a few computer skills. I managed to get into the airline's database and find out what day he was due back. I waited for him in a stolen car and grabbed him just outside his house, making sure that the tailor in the shop opposite saw me and was able to describe me to the police, obviously with the usual tracksuit and slight limp in the right leg. I took Alex to that warehouse in Williamsburg to make it look as if I'd been planning to arrange his body to look like Snoopy. I'd had a tattoo of a demon with butterfly wings drawn on my arm in soluble colours. It might not have been identical to Julius Wong's tattoo, but it was certainly close enough, and in that light it was sure to terrify Alex. I didn't think he'd be paying too much attention to details. Unfortunately, I didn't know he had a weak heart. He died, but not before completing the task I'd given him, which was to set the police on Julius Wong's trail.'

'There's one thing I don't understand. How could you be sure Julius Wong wouldn't have an alibi for the nights when the murders were committed?'

Roscoe pointed to a number of medium-size cylinders in a compartment to his right. 'Nitrous oxide. Colourless, taste-less, odourless.'

'I don't understand.'

'Julius Wong lives in a loft on 14th Street. It's a two-storey building, with a flat roof that can easily be reached from the fire escape in back. All I had to do was connect one of those cylinders to the ventilation system to send him into a dreamless sleep until the following day.'

Roscoe shrugged casually, as if he had just finished telling a friend about a pleasure trip.

'What else is there to say? Nothing, I think.'

Maureen realized that there was no narcissism in his attitude, no pride at the Machiavellian plan he had concocted. Instead, there was the naturalness of a person who feels he has done what is right. And privately, although Maureen cursed herself for the thought, she could not entirely blame him.

'Now you know everything. It's taken me years to get this far and I'm not going to let you ruin it for me now.'

'You've forgotten something,' Maureen told him. 'Didn't it occur to you that, if someone discovered you, you'd have done all this for nothing? Julius Wong would be free and you would go to prison in his place.'

Professor William Roscoe smiled gently. 'No, my dear. I have taken certain precautions, you see. Should that happen, there's a very professional gentleman who'll take care of Julius W—'

Roscoe did not finish the sentence, because at that moment Jordan leaped out from behind the shelter of the bench and threw himself on him.

CHAPTER 51

It all happened in a few seconds, even though to Jordan and Maureen it seemed to last forever, as if they were moving in slow motion.

Jordan, with his one good arm at his disposal, had grabbed Roscoe's right hand and at the same time lifted his leg in order to knock the Professor's wrist against his knee and make him loosen his hold on the gun.

But surprise did not seem to be in William Roscoe's repertoire. If Jordan's unexpected arrival had shaken him in any way, it was not reflected in his reactions. The only result that Jordan did obtain was that his opponent's finger tightened on the trigger and the gun went off, sending a bullet thudding into the tiled floor and raising a cloud of fragments.

Jordan realized immediately that it would not be easy to get the better of Roscoe, not least because he himself was forced to fight with only one arm. He was taller and younger, of course, but from the force with which Roscoe had met his onslaught it was clear that the Professor was in excellent shape – and of course could count on both arms.

Ignoring the agony from his shoulder, Jordan managed to force the Professor's arm backwards and bring his wrist down several times on the tiled edge of the bench.

The gun went off again, and a computer exploded in a shower of sparks.

At last, Roscoe's grip relaxed, and Jordan heard the wonderful sound of the gun clattering to the floor.

Maureen was watching every movement, wondering how she could be of help. Her options were very limited, in that she was still trapped in the chair. One thing she could do, though, was to make it more difficult for Roscoe to reach his gun if he broke free of Jordan. Pressing down on her feet and thrusting her chest forward slightly, she moved the chair as best she could until her feet were close enough to kick it away. The two men who were fighting heard the metallic scrape of the Beretta sliding across the floor, hit the base of the opposite wall, bounce back towards the middle of the room and stop just below the gallery.

Maureen had no idea why Jordan could hardly use his right arm, but it was obvious to her that the fight she was watching was an unequal one.

Roscoe had easily freed himself from Jordan's grip and now was facing him in a defensive posture, like a boxer. It might well have been a sport he had practised as a young man, at university, and it was possible he had continued training over the years.

Unlike Maureen, the doctor had immediately guessed, from the unusual position of Jordan's shoulder, that his attacker had a major weak spot. Every time Jordan came close to hit him with his left hand or attempted a kick, he managed to swerve and hit Jordan directly in the right shoulder, then immediately retreated, to wait for another move from his opponent.

Knowing that Jordan could not keep on taking this punishment, Maureen started moving the chair again, trying to get as close as she could to Roscoe, to trip him with her legs and give Jordan a moment's breather. But when the Professor saw what she was doing, he raised his leg, placed his foot on the chair and gave it a violent push.

The chair went zooming back until it hit the bench and tilted to one side. For a moment, Maureen hung suspended, as if the chair had a will of its own and was desperately trying to regain its balance. Then she saw the white tiles of the floor come closer at a vertiginous speed.

As she hit the floor, she tried to cushion the fall with her shoulder, but despite her efforts, her elbow hit the tiles hard. A kind of electric shock spread up her arm, which immediately turned into a strong burning sensation.

In the meantime, thanks to the diversion offered by Maureen's intervention, Jordan had managed to put his good arm around Roscoe's throat and was squeezing with all the strength he could muster. The Professor responded by hitting him in the stomach with his right elbow.

From her position on the floor, Maureen could not see what was going on. She heard the panting of the two men behind her as they fought for their lives, but could not turn her head to find out who was winning.

She started to wriggle free. Inch by inch, using her legs as much as possible to brace herself, she managed to slide her arms completely off the back of the chair. She turned, still lying on the floor, and kicked the chair away from her.

Now that she could see, however, the two men had disappeared. She could still hear their panting and the noise of the fight, but didn't know where they were. Presumably, they were now fighting, locked together, on the floor next to the refrigeration chamber, behind the central bench.

Raising her head, she saw the gun lying on the floor, on the other side of the room.

Hoisting herself up into a kneeling position she started edging towards the Beretta. When she reached it, she placed her knees on either side of it and bent forward until she was able to take it in her right hand. She did not know how accurate her aim would be if she fired with her hands behind her back, but she hoped she wouldn't have to. All she really needed to do was to be able to hand it to Jordan, to stop any further attempt at resistance from Roscoe.

Unfortunately, things did not go as she had foreseen. All at once, she saw Roscoe rise up over the top of the workbench, thrown backwards as if Jordan had succeeded in placing his feet on his chest and given him a powerful push with his legs. The Professor went sprawling against the big cylinders of liquid nitrogen that fed the refrigeration chamber. The polo shirt he was wearing was all creased, the back of it completely out of his pants, and blood was pouring from his nose. He wiped it with his sleeve, his eyes fixed on his opponent, who was still on the floor, out of sight of Maureen.

Then, about halfway along the bench, a hand appeared over the top, seeking support, and Jordan emerged, panting hard, his face wracked with pain.

Maureen admired his resistance, but could tell that he would not be able to hold out much longer. If his shoulder hurt as much as she supposed, she was surprised that he had not yet fainted.

When he saw Jordan getting up, Roscoe also seemed surprised. A cruel expression distorted his face. To Maureen, he seemed like a man now convulsed by madness, an endless limbo in which the hatred he had harboured all these years had engulfed him.

She saw him bend and grab one of the tubes carrying the liquid nitrogen from the cylinders into the refrigeration chamber. Maureen realized what he was planning to do, and she felt the blood in her veins run cold, as cold perhaps as the liquid running through the cable the Professor was now yanking furiously.

In the meantime, Jordan had got completely to his feet and was advancing towards him.

If Roscoe managed to extract the tube from its base and aim it at him, Jordan would be hit by a jet at almost 200 degrees below zero, which would cause the same burns as a flamethrower.

Maureen had only a fraction of a second to make a decision.

She lay down on the floor and rolled on her side, with her legs towards Roscoe. In that position, she pointed the gun and tried to take aim.

If she missed and hit one of the cylinders, it would explode, and that part of the house would become a small crater covered with the fragments of their bodies.

'Get down, Jordan!' she shouted, and pressed the trigger a fraction of a second after the Professor had managed to extract the tube from its housing.

The gunshot echoed through the room like the tolling of a huge funeral bell.

Roscoe swivelled his head towards Maureen. He looked at her for a moment as if she was someone he thought he knew, but whose name he could not remember.

Then, swaying slightly, he looked down at the bullet-hole in his chest and the bloodstain spreading to cover the Ralph Lauren logo on his polo shirt.

The hand holding the tube, from which a jet of liquid

nitrogen was escaping, lost its grip and the tube tilted downwards. The frozen stream hit Roscoe's calves and feet, yet he seemed not to feel the effects of what must have been a horrendous burning. He fell to his knees and then, after what seemed an eternity, closed his eyes and slid to the floor with his face down, covering the tube with his body and stopping much of the flow with the weight.

As Maureen got to her feet, she found it hard to take her eyes off the corpse of Professor William Roscoe.

Then she turned to look around the lab in search of Jordan, fearing he might have been reached by the liquid nitrogen spreading across the floor.

As soon as Jordan had heard Maureen's warning, he had thrown himself to the floor, on his left side, hoping that the jolt to his dislocated shoulder did not make him faint.

The temperature in the room seemed to be rapidly decreasing, and from somewhere in the distance he could hear Maureen crying, 'The cylinder! Jordan, you have to close the cylinder!'

With the little energy he still had left, he made an effort to get up off the floor. But then, instead of going to the cylinder to close the valve, he moved around to the other side of the bench and grabbed Maureen's arm.

'Let's get out of here, quick.'

They rushed up the three steps of the gallery and, supporting each other, climbed the stairs and emerged out into the open.

CHAPTER 52

'Does your shoulder still hurt?'

Jordan took a sip of coffee and said, 'No. The pain's almost gone.'

Maureen and Jordan were sitting facing each other across a table in Starbucks on Madison Avenue, two figures dusty with fatigue behind a window that reflected the morning traffic. The sleepless night had left marks under their eyes.

There was no sense of elation or triumph in them, only the exhaustion of survivors, and surprise at the fact that they were still alive.

When they had left the house, Jordan had called Burroni and told him where they were and what had happened.

It had not taken long after that for the usual bedlam of lights and yellow tapes and barriers and vans and Medical Examiners to begin. The pair had managed to get away before the inevitable onslaught of reporters. The media would have a field day with this cloak and dagger story that had two outsiders as protagonists.

As they walked away from the big gloomy house on Henry Street, they saw the body of Professor William Roscoe disappear into the back of an ambulance.

Burroni had approached as they were getting in a patrol

car. 'I'd like to know how you managed it, though I suspect I'll never know the truth. Congratulations, anyway.'

He had waved goodbye to them and gone back to his duties, his black hat seeming to float above the bustle of officers and technicians. They had been driven to the Emergency Department at Saint Charles Hospital in Brooklyn, where an orthopaedic consultant had fixed Jordan's shoulder and dressed it with an elastic bandage. On the basis of the X-rays, the doctor had been rather pessimistic about the lesion, saying that Jordan would probably have to undergo a small operation to recover the complete use of his shoulder.

Maureen had been treated for a slight burn on one leg, caused by contact with the fumes from the liquid nitrogen.

Now they were sitting over the coffee they had both felt they needed. What they had needed even more was a pause to take stock of what had happened.

'How did you know it was him?' Jordan asked.

'I told you there was something I couldn't remember, some elusive detail I just couldn't get hold of. Last night, without the help of any vision, I realized what that detail was.'

'Yes? What was it?'

'When Roscoe removed my bandages after the operation and I opened my eyes, for a moment I saw him leaning over me with his hands near my face. Then the image faded out and, as you can imagine, I was really upset. I thought the operation had been a failure, that I would be blind forever. But then the light came back and I saw his face again, very close to mine. I was so relieved that I missed one crucial detail. Between the two figures there was a difference – unfortunately it took me all this time to pinpoint it.'

'Go on.'

401

'In the first image I saw of him, Roscoe wasn't wearing a white coat. When I saw him again, he was. That meant one thing. When he took off the bandages, the face I had in front of me wasn't the first thing I saw, but the last thing Gerald Marsalis saw. The face of his killer.'

Jordan leaned back in his chair. How could it have been otherwise? he thought ironically. An absurd ending to an absurd story. The problem was that after all that had happened to them, they would have to continue living in a world of normal people.

Jordan finished his coffee and threw the paper cup in the trash can. 'What will you do now?'

Maureen shrugged – a powerless but not desolate gesture. 'What can I do? I'll go back to Italy and carry on. What do they say? While there's life, there's hope.'

Both remembered Roscoe's threat. When she had found herself having to choose, Maureen had made her decision in a flash. Jordan was safe and Roscoe was gone, carrying with him any certainty that she would continue to have the use of her eyes.

It might have been just a threat, or it might not. Only time would tell. But Jordan would never forget the choice she had made.

'Don't you want to tell anyone?'

'Why? To run the risk of becoming a freak, having people laugh behind my back when they pass me in the corridor?' Maureen smiled and placed her hand on his arm. 'I'd rather it stayed one of our little secrets, Jordan. Just you and me. Knowing that there's another person in the world who believes I'm not crazy is enough. And you?'

'What about me?'

Maureen was not deceived by his casual tone. 'Jordan, I

know you by now. I'm sorry if it sounds like I'm boasting, but maybe I know you better than you know yourself. Isn't there something you want to talk about?'

'No,' he replied instinctively.

But then it struck him that it was instinct that had got him in trouble before. Right now, he had a desperate need to understand. And to do that he required Maureen's help. This would be another thing that linked them, another little secret to share.

'Actually, yes. There is something I want to talk to you about. There's this person . . .'

'Is her name Lysa, by any chance?'

Jordan was not surprised to hear that name on Maureen's lips. 'Yes, it is. You heard what Roscoe said, the role she played in this story.'

Jordan kept touching his bandaged right shoulder with his good hand, as if checking that the doctor had done a good job. At last, he gathered up his courage and confided everything to Maureen.

As he proceeded with his story, Maureen looked at his eyes. The blue of his gaze seemed, as he spoke, to cleanse itself of all the ugliness he had witnessed lately. By the time he had finished, his eyes were as clear as a May sky and Maureen knew everything.

She knew all about Lysa and what had happened between her and Jordan, and she also knew what Jordan had not yet understood.

With extreme naturalness, she told him.

'It's all so simple, Jordan. Lysa is in love with you and had the courage to tell you. You're clutching at any straw you can find in order not to admit that you're also in love with the woman.'

Jordan was struck by these words. Without even knowing Lysa, Maureen had called her 'a woman'. It was something it had taken him a long time to do.

'She's someone who made a mistake and is paying for it,' Maureen continued. 'Even now, at this moment, while we're sitting here over a coffee, and talking about her.'

She paused, forcing Jordan to lift his head and look at her.

When she spoke again, she tried to put into her voice all the passion she possessed. 'Now it's up to you to make sure she doesn't spend the rest of her life paying.'

Jordan made one last feeble protest. 'But she's—'

'She's love, Jordan. When you find love, wherever it comes from, accept it as a gift and hold tight to it.'

Jordan would never forget the tremulous light of tears in Maureen's eyes as she looked at him and saw someone else.

'Love is so hard to find and so easy to lose . . .'

Jordan turned discreetly to look out at the street, in order not to intrude on that moment of grief.

The coffee break was over, and so was what they had to say to each other.

They left the Starbucks, which was full of people they didn't know, and found themselves out on the sidewalk, among other people they didn't know, people in a hurry, for whom the things they had just lived through would be a headline to be skimmed over as they leafed through the newspaper.

Maureen raised her arm, and was immediately in luck. An empty cab pulled up at the kerb, just past where they were standing.

Jordan walked to it with her. As Maureen opened the door and before getting in, she stood on tiptoe and gave him a kiss on the cheek. 'Good luck, my knight in shining armour.'

When she was seated she looked up at him through the open window.

'Lysa doesn't know it yet, but she's a very lucky person. If I were you, I'd try to make her see that as soon as possible.'

Maureen gave the address to the driver, and the shabby yellow cab moved away from the kerb and edged back into the traffic. As Jordan watched, he thought with a pang in his heart that, even after all that had happened, nothing had changed for her.

Maureen Martini was leaving his life the same way she had entered it.

Alone.

CHAPTER 53

It was late afternoon by now and Jordan stood outside the door of Lysa's room with his helmet in his hand and his backpack over his shoulder. He had been standing there for what seemed like forever, unable to make up his mind to knock. He recalled the words Maureen had spoken that morning, that lesson he had been forced despite himself to learn.

She's love, Jordan. Love is so hard to find and so easy to lose . . .

He finally made up his mind and rapped gently at the door.

He waited for the voice inside to give him permission to enter before opening the door.

Lysa was sitting in bed, propped up by pillows. They had removed the drip, but there was still a blue mark on her arm where the needle had been. Her hair was loose and her face had lost its pallor. She looked beautiful in the light of the sunset coming in through the window.

She was surprised to see him and made an instinctive, typically feminine gesture to straighten her hair.

'Hello, Jordan.'

'Hello, Lysa.'

There was a moment's silence. Lysa was glad there was no monitor by her bed to display the beating of her heart.

'How are you?' Jordan asked, feeling stupid at the question.

'Fine,' Lysa replied, feeling stupid at the answer. Then she pointed to the TV set, which was tuned to NY1, with the sound off. 'I just saw an item about you on the news. You and that girl, Maureen Martini, are the heroes of the hour.'

She had spoken in a tone that was meant to be neutral, but had unconsciously altered her voice as she uttered Maureen's name. Although she knew who Maureen was now, in Lysa's mind, she was still the woman she had seen embracing Jordan, that evening in the Meatpacking District.

'I would have been proud of all that once. Now I think it was just something that had to be done. As for Maureen . . .' Jordan walked to the table and put his backpack and helmet down on it. 'Do you remember Connor Slave, the singer who was kidnapped in Italy with his girlfriend and then killed? The guy in the apartment below ours plays his songs all the time.'

The way Jordan had said the word 'ours' clutched at her heart. It was only one syllable but the whole world was in it. A world she had lost.

'That girlfriend was Maureen.'

Jordan sat down on the aluminium chair, settling comfortably against the back of it to support his bandaged shoulder.

'Now this is all over, I can get my life back. I don't know if she can. I hope so. She deserves to be happy.'

And not only her.

Lysa pointed again at the TV set. 'Look, there's your brother.'

Jordan turned to look at the TV. Christopher had appeared on the screen, standing in front of a lectern studded with

407

microphones in the press conference room at New York City Hall. He was alone in front of an audience of journalists, like a bullfighter in front of a bull. The camera went in for a close-up and Jordan felt sorry for his brother. In the short time that had passed since the death of his son, he appeared to have aged ten years. From what Jordan could see, he must have refused the attentions of the make-up artists his image adviser imposed on him before any television appearance that might include close-ups.

Lysa picked up the remote and turned up the volume just as Mayor Christopher Marsalis was beginning his speech.

'Ladies and gentlemen, before anything else I feel it is my duty to thank you for coming here in such large numbers. That makes what I am about to say both easier and more difficult.'

Christopher paused, silencing any comment and making the tension almost palpable. Jordan was well aware that his ability to communicate wasn't studied, but part of his nature. His voice, though, was tired, like his appearance.

'All of you know about the tragic events that have affected my family recently. The loss of a child is one event that always makes us stop and think. When it happens in such a tragic way, as is the case here, we are led to examine our own actions more deeply and critically. Well, I have done that, and have come to the conclusion that, although I have tried to be a good politician and a good Mayor, I had forgotten – and this is something for which I will never forgive myself – to be a good father. And so I now find myself unable to answer the question any one of you could ask me: *how do you think you can do something for our children, if you weren't capable of doing something for your own?*

'For that reason, and for others of a personal nature, I have decided to tender my resignation. But before I leave the post that the people of this city entrusted to me, I have to perform an act of justice towards my brother, Lieutenant Jordan Marsalis of the New York Police Department. Some years ago, to protect me, he took the blame for an act for which I alone was responsible. I allowed that to happen, and it is another thing for which I will never be able to forgive myself.

'I remember the words he said to me that evening: "A good mayor is much more important than a good cop." The successful outcome of this case is due above all to him, and my reply now to his words then can only be: "An exceptional cop is better than a Mayor who does not deserve to be one." I hope this city will bear this in mind and, if not reinstate him in the post he deserves, at least give him back the respect to which he is entitled.

'That is all I have to say. My decision to resign is irreversible. Ladies and gentlemen, I thank you.'

Christopher turned his back on the audience, which by now was in an uproar, and disappeared through the door at the back of the room.

With the remote, Lysa switched off the TV. Then she turned to Jordan with a smile on her face. 'I'm pleased for you.'

Jordan made a vague gesture. 'Believe me, I don't really care any more. But I'm pleased for him. It wasn't easy to take a decision like that, nor to make that kind of speech in front of tens of thousands of people. I'm glad he found the strength and courage to do it.'

From her place in the bed, Lysa finally pointed to the backpack and helmet she had been unable, despite her efforts, to keep her eyes off.

'Are you leaving the city?'

'I was always going to.'

Lysa would have preferred Jordan not to look at her like that. She would have preferred him to go immediately, so that she could imagine him on his bike as it took him ever further away, minute by minute, because any distance would have been less than the distance she felt between them right now.

'Nothing has changed for you, then,' she whispered.

Jordan shook his head. 'No, something *has* changed and I can't pretend it never happened.'

He stood up, took the backpack and opened it. He searched inside, took out a helmet and placed it on the table next to his. Lysa recognized it immediately. It was the one he had bought her the morning they had gone to Vassar.

'When I leave, I'd like you to put this on and leave with me. If you want to, of course.'

Lysa had to catch her breath before replying. 'Are you sure?'

'Yes. I'm not sure about anything else, but I am sure about that.'

Jordan approached the bed, leaned down, and placed his lips for a moment on Lysa's. She smelled the good masculine smell of his skin and at last felt free to imagine. She bent forward and hid her face in her hands, her eyes full of tears.

She would have liked Jordan to kiss her again, but it struck her that there was plenty of time for that.

PART FOUR

Rome

EPILOGUE

The plane touched down, and through the window, Maureen saw the familiar landscape of Fiumicino airport, somehow homely, on a human scale, so unlike the hi-tech bustle of JFK in New York.

Not better, not worse, only different.

The stewardess welcomed the passengers to Rome in Italian and English. Maureen spoke both languages fluently, but at that moment both sounded foreign to her.

The plane came to a final halt.

Maureen took her hand baggage from the rack and joined the line heading towards the front exit and out of the plane. She then followed the flow to the baggage reclaim area. She knew there was nobody waiting for her outside, and that was fine with her.

Her father had phoned her from Japan, where he'd gone for the opening of a new Martini's in Tokyo. He had heard about the outcome of the investigation in which she had been involved, and in his book, this made her an international star.

From Franco Roberto she had learned that her colleagues from the station had decided to arrive en masse to greet her at the airport. That was why she had brought her departure forward, finding a seat at the last moment on the flight immediately before the one she had booked. She didn't feel triumphant, and didn't want to have people around her to fete her as if she was.

Maureen removed her case from the carousel, put it on a cart and headed for the exit.

She was on her way to the taxi rank when someone came up to her.

'Excuse me, are you Signora Maureen Martini?'

Maureen stopped and looked at him. He was a middle-aged Chinese of slightly above average height.

'Yes. What can I do for you?'

'For me, nothing, *signora*. But I've been asked by someone in America to give you this.'

He held out a small box, covered in plain wrapping paper but with an elegant gilded ribbon around it.

'But what—?'

'The person who asked me to perform this errand told me you would understand. He also told me to thank you, and to tell you he doesn't need a reply. Welcome home, *signora*. Have a good evening.'

Without another word, he gave a little bow, turned and walked away, and was soon swallowed up in the crowd.

Maureen looked at the box for a moment and then slipped it into her hand baggage.

During the taxi ride from Fiumicino, she looked out at the familiar landscape of the Roman *campagna*.

When she had left her mother, Maureen knew that something had changed between them. In the past, they had been so bound up in their professional roles as to forget they were just two women. Her mother had embraced her and Maureen had been grateful to her for having been there to say goodbye in such a physical, emotional way, without worrying about what she was wearing. It was a beginning – a small

414

one, perhaps – but at least not an ending. Only time would tell where it would lead.

She had seen Jordan Marsalis for the last time at Police Headquarters, where they had gone to sign the final statements regarding the case of William Roscoe. They had not discussed the case, but he had seemed in a good mood and had promised to look her up if he came to Italy. That might or might not happen, but one thing was certain: they would never forget each other, or the experience they had shared.

The taxi dropped her outside her building, and the driver helped her carry her luggage to the elevator.

The letter box was full of mail. Maureen took it out and skimmed through it as the elevator carried her up to the top floor. Most of it was junk or bills, but there was a letter from the Ministry of the Interior, plus a few letters from friends. Maureen had no desire to open them.

Only one piece of mail drew her attention.

It was a large brown padded envelope. The postmark indicated that it had been mailed in Baltimore. Inside was a CD and a sheet of paper, folded in two. She opened it and read the letter.

Dear Maureen,

We've never met in person although I've heard so much about you, I feel I know you very well. My name is Brendan Slave and I'm Connor's brother. We are united by our regret for what he took away with him forever, but also by the joy of being able to enjoy the words and music he left as a witness to his genius. Since that tragic event, I've come into possession of all his things and, going through them, I found the enclosed CD. It contains an unpublished song, and from Connor's notes I discovered that he wrote it for you, as you will see from your name on the disc. It seemed only right for you to have it. It's yours, it belongs to you, and you can do with it whatever you like. You can reveal it to the world or keep it as a little secret inheritance of your own.

From what my brother told me, I know the two of you were very much in love, so please allow me to give you a piece of advice. Never forget him, but don't build your life around his memory. I'm sure that's what he would say to you if he could. You're young, beautiful and sensitive. Don't dismiss the possibility that you can live and love again. If you find it difficult, there will always be this last song of Connor's to remind you how it's done.

Kindest regards

Brendan Slave

By the time she had finished reading, the elevator had stopped at her landing, but she stood there, surrounded by her baggage, unable to move, her eyes streaked with tears. Like a child, she wiped them on the sleeves of her blouse, heedless of the marks her make-up left on the material. At last she picked up her bags and stepped out of the elevator. As she was looking for her keys, she felt the box she had been given by the Chinese man at the airport.

As soon as she entered, she went straight to the shutters and opened them, letting the air and the sun and the view of Rome into this apartment she had thought she would never see again.

Standing there, watching the sunset, she loosened the knot on the ribbon and opened the box.

Inside, on a layer of cotton wool, rested a severed human ear. There was an earring still in the lobe – a strange earring in the form of a cross, with a little diamond winking in the middle.

Maureen recognized it immediately.

From someone in America, the Chinaman had said.

Maureen thought again of the words Cesar Wong had uttered, the evening they had taken a short car-ride together, and he had informed her of his son's innocence and asked her to help him prove it.

I assure you that in some way I'll be able to repay you. I don't yet know how, but I assure you I will . . .

Maureen stood looking at that macabre specimen without any emotion. William Roscoe, the evening on which he had died, had claimed that the only thing that could make us superior to God was justice. Maureen did not know if Jordan, just before attacking him, had heard his last words about Julius Wong.

A very professional gentleman will take care of him . . .

If Jordan *had* understood the meaning of this statement, he had shown no sign of it – nor had Maureen. There was also a justice of men, and in this way she and Jordan had become the jury. That would be the third secret they shared. If one day there were accounts to settle with their consciences, they would confront them.

Still holding the box in her hand, Maureen went and threw its contents in the toilet bowl and pressed the flush button. She stood there watching, making sure that the memory of the foul creature who had been Arben Gallani was going to the place most suitable for him – the sewers of Rome.

Then she went to get the brown envelope she had placed on a cabinet and climbed the stairs to the upper floor. She opened the sliding window that showed roofs as far as the eye could see and then went to the stereo and took the CD from the envelope. On the shiny surface were two words, written in indelible ink.

'Underwater'

Maureen

She switched on the CD-player, inserted the disc and pressed *Play*.

There were a few bars of sampled strings, a soft guitar arpeggio and then, against that light background, Connor's violin started moving with the elegance and energy of a skater on ice, drawing spirals in the air with the melody.

And at last she heard his voice, a knife sharpened by pain and joy. Within a moment, Maureen was engrossed in the meaning of the song, a secret song, hidden from the rest of the world, her exclusive property – not because she owned the only copy, but because it had been written specially for her.

> *You were born underwater*
> *underwater was your realm*
> *dancing dreamlike in the waves*
> *dancing round and back again*
>
> *And now you walk the world*
> *hiding within your pain*
> *thinking you left your heart*
> *back there beneath the waves.*

Perhaps you do not know
That light is on your side
Can change the dark of day
into a watery glow

Even underwater
deep down where it is night
A light still shines for you
giving life to your love . . .
. . . your love that hides below,
that would not give up the fight
So stop your grieving, darling,
for when you stop believing
even underwater
there will always be a light.

Once she had grasped the meaning of these words, instead of crying, Maureen smiled.

She sat down on the wicker armchair by the window, arranged the cushions, and let herself be enveloped by the music, the voice, the memory – sure that, whatever happened to her from now on, nobody could ever take away the enormous richness of what she had had. She watched as a triumphant sunset set the sky of Rome aflame, waiting for what was in store, helped only by what she had learned, however unwillingly, and what she was now able to confront.

Maureen Martini closed her eyes. *The darkness and the waiting*, she thought, *are the same colour*.

ACKNOWLEDGEMENTS

I must begin by thanking two remarkable people: Pietro Bartocci and his wife, Dr Mary Elacqua of Samaritan Hospital in Troy. Without them this novel would have had a much more difficult labour, I would have had a much more thankless stay in America, I wouldn't have learned how much a New England parrot can catch in its beak, and above all I wouldn't have been able to give a new meaning to the word 'friendship'.

To them I would like to add:

Andrea Borio, an outstanding cook, affectionately nicknamed 'Cow Borio' for having managed to produce a Piedmontese meat stew in the middle of Manhattan;

Dr Victoria Smith, an exceptional chiropractor and a delightful person, who straightened my shattered back during my stay in New York;

the staff of Via della Pace and the other adorable people I met in the United States: I may not remember all their names, but their faces are indelibly engraved in my memory.

In regard to the scientific aspects of the book, I would like to acknowledge my old friend Dr Gianni Miroglio, and Dr Bartolomeo Marino, Consultant Surgeon at the Civil Hospital in Asti, as well as the multi-talented Dr Rossella Franco, the intensive care anaesthetist of the San Andrea Civil Hospital in La Spezia.

A special thank you to Dr Carlo Vanetti, ocular microsurgeon in Milan, member of the ASCRS (American Society of Cataract and Refractive Surgery), and Professor Giulio Cossu, Director of the Institute for Stem Cell Research of the San Raffaele Scientific Institute in Milan, for both their presence and their patience.

Thanks also to Laura Arghittu, Media Director for the Fondazione San Raffaele del Monte Tabor, who skilfully mediated the onslaught of a writer with dubious credentials.

An affectionate and unstinting salute to Annamaria di Paolo, Head of the State Police, who was indispensable for her ideas and opinions, and invaluable for her friendship and support.

As far as the experienced team that sustains my literary activities is concerned, I must first acknowledge Alessandro Dalai, a man of multi-faceted intelligence and understanding, to whom it is only correct to add:

the invulnerable Cristina Dalai,

the incontrovertible Piero Gelli,

the inescapable Rosaria Guacci,

the indomitable Antonella Fassi,

the dependable Paola Finzi,

the multi-coloured Mara Scanavino,

plus the irreproachable Gianluigi Zecchin to cover everyone's backs.

An honourable mention, finally, to the discerning Piergiorgio Nicolazzini, my valiant agent and capable adviser.

In addition:

Angelo Branduardi and Luisa Zappa for the ritual and propitiatory spoilers in the usual tavern;

Angela Pincelli, who for geographical reasons I see rarely but who for emotional reasons I think of a lot; Armando Attanasi, who's there for me much more than I'm there for him;

Francesco Rapisarda, Media Director for the Ducati Racing Team, who will sooner or later get me to a Grand Prix;

Annarita Nulchis, as unforgettable as her emails and as precious as her smile;

Marco Luci for his kindness and contacts;

Malabar Viaggi for their assistance and distinction.

In conclusion, a hug to all the friends who have earned a lasting place in my life and my unchanging affection with their support and respect and the incorruptible sweetness of things that are real.

And finally on a strictly personal level, a hearfelt THANK YOU in capital letters to Renata Quadro and Jole Gamba for their care, their reassuring presence and the help given to a very dear person at a very difficult time for her and for me.

The characters in this story are purely imaginary.

Fortunately for me, the people I've thanked are not.